By William Burroughs
in Picador
Cities of the Red Night

edited by
John Calder

A
WILLIAM BURROUGHS
READER

Original
published by Pan Books

This collection first published 1982 by Pan Books Ltd,
Cavaye Place, London SW10 9PG
This collection © Pan Books Ltd 1982
The Naked Lunch first published in Great Britain 1964 by John Calder
(Publishers) Ltd
The Soft Machine first published in Great Britain 1968 by Calder & Boyars Ltd
The Ticket That Exploded first published in Great Britain 1968 by
Calder & Boyars Ltd
Nova Express first published in Great Britain 1969 by Jonathan Cape Ltd
The Wild Boys first published in Great Britain 1972 by Calder & Boyars Ltd
Exterminator first published in Great Britain 1974 by Calder & Boyars Ltd
The Third Mind first published in Great Britain 1979 by John Calder
(Publishers) Ltd
Cities of the Red Night first published in Great Britain 1981 by John Calder
(Publishers) Ltd
© John Calder (Publishers) Ltd 1964, 1968, 1969, 1972, 1974, 1979, 1981, 1982

ISBN 0 330 26762 0

Filmset in Great Britain by
Northumberland Press Ltd, Gateshead, Tyne and Wear
Printed and bound by
Richard Clay (The Chaucer Press) Ltd, Bungay, Suffolk

CONTENTS

INTRODUCTION

William Seward Burroughs was born in 1914 in Saint Louis, Missouri. He came from a moderately wealthy family which ran into difficulties during the Depression—the money came from an industrial machine, but not the famous adding-machine company—and managed after leaving the local school to go, first at fifteen to Los Alamos Ranch School in New Mexico, and eventually to Harvard where he graduated in English Literature in 1936. T. S. Eliot was teaching at Harvard at the time and Burroughs' fascination with the poet, who was to influence his style, method and subject matter, stems from those years. From the beginning he wanted to be a writer. His juvenilia were mostly imitative of the ghost stories or gangster novels of the period, subject matter still present in his work today, but his reading included Anatole France, Maupassant, Remy de Gourmont, Oscar Wilde and a variety of good authors of his own and earlier times. He quickly developed a dislike of the American preoccupation with money and profit, partly as a result of the difficulties his family suffered during the Depression, and partly through observation of the ways in which money can be used to exert control over the individual's personal freedom and intellectual independence. His personal ethos was therefore one of revolt against society and this helped to bring him into contact with an inherently outlawed minority, the homosexual world, with which he was able to identify his outlook and one principal direction of his work.

After a visit to Europe in the thirties, which depressed him considerably, and being unable to find an interesting job at home, he returned to the academy to study psychology, and also became involved in martial sports and self-defence, an interest he retains today. He contrived not to enter the army by injuring his trigger finger and ultimately worked at various occupations that were to give him material for his novels and the character of William Lee, his *alter ego* in *The Naked Lunch*. These included stints as private detective, bartender, exterminator (of cockroaches), factory and office worker, advertising and newspaper reporter.

In Mexico he killed his wife with a revolver: they were in the habit of playing William Tell and shooting apples off each other's heads, but he was released after a few days for this *crime d'imprudence*. His experiments with drugs led to addiction. He moved to North Africa, living off a small family remittance from home until, realizing that the money was running out and that he was in danger of total collapse, he flew to London and put himself in the care of a Dr Dent who was experimenting with new forms of curing drug addiction. Burroughs took the apomorphine cure, successfully overcame addiction to heroin and started to write *The Naked Lunch* as a direct result of his cure. A fuller account of Burroughs' life can be found in Eric Mottram's *The Algebra of Need* and Victor Bokriss' *With William Burroughs*.

From his first book *Junkie*, first published in New York in 1953, to *Cities of the Red Night*, published in New York and London in 1981, there is both a development in technique and periodic reversion to earlier forms, but his subject matter varies between straightforward narrative, near-autobiographical reminiscence and the throwing in of other material, often of a haphazard nature, that happens to interest the author at the time. A Burroughs novel is a patchwork quilt of past and present experience, observation of places and people around him, information culled from the daily newspaper, general reading, scholarly and often arcane knowledge and random writing of an often accidental or experimental kind. What is astonishing is that it works. Out of his own colourful, but by no means pleasant, personal experiences and the picture of the world that has developed in his mind, which absorbs, sifts, analyses and draws conclusions in an almost obsessive fashion, he has created an important body of work which has given him the stature of one of the leading creative writers of the present time, comparable to Kafka and Joyce among his immediate predecessors. Although many disagree with Norman Mailer's statement that he is possibly the only living American writer of genius, the remark has been much quoted and is beginning to stick.

William Burroughs now has a world reputation, but he is seen very differently in those countries which have a tradition of experimental writing, and where liaison between the different arts is recognized and understood, from those where art is considered an instinctive professional activity and a branch of the entertainment industry, which means mainly the English-speaking world. The insularity of the British approach to art and the pioneer puritanism of the American psyche are hostile to intellectual analysis and to investigation of the creative process, and indifferent to art history. In contrast Europeans tend to love theory and feel that a cultivated, informed and questioning mind is essential to becoming a successful human being. Europeans have other faults: cliquishness, overanxiety to impress, and frequent resort to charlatanism to hide lack of talent or of any real message. But even these faults ensure that constant debate is carried on among creative artists and their critics, which in a watered-down form becomes the *salon* conversation of the business and professional classes as well.

This explains why William Burroughs fascinates the French, Germans and Italians and is still regarded with incomprehension and suspicion in both Britain and America. The famous fourteen-week correspondence in *The Times Literary Supplement* which followed publication of *Dead Fingers Talk*, Burroughs' literary début in Britain, was initiated by John

Willett, who reviewed the book anonymously in that paper under the heading "Ugh!", thus exemplifying clearly enough the simplistic and philistine approach of most of the British literary establishment. It was an attempt by a British critic, who was also an authority on Brecht, to kill off a writer who had much in common with Brecht but whose technique and subject matter he found objectionable, and whose politics he saw as questionable. Interestingly, Burroughs' European enemies have mainly been Marxists, perhaps because they recognize that his targets are as much of the left as of the right. In America, Burroughs attracted a different form of hostility, being lumped together with writers mostly junior to himself who became known as the "beat generation". The Beats—Allen Ginsberg, Jack Kerouac, Alexander Trocchi, Gregory Corso among others —came under attack for their interest in, and often addiction to, both hard and soft drugs, their advocacy of free sexuality and lack of differentiation between hetero- and homosexuality, and their general bohemianism. They were the heroes of those who benefited from the sexual revolution and who fought the anti-censorship battle. Although William Burroughs is now considered the leader and most important figure among the Beat writers—and it is a reputation that he warrants—this is only a small part of his real importance in the history of the late-twentieth-century novel.

Although his language, style and much of his subject matter are typically American, as might be said of Henry James, he is like James essentially part of the European tradition, and his sources lie principally in the world of European painting and writing, as, for instance, Hieronymus Bosch and the Marquis de Sade, Marcel Duchamp and Tristan Tzara, Georg Grosz and James Joyce. He is an experimenter in the European tradition of experiment, a theorist who not only puts his theories into practice but, like Raymond Roussel and André Breton, has had the willingness and the courage to tell his readers how he does it and to acknowledge the sources of his ideas and techniques. He has increased the number of options open to new writers, partly by adapting to the contemporary novel techniques first developed in painting, partly by freeing the speaking voices of his characters from inhibition in an even more significant way than the autobiographical novels of Henry Miller achieve, and also by deliberately mixing naturalistic and highly entertaining narrative with prose and poetry dredged from the world of dream, hallucination, random stream-of-consciousness and chance observation. So, for instance, he gives full recognition to the unpleasant realities that the civilized mind erases from its own consciousness: racial prejudice, pleasure in cruelty, fascination with excreta. The hatred and sadistic fascination that many Americans (and not only Americans!) feel towards Blacks, Jews and others outside the WASP middle-class norm surfaces in Burroughs' writing as a frequently recurring theme that rings disturbingly true even as he fashions it into high comedy. Burroughs brings out of the subconscious the cruelty that is innate in all of us, and his famous and controversial pornographic passages are deliberately intended to destroy the barriers we build to hide our real feelings, so as to create awareness of why we adopt certain attitudes. The popularity of capital punishment, as Burroughs makes clear, has nothing to do with concern for law and order or any belief in the deterrent value of frightening other potential killers, but simply reflects the continuing presence in our psyche of the same cruel pleasure that made public hangings and beheadings the most popular of public spectacles in the not-so-distant past. Burroughs perfectly explains the rise of Nazism as a twentieth-century Roman festival, popularly supported because it released the cruelty that lies just below the surface in all of us. He believes that it can be consciously eradicated by recognizing it for what it is, and learning to live with it in order to control it or to sublimate it into a positive form, as Burroughs does himself by writing his books.

Burroughs is essentially a political writer who well understands the power struggles that shape political events and the reasons that lie behind the willingness of whole populations to follow or accept dictatorship and to derive positive enjoyment from the oppression and martyrdom of others. All his novels are imaginary histories based on his observation of reality and of the human potential for evil. Among the recurring concepts in his work is the idea of time travel, partly derived, as are the time plays of J. B. Priestley, from the time theories of J. W. Dunne. Many of his characters have the ability to travel back into the distant past to discover the beginnings of human history, or into the future when the race, according to present trends, will have been mechanized and computerized into new patterns of control and tyranny (but, we must hope, with continuing resistance to that tyranny). Burroughs' purpose is to show that nothing ever really changes and that we are probably doomed to repeat the same cycles of war, repression and struggle for liberation that have characterized all the past. He conveys Dunne's sense of time, namely that all the past and all the future continue to exist concurrently with the present.

But he does not deny hope. In one of the stories in *Exterminator* ("Astronaut's Return"), Burroughs not only gives a vision of the past but carries it brilliantly (with occasional use of cut-up or fold-in) into the present and future, going from general to particular, from mass destruction to individual or bureaucratized cruelty by association:

According to ancient legend the white race results from a nuclear explosion in what is now the Gobi desert some 30,000 years ago. The civilization and techniques which made the explosion possible were wiped out. The only survivors were slaves marginal to the area who had no knowledge of its science or techniques. They became albinos as a result of radiation and scattered in different directions. Some of them went into Persia northern India Greece and Turkey. Others moved westward and settled in the caves of Europe. The descendants of the cave-dwelling albinos are the present inhabitants of America and western Europe. In these caves the white settlers contracted a virus passed down along their cursed generation that was to make them what they are today a hideous threat to life on this planet. This virus this ancient parasite is what Freud calls the unconscious spawned in the caves of Europe on flesh already diseased from radiation. Anyone descended from this line is basically different from those who have not had the cave experience and contracted this deadly sickness that lives in your blood and bones and nerves that lives where you used to live before your ancestors crawled into their filthy caves. When they came out of the caves they couldn't mind their own business. They had no business of their own to mind because they didn't belong to themselves any more. They belonged to the virus. They had to kill torture conquer enslave degrade as a mad dog has to bite. At Hiroshima all was lost. The metal sickness dormant 30,000 years stirring now in the blood and bones and bleached flesh. He cut himself shaving looked around for styptic pencil couldn't find one dabbed at his face with a towel remembering the smell and taste of burning metal in the tarnished mirror a teen-aged face crisscrossed with scar tissue pale grey eyes that seemed to be looking at something far away and long ago white white white as far as the eye can see ahead a blinding flash of white the cabin reeks of exploded star white lies the long denial from Christ to Hiroshima white voices always denying excusing the endless white papers why we dropped the atom bomb on Hiroshima how colonial peoples have benefited from our rule why look at all those schools and hospitals over-grown with weeds and vines windows melted dead hand frayed scar tissue lifted on a windy street lying white voices from the Congo to Newark the ancient mineral lie bleached flesh false human voices slow poison of rotting metal lies denials white papers *The Warren Report* he picked up a shirt white wash flapping in the cold spring wind Oppenheimer wipes a tear from one eye with one long finger.

"If it will shorten the war and save white lives ..." (Difficult decision in the Pentagon).

Geologic strata of rotten lies and the vulgar strident affirmation "What are we waiting for? Let's bomb China now."

Nigger killing sheriff chuckling over the notches in his gun the old blind sheriff in his rocking chair.

"Bring me my gun son I wants to feel it."

"Yes father."

This was a ritual between them. Reverently the boy brought the old Colt .44 and put it in his father's twisted arthritic hands knarled fingers feeling the braille of notches and remembering ... Remember the Congo? 15,000,000 blacks were systematically slaughtered by white bounty hunters. At first they were paid on presentation of a matched pair of ears. However some soft-hearted white hunters were just cutting off the ears and not doing the job like.

"Now look black boy I got nothing against you just a job is all wife and kids back in England I'm a nice guy really. Now suppose I just cut off your ears and let you live naturally expect a little something for my trouble. How does that strike you?" "You sure is a good man, boss. You sure is a fair white man." However the fraud came to light and after that the bounty hunters were required to produce severed genitals as proof of performance. It is reported that some favored house niggers were allowed to remain as living eunuchs and that their gratitude was indescribable.

The foreman sits at a long table as the white hunters check in emptying the day's work on the table.

"You know I'm going to hang on to this bag. Give me birds a whiff of it."

Kerosene light his smile through cigarette smoke the foreman counts the genitals and sweeps them into a laundry hamper. He reaches into a drawer and counts out the money.

"There you are Scotty. Good English sterling."

"We're not mercenaries we're missionaries. My motto is 'send a kaffir a day to heaven.'"

"They are just black baboons."

"Just wave a welfare check over the river and them niggers will surface."

"Pass me some of that Redman" said the sheriff.

The officer said "I've been wanting to kill me a nigger for a long time."

"How long sir?"

The victims were Aubrey Pollard 19, Carl Cooper 17, and Fred Temple 18.

"Let's take care of Castro next and let's stay armed to the teeth for years decades centuries."

The Detroit police confirmed that they are investigating the three deaths at the Algiers motel. A riot commission is being set up. Welfare workers are asking questions in their whiney high-pitched voices. An old Jew retires to Miami Beach on fire insurance.

Ugly snarl behind the white lies and excuses. Look at an ugly diseased white face. Look at the smoking mirror. Death rains back a hail of crystal skulls.

DEATH DEATH DEATH

Go out and get the pictures. Get all the pictures of

DEATH DEATH DEATH

For Citizen Kane who didn't like to hear the word spoken in his presence

DEATH DEATH DEATH

So many you can't remember
The boy who used to whistle?
Car accident or was it the war?
Which war?

The boy's room is quite empty now. Do you begin to see there is no face there in the tarnished mirror?

There is little to call optimistic in Burroughs' work, but he at least sees the possibility of a continuing resistance in a world that is basically fascist and likely to become more so. Like Bertrand Russell in his later years he is profoundly pessimistic, but believes it necessary nonetheless to continue the struggle for a free world whatever the odds against success. This occasionally leads him into romantic narrative, as in *Cities of the Red Night*, where he idyllically portrays an eighteenth-century pirate revolt against the Spanish Empire, based on the historical commune established by Captain Mission on the Madagascar coast at that time. Burroughs points out that a great opportunity was missed:

I cite this example of retroactive Utopia since it actually could have happened in terms of the techniques and human resources available at the time. Had Captain Mission lived long enough to set an example for others to follow, mankind might have stepped free from the deadly impasse of insoluble problems in which we now find ourselves.

The chance was there. The chance was missed. The principles of the French and American revolutions became windy lies in the mouths of politicians. The liberal revolutions of 1848 created the so-called republics of Central and South America, with a dreary history of dictatorship, oppression, graft, and bureaucracy, thus closing this vast, underpopulated continent to any possibility of communes along the lines set forth by Captain Mission. In any case South America will soon be crisscrossed by highways and motels. In England, Western Europe, and America, the overpopulation made possible by the Industrial Revolution leaves scant room for communes, which are commonly subject to state and federal law and frequently harassed by the local inhabitants. There is simply no room left for "freedom from the tyranny of government" since city dwellers depend on it for food, power, water, transportation, protection, and welfare. Your right to live where you want, with companions of your choosing, under laws to which you agree, died in the eighteenth century with Captain Mission. Only a miracle or a disaster could restore it.

Unlike Beckett, the contemporary writer with whom I believe he will be most often compared in the future, Burroughs is no Manichaean. He does not see the world as a balance between light and darkness, good and evil, but accepts that nature, and especially human nature, is evil by historical record. The only possibility for good to emerge lies in revolt as a result of creative self-education through understanding our own nature: Burroughs sees his own writing as a weapon to be used with calculation and precision against the enemies of freedom and those who seek to exercise control over others. The ideal society is always within reach but is never likely to be achieved because of political and commercial private interests. But the many communities and styles of communal living that emerged from the "alternative" lifestyle philosophy of many young people in the 1960s are both a reflection of that ideal and a modern model for Burroughs.

Two key words in Burroughs' writing and in his private conversation are "control" and "conspiracy". In the non-political, naïve atmosphere of the 1960s there was a phrase often used which we are not likely to hear again: "the conspiracy theory of history". The Watergate affair which brought about the resignation of Richard Nixon, the revelations that followed the Poulson bankruptcy in Britain, the exposure of spies and Soviet infiltration at all levels of the British establishment, the barely concealed scandals involving prominent public figures during Harold Wilson's premiership and many similar European scandals of recent years have made it clear enough to anyone who follows world news that conspiracy dominates both political and economic history and probably always has. Burroughs is fascinated by the ways in which individuals control others, not only in political terms, but psychologically as well. He devoted many months to studying methods of mind control and even infiltrated the Church of Scientology, first becoming a "clear" and then going through the advanced Scientology course at their special college in Edinburgh. He was no follower of the cult established by L. Ron Hubbard, but believed that he could learn from it. His earlier experiments, which had led to temporary addiction with drugs, had already given him insight into chemical control of the mind. Today, drugs, microbes and poisons are part of the armoury of all secret services and the military, and in some countries of the police and their medical and psychiatric services charged with civilian control as well. Burroughs is convinced that we shall all be increasingly controlled by such methods and that the novelist as well as the journalist has a responsibility to break the barriers of silence and secrecy that hide the truth from us.

The irresponsible scientist has become well known to us from the experiments carried out by Nazi doctors and scientists. Many are still employed in research today that can only lead to mass suffering, destruction and war, unaware or uncaring about the results of their work. Among his characters, Burroughs has included many ambitious or simply curious scientists, some of them indifferent to human suffering, among them Dr Benway, evil master of forensic psychology, and Dr Schafer, compulsive lobotomizer and experimental surgeon who in *The Naked Lunch* even outdoes Benway. After the failure of one of Schafer's more outrageous experiments (see "Meeting of International Conference of Technological Psychiatry"), the following conversation occurs:

BENWAY: "Don't take it so hard, kid.... 'Jeder macht eine kleine Dummheit.'" (Everyone makes a little dumbness.)

SCHAFER: "I tell you I can't escape a feeling ... well, of *evil* about this."

BENWAY: "Balderdash, my boy ... We're scientists.... Pure scientists. Disinterested research and damned be him who cries, 'Hold, *too much!*' Such people are no better than party poops."

SCHAFER: "Yes, yes, of course ... and yet ... I can't get that stench out of my lungs...."

BENWAY (irritably): "None of us can.... Never smelled anything remotely like it.... Where was I? Oh yes, what would be the result of administering curare plus iron lung during acute mania? Possibly the subject, unable to discharge his tensions in motor activity, would succumb on the spot like a jungle rat. Interesting cause of death, what?"

Schafer is not listening. "You know," he says impulsively, "I think I'll go back to plain old-fashioned surgery. The human body is scandalously inefficient. Instead of a mouth and an anus to get out of order why not have one all-purpose hole to eat *and* eliminate? We could seal up nose and mouth, fill in the stomach, make an air hole direct into the lungs where it should have been in the first place. . . ."

The caricature and high farce do not disguise the closeness of much of this to real-life experiments carried out by Nazi doctors in concentration camps, and to the development of sophisticated weapons capable of inflicting appalling suffering, used by some governments today, or manufactured by them for future use.

One reason that there has been so much critical hostility to Burroughs in Britain lies in the way he uses constant juxtaposition of demotic American speech, often deliberately uneducated, ungrammatical and vulgar, together with passages of direct propaganda or scenes of no apparent immediate relevance to his main plot; these flash backwards and forwards for no apparent reason and interlock with narrative, with disjointed descriptive or poetical passages and with other material thrown in, seemingly, on impulse or by chance. To anyone expecting a neat, ordered, logical development of situation or plot, much of Burroughs can only seem a disorganized mess and this applies particularly to his most famous, most successful and most criticized book, *The Naked Lunch*, which whatever the merits of his later work will probably remain his masterpiece. It is no accident that the largest section of this *William Burroughs Reader* comes from that work. Everything written later flows out of it, makes reference to it and to its characters, and echoes the themes that he first introduces there. *The Naked Lunch* starts with an introduction that explains how at the age of forty-five he cured himself of heroin addiction and began to write seriously. It reads like an advertisement for the book itself, using the jargon of the junkie, or as a ringmaster's introduction to a circus about to begin, much as in Wedekind's *Earth Spirit*. From there he takes us straight into a junkie's first-person narrative; the subsequent chapters, which are sometimes in the first person and sometimes in the third, introduce characters set into episodic vignettes that appear to have only the haziest connection with each other. A line of conversation or description, by simple stream-of-consciousness association, often goes off at a tangent to show a possible consequence of what has been said, so that many incidents have anecdotes within anecdotes within anecdotes, set off by a chance remark, much as a disorganized but enthusiastic lecturer will get side-tracked by something that occurs to him away from his main theme while on a favourite subject.

Burroughs must be read, like James Joyce, with concentration, keeping interrupted incidents from his past pages in mind every time the narrative apparently disintegrates or is side-tracked, waiting for it to be continued again without warning, often in the middle of another incident. The technique is not unknown to music and there are parallels in the plastic arts, but it often makes it difficult for the traditional literary reviewer to evaluate what the writer is doing and why.

The sex passages are no longer as controversially shocking as they were in the prurient fifties. *The Naked Lunch* has scenes of both homosexual and heterosexual incident and description, but thereafter his erotic themes have been almost exclusively in the former category. As with other serious homosexual writers, Jean Genet for instance, the heterosexual reader can be erotically drawn in to arousal through empathy and the force of the writing, and it is probably true to say that in relative terms there is less prejudice against Burroughs among heterosexual readers than among homosexuals, who often dislike intensely what he writes and his reasons for doing it. Burroughs is no apologist for militant homosexual causes, keeps his private life strictly private and writes to put over a world view that has no partisan bias other than sounding warnings and revealing the world that he sees around him. But his personal preoccupations and points of interest obviously influence the way in which he writes and what he writes about. When he writes fantasy he uses fantastic characters, expressionistically drawn out of the imagination from his observation. So we get—in addition to Doctors Benway and Schafer—A.J., giver of blue film parties, K.E., super salesman of extraordinary multipurpose gadgets, Mr Bradly Mr Martin, a double single person, characters from Bosch paintings, nigger-lynching Southern sheriffs, judges and rednecks, and as sex objects a series of red-headed, freckled, green-eyed pale-skinned white boys, Arab youths, Mexicans, merman-like green water creatures from other planets, and boy pirates. Sex with Burroughs is never naturalistic but hallucinatory, combining extreme fantasy with the imagery of violent death through hanging, constant ejaculation, buggery, transformation into other persons, other periods and other forms of life; and with mental firework displays symbolising climax, death, regeneration and reincarnation.

There is progression in Burroughs' work from his early narratives *Junkie* and *The Naked Lunch* (the latter using juxtaposed passages of not directly relevant abstract description between and within narrative chapters) and through the novels that follow, particularly *The Soft Machine, The Ticket that Exploded, Nova Express, The Wild Boys* and *Exterminator*. After *The Naked Lunch* his interest in Brion Gysin's development of literary cut-up technique (which will be explained later), as a basis for his own work, became predominant. Nevertheless it is hard to believe that the apparently random abstract passages in *The Naked Lunch* were not composed by cut-up method, but he assures us that it was only after finishing *The Naked Lunch* that he came across and used the method, so we must assume that he adopted it because it was another way of producing mechanically what his own creative processes had previously produced by random association, and that it was because of the similarity of result that he adopted the Gysin method. *The Third Mind*, a book that contains articles by both Burroughs and Gysin, together with interviews, examples of their individual and joint experiments and much else, will ultimately be recognized as one of the important source books of twentieth-century art—comparable to the notebooks of Leonardo da Vinci, which also examine the role of hazard in art, the manifestos of the Dadaists and early Surrealists, and the theories of Duchamp, John Cage, Stockhausen and Boulez, to mention only a few. Burroughs himself, in citing those writers and practitioners of other art disciplines who have influenced his development, emphasizes the difference between those like Roussel, Tzara and himself who have explained their literary method —how and why they did what they did—and others like T. S. Eliot, James Joyce and Celine, who did not. It is significant that the writers who have kept their trade secrets to themselves have a higher reputation critically than those who were generous enough to share them with reviewers and readers.

It will have been realized by now that I believe William Burroughs to be a very important writer indeed and one of the most significant of our time—as innovator, as theorist and as creator of a new form of picaresque novel that stems as much from the history of painting and European art and thought as from his American background and the drug experience that gave the first thrust to his work. He has many American literary ancestors: Walt Whitman, John Dos Passos, Ezra Pound and T. S. Eliot among them, but Americans are few among the authors he claims to have most enjoyed. And although Burroughs' work is often poetic to a high degree, he is not a lyrical writer, but uses romantic imagery as did the novelists of the early nineteenth century, to give colour and atmosphere to his work, to create an imagery, a mystique and a recognizable stylistic signature akin to poetry, but belonging to the very different world of heightened prose.

Burroughs' innovation logically carries literature forward, forging a new link in the chain of artistic development. By nature he is a romantic and an expressionist, whose object is to change a world that is both imperfect and in danger of succumbing to a resurgence of tyranny and perhaps to mass destruction, partly because of the apathy of so many citizens fortunate enough to live in democratic regimes and partly because of the determination of those power-hungry persons—in all societies—who want to exercise control to do so, undermining real (political) education and developing the paraphernalia of a police state to limit and finally remove civil rights. No one has better satirized bureaucratic tyranny:

Every citizen of Annexia was required to apply for and carry on his person at all times a whole portfolio of documents. Citizens were subject to be stopped in the street at any time; and the Examiner, who might be in plain clothes, in various uniforms, often in a bathing suit or pyjamas, sometimes stark naked except for a badge pinned to his left nipple, after checking each paper, would stamp it. On subsequent inspection the citizen was required to show the properly entered stamps of the last inspection. The Examiner, when he stopped a large group, would only examine and stamp the cards of a few. The others were then subject to arrest because their cards were not properly stamped. Arrest meant "provisional detention"; that is, the prisoner would be released if and when his Affidavit of Explanation, properly signed and stamped, was approved by the Assistant Arbiter of Explanations. Since this official hardly ever came to his office, and the Affidavit of Explanation had to be presented in person, the explainers spent weeks and months waiting around in unheated offices with no chairs and no toilet facilities.

Documents issued in vanishing ink faded into old pawn tickets. New documents were constantly required. The citizens rushed from one bureau to another in a frenzied attempt to meet impossible deadlines.

But although an expressionist by nature, sharing the expressionist determination to portray the world as he sees it rather than as it is, Burroughs' technique owes much more to the surrealist preoccupation with special states of the mind, with dream, hallucination and relativism, and he has employed random chance in a similar way to the action painters who were prominent at the time he started writing; the comparison is even closer to the experiments of his compatriot John Cage in music, who has cut up and interwoven musical structures in the same way that Burroughs has done with words. But it was the painter and writer Brion Gysin from whom Burroughs developed his own use of cut-ups. Burroughs has to say on the subject:

At a surrealist rally in the 1920s Tristan Tzara the man from nowhere proposed to create a poem on the spot by pulling words out of a hat. A riot ensued wrecked the theater. André Breton expelled Tristan Tzara from the movement and grounded the cut-ups on the Freudian couch.

In the summer of 1959 Brion Gysin painter and writer cut newspaper articles into sections and rearranged the sections *at random*. "Minutes to Go" resulted from this initial cut-up experiment. "Minutes to Go" contains unedited unchanged cut-ups emerging as quite coherent and meaningful prose.

The cut-up method brings to writers the collage, which has been used by painters for fifty years. And used by the moving and still camera. In fact all street shots from movie or still cameras are by the unpredictable factors of passersby and juxtaposition cut-ups. And photographers will tell you that often their best shots are accidents ... writers will tell you the same. The best writing seems to be done almost by accident by writers until the cut-up method was made explicit—all writing is in fact cut-ups; I will return to this point—had no way to produce the accident of spontaneity.

You cannot *will* spontaneity. But you can introduce the unpredictable spontaneous factor with a pair of scissors.

The method is simple. Here is one way to do it. Take a page. Like this page. Now cut down the middle and across the middle. You have four sections: 1   2   3   4 ... one two three four. Now rearrange the sections placing section four with section one and section two with section three. And you have a new page. Sometimes it says much the same thing. Sometimes something quite different—cutting up political speeches is an interesting exercise—in any case you will find that it says something and something quite definite. Take any poet or writer you fancy. Here, say, or poems you have read over many times. The words have lost meaning and life through years of repetition. Now take the poem and type out selected passages. Fill a page with excerpts. Now cut the page. You have a new poem. As many poems as you like. As many Shakespeare Rimbaud poems as you like. Tristan Tzara said: "Poetry is for everyone." And André Breton called him a cop and expelled him from the movement. Say it again: "Poetry is for everyone." Poetry is a place and it is free to all cut up Rimbaud and you are in Rimbaud's place. Here is a Rimbaud poem cut up.

"Visit of memories. Only your dance and your voice house. On the suburban air improbable desertions ... all harmonic pine for strife.

'The great skies are open. Candor of vapor and tent spitting blood laugh and drunken penance.

"Promenade of wine perfume opens slow bottle.

"The great skies are open. Supreme bugle burning flesh children to mist."

Cut-ups are for everyone. Anybody can make cut-ups. It is experimental in the sense of being *something to do*. Right here write now. Not something to talk and argue about. Greek philosophers assumed logically that an object twice as heavy as another object would fall twice as fast. It did not occur to them to push the two objects off the table and see how they fall. Cut the words and see how they fall. Shakespeare Rimbaud live in their words. Cut the word lines and you will hear their voices. Cut-ups often come through as code messages with special meaning for the cutter. Table tapping? Perhaps. Certainly an improvement on the usual deplorable performance of contacted poets through a medium. Rimbaud announces himself, to be followed by some excruciatingly bad poetry. Cut Rimbaud's words and you are assured of good poetry at least if not personal appearance.

All writing is in fact cut-ups. A collage of words read heard overheard. What else? Use of scissors renders the process explicit and subject to extension and variation. Clear classical prose can be composed entirely of rearranged cut-ups. Cutting and rearranging a page of written words introduces a new dimension into writing enabling the writer to turn images in cinematic variation. Images shift sense under the scissors smell images to sound sight to sound sound to kinesthetic. This is where Rimbaud was going with his color of vowels. And his "systematic derangement of the senses." The place of mescaline hallucination: seeing colors tasting sounds smelling forms.

The cut-ups can be applied to other fields than writing. Dr Neumann in his *Theory of Games and Economic Behavior* introduces the cut-up method of random action into game and military strategy: assume that the worst has happened and act accordingly. If your strategy is at some point determined ... by random factor your opponent will gain no advantage from knowing your strategy since he cannot predict the move. The cut-up method could be used to advantage in processing scientific data. How many discoveries have been made by accident? We cannot produce accidents to order. The cut-ups could add new dimension to films. Cut gambling scene in with a thousand gambling scenes all times and places. Cut back. Cut streets of the world. Cut and rearrange the word and image in films. There is no reason to accept a second-rate product when you can have the best. And the best is there for all. "Poetry is for everyone" ...

Now here are the preceding two paragraphs cut into four sections and rearranged:

ALL WRITING IS IN FACT CUT-UPS OF GAMES AND ECONOMIC BEHAVIOR OVERHEARD? WHAT ELSE? ASSUME THAT THE WORST HAS HAPPENED EXPLICIT AND SUBJECT TO STRATEGY IS AT SOME POINT CLASSICAL PROSE. CUTTING AND REARRANGING FACTOR YOUR OPPONENT WILL GAIN INTRODUCES A NEW DIMENSION YOUR STRATEGY. HOW MANY DISCOVERIES SOUND TO KINESTHETIC? WE CAN NOW PRODUCE ACCIDENT TO HIS COLOR OF VOWELS. AND NEW DIMENSION TO FILMS CUT THE SENSES. THE PLACE OF SAND. GAMBLING SCENES ALL TIMES COLORS TASTING SOUNDS SMELL STREETS OF THE WORLD. WHEN YOU CAN HAVE THE BEST ALL: "POETRY IS FOR EVERYONE" DR NEUMANN IN A COLLAGE OF WORDS READ HEARD INTRODUCED THE CUT-UP SCISSORS RENDERS THE PROCESS GAME AND MILITARY STRATEGY, VARIATION CLEAR AND ACT ACCORDINGLY. IF YOU POSED ENTIRELY OF REARRANGED CUT DETERMINED BY RANDOM A PAGE OF WRITTEN WORDS NO ADVANTAGE FROM KNOWING INTO WRITER PREDICT THE MOVE. THE CUT VARIATION IMAGES SHIFT SENSE ADVANTAGE IN PROCESSING TO SOUND SIGHT TO SOUND. HAVE BEEN MADE BY ACCIDENT IS WHERE RIMBAUD WAS GOING WITH ORDER THE CUT-UPS COULD "SYSTEMATIC DERANGEMENT" OF THE GAMBLING SCENE IN WITH A TEA HALLUCINATION: SEEING AND PLACES. CUT BACK. CUT FORMS. REARRANGE THE WORD AND IMAGE TO OTHER FIELDS THAN WRITING.

Since writing *Exterminator!*, a collection of stories that appeared in 1974 after earlier publication in different journals over the previous eight years, Burroughs has moved back towards more traditional narrative style, only occasionally using cut-up method, and it is possible that free association of the mind now makes it unnecessary for him to use scissors and paste to achieve the same effect. He has claimed that Eliot's *Waste Land* is the first major cut-up, but it was not achieved mechanically, and he obviously feels that Rimbaud, a favourite poet whose work has much of the poetic abstraction that appeals to Burroughs, is in a sense an early "cut-up" writer. The random order of *The Naked Lunch* produces an effect of controlled chaos: Gysin, who was working together with Burroughs at the time he was finishing it, tells us that the manuscript was clapped together in Paris more or less by chance, with pages from earlier work occasionally falling into it by accident. Burroughs himself has always been more interested in the new page in front of him than in going back over earlier work and is indifferent to the niceties of fine style; over the years he has left much of the final editing to his friends and publishers. *Cities of the Red Night*, William Burroughs' twelfth book to appear in Britain, has been through more heavy editing and by more hands than all his previous work put together, but it is by no means free of poetical abstract passages and the order of sequence and episode has been changed many times. Although reviews in America, where it first appeared, and in Britain were mixed, ranging from the dismissive to the ecstatic, it is without question his best-organized book and his major achievement in purely literary terms since *The Naked Lunch*, itself a flawed masterpiece of incredible richness that will always be the book that first comes to mind when Burroughs' name is mentioned, as one thinks first of *Ulysses* with Joyce. *Cities* is a long book, combining a vision of Captain Mission's ideal society in fictional terms with all the Burroughs paraphernalia of hanged boys, buggery, sexual magic and gun technology (Burroughs has always had a special interest in guns), a modern quest for a missing American boy, whose severed head becomes a potent magical juju, by Clem Snide, "Private Asshole" (who first makes a brief appearance in *The Naked Lunch*), the journey of Farnsworth, a British District Health Officer in Waghdas who succumbs to fever, whose dreams may in fact be the substance of the novel, and there are many subplots. No story is every brought to its conclusion except perhaps the failure and end of the Mission colony. A strange fever (akin to scarlet fever) that occurs periodically throughout history is central to the novel and shown as a plague that turns its victims into sexual maniacs. It links the different themes, plots and subplots of *Cities*. Although the novel is metaphorical with many symbolical associations, its main significance may be a metaphor for fanaticism, a principal Burroughs preoccupation.

It is the sexual fantasies and the sadism that most upsets many members of the literary establishment that might otherwise be interested in his ability to create plot and character and even in his experimental methods. The graphic descriptions of homosexual acts, the ritual executions, mostly by hanging, which according to legend inspires erection and ejaculation in the male victim, thereby identifying *le petit mort* with a cruel and violent death, the hallucinatory nature of the orgies, blue film sequences and massacres, all deeply offend the conventional "civilized" mind, and are meant to do so. His use of expressionist caricature is especially apt, cruel and funny, sparing no one, especially not the homosexual community.

"So this elegant faggot comes to New York from Cunt Lick, Texas, and he is the most piss elegant fag of them all. He is taken up by old women of the type batten on young fags, toothless old predators too weak and too slow to run down other prey. Old moth-eaten tigress shit sure turn into a fag eater.... So this citizen, being an arty and crafty fag, begins making costume jewelry and jewelry sets. Every rich old gash in Greater New York wants he should do her sets, and he is making money, 21, El Morocco, Stork, but no time for sex, and all the time worrying about his rep.... He begins playing the horses, supposed to be something manly about gambling God knows why, and he figures it will build him up to be seen at the track. Not many fags play the horses, and those that play lose more than the others, they are lousy gamblers plunge in a losing streak and hedge when they win ... which being the pattern of their lives.... Now every child knows there is one law of gambling: winning and losing come in streaks. Plunge when you win, fold when you lose. (I once knew a fag dip into the till—not the whole two thousand at once on the nose win or Sing Sing. Not our Gertie ... Oh no a deuce at a time ...)

"So he loses and loses and lose some more. One day he is about to put a rock in a set when the obvious occur. 'Of course, I'll replace it later.' Famous last words. So all that winter, one after the other, the diamonds, emeralds, pearls, rubies and star sapphires of the haut monde go in hock and replaced by queer replicas....

"So the opening night of the Met this old hag appear as she thinks resplendent in her diamond tiara. So this other old whore approach and say, 'Oh, Miggles, you're so smart ... to leave the real ones at home.... I mean we're simply mad to go around tempting fate.'

" 'You're mistaken, my dear. These *are* real.'

" 'Oh but Miggles dahling, they're *not*.... I mean ask your jeweler.... Well just ask *anybody*. Haaaaaa.'

"So a Sabbath is hastily called. (Lucy Bradshinkel, look at thy emeralds.) All these old witches examining their rocks like a citizen finds leprosy on himself.

" 'My chicken blood ruby!'

" 'My bleck oopalls!' Old bitch marry so many times so many gooks and spics she don't know her accent from her ass....

" 'My stah sahphire!' shrieks a *poule de luxe*. 'Oh it's all so awful!'

" 'I mean they are strictly from Woolworth's....'

" 'There's only one thing to do. I'm going to call the police,' says a strong-minded, out-spoken old thing; and she clump across the floor on her low heels and calls the fuzz.

"Well, the faggot draws a deuce; and in the box he meets this cat who is some species of cheap hustler, and love sets in or at least a facsimile thereof convince the parties inna first and second parts. As continuity would have it, they are sprung at the same time more or less and take up residence in a flat on the Lower East Side.... And cook in and both are working legit modest jobs.... So Brad and Jim know happiness for the first time.

"Enter the powers of evil.... Lucy Bradshinkel has come to say all is forgiven. She has faith in Brad and wants to set him up in a studio. Of course, he will have to move to the East Sixties.... 'This place is impossible, dahling; and your friend ...' And a safe mob wants Jim back to drive a car. This is a step up, you dig? Offer from citizen hardly see him before.

"Will Jim go back to crime? Will Brad succumb to the blandishments of an aging vampire, a ravening Maw? ... Needless to say, the forces of evil are routed and exit with ominous snarls and mutterings.

" 'The Boss isn't going to like this.'

" 'I don't know why I ever wasted my time with you, you cheap, vulgar little fairy.'

"The boys stand at the tenement window, their arms around each other, looking at the Brooklyn Bridge. A warm spring wind ruffles Jim's black curls and the fine hennaed hair of Brad.

" 'Well, Brad, what's for supper?'

" 'You just go in the other room and wait.' Playfully he shoos Jim out of the kitchen, and puts on his apron.

"Dinner is Lucy Bradshinkel's cunt saignant cooked in kotex papillon. The boys eat happily looking into each other's eyes. Blood runs down their chins."

What offends in a different way is also one of his great virtues, namely his ear for accent, inflection and character portrayal through the speaking voice. The long chapter entitled "The County Clerk" in *The Naked Lunch* is mostly a long monologue by a red neck Southern bigot such as has been depicted in hundreds of American films (Burroughs is a great film addict). The chapter has less interruption and side-track than in most of his other work and is perhaps the most sustained narrative passage to be found anywhere in his work. It is given in full here from page 117. The accuracy of his ear is formidable, even when the prose seems to be an ungrammatical vernacular mess on the page, but it comes to life when read. Burroughs himself has given many readings and delights in these passages, using his voice as Dickens once did to create character and enjoying the roles as an actor would. He recreates what he has heard in terms of caricature that is more faithful to character than the reality.

Magic plays a large part in Burroughs' work and there are times when he gives the appearance that he believes he is creating magic by the manipulation of words. For instance, when working on a fold-in or cut-up one day and aligning different texts so that a new narrative gradually began to appear, he found that he had created the story of a plane crash, described in some detail. The next day the papers carried a report of an identical disaster in South America which had occurred just at the time he was developing his text. He even got the name of the pilot right. In

The Third Mind he relates many incidents where a happening in life suddenly coincides with something he has just read or written, but without making it clear how far he believes in a magical element. It is tempting to see a resemblance between William Burroughs and that other writer-magician, Alistair Crowley, with whom there are many similarities of style and background preoccupation, but Crowley whatever his talent was largely a charlatan, whereas Burroughs is a concerned and rational human being, not devoid of impish humour. The legends about him are numerous and help to create public interest in the enigmatic personality behind the books.

In an age that has come to accept much stranger conceptions than magic and the supernatural—time displacement, black holes and mirror existence for instance—and is beginning to doubt all evidence of the senses where reality is concerned, it is not surprising that a writer of Burroughs' breadths of interest in these things should give his novels the character of science fiction and prophetic utterance as well as involvement in psychology and parapsychology. He embraces all our fears for the future and enables us to recognize the symptoms today of the plagues of tomorrow. The force of the imagery inevitably invites comparison with Bosch and the medieval view of the natural world as being only a small part of the supernatural, a space between Heaven and Hell where all time is unified. His apocalyptic vision is part of his importance as a major modern writer and his virtuosity has established his reputation in the intellectual world except where minds are too closed to overlook the "disgusting" nature of his subject matter. He is reviled in the same terms previously applied to Swift, with whom he has so much in common. But it must be stressed that reading Burroughs is not only a fascinating, if alarming, intellectual adventure, but also a very enjoyable one. A master of dialogue, a creator of character without a contemporary equal, a humourist who gets funnier as his subject-matter gets blacker, and a first-class storyteller, he belongs to that small circle of writers who improve on continued acquaintance and have the ability to extend our awareness of the world in which we live and all its possibilities, good and bad.

J. C.

Note: The reader will note a variation in spelling of words such as gray/grey and nabor/neighbour throughout the book. English and American spellings have both been used by the author at different times and this volume usually follows the author's original.

THE NAKED LUNCH

Many artists have experimented with drugs in order to increase their consciousness, have found the experience intellectually and pleasurably valuable, but have also discovered that although many drugs inspire the desire to write and give insight into consciousness, the ability to write is destroyed by the inhibition of energy and all sense of urgency. In our own time Aldous Huxley, Henri Michaux, Alexander Trocchi and many of William Burroughs' friends and followers have written revealingly about the drug experience, but only Burroughs has been able to create a whole fictional world out of the drug scene, a world that is hardly aware of any other, that lives by its own time clock, its own rules and its own mystique. That world is the antithesis of bourgeois normality and is viewed with horror by all law-abiding members of western society. By contrast there are other societies, mostly Muslim, that are tolerant of hallucinatory and even addictive drugs, but consider alcoholic drinking with equal horror. It is not surprising that members of western society who opt out of it to adopt a lifestyle more appropriate to an Arab country should carry drug-taking to extremes, much as some Arab visitors to the West are unable to use alcohol without similar abuse.

The Naked Lunch, William Burroughs' second novel, starts with an autobiographical introduction which in literary terms describes his condition after emerging from the drug experience without which the book could not have been written, and ends with a paper he wrote for the *British Journal of Addiction.* The first of these texts is given in full, following an extract from the second, because Burroughs' analysis of the different effects of those drugs with which he has experimented should in my opinion be read first for better understanding of the junkie's world. This is followed by what is in effect an abridged version of *The Naked Lunch*, introducing not only those Burroughs characters who are addicts, but also those who encourage the addiction for personal gain, or for reasons of experimentation, and others whose existence is inside a blown-up, caricatured and satirized picture of society that is itself a metaphor for the drug condition. The sickness of the drug society is a microcosm for the sickness of "normal" society, which has its own hallucinatory and addictive poisons. If the addict is a small-time criminal, a danger only to himself except when driven to crime because of the intolerance of society, then society itself is the real criminal because it is dominated by addicts to those other drugs, power-hunger, control-addiction and inhumane experiment, itself part of the alienating process which has created the drug culture. In the nineteenth century, western powers imported opium it is not only the Mafia that benefits from drug addiction, but all those bureaucracies that exist to deny self-dependence to the individual.

Many of the sections that follow show highly unconventional, imaginative and sadistic sexual activity, some of it more erotic to homo- than to heterosexuals, but all intended to stress the connection, now well known to psychiatry and to anthropology, between sex and death and sex and cruelty. Burroughs' purpose, as with Swift's *A Modest Proposal*, is to make his readers aware of the connection between the urge to kill or torture and sexual desire, in order to stop cruelty through self-awareness in the same way as Swift advocated eating babies to cure the Irish famine, shocking those who otherwise would not have been aware that there was a famine or have bothered to think about ending it. The awareness of one's own baser instincts, the reasons for them, and the strong possibility that they are common to a larger number of other people, does not create more cruelty but less, assuming that there is a cultural overlay of learned morality. It is the inability to realize what lies underneath our anger, desire to punish, envy or lust that makes people behave and think in an uncivilized way. Burroughs points out this moral through shock and emotional titillation in the same way as Swift did.

Like Bosch and Swift, Burroughs has a genius for creating monsters, beings that are grotesquely inhuman but have the attributes of humans—mugwumps, Latahs, divisionists, senders, liquefactionists, etc. These belong to medieval diabolism and intermingle with Damon Runyan-like gangsters and denizens of the underworld and the drug society, often with colourful Runyan-like nicknames. Burroughs gets much relish out of them and their speech, as he does out of the Southern "cracker" lawmen and red-necks whose contempt for and cruelty towards Negroes inspires some of his best passages. The County Clerk is an outstanding example of this.

The final section of *The Naked Lunch* has different interpretations and refers to passages that have appeared throughout the book. There is an explosion created by a gasoline can, which simultaneously refers to the burning alive of a black man, the flash of junk hitting the brain cells and the explosion of a nuclear bomb. To Burroughs all these things are identified with sexual orgasm and the moment of death.

The order of *The Naked Lunch* is not consecutive and is different from the order of the extracts that follow, but the rearrangement is by subject and preoccupation. When the reader returns to the complete book, as I am sure he will, he will find that the sporadic sequence of event, association and episode encapsulated in other episodes may take on a different meaning and be more comprehensible as a result of reading the work in the order given here.

FROM THE BRITISH JOURNAL OF ADDICTION vol. 53, no. 2

The use of opium and opium derivatives leads to a state that defines limits and describes "addiction"—(The term is loosely used to indicate anything one is used to or wants. We speak of addiction to candy, coffee, tobacco, warm weather, television, detective stories, crossword puzzles.) So misapplied the term loses any useful precision of meaning. The use of morphine leads to a metabolic dependence on morphine. Morphine becomes a biologic need like water and the user may die if he is suddenly deprived of it. The diabetic will die without insulin, but he is not addicted to insulin. His need for insulin was not brought about by the use of insulin. He needs insulin to maintain a normal metabolism. The addict needs morphine to maintain a morphine metabolism, and so avoid the excruciatingly painful return to a normal metabolism.

I have used a number of "narcotic" drugs over a period of twenty years. Some of these drugs are addicting in the above sense. Most are not:

Opiates.—Over a period of twelve years I have used opium, smoked and taken orally (injection in the skin causes abscesses. Injection in the vein is unpleasant and perhaps dangerous), heroin injected in skin, vein, muscle, sniffed (when no needle was available), morphine, dilaudid, pantopon, eukodol, paracodine, dionine, codeine, demerol, methodone. They are all habit forming in varying degree. Nor does it make much difference how the drug is administered, smoked, sniffed, injected, taken orally, inserted in rectal suppositories, the end result will be the same: addiction. And a smoking habit is as difficult to break as an intravenous injection habit. The concept that injection habits are particularly injurious derives from an irrational fear of needles—("Injections poison the blood stream"—as though the blood stream were any less poisoned by substances absorbed from the stomach, the lungs or the mucous membrane). Demerol is probably less addicting than morphine. It is also less satisfying to the addict, and less effective as a pain killer. While a demerol habit is easier to break than a morphine habit, demerol is certainly more injurious to the health and specifically to the nervous system. I once used demerol for three months and developed a number of distressing symptoms: trembling hands (with morphine my hands are always steady), progressive loss of coordination, muscular contractions, paranoid obsesssions, fear of insanity. Finally I contracted an opportune intolerance for demerol—no doubt a measure of self preservation—and switched to methodone. Immediately all my symptoms disappeared. I may add that demerol is quite as constipating as morphine, that it exerts an even more depressing effect on the appetite and the sexual functions, does not, however, contract the pupils. I have given myself thousands of injections over a period of years with un-sterilized, in fact dirty, needles and never sustained an infection until I used demerol. Then I came down with a series of abscesses one of which had to be lanced and drained. In short demerol seems to me a more dangerous drug than morphine. Methodone is completely satisfying to the addict, an excellent pain killer, at least as addicting as morphine.

I have taken morphine for acute pain. Any opiate that effectively relieves pain to an equal degree relieves withdrawal symptoms. The conclusion is obvious: Any opiate that relieves pain is habit forming, and the more effectively it relieves pain the more habit forming it is. The habit forming molecule, and the pain killing molecule of morphine are probably identical, and the process by which morphine relieves pain is the same process that leads to tolerance and addiction. Non habit forming morphine appears to be a latter day Philosopher's Stone. On the other hand variations of apomorphine may prove extremely effective in controlling the withdrawal syndrome. But we should not expect this drug to a be a pain killer as well.

The phenomena of morphine addiction are well known and there is no reason to go over them here. A few points, it seems to me, have received insufficient attention: The metabolic incompatibility between morphine and alcohol has been observed, but no one, so far as I know, has advanced an explanation. If a morphine addict drinks alcohol he experiences no agreeable or euphoric sensations. There is a feeling of slowly mounting discomfort, and the need for another injection. The alcohol seems to be short-circuited perhaps by the liver. I once attempted to drink in a state of incomplete recovery from an attack of jaundice (I was not using morphine at this time). The metabolic sensation was identical. In one case the liver was partly out of action from jaundice, in the other preoccupied, literally, by a morphine metabolism. In neither case could it metabolize alcohol. If an alcoholic becomes addicted to morphine, morphine invariably and completely displaces alcohol. I have known several alcoholics who began using morphine. They were able to tolerate large doses of morphine immediately (1 grain to a shot) without ill effects, and in a matter of days stopped taking alcohol. The reverse never occurs. The morphine addict can not tolerate alcohol when he is using morphine or suffering from morphine withdrawal. The ability to tolerate alcohol is a sure sign of disintoxication. In consequence alcohol can never be substituted for morphine directly. Of course a disintoxicated addict may start drinking and become an alcoholic.

During withdrawal the addict is acutely aware of his surroundings. Sense impressions are sharpened to the point of hallucination. Familiar objects scem to stir with a writhing furtive life. The addict is subject to a barrage of sensations external and visceral. He may experience flashes of beauty and nostalgia, but the overall impression is extremely painful—(Possibly his sensations are painful because of their intensity. A pleasurable sensation may become intolerable after a certain intensity is reached.)

I have noticed two special reactions of early withdrawal: (1) Everything looks threatening; (2) mild paranoia. The doctors and nurses appear as monsters of evil. In the course of several cures, I have felt myself surrounded by dangerous lunatics. I talked with one of Dr Dent's patients who had just undergone disintoxication for a pethidine habit. He reported an identical experience, told me that for twenty-four hours the nurses and the doctor "seemed brutal and repugnant." And everything looked blue. And I have talked with other addicts who experienced the same reactions. Now the psychological basis for paranoid notions during withdrawal is obvious. The specific similarity of these reactions indicates a common metabolic origin. The similarity between withdrawal phenomena and certain states of drug intoxication, is striking. Hashish, Bannisteria Caapi (harmaline), Peyote (mescaline) produce states of acute sensitivity, with hallucinatory viewpoint. Everything looks alive. Paranoid ideas are frequent. Bannisteria Caapi intoxication specifically reproduces the state of withdrawal. Everything looks threatening. Paranoid ideas are marked, especially with overdose. After taking Bannisteria Caapi, I was convinced that the Medicine Man and his apprentice were conspiring to murder me. It seems that metabolic states of the body can reproduce the effects of various drugs.

In the USA heroin addicts are receiving an involuntary reduction cure from the pushers who progressively dilute their wares with milk, sugar and barbiturates. As a result many of the addicts who scek treatment are lightly addicted so they can be completely disintoxicated in a short time (seven to eight days). They recover rapidly without medication. Meanwhile any tranquillizing, anti-allergic, or sedative drug, will afford some relief, especially if injected. The addict feels better if he knows that some alien substance is coursing through his blood stream. Tolserol, Thorazine and related "tranquillizers," every variety of barbiturate, Chloral and Paraldehyde, anti-histamines, cortisone, reserpine, even shock (can lobotomy be far behind?) have all been used with results usually described as "encouraging." My own experience suggests that these results be accepted with some reserve. Of course, symptomatic treatment is indicated, and all these drugs (with possible exception of the drug most commonly used: barbiturates) have a place in the treatment of the withdrawal syndrome. But none of these drugs is in itself the answer to withdrawal. Withdrawal symptoms vary with individual metabolism and physical type. Pigeon chested, hay fever and asthma liable individuals suffer greatly from allergic symptoms during withdrawal: running nose, sneezing, smarting, watering eyes, difficulty in breathing. In such cases cortisone, and antihistamine drugs may afford definite relief. Vomiting could probably be controlled with anti-nausea drugs like thorazine.

I have undergone ten "cures" in the course of which all these drugs were used. I have taken quick reductions, slow reductions, prolonged sleep, apomorphine, antihistamines, a French system involving a worthless product known as "amorphine," everything but shock. (I would be interested to hear results of further experiments with shock treatment on somebody else.) The success of any treatment depends on the degree and duration of addiction, the stage of withdrawal (drugs which are effective in late or light withdrawal can be disastrous in the acute phase), individual symptoms, health, age, etc. A method of treatment might be completely ineffective at one time, but give excellent results at another. Or a treatment that does me no good may help someone else. I do not presume to pass any final judgements, only to report my own reactions to various drugs and methods of treatment.

Reduction Cures.—This is the commonest form of treatment, and no method yet discovered can entirely replace it in cases of severe addiction. The patient must have some morphine. If there is one rule that applies to all cases of addiction this is it. But the morphine should be withdrawn as quickly as possible. I have taken slow reduction cures and in every case the result was discouragement and eventual relapse. Imperceptible reduction is likely to be endless reduction. When the addict seeks cure, he has, in most cases, already experienced withdrawal symptoms many times. He expects an unpleasant ordeal and he is prepared to endure it. But if the pain of withdrawal is spread over two months instead of ten days he may not be able to endure it. It is not the intensity but the duration of pain that breaks the will to resist. If the addict habitually takes any quantity, however small, of any opiate to alleviate the weakness, insomnia, boredom, restlessness, of late withdrawal, the withdrawal symptoms will be prolonged indefinitely and complete relapse is almost certain.

Prolonged Sleep.—The theory sounds good. You go to sleep and wake up cured. Industrial doses of chloral hydrate, barbiturates, thorazine, only produced a nightmare state of semi-consciousness. Withdrawal of sedation, after five days, occasioned a severe shock. Symptoms of acute morphine deprivation supervened. The end result was a combined syndrome of unparalleled horror. No cure I ever took was as painful as this allegedly painless method. The cycle of sleep and wakefulness is always deeply disturbed during withdrawal. To further disturb it with massive sedation seems contraindicated to say the least. Withdrawal of morphine is sufficiently traumatic without adding to it withdrawal of barbiturates. After two weeks in the hospital (five days sedation, ten days "rest") I was still so weak that I fainted when I tried to walk up a slight incline. I consider prolonged sleep the worst possible method of treating withdrawal.

Anti-histamines.—The use of anti-histamines is based on the allergic theory of withdrawal. Sudden withdrawal of morphine precipitates an overproduction of histamine with consequent allergic symptoms. (In shock resulting from traumatic injury with acute pain large quantities of histamine are released in the blood. In acute pain as in addiction toxic doses of morphine are readily tolerated. Rabbits, who have a high histamine content in the blood, are extremely resistant to morphine.) My own experience with anti-histamines has not been conclusive. I once took a cure in which only anti-histamines were used, and the results were good. But I was lightly addicted at that time, and had been without morphine for seventy-two hours when the cure started. I have frequently used anti-histamines since then for withdrawal symptoms with disappointing results. In fact they seem to increase my depression and irritability (I do not suffer from typical allergic symptoms).

Apomorphine.—Apomorphine is certainly the best method of

treating withdrawal that I have experienced. It does not completely eliminate the withdrawal symptoms, but reduces them to an endurable level. The acute symptoms such as stomach and leg cramps, convulsive or maniac states are completely controlled. In fact apomorphine treatment involves less discomfort than a reduction cure. Recovery is more rapid and more complete. I feel that I was never completely cured of the craving for morphine until I took apomorphine treatment. Perhaps the "psychological" craving for morphine that persists after a cure is not psychological at all, but metabolic. More potent variations of the apomorphine formula might prove qualitatively more effective in treating all forms of addiction.

Cortisone.—Cortisone seems to give some relief especially when injected intravenously.

Thorazine.—Provides some relief from withdrawal symptoms, but not much. Side effects of depression, disturbances of vision, indigestion offset dubious benefits.

Reserpine.—I never noticed any effect whatever from this drug except a slight depression.

Tolserol.—Negligible results.

Barbiturates.—It is common practice to prescribe barbiturates for the insomnia of withdrawal. Actually the use of barbiturates delays the return of normal sleep, prolongs the whole period of withdrawal, and may lead to relapse. (The addict is tempted to take a little codeine or paregoric with his nembutal. Very small quantities of opiates, that would be quite innocuous for a normal person, immediately re-establish addiction in a cured addict.) My experience certainly confirms Dr Dent's statement that barbiturates are contraindicated.

Chloral and paraldehyde.—Probably preferable to barbiturates if a sedative is necessary, but most addicts will vomit up paraldehyde at once. I have also tried, on my own initiative, the following drugs during withdrawal:

Alcohol.—Absolutely contraindicated at any stage of withdrawal. The use of alcohol invariably exacerbates the withdrawal symptoms and leads to relapse. Alcohol can only be tolerated after metabolism returns to normal. This usually takes one month in cases of severe addiction.

Benzedrine.—May relieve temporarily the depression of late withdrawal, disastrous during acute withdrawal, contraindicated at any stage because it produces a state of nervousness for which morphine is the physiological answer.

Cocaine.—The above goes double for cocaine.

Cannabis indica (marijuana).—In late or light withdrawal relieves depression and increases the appetite, in acute withdrawal an unmitigated disaster. (I once smoked marijuana during early withdrawal with nightmarish results.) Cannabis is a sensitizer. If you feel bad already it will make you feel worse. Contraindicated.

Peyote, *Bannisteria caapi*.—I have not ventured to experiment. The thought of Bannisteria intoxication superimposed on acute withdrawal makes the brain reel. I know of a man who substituted peyote during late withdrawal, claimed to lose all desire for morphine, ultimately died of peyote poisoning.

In cases of severe addiction, definite, physical, withdrawal symptoms persist for one month at least.

I have never seen or heard of a psychotic morphine addict, I mean anyone who showed psychotic symptoms while addicted to an opiate. In fact addicts are drearily sane. Perhaps there is a metabolic incompatibility between schizophrenia and opiate addiction. On the other hand the withdrawal of morphine often precipitates psychotic reactions—usually mild paranoia. Interesting that drugs and methods of treatment that give results in schizophrenia, are also of some use in withdrawal: anti-histamines, tranquillizers, apomorphine, shock.

Sir Charles Sherington defines pain as "the psychic adjunct of an imperative protective reflex."

The vegetative nervous system expands and contracts in response to visceral rhythms and external stimuli, expanding to stimuli which are experienced as pleasurable—sex, food, agreeable social contacts, etc.—contracting from pain, anxiety, fear, discomfort, boredom. Morphine alters the whole cycle of expansion and contraction, release and tension. The sexual function is deactivated, peristalsis inhibited, the pupils cease to react in response to light and darkness. The organism neither contracts from pain nor expands to normal sources of pleasure. It adjusts to a morphine cycle. The addict is immune to boredom. He can look at his shoe for hours or simply stay in bed. He needs no sexual outlet, no social contacts, no work, no diversion, no exercise, nothing but morphine. Morphine may relieve pain by imparting to the organism some of the qualities of a plant. (Pain could have no function for plants which are, for the most part, stationary, incapable of protective reflexes.)

Scientists look for a non-habit forming morphine that will kill pain without giving pleasure, addicts want—or think they want—

euphoria without addiction. I do not see how the functions of morphine can be separated, I think that any effective pain killer will depress the sexual function, induce euphoria and cause addiction. The perfect pain killer would probably be immediately habit forming. (If anyone is interested to develop such a drug, dehydro-oxy-heroin might be a good place to start.)

The addict exists in a painless, sexless, timeless state. Transition back to the rhythms of animal life involves the withdrawal syndrome. I doubt if this transition can ever be made in comfort. Painless withdrawals can only be approached.

Cocaine.—Cocaine is the most exhilarating drug I have ever used. The euphoria centres in the head. Perhaps the drug activates pleasure connections directly in the brain. I suspect that an electric current in the right place would produce the same effect. The full exhilaration of cocaine can only be realised by an intravenous injection. The pleasurable effects do not last more than five or ten minutes. If the drug is injected in the skin, rapid elimination vitiates the effects. This goes doubly for sniffing.

It is standard practice for cocaine users to sit up all night shooting cocaine at one minute intervals, alternating with shots of heroin, or cocaine and heroin mixed in the same injection to form a "speed ball." (I have never known an habitual cocaine user who was not a morphine addict.)

The desire for cocaine can be intense. I have spent whole days walking from one drug store to another to fill a cocaine prescription. You may want cocaine intensely, but you don't have any metabolic need for it. If you can't get cocaine you eat, you go to sleep and forget it. I have talked with people who used cocaine for years, then were suddenly cut off from their supply. None of them experienced any withdrawal symptoms. Indeed it is difficult to see how a front brain stimulant could be addicting. Addiction seems to be a monopoly of sedatives.

Continued use of cocaine leads to nervousness, depression, sometimes drug psychosis with paranoid hallucinations. The nervousness and depression resulting from cocaine use are not alleviated by more cocaine. They are effectively relieved by morphine. The use of cocaine by a morphine addict, always leads to larger and more frequent injections of morphine.

Cannabis indica (hashish, marijuana).—The effects of this drug have been frequently and luridly described: disturbance of space-time perception, acute sensitivity to impressions, flight of ideas, laughing jags, silliness. Marijuana is a sensitizer, and the results are not always pleasant. It makes a bad situation worse. Depression becomes despair, anxiety panic. I have already mentioned my horrible experience with marijuana during acute morphine withdrawal. I once gave marijuana to a guest who was mildly anxious about something ("On bum kicks" as he put it). After smoking half a cigarette he suddenly leapt to his feet screaming "I got the fear!" and rushed out of the house.

An especially unnerving feature of marijuana intoxication is a disturbance of the affective orientation. You do not know whether you like something or not, whether a sensation is pleasant or unpleasant.

The use of marijuana varies greatly with the individual. Some smoke it constantly, some occasionally, not a few dislike it intensely. It seems to be especially unpopular with confirmed morphine addicts, many of whom take a puritanical view of marijuana smoking.

The ill effects of marijuana have been grossly exaggerated in the US. Our national drug is alcohol. We tend to regard the use of any other drug with special horror. Anyone given over to these alien vices deserves the complete ruin of his mind and body. People believe what they want to believe without regard for the facts. Marijuana is not habit forming. I have never seen evidence of any ill effects from moderate use. Drug psychosis may result from prolonged and excessive use.

Barbiturates.—The barbiturates are definitely addicting if taken in large quantities over any period of time (about a gramme a day will cause addiction). Withdrawal syndrome is more dangerous than morphine withdrawal, consisting of hallucinations with epilepsy type convulsions. Addicts often injure themselves flopping about on concrete floors (concrete floors being a usual corollary of abrupt withdrawal). Morphine addicts often take barbiturates to potentiate inadequate morphine rations. Some of them become barbiturate addicts as well.

I once took two nembutal capsules (one and a half grains each) every night for four months and suffered no withdrawal symptoms. Barbiturate addiction is a question of quantity. It is probably not a metabolic addiction like morphine, but a mechanical reaction from excessive front brain sedation.

The barbiturate addict presents a shocking spectacle. He can not coordinate, he staggers, falls off bar stools, goes to sleep in the middle of a sentence, drops food out of his mouth. He is confused, quarrelsome and stupid. And he almost always uses other drugs, anything he can lay hands on: alcohol, benzedrene, opiates, marijuana. Barbiturate users are looked down on in addict society: "Goof ball bums. They got no class to them." The next step down is coal gas and milk, or sniffing ammonia in a bucket—"The scrub woman's kick."

It seems to me that barbiturates cause the worst possible form of addiction, unsightly, deteriorating, difficult to treat.

Benzedrene.—This is a cerebral stimulant like cocaine. Large doses cause prolonged sleeplessness with feelings of exhilaration. The period of euphoria is followed by a horrible depression. The drug tends to increase anxiety. It causes indigestion and loss of appetite.

I know of only one case where definite symptoms followed the withdrawal of benzedrene. This was a woman of my acquaintance who used incredible quantities of benzedrene for six months. During this period she developed a drug psychosis and was hospitalized for ten days. She continued the use of benzedrene, but was suddenly cut off. She suffered an asthma type seizure. She could not get her breath and turned blue. I gave her a dose of antihistamine (thepherene) which afforded immediate relief. The symptoms did not return.

Peyote (mescaline).—This is undoubtedly a stimulant. It dilates the pupils, keeps one awake. Peyote is extremely nauseating. Users experience difficulty keeping it down long enough to realize the effect, which is similar, in some respects, to marijuana. There is increased sensitivity to impression, especially to colours. Peyote intoxication causes a peculiar vegetable consciousness or identification with the plant. Everything looks like a peyote plant. It is easy to understand why the Indians believe there is a resident spirit in the peyote cactus.

Overdose of peyote may lead to respiratory paralysis and death. I know of one case. There is no reason to believe that peyote is addicting.

Bannisteria caapi (Harmaline, Banisterine, Telepathine).— Bannisteria caapi is a fast growing vine. The active principle is apparently found throughout the wood of the fresh cut vine. The inner bark is considered most active, and the leaves are never used.

It takes a considerable quantity of the vine to feel the full effects of the drug. About five pieces of vine each eight inches long are needed for one person. The vine is crushed and boiled for two or more hours with the leaves of a bush identified as *Palicourea sp. rubiaceae*.

Yage or Ayuahuaska (the most commonly used Indian names for Bannisteria caapi) is a hallucinating narcotic that produces a profound derangement of the senses. In overdose it is a convulsant poison. The antidote is a barbiturate or other strong, anti-convulsant sedative. Anyone taking Yage for the first time should have a sedative ready in the event of an overdose.

The hallucinating properties of Yage have led to its use by Medicine Men to potentiate their powers. They also use it as a cure-all in the treatment of various illnesses. Yage lowers the body temperature and consequently is of some use in the treatment of fever. It is a powerful antihelminthic, indicated for treatment of stomach or intestinal worms. Yage induces a state of conscious anaesthesia, and is used in rites where the initiates must undergo a painful ordeal like whipping with knotted vines, or exposure to the sting of ants.

So far as I could discover only the fresh cut vine is active. I found no way to dry, extract or preserve the active principal. No tinctures proved active. The dried vine is completely inert. The pharmacology of Yage requires laboratory research. Since the crude extract is such a powerful, hallucinating narcotic, perhaps even more spectacular results could be obtained with synthetic variations. Certainly the matter warrants further research.*

I did not observe any ill effects that could be attributed to the use of Yage. The Medicine Men who use it continuously in line of duty seem to enjoy normal health. Tolerance is soon acquired so that one can drink the extract without nausea or other ill effect.

Yage is a unique narcotic. Yage intoxication is in some respects similar to intoxication with hashish. In both instances there is a shift of viewpoint, an extension of consciousness beyond ordinary experience. But Yage produces a deeper derangement of the senses with actual hallucinations. Blue flashes in front of the eyes is peculiar to Yage intoxication.

There is a wide range of attitude in regard to Yage. Many Indians and most White users seem to regard it simply as another intoxicant like liquor. In other groups it has ritual use and significance. Among

* Since this was published I have discovered that the alkaloid of Bannisteria are closely related to LSD6 which has been used to produce experimental psychosis. I think they are up to LSD25 already.

the Jivaro, young men take Yage to contact the spirits of their ancestors and get a briefing for their future life. It is used during initiations to anaesthetize the initiates for painful ordeals. All Medicine Men use it in their practice to foretell the future, locate lost or stolen objects, name the perpetrator of a crime, to diagnose and treat illness.

The alcaloid of Bannisteria caapi was isolated in 1923 by Fisher Cardenas. He called the alcaloid Telepathine alternately Banisterine. Rumf showed that Telepathine was identical with Harmine, the alcaloid of Perganum Harmala.

Bannisteria caapi is evidently not habit forming.

Nutmeg.—Convicts and sailors sometimes have recourse to nutmeg. About a tablespoon is swallowed with water. Results are vaguely similar to marijuana with side effects of headache and nausea. Death would probably supervene before addiction if such addiction is possible. I have only taken nutmeg once.

There are a number of narcotics of the nutmeg family in use among the Indians of South America. They are usually administered by sniffing a dried powder of the plant. The Medicine Men take these noxious substances, and go into convulsive states. Their twitchings and mutterings are thought to have prophetic significance. A friend of mine was violently sick for three days after experimenting with a drug of the nutmeg family in South America.

Datura-scopolamine.—Morphine addicts are frequently poisoned by taking morphine in combination with scopolamine.

I once obtained some ampoules each of which contained one-sixth grain of morphine and one-hundredth grain of scopolamine. Thinking that one-hundredth grain was a negligible quantity, I took six ampoules in one injection. The result was a psychotic state lasting some hours during which I was opportunely restrained by my long suffering landlord. I remembered nothing the following day.

Drugs of the datura group are used by the Indians of South America and Mexico. Fatalities are said to be frequent.

Scopolamine has been used by the Russians as a confession drug with dubious results. The subject may be willing to reveal his secrets, but quite unable to remember them. Often cover story and secret information are inextricably garbled. I understand that mescaline has been very successful in extracting information from suspects.

Morphine addiction is a metabolic illness brought about by the use of morphine. In my opinion psychological treatment is not only useless it is contraindicated. Statistically the people who become addicted to morphine are those who have access to it: doctors, nurses, anyone in contact with black market sources. In Persia where opium is sold without control in opium shops, seventy per cent of the adult population is addicted. So we should psychoanalyse several million Persians to find out what deep conflicts and anxieties have driven them to the use of opium? I think not. According to my experience most addicts are not neurotic and do not need psychotherapy. Apomorphine treatment and access to apomorphine in the event of relapse would certainly give a higher percentage of permanent cures than any programme of "psychological rehabilitation".

DEPOSITION: TESTIMONY CONCERNING A SICKNESS

I awoke from The Sickness at the age of forty-five, calm and sane, and in reasonably good health except for a weakened liver and the look of borrowed flesh common to all who survive The Sickness ... Most survivors do not remember the delirium in detail. I apparently took detailed notes on sickness and delirium. I have no precise memory of writing the notes which have now been published under the title *Naked Lunch*. The title was suggested by Jack Kerouac. I did not understand what the title meant until my recent recovery. The title means exactly what the words say: NAKED Lunch—a frozen moment when everyone sees what is on the end of every fork.

The Sickness is drug addiction and I was an addict for fifteen years. When I say addict I mean an addict to junk (generic term for opium and/or derivatives including all synthetics from demerol to palfium). I have used junk in many forms: morphine, heroin, delaudid, eukodal, pantopon, diocodid, diosane, opium, demerol, dolophine, palfium. I have smoked junk, eaten it, sniffed it, injected it in vein-skin-muscle, inserted it in rectal suppositories. The needle is not important. Whether you sniff it smoke it eat it or shove it up your ass the result is the same: addiction. When I speak of drug addiction I do not refer to keif, marijuana or any preparation of hashish, mescaline, *Bannisteria Caapi*, LSD6, Sacred Mushrooms or any other drug of the hallucinogen group ... There is no evidence that the use of any hallucinogen results in physical dependence. The action of these drugs in physiologically opposite to the action of junk. A lamentable confusion between the two classes of drugs has arisen owing to the zeal of the US and other narcotic departments.

I have seen the exact manner in which the junk virus operates through fifteen years of addiction. The pyramid of junk, one level eating the level below (it is no accident that junk higher-ups are always fat and the addict in the street is always thin) right up to the top or tops since there are many junk pyramids feeding on peoples of the world and all built on basic principles of monopoly:

1—Never give anything away for nothing.
2—Never give more than you have to give (always catch the buyer hungry and always make him wait).

3—Always take everything back if you possibly can.

The Pusher always gets it all back. The addict needs more and more junk to maintain a human form ... buy off the Monkey.

Junk is the mold of monopoly and possession. The addict stands by while his junk legs carry him straight in on the junk beam to relapse. Junk is quantitative and accurately measurable. The more junk you use the less you have and the more you have the more you use. All the hallucinogen drugs are considered sacred by those who use them—there are Peyote Cults and Bannisteria Cults, Hashish Cults and Mushroom Cults—"the Sacred Mushrooms of Mexico enable a man to see God"—but no one ever suggested that junk is sacred. There are no opium cults. Opium is profane and quantitative like money. I have heard that there was once a beneficent non-habit-forming junk in India. It was called *soma* and is pictured as a beautiful blue tide. If *soma* ever existed the Pusher was there to bottle it and monopolize it and sell it and it turned into plain old time JUNK.

Junk is the ideal product ... the ultimate merchandise. No sales talk necessary. The client will crawl through a sewer and beg to buy ... The junk merchant does not sell his product to the consumer, he sells the consumer to his product. He does not improve and simplify his merchandise. He degrades and simplifies the client. He pays his staff in junk.

Junk yields a basic formula of "evil" virus: *The Algebra of Need*. The face of "evil" is always the face of total need. A dope fiend is a man in total need of dope. Beyond a certain frequency need knows absolutely no limit or control. In the words of total need: "*Wouldn't you?*" Yes you would. You would lie, cheat, inform on your friends, steal, do *anything* to satisfy total need. Because you would be in a state of total sickness, total possession, and not in a position to act in any other way. Dope fiends are sick people who cannot act other than they do. A rabid dog cannot choose but bite. Assuming a self-righteous position is nothing to the purpose unless your purpose be to keep the junk virus in operation. And junk is a big industry.

Look down LOOK DOWN along that junk road before you travel there and get in with the Wrong Mob ...

A word to the wise guy.

—*William S. Burroughs*

THE DRUG SCENE

I

When they walked in on me that morning at eight o'clock, I knew
that it was my last chance, my only chance. But they didn't know.
How could they? Just a routine pick-up. But not quite routine.

Hauser had been eating breakfast when the Lieutenant called: "I
want you and your partner to pick up a man named Lee, William
Lee, on your way down-town. He's in the Hotel Lamprey. 103 just
off B way."

"Yeah I know where it is. I remember him too."

"Good. Room 606. Just pick him up. Don't take time to shake
the place down. Except bring in all books, letters, manuscripts.
Anything printed, typed or written. Ketch?"

"Ketch. But what's the angle. . . . Books . . .'

"Just do it." The Lieutenant hung up.

Hauser and O'Brien. They had been on the City Narcotic Squad
for twenty years. Oldtimers like me. I been on the junk for sixteen
years. They weren't bad as laws go. At least O'Brien wasn't.
O'Brien was the conman, and Hauser the tough guy. A vaudeville
team. Hauser had a way of hitting you before he said anything just
to break the ice. Then O'Brien gives you an Old Gold—just like a
cop to smoke Old Golds somehow . . . and starts putting down a cop
con that was really bottled in bond. Not a bad guy, and I didn't want
to do it. But it was my only chance.

I was just tying up for my morning shot when they walked in with
a pass key. It was a special kind you can use even when the door
is locked from the inside with a key in the lock. On the table in front
of me was a packet of junk, spike, syringe—I got the habit of using
a regular syringe in Mexico and never went back to using a dropper
—alcohol, cotton and a glass of water.

"Well well," says O'Brien. . . . "Long time no see eh?"

"Put on your coat, Lee," says Hauser. He had his gun out. He
always has it out when he makes a pinch for the psychological effect
and to forestall a rush for toilet sink or window.

"Can I take a bang first, boys?" I asked. . . . "There's plenty here
for evidence. . . ."

I was wondering how I could get to my suitcase if they said no.
The case wasn't locked, but Hauser had the gun in his hand.

"He wants a shot," said Hauser.

"Now you know we can't do that, Bill," said O'Brien in his sweet con voice, dragging out the name with an oily, insinuating familiarity, brutal and obscene.

He meant, of course, "What can you do for *us*, Bill?" He looked at me and smiled. The smile stayed there too long, hideous and naked, the smile of an old painted pervert, gathering all the negative evil of O'Brien's ambiguous function.

"I might could set up Marty Steel for you," I said.

I knew they wanted Marty bad. He'd been pushing for five years, and they couldn't hang one on him. Marty was an oldtimer, and very careful about who he served. He had to know a man and know him well before he would pick up his money. No one can say they ever did time because of me. My rep is perfect, but still Marty wouldn't serve me because he didn't know me long enough. That's how skeptical Marty was.

"Marty!" said O'Brien. "Can you score from him?"

"Sure I can."

They were suspicious. A man can't be a cop all his life without developing a special set of intuitions.

"OK," said Hauser finally. "But you'd better deliver, Lee."

"I'll deliver all right. Believe me I appreciate this."

I tied up for a shot, my hands trembling with eagerness, an archetype dope fiend.

"Just an old junky, boys, a harmless old shaking wreck of a junky." That's the way I put it down. As I had hoped, Hauser looked away when I started probing for a vein. It's a wildly unpretty spectacle.

O'Brien was sitting on the arm of a chair smoking an Old Gold, looking out the window with that dreamy what I'll do when I get my pension look.

I hit a vein right away. A column of blood shot up into the syringe for an instant sharp and solid as a red cord. I pressed the plunger down with my thumb, feeling the junk pound through my veins to feed a million junk-hungry cells, to bring strength and alertness to every nerve and muscle. They were not watching me. I filled the syringe with alcohol.

Hauser was juggling his snub-nosed detective special, a Colt, and looking around the room. He could smell danger like an animal. With his left hand he pushed the closet door open and glanced inside. My stomach contracted. I thought, 'If he looks in the suitcase now I'm done."

Hauser turned to me abruptly. "You through yet?" he snarled. "You'd better not try to shit us on Marty." The words came out so ugly he surprised and shocked himself.

I picked up the syringe full of alcohol, twisting the needle to make sure it was tight.

"Just two seconds," I said.

I squirted a thin jet of alcohol, whipping it across his eyes with a sideways shake of the syringe. He let out a bellow of pain. I could see him pawing at his eyes with the left hand like he was tearing off an invisible bandage as I dropped to the floor on one knee, reaching for my suitcase. I pushed the suitcase open, and my left hand closed over the gun butt—I am righthanded but I shoot with my left hand. I felt the concussion of Hauser's shot before I heard it. His slug slammed into the wall behind me. Shooting from the floor, I snapped two quick shots into Hauser's belly where his vest had pulled up showing an inch of white shirt. He grunted in a way I could feel and doubled forward. Stiff with panic, O'Brien's hand was tearing at the gun in his shoulder holster. I clamped my other hand around my gun wrist to steady it for the long pull—this gun has the hammer filed off round so you can only use it double action—and shot him in the middle of his red forehead about two inches below the silver hairline. His hair had been grey the last time I saw him. That was about fifteen years ago. My first arrest. His eyes went out. He fell off the chair onto his face. My hands were already reaching for what I needed, sweeping my notebooks into a briefcase with my works, junk, and a box of shells. I stuck the gun into my belt, and stepped out into the corridor putting on my coat.

I could hear the desk clerk and the bell boy pounding up the stairs. I took the self-service elevator down, walked through the empty lobby into the street.

It was a beautiful Indian Summer day. I knew I didn't have much chance, but any chance is better than none, better than being a subject for experiments with ST (6) or whatever the initials are.

I had to stock up on junk fast. Along with airports, RR stations and bus terminals, they would cover all junk areas and connections. I took a taxi to Washington Square, got out and walked along 4th Street till I spotted Nick on a corner. You can always find the pusher. Your need conjures him up like a ghost. "Listen, Nick," I said, "I'm leaving town. I want to pick up a pice of H. Can you make it right now?"

We were walking along 4th Street. Nick's voice seemed to drift into my consciousness from no particular place. An eerie, disembodied voice. "Yes, I think I can make it. I'll have to make a run uptown."

"We can take a cab."

"OK, but I can't take you in to the guy, you understand."

"I understand. Let's go."

We were in the cab heading North. Nick was talking in his flat, dead voice.

"Some funny stuff we're getting lately. It's not weak exactly.... I don't know.... It's different. Maybe they're putting some synthetic shit in it.... Dollies or something...."

"What!!!? Already?"

"Huh?... But this I'm taking you to now is OK. In fact it's about the best deal around that I know of.... Stop here."

"Please make it fast," I said.

"It should be a matter of ten minutes unless he's out of stuff and has to make a run.... Better sit down over there and have a cup of coffee.... This is a hot neighborhood."

I sat down at a counter and ordered coffee, and pointed to a piece of Danish pastry under a plastic cover. I washed down the stale rubbery cake with coffee, praying that just this once, please God, let him make it now, and not come back to say the man is all out and has to make a run to East Orange or Greenpoint.

Well here he was back, standing behind me. I looked at him, afraid to ask. Funny, I thought, here I sit with perhaps one chance in a hundred to live out the next twenty-four hours—I had made up my mind not to surrender and spend the next three or four months in death's waiting room. And here I was worrying about a junk score. But I only had about five shots left, and without junk I would be immobilized.... Nick nodded his head.

"Don't give it to me here," I said. "Let's take a cab."

We took a cab and started downtown. I held out my hand and copped the package, then I slipped a fifty-dollar bill into Nick's palm. He glanced at it and showed his gums in a toothless smile: "Thanks a lot.... This will put me in the clear...."

I sat back letting my mind work without pushing it. Push your mind too hard, and it will fuck up like an overloaded switch-board, or turn on you with sabotage.... And I had no margin for error. Americans have a special horror of giving up control, of letting things happen in their own way without interference. They would like to jump down into their stomachs and digest the food and shovel the shit out.

Your mind will answer most questions if you learn to relax and wait for the answer. Like one of those thinking machines, you feed in your question, sit back, and wait. . . .

I was looking for a name. My mind was sorting through names, discarding at once FL—Fuzz Lover, BW—Born Wrong, NCBC—Nice Cat But Chicken; putting aside to reconsider, narrowing, sifting, feeling for the name, the answer.

"Sometimes, you know, he'll keep me waiting three hours. Sometimes I make it right away like this." Nick had a deprecating little laugh that he used for punctuation. Sort of an apology for talking at all in the telepathizing world of the addict where only the quantity factor—How much $? How much junk?—requires verbal expression. He knew and I knew all about waiting. At all levels the drug trade operates without schedule. Nobody delivers on time except by accident. The addict runs on junk time. His body is his clock, and junk runs through it like an hour-glass. Time has meaning for him only with reference to his need. Then he makes his abrupt intrusion into the time of others, and, like all Outsiders, all Petitioners, he must wait, unless he happens to mesh with non-junk time.

"What can I say to him? He knows I'll wait," Nick laughed.

I spent the night in the Ever Hard Baths—(homosexuality is the best all-around cover story an agent can use)—where a snarling Italian attendant creates such an unnerving atmosphere sweeping the dormitory with infra red see in the dark fieldglasses.

("All right in the North East corner! I see you!" switching on floodlights, sticking his head through trapdoors in the floor and wall of the private rooms, that many a queen has been carried out in a straitjacket. . . .)

I lay there in my open top cubicle room looking at the ceiling . . . listened to the grunts and squeals and snarls in the nightmare half light of random, broken lust. . . .

"Fuck off you!"

"Put on two pairs of glasses and maybe you can see something!"

Walked out in the precise morning and bought a paper. . . . Nothing. . . . I called from a drugstore phone booth . . . and asked for Narcotics:

"Lieutenant Gonzales . . . who's calling?"

"I want to speak to O'Brien." A moment of static, dangling wires, broken connections . . .

"Nobody of that name in this department. . . . Who are *you*?"

"Well let me speak to Hauser."

"Look, Mister, no O'Brien no Hauser in this Bureau. Now what do you want?"

"Look, this is important.... I've got info on a big shipment of H coming in.... I want to talk to Hauser or O'Brien.... I don't do business with anybody else...."

"Hold on.... I'll connect you with Alcibiades."

I began to wonder if there was an Anglo-Saxon name left in the Department....

"I want to speak to Hauser or O'Brien."

"How many times I have to tell you no Hauser no O'Brien in this department.... Now who is this calling?"

I hung up and took a taxi out of the area.... In the cab I realized what had happened.... I had been occluded from space-time like an eel's ass occludes when he stops eating on the way to Sargasso.... Locked out.... Never again would I have a Key, a Point of Intersection.... The Heat was off me from here on out ... relegated with Hauser and O'Brien to a landlocked junk past where heroin is always twenty-eight dollars an ounce and you can score for yen pox in the Chink Laundry of Sioux Falls.... Far side of the world's mirror, moving into the past with Hauser and O'Brien ... clawing at a not-yet of Telepathic Bureaucracies, Time Monopolies, Control Drugs, Heavy Fluid Addicts:

"I thought of that three hundred years ago."

"Your plan was unworkable then and useless now.... Like Da Vinci's flying machine plans...."

II

I can feel the heat closing in, feel them out there making their moves, setting up their devil doll stool pigeons, crooning over my spoon and dropper I throw away at Washington Square Station, vault a turnstile and two flights down the iron stairs, catch an uptown A train ... Young, good looking, crew cut, Ivy League, advertising exec type fruit holds the door back for me. I am evidently his idea of a character. You know the type comes on with bartenders and cab drivers, talking about right hooks and the Dodgers, call the counterman in Nedick's by his first name. A real asshole. And right on time this narcotics dick in a white trench coat (imagine tailing somebody in a white trench coat—trying to pass as a fag I guess) hit the platform. I can hear the way he would say it holding my outfit in his left hand, right hand on his piece: "I think you dropped something, fella."

But the subway is moving.

"So long flatfoot!" I yell, giving the fruit his B production. I look into the fruit's eyes, take in the white teeth, the Florida tan, the two hundred dollar sharkskin suit, the button-down Brooks Brothers shirt and carrying *The News* as a prop. "Only thing I read is Little Abner."

A square wants to come on hip. . . . Talks about "pod," and smoke it now and then, and keeps some around to offer the fast Hollywood types.

"Thanks, kid," I say, "I can see you're one of our own." His face lights up like a pinball machine, with stupid, pink effect.

"Grassed on me he did," I said morosely. (Note: Grass is English thief slang for inform.) I drew closer and laid my dirty junky fingers on his sharkskin sleeve. "And us blood brothers in the same dirty needle. I can tell you in confidence he is due for a hot shot." (Note: This is a cap of poison junk sold to addict for liquidation purposes. Often given to informers. Usually the hot shot is strychnine since it tastes and looks like junk.)

"Ever see a hot shot hit, kid? I saw the Gimp catch one in Philly. We rigged his room with a one-way whorehouse mirror and charged a sawski to watch it. He never got the needle out of his arm. They don't if the shot is right. That's the way they find them, dropper full of clotted blood hanging out of a blue arm. The look in his eyes when it hit—Kid, it was tasty. . . .

"Recollect when I am travelling with the Vigilante, best Shake Man in the industry. Out in Chi ... We is working the fags in Lincoln Park. So one night the Vigilante turns up for work in cowboy boots and a black vest with a hunka tin on it and a lariat slung over his shoulder.

"So I says: 'What's with you? You wig already?'

"He just looks at me and says: 'Fill your hand stranger' and hauls out an old rusty six shooter and I take off across Lincoln Park, bullets cutting all around me. And he hang three fags before the fuzz nail him. I mean the Vigilante earned his moniker. . . .

"Ever notice how many expressions carry over from queers to con men? Like 'raise,' letting someone know you are in the same line?

" 'Get her!'

" 'Get the Paregoric Kid giving that mark the build up!'

" 'Eager Beaver wooing him much too fast.'

"The Shoe Store Kid (he got that moniker shaking down fetishists in shoe stores) say: 'Give it to a mark with KY and he will come back moaning for more.' And when the Kid spots a mark he begin to breathe heavy. His face swells and his lips turn purple like an Eskimo in heat. Then slow, slow he comes on the mark, feeling for him, palpating him with fingers of rotten ectoplasm."

III

Mexico City where Lupita sits like an Aztec Earth Goddess doling out her little papers of lousy shit.

"Selling is more of a habit than using," Lupita says. Nonusing pushers have a contact habit, and that's one you can't kick. Agents get it too. Take Bradley the Buyer. Best narcotics agent in the industry. Anyone would make him for junk. (Note: Make in the sense of dig or size up.) I mean he can walk up to a pusher and score direct. He is so anonymous, grey and spectral the pusher don't remember him afterwards. So he twists one after the other. . . .

Well the Buyer comes to look more and more like a junky. He can't drink. He can't get it up. His teeth fall out. (Like pregnant women lose their teeth feeding the stranger, junkies lose their yellow fangs feeding the monkey.) He is all the time sucking on a candy bar. Babe Ruths he digs special. "It really disgust you to see the Buyer sucking on them candy bars so nasty," a cop says.

The Buyer takes on an ominous grey-green color. Fact is his body is making its own junk or equivalent. The Buyer has a steady connection. A Man Within you might say. Or so he thinks. "I'll just sit in my room," he says. "Fuck 'em all. Squares on both sides. I am the only complete man in the industry."

But a yen comes on him like a great black wind through the bones. So the Buyer hunts up a young junky and gives him a paper to make it.

"Oh all right," the boy says. "So what you want to make?"

"I just want to rub up against you and get fixed."

"Ugh . . . Well all right. . . . But why cancha just get physical like a human?"

Later the boy is sitting in a Waldorf with two colleagues dunking pound cake. "Most distasteful thing I ever stand still for," he says. "Some way he make himself all soft like a blob of jelly and surround me so nasty. Then he gets wet all over like with green slime. So I guess he come to some kinda awful climax. . . . I come near wigging with that green stuff all over me, and he stink like a old rotten canteloupe."

"Well it's still an easy score."

The boy sighed resignedly; "Yes, I guess you can get used to anything. I've got a meet with him again tomorrow."

The Buyer's habit keeps getting heavier. He needs a recharge every half hour. Sometimes he cruises the precincts and bribes the turnkey to let him in with a cell of junkies. It get to where no amount of contact will fix him. At this point he receives a summons from the District Supervisor:

"Bradley, your conduct has given rise to rumors—and I hope for your sake they are no more than that—so unspeakably distasteful that . . . I mean Caesar's wife . . . hrump . . . that is, the Department must be above suspicion . . . certainly above such suspicions as you have seemingly aroused. You are lowering the entire tone of the industry. We are prepared to accept your immediate resignation."

The Buyer throws himself on the ground and crawls over to the DS "No, Boss Man, no . . . The Department is my very lifeline."

He kisses the DS's hand thrusting his fingers into his mouth (the DS must feel his toothless gums) complaining he has lost his teeth "inna thervith." "Please Boss Man, I'll wipe your ass, I'll wash out your dirty condoms, I'll polish your shoes with the oil on my nose. . . ."

"Really, this is most distasteful! Have you no pride? I must tell you I feel a distinct revulsion. I mean there is something, well, rotten about you, and you smell like a compost heap." He put a scented handkerchief in front of his face. "I must ask you to leave this office at once."

"I'll do anything, Boss, *anything*." His ravaged green face splits in a horrible smile. "I'm still young, Boss, and I'm pretty strong when I get my blood up."

The DS retches into his handkerchief and points to the door with a limp hand. The Buyer stands up looking at the DS dreamily. His body begins to dip like a dowser's wand. He flows forward. . . .

"No! No!" screams the DS.

"Schlup . . . schlup schlup." An hour later they find the Buyer on the nod in the DS's chair. The DS has disappeared without a trace.

The Judge: "Everything indicates that you have, in some un-speakable manner uh . . . assimilated the District Supervisor. Unfortunately there is no proof. I would recommend that you be confined or more accurately contained in some institution, but I know of no place suitable for a man of your calibre. I must reluct-antly order your release."

"That one should stand in an aquarium," says the arresting officer.

The Buyer spreads terror throughout the industry. Junkies and agents disappear. Like a vampire bat he gives off a narcotic effluvium, a dank green mist that anesthetizes his victims and renders them helpless in his enveloping presence. And once he has scored he holes up for several days like a gorged boa constrictor. Finally he is caught in the act of digesting the Narcotics Commissioner and destroyed with a flame thrower—the court of inquiry ruling that such means were justified in that the Buyer had lost his human citizenship and was, in consequence, a creature without species and a menace to the narcotics industry on all levels.

IV

"We friends, yes?"

The shoe shine boy put on his hustling smile and looked up into the Sailor's dead, cold, undersea eyes, eyes without a trace of warmth or lust or hate or any feeling the boy had ever experienced in himself or seen in another, at once cold and intense, impersonal and predatory.

The sailor leaned forward and put a finger on the boy's inner arm at the elbow. He spoke in his dead, junky whisper.

"With veins like that, Kid, I'd have myself a time!"

He laughed, black insect laughter that seemed to serve some obscure function of orientation like a bat's squeak. The Sailor laughed three times. He stopped laughing and hung there motionless listening down into himself. He had picked up the silent frequency of junk. His face smoothed out like yellow wax over the high cheek-bones. He waited half a cigarette. The Sailor knew how to wait. But his eyes burned in a hideous dry hunger. He turned his face of controlled emergency in a slow half pivot to case the man who had just come in. "Fats" Terminal sat there sweeping the café with blank, periscope eyes. When his eyes passed the Sailor he nodded minutely. Only the peeled nerves of junk sickness would have registered a movement.

The Sailor handed the boy a coin. He drifted over to Fats table with his floating walk and sat down. They sat a long time in silence. The café was built into one side of a stone ramp at the bottom of a high white canyon of masonry. Faces of The City poured through silent as fish, stained with vile addictions and insect lusts. The lighted café was a diving bell, cable broken, settling into black depths.

The Sailor was polishing his nails on the lapels of his glen plaid suit. He whistled a little tune through his shiny, yellow teeth.

When he moved an effluvia of mold drifted out of his clothes, a musty smell of deserted locker rooms. He studied his nails with phosphorescent intensity.

"Good thing here, Fats. I can deliver twenty. Need an advance of course."

"On spec?"

"So I don't have the twenty eggs in my pocket. I tell you it's jellied consommé. One little whoops and a push." The Sailor looked at his nails as if he were studying a chart. "You know I always deliver."

"Make it thirty. And a ten tube advance. This time tomorrow."

"Need a tube now, Fats."

"Take a walk, you'll get one."

The Sailor drifted down into the Plaza. A street boy was shoving a newspaper in the Sailor's face to cover his hand on the Sailor's pen. The Sailor walked on. He pulled the pen out and broke it like a nut in his thick, fibrous, pink fingers. He pulled out a lead tube. He cut one end of the tube with a little curved knife. A black mist poured out and hung in the air like boiling fur. The Sailor's face dissolved. His mouth undulated forward on a long tube and sucked in the black fuzz, vibrating in supersonic peristalsis disappeared in a silent, pink explosion. His face came back into focus unbearably sharp and clear, burning yellow brand of junk searing the grey haunch of a million screaming junkies.

"This will last a month," he decided, consulting an invisible mirror.

All streets of the City slope down between deepening canyons to a vast, kidney-shaped plaza full of darkness. Walls of street and plaza are perforated by dwelling cubicles and cafés, some a few feet deep, others extending out of sight in a network of rooms and corridors.

At all levels criss-cross of bridges, cat walks, cable cars. Catatonic youths dressed as women in gowns of burlap and rotten rags, faces heavily and crudely painted in bright colors over a strata of beatings, arabesques of broken, suppurating scars to the pearly bone, push against the passer-by in silent clinging insistence.

Traffickers in the Black Meat, flesh of the giant aquatic black centipede—sometimes attaining a length of six feet—found in a lane of black rocks and iridescent, brown lagoons, exhibit paralyzed crustaceans in camouflage pockets of the Plaza visible only to the Meat Eaters.

Followers of obsolete unthinkable trades, doodling in Etruscan, addicts of drugs not yet synthesized, black marketeers of World

War III, excisors of telepathic sensitivity, osteopaths of the spirit, investigators of infractions denounced by bland paranoid chess players, servers of fragmentary warrants taken down in hebephrenic short-hand charging unspeakable mutilations of the spirit, officials of unconstituted police states, brokers of exquisite dreams and nostalgias tested on the sensitized cells of junk sickness and bartered for raw materials of the will, drinkers of the Heavy Fluid sealed in translucent amber of dreams.

The Meet Café occupies one side of the Plaza, a maze of kitchens, restaurants, sleeping cubicles, perilous iron balconies and basements opening into the underground baths.

On stools covered in white satin sit naked Mugwumps sucking translucent, colored syrups through alabaster straws. Mugwumps have no liver and nourish themselves exclusively on sweets. Thin, purple-blue lips cover a razor-sharp beak of black bone with which they frequently tear each other to shreds in fights over clients. These creatures secrete an addicting fluid from their erect penises which prolongs life by slowing metabolism. (In fact all longevity agents have proved addicting in exact ratio to their effectiveness in prolonging life.) Addicts of Mugwump fluid are known as Reptiles. A number of these flow over chairs with their flexible bones and black-pink flesh. A fan of green cartilage covered with hollow, erectile hairs through which the Reptiles absorb the fluid sprouts from behind each ear. The fans, which move from time to time touched by invisible currents, serve also some form of communication known only to Reptiles.

During the biennial Panics when the raw, pealed Dream Police storm the City, the Mugwumps take refuge in the deepest crevices of the wall sealing themselves in clay cubicles and remain for weeks in biostasis. In those days of grey terror the Reptiles dart about faster and faster, scream past each other at supersonic speed, their flexible skulls flapping in black winds of insect agony.

The Dream Police disintegrate in globs of rotten ectoplasm swept away by an old junky, coughing and spitting in the sick morning. The Mugwump Man comes with alabaster jars of fluid and the Reptiles get smoothed out.

The air is once again still and clear as glycerine.

The Sailor spotted his Reptile. He drifted over and ordered a green syrup. The Reptile had a little, round disk mouth of brown gristle, expressionless green eyes almost covered by a thin membrane of eyelid. The Sailor waited an hour before the creature picked up his presence.

"Any eggs for Fats?" he asked, his words stirring through the Reptile's fan hairs.

It took two hours for the Reptile to raise three pink transparent fingers covered with black fuzz.

Several Meat Eaters lay in vomit, too weak to move. (The Black Meat is like a tainted cheese, overpoweringly delicious and nauseating so that the eaters eat and vomit and eat again until they fall exhausted.)

A painted youth slithered in and seized one of the great black claws sending the sweet, sick smell curling through the café.

DOCTORS AND SCIENTISTS

I

So I am assigned to engage the services of Doctor Benway for Islam Inc.

Dr Benway had been called in as advisor to the Freeland Republic, a place given over to free love and continual bathing. The citizens are well adjusted, cooperative, honest, tolerant and above all clean. But the invoking of Benway indicates all is not well behind that hygienic façade: Benway is a manipulator and coordinator of symbol systems, an expert on all phases of ˙nterrogation, brainwashing and control. I have not seen Benway since his precipitate departure from Annexia, where his assignment had been TD—Total Demoralization. Benway's first act was to abolish concentration camps, mass arrest and, except under certain limited and special circumstances, the use of torture.

"I deplore brutality," he said. "It's not efficient. On the other hand, prolonged mistreatment, short of physical violence, gives rise, when skilfully applied, to anxiety and a feeling of special guilt. A few rules or rather guiding principles are to be borne in mind. The subject must not realize that the mistreatment is a deliberate attack of an anti-human enemy on his personal identity. He must be made to feel that he deserves *any* treatment he receives because there is something (never specified) horribly wrong with him. The naked need of the control addicts must be decently covered by an arbitrary and intricate bureaucracy so that the subject cannot contact his enemy direct."

Every citizen of Annexia was required to apply for and carry on his person at all times a whole portfolio of documents. Citizens were subject to be stopped in the street at any time; and the Examiner, who might be in plain clothes, in various uniforms, often in a bathing suit or pyjamas, sometimes stark naked except for a badge pinned to his left nipple, after checking each paper, would stamp it. On subsequent inspection the citizen was required to show the properly entered stamps of the last inspection. The Examiner, when he stopped a large group, would only examine and stamp the cards of a few. The others were then subject to arrest because their cards were not properly stamped. Arrest meant "provisional detention"; that is, the prisoner would be released if and when his

Affidavit of Explanation, properly signed and stamped, was approved by the Assistant Arbiter of Explanations. Since this official hardly ever came to his office, and the Affidavit of Explanation had to be presented in person, the explainers spent weeks and months waiting around in unheated offices with no chairs and no toilet facilities.

Documents issued in vanishing ink faded into old pawn tickets. New documents were constantly required. The citizens rushed from one bureau to another in a frenzied attempt to meet impossible deadlines.

All benches were removed from the city, all fountains turned off, all flowers and trees destroyed. Huge electric buzzers on the top of every apartment house (everyone lived in apartments) rang the quarter hour. Often the vibrations would throw people out of bed. Searchlights played over the town all night (no one was permitted to use shades, curtains, shutters or blinds).

No one ever looked at anyone else because of the strict law against importuning, with or without verbal approach, anyone for any purpose, sexual or otherwise. All cafés and bars were closed. Liquor could only be obtained with a special permit, and the liquor so obtained could not be sold or given or in any way transferred to anyone else, and the presence of anyone else in the room was considered *prima facie* evidence of conspiracy to transfer liquor.

No one was permitted to bolt his door, and the police had pass keys to every room in the city. Accompanied by a mentalist they rush into someone's quarters and start "looking for it."

The mentalist guides them to whatever the man wishes to hide: a tube of vaseline, an enema, a handkerchief with come on it, a weapon, unlicensed alcohol. And they always submitted the suspect to the most humiliating search of his naked person on which they make sneering and derogatory comments. Many a latent homosexual was carried out in a straitjacket when they planted vaseline in his ass. Or they pounce on any object. A pen wiper or a shoe tree.

"And what is this supposed to be for?"

"It's a pen wiper."

"A pen wiper, he says."

"I've heard everything now."

"I guess this is all we need. Come on, you."

After a few months of this the citizens cowered in corners like neurotic cats.

Of course the Annexia police processed suspected agents,

saboteurs and political deviants on an assembly line basis. As regards the interrogation of suspects, Benway has this to say:

"While in general I avoid the use of torture—torture locates the opponent and mobilizes resistance—the threat of torture is useful to induce in the subject the appropriate feeling of helplessness and gratitude to the interrogator for withholding it. And torture can be employed to advantage as a penalty when the subject is far enough along with the treatment to accept punishment as deserved. To this end I devised several forms of disciplinary procedure. One was known as The Switchboard. Electric drills that can be turned on at any time are clamped against the subject's teeth; and he is instructed to operate an arbitrary switchboard, to put certain connections in certain sockets in response to bells and lights. Every time he makes a mistake the drills are turned on for twenty seconds. The signals are gradually speeded up beyond his reaction time. Half an hour on the switchboard and the subject breaks down like an overloaded thinking machine.

"The study of thinking machines teaches us more about the brain than we can learn by introspective methods. Western man is externalizing himself in the form of gadgets. Ever pop coke in the mainline? It hits you right in the brain, activating connections of pure pleasure. The pleasure of morphine is in the viscera. You listen down into yourself after a shot. But C is electricity through the brain, and the C yen is of the brain alone, a need without body and without feeling. The C-charged brain is a berserk pinball machine, flashing blue and pink lights in electric orgasm. C pleasure could be felt by a thinking machine, the first stirrings of hideous insect life. The craving for C lasts only a few hours, as long as the C channels are stimulated. Of course the effect of C could be produced by an electric current activating the C channels. . . .

"So after a bit the channels wear out like veins, and the addict has to find new ones. A vein will come back in time, and by adroit vein rotation a junky can piece out the odds if he don't become an oil burner. But brain cells don't come back once they're gone, and when the addict runs out of brain cells he is in a terrible fucking position.

"Squatting on old bones and excrement and rusty iron, in a white blaze of heat, a panorama of naked idiots stretches to the horizon. Complete silence—their speech centers are destroyed—except for the crackle of sparks and the popping of singed flesh as they apply electrodes up and down the spine. White smoke of burning flesh hangs in the motionless air. A group of children have tied an idiot to a post with barbed wire and built a fire between his legs and stand watching with bestial curiosity as the flames lick his thighs. His flesh jerks in the fire with insect agony.

"I digress as usual. Pending more precise knowledge of brain electronics, drugs remain an essential tool of the interrogator in his assault on the subject's personal identity. The barbiturates are, of course, virtually useless. That is, anyone who can be broken down by such means would succumb to the puerile methods used in an American precinct. Scopolamine is often effective in dissolving resistance, but it impairs the memory: an agent might be prepared to reveal his secrets but quite unable to remember them, or cover story and secret life info might be inextricably garbled. Mescaline, harmaline, LSD6, bufotenine, muscarine successful in many cases. Bulbocapnine induces a state approximating schizophrenic catatonia ... instances of automatic obedience have been observed. Bulbocapnine is a backbrain depressant probably putting out of action the centers of motion in the hypothalamus. Other drugs that have produced experimental schizophrenia—mescaline, harmaline, LSD6—are backbrain stimulants. In schizophrenia the backbrain is alternatively stimulated and depressed. Catatonia is often followed by a period of excitement and motor activity during which the nut rushes through the wards giving everyone a bad time. Deteriorated schizos sometimes refuse to move at all and spend their lives in bed. A disturbance of the regulatory function of the hypothalamus is indicated as the "cause" (casual thinking never yields accurate description of metabolic process—limitations of existing language) of schizophrenia. Alternate doses of LSD6 and bulbocapnine—the bulbocapnine potientiated with curare—give the highest yield of automatic obedience.

"There are other procedures. The subject can be reduced to deep depression by administering large doses of benzedrine for several days. Psychosis can be induced by continual large doses of cocaine or demerol or by the abrupt withdrawal of barbiturates after prolonged administration. He can be addicted by dihydro-oxy-heroin and subjected to withdrawal (this compound should be five times as addicting as heroin, and the withdrawal proportionately severe).

"There are various 'psychological' methods, compulsory psychoanalysis, for example. The subject is requested to free-associate for one hour every day (in cases where time is not of the essence). 'Now, now. Let's not be negative, boy. Poppa call nasty man. Take baby walkabout switchboard.'

"The case of a female agent who forgot her real identity and merged with her cover story—she is still a fricoteuse in Annexia—put me onto another gimmick. An agent is trained to deny his agent identity by asserting his cover story. So why not use psychic jiu-jitsu and go along with him? Suggest that his cover story is his identity and that he has no other. His agent identity becomes unconscious, that is, out of his control; and you can dig it with drugs and hypnosis. You can make a square heterosex citizen queer with this angle ... that is, reinforce and second his rejection of normally latent homosexual trends—at the same time depriving him of cunt and subjecting him to homosex stimulation. Then drugs, hypnosis, and—" Benway flipped a limp wrist.

"Many subjects are vulnerable to sexual humiliation. Nakedness, stimulation with aphrodisiacs, constant supervision to embarrass subject and prevent relief of masturbation (erections during sleep automatically turn on an enormous vibrating electric buzzer that throws the subject out of bed into cold water, thus reducing the incidence of wet dreams to a minimum). Kicks to hypnotize a priest and tell him he is about to consummate a hypostatic union with the Lamb—then steer a randy old sheep up his ass. After that the Interrogator can gain complete hypnotic control—the subject will come at his whistle, shit on the floor if he but say Open Sesame. Needless to say, the sex humiliation angle is contraindicated for overt homosexuals. (I mean let's keep our eye on the ball here and remember the old party line ... never know who's listening in.) I recall this one kid, I condition to shit at sight of me. Then I wash his ass and screw him. It was real tasty. And he was a lovely fellah too. And some times a subject will burst into boyish tears because he can't keep from ejaculate when you screw him. Well, as you can plainly see, the possibilities are endless like meandering paths in a great big beautiful garden. I was just scratching that lovely surface when I am urged by Party Poops. . . . 'Well, son cosas de la vida.' "

I reach Freeland, which is clean and dull my God. Benway is directing the RC, Reconditioning Center. I drop around, and, "What happened to so and so?" sets in like: "Sidi Idriss 'The Nark' Smithers crooned to the Senders for a longevity serum. No fool like an old queen." "Lester Stroganoff Smuunn—'El Hassein' —turned himself into a Latah trying to perfect AOP, Automatic Obedience Processing. A martyr to the industry ..." (Latah is a condition occurring in South East Asia. Otherwise sane, Lafahs compulsively imitate every motion once their attention is attracted by snapping the fingers or calling sharply. A form of compulsive involuntary hypnosis. They sometimes injure themselves trying to imitate the motions of several people at once.)

"Stop me if you've heard this atomic secret. . . ."

Benway's face retains its form in the flash bulb of urgency, subject at any moment to unspeakable cleavage or metamorphoses. It flickers like a picture moving in and out of focus.

"Come on," says Benway, "and I'll show you around the RC."

We are walking down a long white hall. Benway's voice drifts into my consciousness from no particular place . . . a disembodied voice that is sometimes loud and clear, sometimes barely audible like music down a windy street.

"Isolated groups like natives of the Bismarck Archipelago. No overt homosexuality among them. God damned matriarchy. All matriarchies anti-homosexual, conformist and prosaic. Find yourself in a matriarchy walk don't run to the nearest frontier. If you run, some frustrate latent queer cop will likely shoot you. So somebody wants to establish a beach head of homogeneity in a shambles of potentials like West Europe and USA? Another fucking matriarchy. Margaret Mead notwithstanding . . . Spot of bother there. Scalpel fight with a colleague in the operating room. And my baboon assistant leaped on the patient and tore him to pieces. Baboons always attack the weakest party in an altercation. Quite right too. We must never forget our glorious simian heritage. Doc Browbeck was party inna second part. A retired abortionist and junk pusher (he was a veterinarian actually) recalled to service during the manpower shortage. Well, Doc had been in the hospital kitchen all morning goosing the nurses and tanking up on coal gas and Klim—and just before the operation he sneaked a double shot of nutmeg to nerve himself up."

(In England and especially in Edinburgh the citizens bubble coal gas through Klim—a horrible form of powdered milk tasting like rancid chalk—and pick up on the results. They hock everything to pay the gas bill, and when the man comes around to shut it off for the non-payment, you can hear their screams for miles. When a citizen is sick from needing it he says, "I got the klinks" or "That old stove climbing up my back."

Nutmeg. I quote from the author's article on narcotic drugs in the *British Journal of Addiction* (see page 40): "Convicts and sailors sometimes have recourse to nutmeg. About a tablespoon is swallowed with water. Result vaguely similar to marijuana with side effects of headache and nausea. There are a number of narcotics of the nutmeg family in use among the Indians of South America.

They are usually administered by sniffing a dried powder of the plant. The medicine men take these noxious substances and go into convulsive states. Their twitchings and mutterings are thought to have prophetic significance.")

"I had a Yage hangover, me, and in no condition to take any of Browbeck's shit. First thing he comes on with I should start the incision from the back instead of the front, muttering some garbled nonsense about being sure to cut out the gall bladder it would fuck up the meat. Thought he was on the farm cleaning a chicken. I told him to go put his head back in the oven, whereupon he had the effrontery to push my hand severing the patient's femoral artery. Blood spurted up and blinded the anesthetist, who ran out through the halls screaming. Browbeck tried to knee me in the groin, and I managed to hamstring him with my scalpel. He crawled about the floor stabbing at my feet and legs. Violet, that's my baboon assistant —only woman I ever cared a damn about—really wigged. I climbed up on the table and poise myself to jump on Browbeck with both feet and stomp him when the cops rushed in.

"Well, this rumble in the operating room, 'this unspeakable occurrence' as the Super called it, you might say was the blow off. The wolf pack was closing for the kill. A crucifixion, that's the only word for it. Of course I'd made a few 'dummheits' here and there. Who hasn't? There was the time me and the anesthetist drank up all the ether and the patient came up on us, and I was accused of cutting the cocaine with Saniflush. Violet did it actually. Had to protect her of course....

"So the wind-up is we are all drummed out of the industry. Not that Violet was a *bona fide* croaker, neither was Browbeck for that matter, and even my own certificate was called in question. But Violet knew more medicine than the Mayo Clinic. She had an extraordinary intuition and a high sense of duty.

"So there I was flat on my ass with no certificate. Should I turn to another trade? No. Doctoring was in my blood. I managed to keep up my habits performing cutrate abortions in subway toilets. I even descended to hustling pregnant women in the public streets. It was positively unethical. Than I met a great guy, Placenta Juan the After Birth Tycoon. Made his in slunks during the war. (Slunks are underage calves trailing afterbirths and bacteria, generally in an unsanitary and unfit condition. A calf may not be sold as food until it reaches a minimum age of six weeks. Prior to that time it is classified as a slunk. Slunk trafficking is subject to a heavy penalty.) Well, Juanito controlled a fleet of cargo boats he register under the

Abyssinian flag to avoid bothersome restrictions. He gives me a job as ship's doctor on the SS *Filiarisis*, as filthy a craft as ever sailed the seas. Operating with one hand, beating the rats offa my patient with the other and bed-bugs and scorpions rain down from the ceiling.

"So somebody wants homogeneity at this juncture. Can do but it costs. Bored with the whole project, me. . . . Here we are. . . . Drag Alley."

Benway traces a pattern in the air with his hand and a door swings open. We step through and the door closes. A long ward gleaming with stainless steel, white tile floors, glass brick walls. Beds along one wall. No one smokes, no one reads, no one talks.

"Come and take a close look," says Benway. "You won't embarrass anybody."

I walk over and stand in front of a man who is sitting on his bed. I look at the man's eyes. Nobody, nothing looks back.

"INDs," says Benway, "Irreversible Neural Damage. Overliberated, you might say . . . a drag on the industry."

I pass a hand in front of the man's eyes.

"Yes," says Benway, "they still have reflexes. Watch this." Benway takes a chocolate bar from his pocket, removes the wrapper and holds it in front of the man's nose. The man sniffs. His jaws begin to work. He makes snatching motions with his hands. Saliva drips from his mouth and hangs off his chin in long streamers. His stomach rumbles. His whole body writhes in peristalsis. Benway steps back and holds up the chocolate. The man drops to his knees, throws back his head and barks. Benway tosses the chocolate. The man snaps at it, misses, scrambles around on the floor making slobbering noises. He crawls under the bed, finds the chocolate and crams it into his mouth with both hands.

"Jesus! These IDs got no class to them."

Benway calls over the attendant who is sitting at one end of the ward reading a book of J. M. Barrie's plays.

"Get these fucking IDs outa here. It's a bring down already. Bad for the tourist business."

"What should I do with them?"

"How in the fuck should I know? I'm a scientist. A *pure* scientist. Just get them outa here. I don't hafta look at them is all. They constitute an albatross."

"But what? Where?"

"Proper channels. Buzz the District Coordinator or whatever he calls himself . . . new title every week. Doubt if he exists."

Doctor Benway pauses at the door and looks back at the INDs. "Our failure," he says. "Well, it's all in the day's work."

"Do they ever come back?"

"They don't come back, won't come back, once they're gone," Benway sings softly. "Now this ward has some innarest."

The patients stand in groups talking and spitting on the floor. Junk hangs in the air like a grey haze.

"A heart-warming sight," says Benway, "those junkies standing around waiting for the Man. Six months ago they were all schizophrenic. Some of them hadn't been out of bed for years. Now look at them. In all the course of my practices, I have never seen a schizophrenic junky, and junkies are mostly of the schizo physical type. Want to cure anybody of anything, find out who doesn't have it. So who don't got it? Junkies don't got it. Oh, incidentally, there's an area in Bolivia with no psychosis. Right sane folk in them hills. Like to get in there, me, before it is loused up by literacy, advertising, TV and drive-ins. Make a study strictly from metabolism: diet, use of drugs and alcohol, sex, etc. Who cares what they think? Same nonsense everybody thinks, I daresay.

"And why don't junkies got schizophrenia? Don't know yet. A schizophrenic can ignore hunger and starve to death if he isn't fed. No one can ignore heroin withdrawal. The fact of addiction imposes contact.

"But that's only one angle. Mescaline, LSD6, deteriorated adrenalin, harmaline can produce an approximate schizophrenia. The best stuff is extracted from the blood of schizos; so schizophrenia is likely a drug psychosis. They got a metabolic connection, a Man Within you might say. (Interested readers are referred to Appendix.)

"In the terminal stage of schizophrenia the backbrain is permanently depressed, and the front brain is almost without content since the front brain is only active in response to backbrain stimulation.

"Morphine calls forth the antidote of backbrain stimulation similar to schizo substance. (Note similarity between withdrawal syndrome and intoxication with Yage or LSD6.) Eventual result of junk use—especially true of heroin addiction where large doses are available to the addict—is permanent backbrain depression and a state much like terminal schizophrenia: complete lack of affect, autism, virtual absence of cerebral event. The addict can spend eight hours looking at a wall. He is conscious of his surroundings, but they have no emotional connotation and in consequence no interest. Remembering a period of heavy addiction is like playing back a tape recording of events experienced by the front brain alone. Flat statements of external events. 'I went to the store and bought some brown sugar. I came home and ate half the box. I took a three grain shot etc.' Complete absence of nostalgia in these memories. However, as soon as junk intake falls below par, the withdrawal substance floods the body.

"If all pleasure is relief from tension, junk affords relief from the whole life process, in disconnecting the hypothalamus, which is the center of psychic energy and libido.

"Some of my learned colleagues (nameless assholes) have suggested that junk derives its euphoric effect from direct stimulation of the orgasm center. It seems more probable that junk suspends the whole cycle of tension, discharge and rest. The orgasm has no function in the junky. Boredom, which always indicates an undischarged tension, never troubles the addict. He can look at his shoe for eight hours. He is only roused to action when the hourglass of junk runs out."

At the far end of the ward an attendant throws up an iron shutter and lets out a hog call. The junkies rush up grunting and squealing.

"Wise guy," says Benway. "No respect for human dignity. Now I'll show you the mild deviant and criminal ward. Yes, a criminal is a mild deviant here. He doesn't deny the Freeland contract. He merely seeks to circumvent some of the clauses. Reprehensible but not too serious. Down this hall ... We'll skip wards 23, 86, 57 and 97 ... and the laboratory."

"Are homosexuals classed as deviants?"

"No. Remember the Bismarck Archipelago. No overt homosexuality. A *functioning* police state needs no police. Homosexuality does not occur to anyone as conceivable behaviour.... Homosexuality is a *political* crime in a matriarchy. No society tolerates overt rejection of its basic tenets. We aren't a matriarchy here, *Insh'allah*. You know the experiment with rats where they are subject to this electric shock and dropped in cold water if they so much as move at a female. So they all become fruit rats and that's the way it is with the etiology. And shall such a rat squeak out, 'I'm queah and I luuuuuuuuve it' or 'Who cut yours off, you two-holed freak?' 'twere a square rat so to squeak. During my rather brief experience as a psychoanalyst—spot of bother with the Society—one patient ran amok in Grand Central with a flame thrower, two committed suicide and one died on the couch like a jungle rat (jungle rats are subject to die if confronted suddenly with a hopeless situation). So his relations beef and I tell them, 'It's all in the day's work. Get this stiff outa here. It's a bring down for my live patients'—I noticed that all my homosexual patients manifested strong unconscious heterosex trends and all my hetero patients unconscious homosexual trends. Makes the brain reel, don't it?'

"And what do you conclude from that?"

"Conclude? Nothing whatever. Just a passing observation."

We are eating lunch in Benway's office when he gets a call.

"What's that? . . . Monstrous! Fantastic! . . . Carry on and stand by."

He puts down the phone. "I am prepared to accept immediate assignment with Islam Incorporated. It seems the electronic brain went berserk playing six-dimensional chess with the Technician and released every subject in the RC. Leave us adjourn to the roof. Operation Helicopter is indicated."

From the roof of the RC we survey a scene of unparalleled horror. INDs stand around in front of the café tables, long streamers of saliva hanging off their chins, stomachs noisily churning, others ejaculate at the sight of women. Latahs imitate the passers-by with monkey-like obscenity. Junkies have looted the drugstores and fix on every street corner. . . . Catatonics decorate the parks. . . . Agitated schizophrenics rush through the streets with mangled, inhuman cries. A group of PRs—Partially Reconditioned—have surrounded some homosexual tourists with horrible knowing smiles showing the Nordic skull beneath in double exposure.

"What do you want?" snaps one of the queens.

"We want to *understand* you."

A contingent of howling simopaths swing from chandeliers, balconies and trees, shitting and pissing on passers-by. (A simopath—the technical name for this disorder escapes me—is a citizen convinced he is an ape or other simian. It is a disorder peculiar to the army, and discharge cures it.) Amoks trot along cutting off heads, faces sweet and remote with a dreamy half smile. . . . Citizens with incipient Bang-utot clutch their penises and call on the tourists for help. . . . Arab rioters yipe and howl, castrating, disembowelling, throw burning gasoline. . . . Dancing boys strip-tease with intestines, women stick severed genitals in their cunts, grind, bump and flick it at the man of their choice. . . . Religious fanatics harangue the crowd from helicopters and rain stone tablets on their heads, inscribed with meaningless messages. . . . Leopard Men tear people to pieces with iron claws, coughing and grunting. . . . Kwakiutl Cannibal Society initiates bite off noses and ears. . . .

A coprophage calls for a plate, shits on it and eats the shit, exclaiming, "Mmmm, that's my rich substance."

A battalion of rampant bores prowls the streets and hotel lobbies in search of victims. An intellectual avant-gardist—"Of course the only writing worth considering now is to be found in scientific reports and periodicals"—has given someone a bulbocapnine injection and is preparing to read him a bulletin on "the use of neohemoglobin in the control of multiple degenerative granuloma." (Of course, the reports are all gibberish he has concocted and printed up.)

His opening words: "You look to me like a man of intelligence." (Always ominous words, my boy ... When you hear them stay not on the order of your going but go at once.)

An English colonial, assisted by five police boys, has detained a subject in the club bar: "I say, do you know Mozambique?" and he launches into the endless saga of his malaria. "So the doctor said to me, 'I can only advise you to leave the area. Otherwise I shall bury you.' This croaker does a little undertaking on the side. Piecing out the odds you might say, and throwing himself a spot of business now and then." So after the third pink gin when he gets to know you, he shifts to dysentery. "Most extraordinary discharge. More or less of a white yellow color like rancid jism and stringy you know."

An explorer in sun helmet has brought down a citizen with blow gun and curare dart. He administers artificial respiration with one foot. (Curare kills by paralyzing the lungs. It has no other toxic effect, is not, strictly speaking, a poison. If artificial respiration is administered the subject will not die. Curare is eliminated with great rapidity by the kidneys.) "That was the year of the rindpest when everything died, even the hyenas.... So there I was completely out of KY in the headwaters of the Baboonsasshole. When it came through by air drop my gratitude was indescribable.... As a matter of fact, and I have never told this before to a living soul—elusive blighters"—his voice echoes through a vast empty hotel lobby in 1890 style, red plush, rubber plants, gilt and statues —"I was the only white man ever initiated into the infamous Agouti Society, witnessed and participated in their unspeakable rites."

The Agouti Society has turned out for a Chimu Fiesta. (The Chimu of ancient Peru were much given to sodomy and occasionally staged bloody battles with clubs, running up several hundred casualties in the course of an afternoon.) The youths, sneering and goosing each other with clubs, troop out to the field. Now the battle begins.

Gentle reader, the ugliness of that spectacle buggers description. Who can be a cringing pissing coward, yet vicious as a purple-assed mandril, alternating these deplorable conditions like vaudeville skits? Who can shit on a fallen adversary who, dying, eats the shit and screams with joy? Who can hang a weak passive and catch his sperm in mouth like a vicious dog? Gentle reader, I fain would spare you this, but my pen hath its will like the Ancient Mariner. Oh Christ what a scene is this! Can tongue or pen accommodate these scandals? A beastly young hooligan has gouged out the eye of his confrere and fuck him in the brain. "This brain atrophy already, and dry as grandmother's cunt."

He turns into Rock and Roll hoodlum. "I screw the old gash— like a crossword puzzle what relation to me is the outcome if it outcome? My father already or not yet? I can't screw you, Jack, you is about to become my father, and better 'twere to cut your throat and screw my mother playing it straight than fuck my father or *vice versa mutatis mutandis* as the case may be, and cut my mother's throat, that sainted gash, though it be the best way I know to stem her word horde and freeze her asset. I mean when a fellow be caught short in the switches and don't know is he to offer up his ass to 'great big daddy' or commit a torso job on the old lady. Give me two cunts and a prick of steel and keep your dirty finger out of my sugar bum what you think I am a purple-assed reception already fugitive from Gibraltar? Male and female castrated he them. Who can't distinguish between the sexes? I'll cut your throat you white mother fucker. Come out in the open like my grandchild and meet thy unborn mother in dubious battle. Confusion hath fuck his masterpiece. I have cut the janitor's throat quite by mistake of identity, he being such a horrible fuck like the old man. And in the coal bin all cocks are alike."

II

The lavatory has been locked for three hours solid. . . . I think they are using it for an operating room. . . .

NURSE: "I can't find her pulse, doctor."

DR BENWAY: "Maybe she got it up her snatch in a finger stall."

NURSE: "Adrenalin, doctor?"

DR BENWAY: "The night porter shot it all up for kicks." He looks around and picks up one of those rubber vacuum cups at the end of a stick they use to unstop toilets. . . . He advances on the patient. . . .

"Make an incision, Doctor Limpf," he says to his appalled assistant.... "I'm going to massage the heart."

Dr Limpf shrugs and begins the incision. Dr Benway washes the suction cup by swishing it around in the toilet-bowl....

NURSE: "Shouldn't it be sterilized, doctor?"

DR BENWAY: "Very likely, but there's no time." He sits on the suction cup like a cane seat watching his assistant make the incision.... "You young squirts couldn't lance a pimple without an electric vibrating scalpel with automatic drain and suture.... Soon we'll be operating by remote control on patients we never see.... We'll be nothing but button pushers. All the skill is going out of surgery.... All the know-how and make-do ... Did I ever tell you about the time I performed an appendectomy with a rusty sardine can? And once I was caught short without instrument one and removed a uterine tumor with my teeth. That was in the Upper Effendi, and besides ..."

DR LIMPF: "The incision is ready, doctor."

Dr Benway forces the cup into the incision and works it up and down. Blood spurts all over the doctors, the nurse the wall ... The cup makes a horrible sucking sound.

NURSE: "I think she's gone, doctor."

DR BENWAY: "Well, it's all in the day's work." He walks across the room to a medicine cabinet.... "Some fucking drug addict has cut my cocaine with Saniflush! Nurse! Send the boy out to fill this RX on the double!"

Dr Benway is operating in an auditorium filled with students: "Now, boys, you won't see this operation performed very often and there's a reason for that.... You see it has absolutely no medical value. No one knows what the purpose of it originally was or if it had a purpose at all. Personally I think it was a pure artistic creation from the beginning.

"Just as a bull fighter with his skill and knowledge extricates himself from danger he has himself invoked, so in this operation the surgeon deliberately endangers his patient, and then, with incredible speed and celerity, rescues him from death at the last possible split second.... Did any of you ever see Dr Tetrazzini perform? I say perform advisedly because his operations were performances. He would start by throwing a scalpel across the room into the patient and then make his entrance like a ballet dancer. His speed was incredible: 'I don't give them time to die,' he would say. Tumors put him in a frenzy of rage. 'Fucking undisciplined cells!' he would snarl, advancing on the tumor like a knife-fighter."

A young man leaps down into the operating theatre and, whipping out a scalpel, advances on the patient.

DR BENWAY: "An espontaneo! Stop him before he guts my patient!"

(Espontaneo is a bull-fighting term for a member of the audience who leaps down into the ring, pulls out a concealed cape and attempts a few passes with the bull before he is dragged out of the ring.)

The orderlies scuffle with the espontaneo, who is finally ejected from the hall. The anesthetist takes advantage of the confusion to pry a large gold filling from the patient's mouth....

I am passing room 10 they moved me out of yesterday.... Maternity case I assume ... Bedpans full of blood and Kotex and nameless female substances, enough to pollute a continent ... If someone comes to visit me in my old room he will think I gave birth to a monster and the State Department is trying to hush it up....

Music from *I Am an American* ... An elderly man in the striped pants and cutaway of a diplomat stands on a platform draped with the American flag. A decayed, corseted tenor—bursting out of a Daniel Boone costume—is singing the *Star Spangled Banner*, accompanied by a full orchestra. He sings with a slight lisp....

THE DIPLOMAT (reading from a great scroll of ticker tape that keeps growing and tangling around his feet): "And we categorically deny that *any* male citizen of the United States of America ..."

TENOR: "Oh thay can you thee ..." His voice breaks and shoots up to a high falsetto.

In the control room the Technician mixes a bicarbonate of soda and belches into his hand: "God damned tenor's a brown artist," he mutters sourly. "Mike! rumph," the shout ends in a belch. "Cut that swish fart off the air and give him his purple slip. He's through as of right now.... Put in that sex-changed Liz athlete.... She's a fulltime tenor at least.... *Costume*? How in the fuck should I know? I'm no dress designer swish from the costume department! *What's that?* The entire costume department occluded as a security risk? What am I, an octopus? Let's see ... How about an Indian routine? Pocahontas or Hiawatha? ... No, that's not right. Some citizen cracks wise about giving it back to the Indians.... A Civil War uniform, the coat North and the pants South like it show they got together again? She can come on like Buffalo Bill or Paul Revere or that citizen wouldn't give up the shit, I mean the ship, or a GI or a Doughboy or the unknown Soldier.... That's the best deal.... Cover her with a monument, that way nobody has to look at her...."

The Lesbian, concealed in a *papier mâché* Arc de Triomphe fills her great lungs and looses a tremendous bellow.

"Oh say do that Star Spangled Banner yet wave ..."
A great rent rips the Arc de Triomphe from top to bottom. The Diplomat puts a hand to his forehead....

THE DIPLOMAT: "That any male citizen of the United States has given birth in Interzone or at any other place...."

"O'er the land of the FREEEEEEEEEEE ..."
The Diplomat's mouth is moving but no one can hear him. The Technician clasps his hands over his ears "Mother of God!" he screams. His plate begins to vibrate like a Jew's harp, suddenly flies out of his mouth.... He snaps at it irritably, misses and covers his mouth with one hand.

The Arc de Triomphe falls with a ripping, splintering crash, reveals the Lesbian standing on a pedestal clad only in a leopard-skin jockstrap with enormous falsie basket.... She stands there smiling stupidly and flexing her huge muscles.... The Technician is crawling around on the control room floor looking for his plate and shouting unintelligible orders: "Thess thupper thonic!! Thut ur oth thu thair!"

THE DIPLOMAT (wiping sweat from his brow): "To any creature of any type or description ..."

"And the home of the brave."
The diplomat's face is grey. He staggers, trips in the scroll, sags against the rail, blood pouring from eyes, nose and mouth, dying of cerebral hemorrhage.

THE DIPLOMAT (barely audible): "The Department denies ... un-American ... It's been destroyed ... I mean it never was ... Categor ..." *Dies*.

In the Control Room instrument panels are blowing out ... great streamers of electricity crackle through the room.... The Technician, naked, his body burned black, staggers about like a figure in Götterdämmerung, screaming: "Thubber thonic!! Oth thu thair!!!" A final blast reduces the Technician to a cinder.

> *Gave proof through the night*
> *That our flag was still there....*

III

MEETING OF INTERNATIONAL
CONFERENCE OF
TECHNOLOGICAL PSYCHIATRY

Doctor "Fingers" Schafer, the Lobotomy Kid, rises and turns on the Conferents the cold blue blast of his gaze:

"Gentlemen, the human nervous system can bereduced to a compact and abbreviated spinal column. The brain, front, middle and rear must follow the adenoid, the wisdom tooth, the appendix.... I give you my Master Work: *The Complete All American De-anxietized Man....*"

Blast of trumpets: The Man is carried in naked by two Negro Bearers who drop him on the platform with bestial, sneering brutality.... The Man wriggles.... His flesh turns to viscid, transparent jelly that drifts away in green mist, unveiling a monster black centipede. Waves of unknown stench fill the room, searing the lungs, grabbing the stomach....

Schafer wrings his hands sobbing: "Clarence!! How can you do this to me?? Ingrates!! Every one of them ingrates!!"

The Conferents start back muttering in dismay:

"I'm afraid Schafer had gone a bit too far...."

"I sounded a word of warning...."

"Brilliant chap Schafer ... but...."

"Man will do anything for publicity...."

"Gentlemen, this unspeakable and in every sense illegitimate child of Doctor Schafer's perverted brain must not see the light.... Our duty to the human race is clear...."

"Man he done seen the light," said one of the Negro Bearers.

"We must stomp out the Un-American crittah," says a fat, frog-faced Southern doctor who has been drinking corn out of a mason jar. He advances drunkenly, then halts, appalled by the formidable size and menacing aspect of the centipede....

"Fetch gasoline!" he bellows. "We gotta burn the son of a bitch like an uppity Nigra!"

"I'm not sticking my neck out, me," says a cool hip young doctor high on LSD25.... "Why a smart DA could ..."

Fadeout. "Order in The Court!"

DA: "Gentlemen of the jury, these 'learned gentlemen' claim that the innocent human creature they have so wantonly slain suddenly turned himself into a huge black centipede and it was 'their duty to the human race' to destroy this monster before it could, by any means at its disposal, perpetrate its kind. . . .

"Are we to gulp down this tissue of horse shit? Are we to take these glib lies like a greased and nameless asshole? Where *is* this wondrous centipede?

" 'We have destroyed it,' they say smugly. . . . And I would like to remind you, Gentlemen and Hermaphrodites of the Jury, that this Great Beast"—he points to Doctor Schafer—"has, on several previous occasions, appeared in this court charged with the unspeakable crime of brain rape. . . . In plain English"—he pounds the rail of the jury box, his voice rises to a scream—"in plain English, Gentlemen, *forcible lobotomy*. . . ."

The Jury gasps. . . . One dies of a heart attack. . . . Three fall to the floor writhing in orgasms of prurience. . . .

The DA points dramatically: "He it is. . . . He and no other who has reduced whole provinces of our fair land to a state bordering on the far side of idiocy. . . . He it is who has filled great warehouses with row on row, tier on tier of helpless creatures who must have their every want attended. . . . 'The Drones' he calls them with a cynical leer of pure educated evil. . . . Gentlemen, I say to you that the wanton murder of Clarence Cowie must not go unavenged: This foul crime shrieks like a wounded faggot for justice at least!"

The centipede is rushing about in agitation.

"Man, that mother fucker's hungry," screams one of the Bearers.

"I'm getting out of here, me."

A wave of electric horror sweeps through the Conferents. . . . They storm the exits screaming and clawing. . . .

IV

BENWAY: "Don't take it so hard, kid. . . . 'Jeder macht eine kleine Dummheit.' " (Everyone makes a little dumbness.)

SCHAFER: "I tell you I can't escape a feeling . . . well, of *evil* about this."

BENWAY: "Balderdash, my boy . . . We're scientists. . . . Pure scientists. Disinterested research and damned be him who cries, 'Hold, *too much*!' Such people are no better than party poops."

SCHAFER: "Yes, yes, of course . . . and yet . . . I can't get that stench out of my lungs. . . ."

BENWAY (irritably): "None of us can. . . . Never smelled anything remotely like it. . . . Where was I? Oh yes, what would be the result of administering curare plus iron lung during acute mania? Possibly the subject, unable to discharge his tensions in motor activity, would succumb on the spot like a jungle rat. Interesting cause of death, what?"

Schafer is not listening. "You know," he says impulsively, "I think I'll go back to plain old-fashioned surgery. The human body is scandalously inefficient. Instead of a mouth and an anus to get out of order why not have one all-purpose hole to eat *and* eliminate? We could seal up nose and mouth, fill in the stomach, make an air hole direct into the lungs where it should have been in the first place...."

BENWAY: "Why not one all-purpose blob? Did I ever tell you about the man who taught his asshole to talk? His whole abdomen would move up and down you dig farting out the words. It was unlike anything I ever heard.

"This ass talk had a sort of gut frequency. It hit you right down there like you gotta go. You know when the old colon gives you the elbow and it feels sorta cold inside, and you know all you have to do is turn loose? Well this talking hit you right down there, a bubbly, thick stagnant sound, a sound you could *smell*.

"This man worked for a carnival you dig, and to start with it was like a novelty ventriloquist act. Really funny, too, at first. He had a number he called 'The Better 'Ole' that was a scream, I tell you. I forget most of it but it was clever. Like, 'Oh I say, are you still down there, old thing?'

"'Nah! I had to go relieve myself.'

"After a while the ass started talking on its own. He would go in without anything prepared and his ass would ad-lib and toss the gags back at him every time.

"Then it developed sort of teeth-like little raspy incurving hooks and started eating. He thought this was cute at first and built an act around it, but the asshole would eat its way through his pants and start talking on the street, shouting out it wanted equal rights. It would get drunk, too, and have crying jags nobody loved it and it wanted to be kissed same as any other mouth. Finally it talked all the time day and night, you could hear him for blocks screaming at it to shut up, and beating it with his fist, and sticking candles up it, but nothing did any good and the asshole said to him: 'It's you who will shut up in the end. Not me. Because we don't need you around here any more. I can talk and eat *and* shit.'

"After that he began waking up in the morning with a transparent jelly like a tadpole's tail all over his mouth. This jelly was what the scientists call un-DT, Undifferentiated Tissue, which can grow into any kind of flesh on the human body. He would tear it off his mouth and the pieces would stick to his hands like burning gasoline jelly and grow there, grow anywhere on him a glob of it fell. So finally his mouth sealed over, and the whole head would have amputated spontaneous—(did you know there is a condition occurs in parts of Africa and only among Negroes where the little toe amputates spontaneously?)—except for the *eyes* you dig. That's one thing the asshole *couldn't* do was see. It needed the eyes. But nerve connections were blocked and infiltrated and atrophied so the brain couldn't give orders any more. It was trapped in the skull, sealed off. For a while you could see the silent, helpless suffering of the brain behind the eyes, then finally the brain must have died, because the eyes *went out*, and there was no more feeling in them than a crab's eye on the end of a stalk.

"That's the sex that passes the censor, squeezes through between bureaus, because there's always a space *between*, in popular songs and Grade B movies, giving away the basic American rottenness, spurting out like breaking boils, throwing out globs of that un-DT to fall anywhere and grow into some degenerate cancerous life-form, reproducing a hideous random image. Some would be entirely made of penis-like erectile tissue, others viscera barely covered over with skin, clusters of 3 and 4 eyes together, criss-cross of mouth and assholes, human parts shaken around and poured out any way they fell.

"The end result of complete cellular representation is cancer. Democracy is cancerous, and bureaus are its cancer. A bureau takes root anywhere in the state, turns malignant like the Narcotic Bureau, and grows and grows, always reproducing more of its own kind, until it chokes the host if not controlled or excised. Bureaus cannot live without a host, being true parasitic organisms. (A cooperative on the other hand *can* live without the state. That is the road to follow. The building up of independent units to meet needs of the people who participate in the functioning of the unit. A bureau operates on opposite principle of *inventing needs* to justify its existence.) Bureaucracy is wrong as a cancer, a turning away from the human evolutionary direction of infinite potentials and differentiation and independent spontaneous action, to the complete parasitism of a virus.

"(It is thought that the virus is a degeneration from a more complex life form. It may at one time have been capable of independent life. Now it has fallen to the borderline between living and

76

dead matter. It can exhibit living qualities only in a host, by using the life of another—the renunciation of life itself, a *falling* towards inorganic, inflexible machine, towards dead matter.)

"Bureaus die when the structure of the state collapses. They are as helpless and unfit for independent existences as a displaced tapeworm, or a virus that has killed the host.

"In Timbuctu I once saw an Arab boy who could play a flute with his ass, and the fairies told me he was really an individual in bed. He could play a tune up and down the organ hitting the most erogenously sensitive spots, which are different on everyone, of course. Every lover had his special theme song which was perfect for him and rose to his climax. The boy was a great artist when it came to improving new combines and special climaxes, some of them notes in the unknown, tie-ups of seeming discords that would suddenly break through each other and crash together with a stunning, hot sweet impact."

V

Dr Berger's Mental Hour.... Fadeout.

TECHNICIAN: "Now listen, I'll say it again, and I'll say it slow. 'Yes.'" He nods. "And make with the smile.... The *smile*." He shows his false teeth in hideous parody of a toothpaste ad. "'We like apple pie, and we like each other. It's just as simple as that,' and make it sound *simple*, country simple.... Look bovine, whyncha? You want the switchboard again? Or the pail?"

SUBJECT—Cured Criminal Psychopath—"No!... No!... What's this bovine?"

TECHNICIAN: "Look like a cow."

SUBJECT—with cow's head—"Moooo Moooo."

TECHNICIAN (starting back): "Too much!! No! Just look square, you dig, like a nice popcorn John...."

SUBJECT: "A mark?"

TECHNICIAN: "Well, not exactly a mark. Not enough larceny in this citizen. He is after light concussion.... You know the type. Telepathic sender and receiver excised. The Service Man Look ... Action, camera."

SUBJECT: "Yes, we like apple pie." His stomach rumbles loud and long. Streamers of saliva hang off his chin....

Dr Berger looks up from some notes. He look like Jewish owl with black glasses, the light hurt his eyes: "I think he is an unsuitable subject.... See he reports to Disposal."

TECHNICIAN: "Well, we could cut that rumble out of the sound track, stick a drain in his mouth and . . ."

DR BERGER: "No . . . He's *unsuitable*." He looks at the subject with distaste as if he commit some terrible faux-pas like look for crabs in Mrs Worldly's drawing room.

TECHNICIAN (resigned and exasperated): "Bring in the cured swish."

The cured homosexual is brought in. . . . He walks through invisible contours of hot metal. He sits in front of the camera and starts arranging his body in a countrified sprawl. Muscles move into place like autonomous parts of a severed insect. Blank stupidity blurs and softens his face: "Yes," he nods and smiles, "we like apple pie and we like each other. It's just as simple as that." He nods and smiles and nods and smiles and—

"Cut! . . ." screams the Technician. The cured homosexual is led out nodding and smiling.

"Play it back."

The Artistic Adviser shakes his head: "It lacks something. To be specific, it lacks health."

BERGER (leaps to his feet): "Preposterous! It's health incarnate! . . ."

ARTISTIC ADVISER (primly): "Well if you have anything to enlighten me on this subject I'll be very glad to hear it, *Doctor* Berger. . . . If you with your brilliant mind can carry the project alone, I don't know why you *need* an Art Adviser at *all*." He exits with hand on hip singing softly: "I'll be around when you're gone."

TECHNICIAN: "Send in the cured writer. . . . He's got *what*? Buddhism? . . . Oh, he can't talk. Say so at first, whyncha?" He turns to Berger: "The writer can't talk. . . . Overliberated, you might say. Of course we can dub him. . . ."

BERGER (sharply): "No, that wouldn't do at all. . . . Send in someone else."

TECHNICIAN: "Those two was my white-haired boys. I put in a hundred hours overtime on those kids for which I am not yet compensate. . . ."

BERGER: "Apply triplicate. . . . Form 6090."

TECHNICIAN: "You tell me how to apply already? Now look, Doc, you say something once. 'To speak of a healthy homosexual it's like how can a citizen be perfectly healthy with terminal cirrhosis.' Remember?"

BERGER: "Oh yes. Very well put, of course," he snarls viciously.

"I don't pretend to be a *writer*." He spits the word out with such ugly hate that the Technician reels back appalled. . . .

TECHNICIAN (aside): "I can't bear the smell of him. Like old rotten replica cultures. . . . Like the farts of a maneating plant. . . . Like Schafer's hurumph" (parodies academic manner). "Strange Serpent . . . What I'm getting at, Doc, is how can you expect a body to be healthy with its brains washed out? . . . Or put it another way. Can a subject be healthy *in abstentia* by proxy already?"

BERGER (leaps up): "I got the health! . . . All the health! Enough health for the whole world, the whole fucking world!! I cure everybody!"

The Technician looks at him sourly. He mixes a bicarbonate of soda and drinks it and belches into his hand. "Twenty years I've been a martyr to dyspepsia."

Lovable Lu your brainwashed poppa say: "I'm strictly for fish, and I luuuuuve it. . . . Confidentially, girls, I use Steely Dan's Yokohama, wouldn't you? Danny Boy never lets you down. Besides it's more hygenic that way and avoids all kinda awful contacts leave a man paralyzed from the waist down. Women have poison juices. . . ."

"So I told him, I said '*Doctor* Berger, don't think you can pass your tired old brainwashed belles on me. I'm the oldest faggot in the Upper Baboon's Asshole . . . .' "

VI

Carl Peterson found a postcard in his box requesting him to report for a ten o'clock appointment with Doctor Benway in the Ministry of Mental Hygiene and Prophylaxis. . . .

"What on earth could they want with me?" he thought irritably. . . . "A mistake most likely." But he knew they didn't make mistakes. . . . Certainly not mistakes of identity. . . .

It would not have occurred to Carl to disregard the appointment even though failure to appear entailed no penalty. . . . Freeland was a welfare state. If a citizen wanted anything from a load of bone meal to a sexual partner some department was ready to offer effective aid. The threat implicit in this enveloping benevolence stifled the concept of rebellion. . . .

Carl walked through the Town Hall Square. . . . Nickel nudes sixty feet high with brass genitals soaped themselves under gleaming showers. . . . The Town Hall cupola, of glass brick and copper crashed into the sky.

Carl stared back at a homosexual American tourist who dropped his eyes and fumbled with the light filters of his Leica. . . .

Carl entered the steel enamel labyrinth of the Ministry, strode to the information desk . . . and presented his card.

"Fifth floor . . . Room twenty-six . . ."

In room twenty-six a nurse looked at him with cold undersea eyes.

"Doctor Benway is expecting you," she said smiling. "Go right in."

"As if he had nothing to do but wait for me," thought Carl. . . .

The office was completely silent, and filled with milky light. The doctor shook Carl's hand, keeping his eyes on the young man's chest. . . .

"I've seen this man before," Carl thought. . . . "But where?"

He sat down and crossed his legs. He glanced at an ashtray on the desk and lit a cigarette. . . . He turned to the doctor a steady inquiring gaze in which there was more than a touch of insolence.

The doctor seemed embarrassed. . . . He fidgeted and coughed . . . and fumbled with papers. . . .

"Hurumph," he said finally. . . . "Your name is Carl Peterson I believe. . . ." His glasses slid down onto his nose in parody of the academic manner. . . . Carl nodded silently. . . . The doctor did not look at him but seemed none the less to register the acknowledgement. . . . He pushed his glasses back into place with one finger and opened a file on the white enamelled desk.

"Mmmmmmmm. Carl Peterson," he repeated the name caressingly, pursed his lips and nodded several times. He spoke again abruptly: "You know of course that we are trying. We are all trying. Sometimes of course we don't succeed." His voice trailed off thin and tenuous. He put a hand to his forehead. "To adjust the state—simply a tool—to the needs of each individual citizen." His voice boomed out so unexpectedly deep and loud that Carl started. "That is the only function of the state as we see it. Our knowledge . . . incomplete, of course," he made a slight gesture of depreciation. . . . "For example . . . *for example* . . . take the matter of uh *sexual deviation*." The doctor rocked back and forth in his chair. His glasses slid down onto his nose. Carl felt suddenly uncomfortable.

"We regard it as a misfortune . . . a sickness . . . certainly nothing to be censored or uh sanctioned any more than say . . . tuberculosis. . . . Yes," he repeated firmly as if Carl had raised an objection. . . . "Tuberculosis. On the other hand you can readily see that *any* illness imposes certain, should we say *obligations*, certain *necessities* of a prophylactic nature on the authorities concerned with public health, such necessities to be imposed, needless to say, with a minimum of inconvenience and hardship to the unfortunate individual who has, through no fault of his own, become uh infected.... That is to say, of course, the minimum hardship compatible with adequate protection of other individuals who are not so infected.... We do not find obligatory vaccination for smallpox an unreasonable measure.... Nor isolation for certain contagious diseases.... I am sure you will agree that individuals infected with hurumph what the French call 'Les Maladies galantes' heh heh heh should be compelled to undergo treatment if they do not report voluntarily." The doctor went on chuckling and rocking in his chair like a mechanical toy.... Carl realized that he was expected to say something.

"That seems reasonable," he said.

The doctor stopped chuckling. He was suddenly motionless. "Now to get back to this uh matter of sexual deviation. Frankly we don't pretend to understand—at least not completely—why some men and women prefer the uh sexual company of their own sex. We do know that the uh phenomena is common enough, and, under certain circumstances a matter of uh concern to this department."

For the first time the doctor's eyes flickered across Carl's face. Eyes without a trace of warmth or hate or any emotion that Carl had ever experienced in himself or seen in another, at once cold and intense, predatory and impersonal. Carl suddenly felt trapped in this silent underwater cave of a room, cut off from all sources of warmth and certainty. His picture of himself sitting there calm, alert with a trace of well mannered contempt went dim, as if vitality were draining out of him to mix with the milky grey medium of the room.

"Treatment of these disorders is, at the present time, hurmph symptomatic." The doctor suddenly threw himself back in his chair and burst into peals of metallic laughter. Carl watched him appalled. ... "The man is insane," he thought. The doctor's face went blank as a gambler's. Carl felt an odd sensation in his stomach like the sudden stopping of an elevator.

The doctor was studying the file in front of him. He spoke in a tone of slightly condescending amusement:

"Don't look so frightened, young man. Just a professional joke. To say treatment is symptomatic means there is none, except to make the patient feel as comfortable as possible. And that is precisely what we attempt to do in these cases." Once again Carl felt the impact of that cold interest on his face. "That is to say reassurance when reassurance is necessary ... and, of course, suitable outlets with other individuals of similar tendencies. No isolation is indicated ... the condition is no more directly contagious than cancer. Cancer, my first love," the doctor's voice receded. He seemed actually to have gone away through an invisible door leaving his empty body sitting there at the desk.

Suddenly he spoke again in a crisp voice. "And so you may well wonder why we concern ourselves with the matter at all?" He flashed a smile bright and cold as snow in sunlight.

Carl shrugged: "That is not my business ... what I am wondering is why you have asked me to come here and why you tell me all this ... this ..."

"Nonsense?"

Carl was annoyed to find himself blushing.

The doctor leaned back and placed the ends of his fingers together:

"The young," he said indulgently. "Always they are in a hurry. One day perhaps you will learn the meaning of patience. No, Carl.... I may call you Carl? I am not evading your question. In cases of suspected tuberculosis we—that is the appropriate department—may ask, even *request*, someone to appear for a fluoroscopic examination. This is routine, you understand. Most of such examinations turn up negative. So you have been asked to report here for, should I say a psychic fluoroscope???? I may add that after talking with you I feel *relatively* sure that the result will be, for practical purposes, negative...."

"But the whole thing is ridiculous. I have always interested myself only in girls. I have a steady girl now and we plan to marry."

'Yes Carl, I know. And that is why you are here. A blood test prior to marriage, this is reasonable, no?"

"Please doctor, speak directly."

The doctor did not seem to hear. He drifted out of his chair and began walking around behind Carl, his voice languid and intermittent like music down a windy street.

"I may tell you in strictest confidence that there is definite evidence of a hereditary factor. Social pressure. Many homosexuals latent and overt do, unfortunately, marry. Such marriages often result in ... Factor of infantile environment." The doctor's voice went on and on. He was talking about schizophrenia, cancer, hereditary disfunction of the hypothalamus.

Carl dozed off. He was opening a green door. A horrible smell grabbed his lungs and he woke up with a shock. The doctor's voice was strangely flat and lifeless, a whispering junky voice:

'The Kleiberg-Stanislouski semen floculation test ... a diagnostic tool ... indicative at least in a negative sense. In certain cases useful—taken as part of the whole picture. . . . Perhaps under the uh *circumstances.*" The doctor's voice shot up to a pathic scream. "The nurse will take your uh *specimen.*"

"This way please. . . ." The nurse opened the door into a bare white walled cubicle. She handed him a jar.

"Use this please. Just yell when you're ready."

There was a jar of KY on a glass shelf. Carl felt ashamed as if his mother had laid out a handkerchief for him. Some coy little message stitched on like: "If I was a cunt we could open a dry goods store."

Ignoring the KY, he ejaculated into the jar, a cold brutal fuck of the nurse standing her up against a glass brick wall. "Old Glass Cunt," he sneered, and saw a cunt full of colored glass splinters under the Northern Lights.

He washed his penis and buttoned up his pants.

Something was watching his every thought and movement with cold, sneering hate, the shifting of his testes, the contractions of his rectum. He was in a room filled with green light. There was a stained wood double bed, a black wardrobe with full length mirror. Carl could not see his face. Someone was sitting in a black hotel chair. He was wearing a stiff bosomed white shirt and a dirty paper tie. The face swollen, skull-less, eyes like burning pus.

"Something wrong?" said the nurse indifferently. She was holding a glass of water out to him. She watched him drink with aloof contempt. She turned and picked up the jar with obvious distaste.

The nurse turned to him: "Are you waiting for something special?" she snapped. Carl had never been spoken to like that in his adult life. "Why no. . . ." "You can go then," she turned back to the jar. With a little exclamation of disgust she wiped a gob of semen off her hand. Carl crossed the room and stood at the door.

"Do I have another appointment?"

She looked at him in disapproving surprise: "You'll be notified *of course.*" She stood in the doorway of the cubicle and watched him walk through the outer office and open the door. He turned and attempted a jaunty wave. The nurse did not move or change her expression. As he walked down the stairs the broken, false grin burned his face with shame. A homosexual tourist looked at him and raised a knowing eyebrow. "Something *wrong?*"

83

Carl ran into a park and found an empty bench beside a bronze faun with cymbals.

"Let your hair down, chicken. You'll feel better." The tourist was leaning over him, his camera swinging in Carl's face like a great dangling tit.

"Fuck off you!"

Carl saw something ignoble and hideous reflected back in the queen's spayed animal brown eyes.

"Oh! I wouldn't be calling any names if I were you, chicken. You're hooked too. I saw you coming out of The Institute."

"What do you mean by that?" Carl demanded.

"Oh nothing. Nothing at all."

"Well, Carl," the doctor began smiling and keeping his eyes on a level with Carl's mouth. "I have some good news for you." He picked up a slip of blue paper off the desk and went through an elaborate pantomime of focusing his eyes on it. "Your uh test ... the Robinson-Kleiberg floculation test ..."

"I thought it was a Blomberg-Stanlouski test."

The doctor tittered. "Oh dear no. ... You are getting ahead of me young man. You might have misunderstood. The Blomberg-Stanlouski, weeell that's a different sort of test altogether. I *do hope* ... not necessary. ..." He tittered again: "But as I was saying before I was so charmingly interrupted ... by my hurumph learned young colleague. Your KS seems to be ..." He held the slip at arm's length. "... completely uh negative. So perhaps we won't be troubling you any further. And so ..." He folded the slip carefully into a file. He leafed through the file. Finally he stopped and frowned and pursed his lips. He closed the file and put his hand flat on it and leaned forward.

"Carl, when you were doing your military service ... There must have been ... in fact there were long periods when you found yourself deprived of the uh consolations and uh *facilities* of the fair sex. During these no doubt trying and difficult periods you had perhaps a pin up girl?? Or more likely a pin up harem?? Heh heh heh ..."

Carl looked at the doctor with overt distaste. "Yes, of course," he said. "We all did."

"And now, Carl, I would like to show you some pin up girls." He pulled an envelope out of a drawer. "And ask you to please pick out the one you would most like to uh make heh heh heh. ..." He suddenly leaned forward fanning the photographs in front of Carl's face. "Pick a girl, any girl!"

Carl reached out with numb fingers and touched one of the photographs. The doctor put the photo back into the pack and shuffled and cut and he placed the pack on Carl's file and slapped it smartly. He spread the photos face up in front of Carl. "Is she there?"

Carl shook his head.

"Of course not. She is in here where she belongs. A woman's place what???" He opened the file and held out the girl's photo attached to a Rorshach plate.

"Is that her?"

Carl nodded silently.

"You have good taste, my boy. I may tell you in strictest confidence that some of these girls ..." with gambler fingers he shifts the photos in Three Card Monte Passes—"are really *boys*. In uh *drag* I believe is the word???" His eyebrows shot up and down with incredible speed. Carl could not be sure he had seen anything unusual. The doctor's face opposite him was absolutely immobile and expressionless. Once again Carl experienced the floating sensation in his stomach and genitals of a sudden elevator stop.

"Yes, Carl, you seem to be running our little obstacle course with flying colors. . . . I guess you think this is all pretty silly don't you now . . . ???"

"Well, to tell the truth . . . Yes . . ."

"You are frank, Carl. . . . This is good. . . . And now . . . Carl . . ." He dragged the name out caressingly like a sweet con dick about to offer you an Old Gold—(just like a cop to smoke Old Golds somehow) and go into his act. . . .

The con dick does a little dance step.

"Why don't you make The Man a proposition?" he jerks a head towards his glowering super-ego who is always referred to in the third person as "The Man" or "The Lieutenant."

"That's the way the Lieutenant is, you play fair with him and he'll play fair with you. . . . We'd like to go light on you. . . . If you could help us in some way." His words open out into a desolate waste of cafeterias and street corners and lunch rooms. Junkies look the other way munching pound cake.

"The Fag is wrong."

The Fag slumps in a hotel chair knocked out on goof balls with his tongue lolling out.

He gets up in a goof ball trance, hangs himself without altering his expression or pulling his tongue in.

The dick is diddling on a pad.

"Know Marty Steel?" Diddle.

"Yes."

"Can you score off him?" Diddle? Diddle?

"He's skeptical."

"But you can score." Diddle diddle. "You scored off him last week didn't you?" Diddle???

"Yes."

"Well you can score off him this week." Diddle ... Diddle ... Diddle ... "You can score off him today." No diddle.

"No! No! Not that!!"

"Now look are you going to cooperate"—three vicious diddles—"or does the ... does the Man cornhole you???" He raises a fay eyebrow.

"And so Carl you will please oblige to tell me how many times and under what circumstances you have uh indulged in homosexual acts???" His voice drifts away. "If you have never done so I shall be inclined to think of you as a somewhat atypical young man." The doctor raises a coy admonishing finger. "In any case ..." He tapped the file and flashed a hideous leer. Carl noticed that the file was six inches thick. In fact it seemed to have thickened enormously since he entered the room.

"Well, when I was doing my military service ... These queers used to proposition me and sometimes ... when I was blank ..."

"Yes, of course, Carl," the doctor brayed heartily. 'In your position I would have done the same I don't mind telling you heh heh heh.... Well, I guess we can uh *dismiss as irrelevant* these uh understandable means of replenishing the uh *exchequer*. And now, Carl, there were perhaps"—one finger tapped the file which gave out a faint effluvia of moldy jock straps and chlorine—"occasions. When no uh economic factors were involved."

A green flare exploded in Carl's brain. He saw Hans' lean brown body—twisting towards him, quick breath on his shoulder. The flare went out. Some huge insect was squirming in his hand.

His whole being jerked away in an electric spasm of revulsion.

Carl got to his feet shaking with rage.

"What are you writing there?" he demanded.

"Do you often doze off like that??? in the middle of a conversation ...?"

"I wasn't asleep that is."

"You weren't?"

"It's just that the *whole thing* is unreal.... I'm going now. I don't care. You can't force me to stay."

He was walking across the room towards the door. He had been walking a long time. A creeping numbness dragged his legs. The door seemed to recede.

"Where can you go, Carl?" The doctor's voice reached him from a great distance.

"Out ... Away ... Through the door ..."

"The Green Door, Carl?"

The doctor's voice was barely audible. The whole room was exploding out into space.

TECHNOLOGY AND CONTROL

I

Now a word about the parties of Interzone....

It will be immediately clear that the Liquefaction Party is, except for one man, entirely composed of dupes, it not being clear until the final absorption who is whose dupe.... The Liquefactionists are much given to every form of perversion, especially sado-masochistic practices.

Liquefactionists in general know what the score is. The Senders, on the other hand, are notorious for their ignorance of the nature and terminal state of sending, for barbarous and self-righteous manners, and for rabid fear of any *fact*. It was only the intervention of the Factualists that prevented the Senders from putting Einstein in an institution and destroying his theory. It may be said that only a very few Senders know what they are doing and these top Senders are the most dangerous and evil men in the world.... Techniques of Sending were crude at first. Fadeout to the National Electronic Conference in Chicago.

The Conferents are putting on their overcoats.... The speaker talks in a flat shopgirl voice:

"In closing I want to sound a word of warning.... The logical extension of encephalographic research is biocontrol; that is control of physical movement, mental processes, emotional reactions and *apparent* sensory impressions by means of bioelectric signals injected into the nervous system of the subject."

"Louder and funnier!" The Conferents are trouping out in clouds of dust.

"Shortly after birth a surgeon could install connections in the brain. A miniature radio receiver could be plugged in and the subject controlled from State-controlled transmitters."

Dust settles through the windless air of a vast empty hall—smell of hot iron and steam; a radiator sings in the distance.... The Speaker shuffles his notes and blows dust off them....

"The biocontrol apparatus is prototype of one-way telepathic control. The subject could be rendered susceptible to the transmitter by drugs or other processing without installing any apparatus. Ultimately the Senders will use telepathic transmitting exclusively.... Ever dig the Mayan codices? I figure it like this: the priests—about one per cent of population—made with one-way telepathic broadcasts instructing the workers what to feel and when.... A telepathic sender has to send all the time. He can never receive, because if he receives that means someone else who has feelings of his own could louse up his continuity. The sender has to send all the time, but he can't ever recharge himself by contact. Sooner or later he's got no feelings to send. You can't have feelings alone. Not alone like the Sender is alone—and you dig there can only be one Sender at one place-time.... Finally the screen goes dead.... The Sender has turned into a huge centipede.... So the workers come in on the beam and burn the centipede and elect a new Sender by consensus of the general will.... The Mayans were limited by isolation.... Now one Sender could control the planet.... *You see control can never be a means to any practical end.... It can never be a means to anything but more control.... Like junk ...*"

The Divisionists occupy a mid-way position, could in fact be termed moderates.... They are called Divisionists because they literally divide. They cut off tiny bits of their flesh and grow exact replicas of themselves in embryo jelly. It seems probable, unless the process of division is halted, that eventually there will be only one replica of one sex on the planet: that is one person in the world with millions of separate bodies.... Are these bodies actually independent, and could they in time develop varied characteristics? I doubt it. Replicas must periodically recharge with the Mother Cell. This is an article of faith with the Divisionists, who live in fear of a replica revolution.... Some Divisionists think that the process can be halted short of the eventual monopoly of one replica. They say: "Just let me plant a few more replicas all over so I won't be lonely when I travel.... And we must strictly control the division of Undesirables...." Every replica but your own is eventually an "Undesirable." Of course if someone starts inundating an area with Identical Replicas, everyone knows what is going on. The other citizens are subject to declare a "Schluppit" (wholesale massacre of all identifiable replicas). To avoid extermination of their replicas, citizens dye, distort, and alter them with face and body molds. Only the most abandoned and shameless characters venture to manufacture IRs—Identical Replicas.

A cretinous albino Caid, product of a long line of recessive genes (tiny toothless mouth lined with black hairs, body of a huge crab, claws instead of arms, eyes projected on stalks) accumulated 20,000 IRs.

"As far as the eye can see, nothing but replicas," he says, crawling around on his terrace and speaking in strange insect chirps. "I don't have to skulk around like a nameless asshole growing replicas in my cesspool and sneaking them out disguised as plumbers and delivery men.... My replicas don't have their dazzling beauty marred by plastic surgery and barbarous dye and bleach processes. They stand forth naked in the sun for all to see, in their incandescent loveliness of body, face and soul. I have made them in my image and enjoined them to increase and multiply geometric for they shall inherit the earth."

A professional witch was called in to make Sheik Aracknid's replica cultures forever sterile.... As the witch was preparing to loose a blast of anti-orgones, Benway told him: "Don't knock yourself out. Frederick's ataxia will clean out that replica nest. I studied neurology under Professor Fingerbottom in Vienna ... and he knew every nerve in your body. Magnificent old thing ... Came to a sticky end.... His falling piles blew out the Duc de Ventre's Hispano Suiza and wrapped around the rear wheel. He was completely gutted, leaving an empty shell sitting there on the giraffe skin upholstery.... Even the eyes and brain went with a horrible schlupping sound. The Duc de Ventre says he will carry that ghastly schlup to his mausoleum."

Since there is no sure way to detect a disguised replica (though every Divisionist has some method he considers infallible) the Divisionists are hysterically paranoid. If some citizen ventures to express a liberal opinion another citizen invariably snarls: "What are you? Some stinking Nigger's bleached-out replica?"

The casualties in barroom fights are staggering. In fact the fear of Negro replicas—which may be blond and blue-eyed—has depopulated whole regions. The Divisionists are all latent or overt homosexuals. Evil old queens tell the young boys: "If you go with a woman your replicas won't grow." And citizens are forever putting the hex on someone else's replica cultures. Cries of: "Hex my culture will you, Biddy Blair!" followed by sound effects of mayhem, continually ring through the quarter.... The Divisionists are much given to the practice of black magic in general, and they have innumerable formulas of varying efficacy for destroying the Mother Cell, also known as the Protoplasm Daddy, by torturing or killing a captured replica.... The authorities have finally given up the attempt to control, among the Divisionists, the crimes of murder and unlicensed production of replicas. But they do stage pre-election raids and destroy vast replica cultures in the mountainous regions of the Zone where replica moonshiners hole up.

Sex with a replica is strictly forbidden and almost universally practised. There are queer bars where shameless citizens openly consort with their replicas. House detectives stick their heads into hotel rooms saying: "Have you got a replica in here?"

Bars subject to be inundated by low class replica lovers put up signs in ditto marks: " " " "s Will Not Be Served Here.... It may be said that the average Divisionist lives in a continual crisis of fear and rage, unable to achieve either the self-righteous complacency of the Senders or the relaxed depravity of the Liquefactionists.... However the parties are not in practice separate but blend in all combinations.

The Factualists are Anti-Liquefactionist, Anti-Divisionist, and above all Anti-Sender.

Bulletin of the Coordinate Factualist on the subject of replicas: "We must reject the facile solution of flooding the planet with 'desirable replicas.' It is highly doubtful if there are any desirable replicas, such creatures constituting an attempt to circumvent process and change. Even the most intelligent and genetically perfect replicas would in all probability constitute an unspeakable menace to life on this planet...."

TB—Tentative Bulletin-Liquefaction: "We must not reject or deny our protoplasmic core, striving at all times to maintain a maximum of flexibility without falling into the morass of lique-faction...." Tentative and Incomplete Bulletin: "Emphatically we do not oppose telepathic research. In fact, telepathy properly used and understood could be the ultimate defense against any form of organized coercion or tyranny on the part of pressure groups or individual control addicts. We oppose, as we oppose atomic war, the use of such knowledge to control, coerce, debase, exploit or annihilate the individuality of another living creature. Telepathy is not, by its nature, a one-way process. To attempt to set up a one-way telepathic broadcast must be regarded as an unqualified evil...."

DB—Definitive Bulletin: "The Sender will be defined by negatives. A low pressure area, a sucking emptiness. He will be portentously anonymous, faceless, colorless. He will—probably—be born with smooth disks of skin instead of eyes. He always knows where he is going like a virus knows. He doesn't need eyes."

"Couldn't there be more than one Sender?"

"Oh yes, many of them at first. But not for long. Some maudlin citizens will think they can send something edifying, not realizing that sending *is* evil. Scientists will say: 'sending is like atomic power.... If properly harnessed.' At this point an anal technician mixes a bicarbonate of soda and pulls the switch that reduces the earth to cosmic dust. ('Belch ... They'll hear this fart on Jupiter.') ... Artists will confuse sending with creation. They will camp around screeching 'A new medium' until their rating drops off.... Philosophers will bat around the ends and means hassle not knowing that *sending can never be a means to anything but more sending, like Junk.* Try using junk as a means to something else.... Some citizens with 'Coca Cola and aspirin' control habits will be talking about the evil glamor of sending. But no one will talk about anything very long. *The Sender*, he don't like talking."

The Sender is not a human individual.... It is The Human Virus. (All virus are deteriorated cells leading a parasitic existence.... They have specific affinity for the Mother Cell; thus deteriorated liver cells seek the home place of hepatitis, etc. So every species has a Master Virus: Deteriorated Image of that species.)

The broken image of Man moves in minute by minute and cell by cell.... Poverty, hatred, war, police-criminals, bureaucracy, insanity, all symptoms of The Human Virus.

The Human Virus can now be isolated and treated.

II

The only native in Interzone who is neither queer nor available is Andrew Kief's chauffeur, which is not affectation or perversity on Keif's part, but a useful pretext to break off relations with anyone he doesn't want to see: "You made a pass at Aracknid last night. I can't have you to the house again." People are always blacking out in the Zone, whether they drink or not, and no one can say for sure he didn't make a pass at Aracknid's unappetizing person.

Aracknid is a worthless chauffeur, barely able to drive. On one occasion he ran down a pregnant woman in from the mountains with a load of charcoal on her back, and she miscarriaged a bloody, dead baby in the street, and Keif got out and sat on the curb stirring the blood with a stick while the police questioned Aracknid and finally arrested the woman for a violation of the Sanitary Code.

Aracknid is a grimly unattractive young man with a long face of a strange, slate-blue color. He has a big nose and great yellow teeth like a horse. Anybody can find an attractive chaffeur, but only Andrew Keif could have found Aracknid; Keif the brilliant, decadent young novelist who lives in a remodeled pissoir in the red light district of the Native Quarter.

The Zone is a single, vast building. The rooms are made of a plastic cement that bulges to accommodate people, but when too many crowd into one room there is a soft plop and someone squeezes through the wall right into the next house, the next bed that is, since the rooms are mostly bed where the business of the Zone is transacted. A hum of sex and commerce shakes the Zone like a vast hive:

"Two thirds of one percent. I won't budge from that figure; not even for my bumpkins."

"But where are the bills of lading, lover?"

"Not where you're looking, pet. That's too obvious."

"A bale of levis with built-in falsie baskets. Made in Hollywood."

"Hollywood, Siam."

"Well American *style*."

"What's the commission? ... The commission.... The Commission."

"Yes, nugget, a shipload of KY made of genuine whale dreck in the South Atlantic at present quarantined by the Board of Health in Tierra del Fuego. The commission, my dear! If we can pull this off we'll be in clover." (Whale dreck is reject material that accumulates in the process of cutting up a whale and cooking it down. A horrible, fishy mess you can smell for miles. No one has found any use for it.)

Interzone Imports Unlimited, which consists of Marvie and Leif The Unlucky, had latched onto the KY deal. In fact they specialize in pharmaceuticals and run a 24-hour Pro station, six ways coverage fore and aft, as a side line. (Six separate venereal diseases have been identified to date.)

They plunge into the deal. They form unmentionable services for a spastic Greek shipping agent, and one entire shift of Customs inspectors. The two partners fall out and finally denounce each other in the Embassy where they are referred to the We Don't Want To Hear About It Department, and eased out a back door into a shit-strewn vacant lot, where vultures fight over fish heads. They flail at each other hysterically.

"You're trying to fuck me out of my commission!"

"*Your* commission! Who smelled out this good thing in the first place?"

"But I have the bill of lading."

"Monster! But the check will be made out in my name."

"Bawstard! You'll never see the bill of lading until my cut is deposited in escrow."

"Well, might as well kiss and make up. There's nothing mean or petty about me."

They shake hands without enthusiasm and peck each other on the cheek. The deal drags on for months. They engage the services of an Expeditor. Finally Marvie emerges with a check for 42 Turkestan kurds drawn on an anonymous bank in South America, to clear through Amsterdam, a procedure that will take eleven months more or less.

Now we can relax in the cafés of The Plaza. He shows a photostatic copy of the check. He would never show the original of course, lest some envious citizen spit ink eradicator on the signature or otherwise mutilate the check.

Everyone asks him to buy drinks and celebrate, but he laughs jovially and says, "Fact is I can't afford to buy myself a drink. I already spent every kurd of it buying Penstrep for Ali's clap. He's down with it fore and aft again. I came near kicking the little bastard right through the wall into the next bed. But you all know what a sentimental old thing I am."

Marvie does buy himself a shot glass of beer, squeezing a blackened coin out of his fly onto the table. "Keep the change." The waiter sweeps the coin into a dust pan, he spits on the table and walks away.

"Sore head! He's envious of my check."

Marvie has been in Interzone since "the year before one" as he put it. He had been retired from some unspecified position in the State Dept "for the good of the service." Obviously he had once been very good looking in a crew-cut, college boy way, but his face had sagged and formed lumps under the chin like melting paraffin. He was getting heavy around the hips.

Leif The Unlucky was a tall, thin Norwegian, with a patch over one eye, his face congealed in a permanent, ingratiating smirk. Behind him lay an epic saga of unsuccessful enterprises. He had failed at raising frogs, chinchilla, Siamese fighting fish, rami and culture pearls. He had attempted, variously and without success, to promote a Love Bird Two-in-a-Coffin Cemetery, to corner the condom market during the rubber shortage, to run a mail order whore house, to issue penicillin as a patent medicine. He had followed disastrous betting systems in the casinos of Europe and the race tracks of the US. His reverses in business were matched by the incredible mischances of his personal life. His front teeth had been stomped out by bestial American sailors in Brooklyn. Vultures had eaten out an eye when he drank a pint of paregoric and passed out in a Panama City park. He had been trapped between floors in an elevator for five days with an oil-burning junk habit and sustained an attack of DTs while stowing away in a foot locker. Then there was the time he collapsed with strangulated intestines, perforated ulcers and peritonitis in Cairo and the hospital was so crowded they bedded him in the latrine, and the Greek surgeon goofed and sewed up a live monkey in him, and he was gang-fucked by the Arab attendants, and one of the orderlies stole the penicillin substituting Saniflush; and the time he got clap in his ass and a self-righteous English doctor cured him with an enema of hot, sulphuric acid, and the German practitioner of Technological Medicine who removed his appendix with a rusty can opener and a pair of tin snips (he considered the germ theory "a nonsense"). Flushed with success he then began snipping and cutting out everything in sight: "The human body is filled up vit unnecessitated parts. You can get by vit one kidney. Vy have two? Yes dot is a kidney.... The inside parts should not be so close in together crowded. They need lebensraum like the Vaterland."

The Expeditor had not yet been paid, and Marvie was faced by the prospect of stalling him for eleven months until the check cleared. The Expeditor was said to have been born on the Ferry between the Zone and the Island. His profession was to expedite the delivery of merchandise. No one knew for sure whether his services were of any use or not, and to mention his name always precipitated an argument. Cases were cited to prove his miraculous ficiency and utter worthlessness.

The Island was a British Military and Naval station directly opposite the Zone. England holds the Island on yearly rent-free lease, and every year the lease and permit of residence is formally renewed. The entire population turns out, attendance is compulsory, and gathers at the municipal dump. The President of the Island is required by custom to crawl across the garbage on his stomach and deliver the Permit of Residence and Renewal of the Lease, signed by every citizen of the Island, to The Resident Governor who stands resplendent in dress uniform. The Governor takes the permit and shoves it into his coat pocket:

"Well," he says with a tight smile, "so you've decided to let us stay another year have you? Very good of you. And everyone is happy about it? ... Is there anyone who isn't happy about it?"

Soldiers in jeeps sweep mounted machine-guns back and forth across the crowd with a slow, searching movement.

"Everybody happy. Well that's fine." He turns jovially to the prostrate President. "I'll keep your papers in case I get caught short. Haw Haw Haw." His loud, metallic laugh rings out across the dump, and the crowd laughs with him under the searching guns.

The forms of democracy are scrupulously enforced on the Island. There is a Senate and a Congress who carry on endless sessions discussing garbage disposal and outhouse inspection, the only two questions over which they have jurisdiction. For a brief period in the mid-nineteenth century, they had been allowed to control the dept of Baboon Maintenance, but this privilege had been withdrawn owing to absenteeism in the Senate.

The purple-assed Tripoli baboons had been brought to the Island by pirates in the 17th century. There was a legend that when the baboons left the Island it would fall. To whom or in what way is not specified, and it is a capital offense to kill a baboon, though the noxious behaviour of these animals harries the citizens almost beyond endurance. Occasionally someone goes berserk, kills several baboons and himself.

The post of President is always forced on some particularly noxious and unpopular citizen. To be elected President is the greatest misfortune and disgrace that can befall an Islander. The humiliations and ignominy are such that few Presidents live out their full term of office, usually dying of a broken spirit after a year or two. The Expeditor had once been President and served the full five years of his term. Subsequently he changed his name and underwent plastic surgery, to blot out, as far as possible, the memory of his disgrace.

"Yes of course ... we'll pay you," Marvie was saying to the Expeditor.

"But take it easy. It may be a little while yet...."

"Take it easy! A little while! ... Listen."

"Yes I know it all. The finance company is repossessing your wife's artificial kidney.... They are evicting your grandmother from her iron lung."

"That's in rather bad taste, old boy.... Frankly I wish I had never involved myself in this uh matter. That bloody grease has too much carbolic in it. I was down to customs one day last week. Stuck a broom handle into a drum of it, and the grease ate the end off straight away. Besides, the stink is enough to knock a man on his bloody ass. You should take a walk down by the port."

"I'll do no such thing," Marvie screetched. It is a mark of caste in the Zone never to touch or even go near what you are selling. To do so gives rise to suspicion of retailing, that is of being a common peddler. A good part of the merchandise in the Zone is sold through street peddlers.

"Why do you tell me all this? It's too sordid! Let the retailers worry about it."

"Oh it's all very well for you chaps, you can scud out from under. But I have a reputation to maintain.... There'll be a spot of bother about this."

"Do you suggest there is something *illegitimate* in this operation?"

"Not *illegitimate* exactly. But shoddy. Definitely shoddy."

"Oh go back to your Island before it falls! We knew you when you were peddling your purple ass in the Plaza pissoirs for five pesetas."

"And not many takers either," Leif put in. He pronounced it ither. This reference to his Island origin was more than the Expeditor could stand.... He was drawing himself up, mobilizing his most frigid impersonation of an English aristocrat, preparing to deliver an icy, clipped "crusher," but instead, a whining, whimpering, kicked dog snarl broke from his mouth. His presurgery face emerged in an arc-light of incandescent hate.... He began to spit curses in the hideous, strangled gutturals of the Island dialect.

The Islanders all profess ignorance of the dialect or flatly deny its existence. "We are Breetish," they say. "We don't got no bloody dealect."

Froth gathered at the corners of the Expeditor's mouth. He was spitting little balls of saliva like pieces of cotton. The stench of spiritual vileness hung in the airs about him like a green cloud. Marvie and Leif fell back twittering in alarm.

"He's gone *mad*," Marvie gasped. "Let's get *out* of here." Hand in hand they skip away into the mist that covers the Zone in the winter months like a cold Turkish Bath.

III

Luncheon of Nationalist Party on balcony overlooking the Market. Cigars, scotch, polite belches.... The Party Leader strides about in a Jellaba smoking a cigar and drinking Scotch. He wears expensive English shoes, loud socks, garters, muscular, hairy legs—overall effect of successful gangster in drag.

PL (pointing dramatically): "Look out there. What do you see?"

LIEUTENANT: "Huh? Why, I see the Market."

PL: "No you don't. You see men and women. *Ordinary* man and women going about their ordinary everyday tasks. Leading their ordinary lives. That's what we need. . . ."

A street boy climbs over the balcony rail.

LIEUTENANT: "No we do not want to buy any used condoms! Cut!"

PL: "Wait! . . . Come in, my boy. Sit down. . . . Have a cigar. . . . Have a drink."

He paces around the boy like an aroused tom cat.

"What do you think about the French?"

"Huh?"

"The French. The Colonial bastards who is sucking your live corpuscles."

"Look mister. It cost two hundred francs to suck my corpuscle. Haven't lowered my rates since the year of the rindpest when all the tourists died, even the Scandinavians."

PL: "You see? This is pure uncut boy in the street."

"You sure can pick'em, boss."

"MI never misses."

PL: "Now look, kid, let's put it this way. The French have dispossessed you of your birthright."

"You mean like Friendly Finance? . . . They got this toothless Egyptian eunuch does the job. They figure he arouse less antagonism, you dig, he always take down his pants to show you his condition. 'Now I'm just a poor old eunuch trying to keep up my habit. Lady, I'd like to give you an extension on that artificial kidney, I got a job to do is all. . . . Disconnect her, boys,' He shows his gums in a feeble snarl. . . . 'Not for nothing am I known as Nellie the Repossessor.'

"So they disconnect my own mother, the sainted old gash, and she swell up and turn black and the whole souk stink of piss and the neighbours beef to the Board of Health and my father say: 'It's the will of Allah. She won't piss any more of my loot down the drain.'

"Sick people disgust me already. When some citizen start telling me about his cancer of the prostate or his rotting septum make with that purulent discharge I tell him: 'You think I am innarested to hear about your horrible old condition? I am not innarested at all.' "

PL: "All *right*. Cut . . . You hate French, don't you?"

"Mister, I hate everybody. Doctor Benway says it's metabolic, I got this condition of the blood.... Arabs and Americans got it special.... Doctor Benway is concocting this serum."

PL: "Benway is an infiltrating Western Agent."

L1: "A rampant French Jew ..."

L2: "A hog-balled, black-assed Communist Jew Nigger."

PL: "Shut up, you fool!"

L2: "Sorry, chief. I am after being stationed in Pigeonhole."

PL: "Don't go near Benway." (Aside: "I wonder if this will go down. You never know how primitive they are....") "Confidentially he's a black magician."

L1: "He's got this resident djinn."

"Uhuh ... Well I got a date with a high-type American client. A real classy fellah."

PL: "Don't you know it's shameful to peddle your ass to the alien unbelieving pricks?"

"Well that's a point of view. Have fun."

PL: "Likewise." Exit boy. "They're hopeless I tell you. Hopeless."

L1: "What's with this serum?"

PL: "I don't know, but it sounds ominous. We better put a telepathic direction finder on Benway. The man's not to be trusted. Might do almost anything.... Turn a massacre into a sex orgy...."

"Or a joke."

"Precisely. Arty type ... No principles ..."

AMERICAN HOUSEWIFE (opening a box of LUX): "Why don't it have an electric eye the box flip open when it see me and hand itself to the Automat Handy Man he should put it inna water already.... The Handy Man is outa control since Thursday, he been getting physical with me and I didn't put it in his combination at all.... And the Garbage Disposal Unit snapping at me, and the nasty old Mixmaster keep trying to get up under my dress.... I got the most awful cold, and my intestines is all constipated.... I'm gonna put it in the Handy Man's combination he should administer me a high colonic awready."

SALESMAN (he is something between an aggressive Latah and a timid Sender): "Recollect when I am travelling with K.E., hottest idea man in the gadget industry.

" 'Think of it!' he snaps. 'A cream separator in your own kitchen!'

" 'K.E., my brain reels at the thought.'

" 'It's five, maybe ten, yes, maybe twenty years away.... But it's coming.'

" 'I'll wait, K.E. No matter how long it is I'll wait. When the priority numbers are called up yonder I'll be there.'

"It was K.E. put out the Octopus Kit for Massage Parlors, Barber Shops and Turkish Baths, with which you can administer a high colonic, an unethical massage, a shampoo, whilst cutting the client's toenails and removing his blackheads. And the MD's Can Do Kit for busy practitioners will take out your appendix, tuck in a hernia, pull a wisdom tooth, extomize your piles and circumcise you. Well, K.E. is such an atomic salesman if he runs out of Octopus Kits he is subject, by sheer chance, to sell an MD Can Do to a barber shop and some citizen wakes up with his piles cut out....

" 'Jesus, Homer, what kinda creep joint you running here? I been gang fucked.'

" 'Well, landsake, Si, I was just aiming to administer our complimentary high colonic free and gratis on Thanksgiving Day. K.E. musta sold me the wrong kit again....' "

EROS AND THANATOS

I

Gilt and red plush. Rococo bar backed by pink shell. The air is cloyed with a sweet evil substance like decayed honey. Men and women in evening dress sip pousse-cafés through alabaster tubes. A Near East Mugwump sits naked on a bar stool covered in pink silk. He licks warm honey from a crystal goblet with a long black tongue. His genitals are perfectly formed—circumcized cock, black shiny pubic hairs. His lips are thin and purple-blue like the lips of a penis, his eyes blank with insect calm. The Mugwump has no liver, maintaining himself exclusively on sweets. Mugwump push a slender blond youth to a couch and strip him expertly.

"Stand up and turn around," he orders in telepathic pictographs. He ties the boy's hands behind him with a red silk cord. "Tonight we make it all the way."

"No, no!" screams the boy.

"Yes. Yes."

Cocks ejaculate in silent "yes." Mugwump part silk curtains, reveal a teak wood gallows against lighted screen of red flint. Gallows is on a dais of Aztec mosaics.

The boy crumples to his knees with a long "OOOOOOOOH," shitting and pissing in terror. He feels the shit warm between his thighs. A great wave of hot blood swells his lips and throat. His body contracts into a foetal position and sperm spurts hot into his face. The Mugwump dips hot perfumed water from alabaster bowl, pensively washes the boy's ass and cock, drying him with a soft blue towel. A warm wind plays over the boy's body and the hairs float free. The Mugwump puts a hand under the boy's chest and pulls him to his feet. Holding him by both pinioned elbows, propels him up the steps and under the noose. He stands in front of the boy holding the noose in both hands.

The boy looks into Mugwump eyes blank as obsidian mirrors, pools of black blood, glory holes in a toilet wall closing on the Last Erection.

An old garbage collector, face fine and yellow as Chinese ivory, blows The Blast on his dented brass horn, wakes the Spanish pimp with a hard-on. Whore staggers out through dust and shit and litter of dead kittens, carrying bales of aborted foetuses, broken condoms, bloody Kotex, shit wrapped in bright color comics.

A vast still harbor of iridescent water. Deserted gas well flares on the smoky horizon. Stink of oil and sewage. Sick sharks swim through the black water, belch sulphur from rotting livers, ignore a bloody, broken Icarus. Naked Mr America, burning frantic with self bone love, screams out: "My asshole confounds the Louvre! I fart ambrosia and shit pure gold turds! My cock spurts soft diamonds in the morning sunlight!" He plummets from the eyeless lighthouse, kissing and jacking off in face of the black mirror, glides oblique down with cryptic condoms and mosaic of a thousand newspapers through a drowned city of red brick to settle in black mud with tin cans and beer bottles, gangsters in concrete, pistols pounded flat and meaningless to avoid short-arm inspection of prurient ballistic experts. He waits the slow striptease of erosion with fossil loins.

The Mugwump slips the noose over the boy's head and tightens the knot caressingly behind the left ear. The boy's penis is retracted, his balls tight. He looks straight ahead breathing deeply. The Mugwump sidles around the boy goosing him and caressing his genitals in hieroglyphs of mockery. He moves in behind the boy with a series of bumps and shoves his cock up the boy's ass. He stands there moving in circular gyrations.

The guests shush each other, nudge and giggle.

Suddenly the Mugwump pushes the boy forward into space, free of his cock. He steadies the boy with hands on the hip bones, reaches up with his stylized hieroglyph hands and snaps the boy's neck. A shudder passes through the boy's body. His penis rises in three great surges pulling his pelvis up, ejaculates immediately.

Green sparks explode behind his eyes. A sweet toothache pain shoots through his neck down the spine to the groin, contracting the body in spasms of delight. His whole body squeezes out through his cock. A final spasm throws a great spurt of sperm across the red screen like a shootingstar.

The boy falls with soft gutty suction through a maze of penny arcades and dirty pictures.

A sharp turd shoots clean out of his ass. Farts shake his slender body. Skyrockets burst in green clusters across a great river. He hears the faint put-put of a motor boat in jungle twilight. . . . Under silent wings of the anopheles mosquito.

The Mugwump pulls the boy back onto his cock. The boy squirms, impaled like a speared fish. The Mugwump swings on the boy's back, his body contracting in fluid waves. Blood flows down the boy's chin from his mouth, half-open, sweet, and sulky in death. The Mugwump falls with a fluid, sated plop.

Windowless cubicle with blue walls. Dirty pink curtain cover the door. Red bugs crawl on the wall, cluster in corners. Naked boy in the middle of the room twang a two-string ouad, trace an arabesque on the floor. Another boy lean back on the bed smoking keif and blow smoke over his erect cock. They play game with tarot cards on the bed to see who fuck who. Cheat. Fight. Roll on the floor snarling and spitting like young animals. The loser sit on the floor chin on knees, licks a broken tooth. The winner curls up on the bed pretending to sleep. Whenever the other boy come near kick at him. Ali seize him by one ankle, tuck the ankle under the arm pit, lock his arm around the calf. The boy kick desperately at Ali's face. Other ankle pinioned. Ali tilt the boy back on his shoulders. The boy's cock extends along his stomach, float free pulsing. Ali put his hands over his head. Spit on his cock. The other sighs deeply as Ali slides his cock in. The mouths grind together smearing blood. Sharp musty odor of penetrated rectum. Nimun drive in like a wedge, force jism out the other cock in long hot spurts. (The author has observed that Arab cocks tend to be wide and wedge shaped.)

Satyr and naked Greek lad in aqualungs trace a ballet in pursuit in a monster vase of transparent alabaster. The Satyr catches the boy from in front and whirls him around. They move in fish jerks. The boy releases a silver stream of bubbles from his mouth. White sperm ejaculates into the green water and floats lazily around the twisting bodies.

Negro gently lifts exquisite Chinese boy into a hammock. He pushes the boy's legs up over his head and straddles the hammock. He slides his cock up the boy's slender tight ass. He rocks the hammock gently back and forth. The boy screams, a weird high wail of unendurable delight.

A Javanese dancer in ornate teak swivel chair, set in a socket of limestone buttocks, pulls an American boy—red hair, bright green eyes—down onto his cock with ritual motions. The boy sits impaled facing the dancer who propels himself in circular gyrations, lending fluid substance to the chair. "Weeeeeeeeee!" scream the boy as his sperm spurt up over the dancer's lean brown chest. One gob hit the corner of the dancer's mouth. The boy push it in with his finger and laugh: "Man, that's what I call suction!"

Two Arab women with bestial faces have pulled the shorts off a little blond French boy. They are screwing him with red rubber cocks. The boy snarls, bites, kicks, collapses in tears as his cock rises and ejaculates.

Hassan's face swells, tumescent with blood. His lips turn purple. He strip off his suit of banknotes and throw it into an open vault that closes soundless.

"Freedom Hall here, folks!" he screams in his phoney Texas accent. Ten-gallon hat and cowboy boots still on, he dances the Liquefactionist Jig, ending with a grotesque can-can to the tune of *She Started a Heat Wave.*

"Let it be! And no holes barred!!!"

Couples attached to baroque harness with artificial wings copulate in the air, screaming like magpies.

Aerialists ejaculate each other in space with one sure touch.

Equilibrists suck each other off deftly, balanced on perilous poles and chairs tilted over the void. A warm wind brings the smell of rivers and jungle from misty depths.

Boys by the hundred plummet through the roof, quivering and kicking at the end of ropes. The boys hang at different levels, some near the ceiling and others a few inches off the floor. Exquisite Balinese and Malays, Mexican Indians with fierce innocent faces and bright red gums. Negroes (teeth, fingers, toe nails and pubic hair gilded), Japanese boys smooth and white as China, Titian-haired Venetian lads, Americans with blond or black curls falling across the forehead (the guests tenderly shove it back), sulky blond Pollacks with animal brown eyes, Arab and Spanish street boys, Austrian boys pink and delicate with a faint shadow of blond pubic hair, sneering German youths with bright eyes scream "Heil Hitler!" as the trap falls under them. Sollubis shit and whimper.

Mr Rich-and-Vulgar chews his Havana lewd and nasty, sprawled on a Florida beach surrounded by simpering blond catamites:

"This citizen have a Latah he import from Indo-China. He figure to hang the Latah and send a Xmas TV short to his friends. So he fix up two ropes—one gimmicked to stretch, the other the real McCoy. But that Latah get up in feud state and put on his Santa Claus suit and make with the switcheroo. Come the dawning. The citizen put one rope on and the Latah, going along the way Latahs will, put on the other. When the traps arc down the citizen hang for real and the Latah stand with the carny-rubber stretch rope. Well, the Latah imitate every twitch and spasm. Come three times.

"Smart young Latah keep his eye on the ball. I got him working in one of my plants as an expeditor."

Aztec priests strip blue feather robe from the Naked Youth. They bend him back over a limestone altar, fit a crystal skull over his head, securing the two hemispheres back and front with crystal screws. A waterfall pour over the skull snapping the boy's neck. He ejaculate in a rainbow against the rising sun.

Sharp protein odor of semen fills the air. The guests run hands over twitching boys, suck their cocks, hang on their backs like vampires.

Naked lifeguards carry in iron-lungs full of paralyzed youths.

Blind boys grope out of huge pies, deteriorated schizophrenics pop from under a rubber cunt, boys with horrible skin diseases rise from a black pond (sluggish fish nibble yellow turds on the surface).

A man with white tie and dress shirt, naked from the waist down except for black garters, talks to the Queen Bee in elegant tones. (Queen Bees are old women who surround themselves with fairies to form a "swarm." It is a sinister Mexican practice.)

"But where is the statuary?" He talks out of one side of his face, the other is twisted by the Torture of a Million Mirrors. He masturbates wildly. The Queen Bee continues the conversation, notices nothing.

Couches, chairs, the whole floor begins to vibrate, shaking the guests to blurred grey ghosts shrieking in cock-bound agony.

Two boys jacking off under railroad bridge. The train shakes through their bodies, ejaculate them, fades with distant whistle. Frogs croak. The boys wash semen off lean brown stomachs.

Train compartment: two sick young junkies on their way to Lexington tear their pants down in convulsions of lust. One of them soaps his cock and works it up the other's ass with a corkscrew motion. "Jeeeeeeeeeeeeeesus!" Both ejaculate at once standing up. They move away from each other and pull up their pants.

"Old croaker in Marshall writes for tincture and sweet oil."

"The piles of an aged mother shriek out raw and bleeding for the Black Shit.... Doc, suppose it was your mother, rimmed by resident leaches, squirming around so nasty.... De-active that pelvis, mom, you disgust me already."

"Let's stop over and make him for an RX."

The train tears on through the smoky, neon-lighted June night.

Pictures of men and women, boys and girls, animals, fish, birds, the copulating rhythm of the universe flows through the room, a great blue tide of life. Vibrating, soundless hum of deep forest— sudden quiet of cities when the junky copes. A moment of stillness and wonder. Even the Commuter buzzes clogged lines of cholesterol for contact.

Hassan shrieks out: "This is your doing, A.J.! You poopa my party!"

A.J. looks at him, face remote as limestone: "Uppa your ass, you liquefying gook."

A horde of lust-mad American women rush in. Dripping cunts, from farm and dude ranch, factory, brothel, country club, penthouse and suburb, motel and yacht and cocktail bar, strip off riding clothes, ski togs, evening dresses, levis, tea gowns, print dresses, slacks, bathing suits and kimonos. They scream and yipe and howl, leap on the guests like bitch dogs in heat with rabies. They claw at the hanged boys shrieking: "You fairy! You bastard! Fuck me! Fuck me! Fuck me!" The guests flee screaming, dodge among the hanged boys, overturn iron lungs.

A.J.: "Call out my Sweitzers, God damn it! Guard me from these she-foxes!"

Mr Hyslop, A.J.'s secretary, looks up from his comic book: "The Sweitzers liquefy already."

(Liquefaction involves protein cleavage and reduction to liquid which is absorbed into someone else's protoplasmic being. Hassan, a notorious liquefactionist, is probably the beneficiary in this case.)

A.J.: "Gold-bricking cocksuckers! Where's a man without his Sweitzers? Our backs are to the wall, Gentlemen. Our very cocks at stake. Stand by to resist boarders, Mr Hyslop, and issue short arms to the men."

A.J. whips out a cutlass and begins decapitating the American Girls. He sings lustily:

> *Fifteen men on the dead man's chest*
> *Yo Ho Ho and a bottle of rum.*
> *Drink and the devil had done for the rest*
> *Yo Ho Ho and a bottle of rum.*

Mr Hyslop, bored and resigned: "Oh Gawd! He's at it again." He waves the Jolly Roger listlessly.

A.J. surrounded and fighting against overwhelming odds, throws back his head and makes with the hog-call. Immediately a thousand rutting Eskimos pour in grunting and squealing, faces tumescent, eyes hot and red, lips purple, fall on the American women.

(Eskimos have a rutting season when the tribes meet in short Summer to disport themselves in orgies. Their faces swell and lips turn purple.)

A House Dick with cigar two feet long sticks his head in through the wall: "Have you got a menagerie in here?"

Hassan wrings his hands: "A shambles! A filthy shambles! By Allah I never see anything so downright nasty!"

He whirls on A.J. who is sitting on a sea chest, parrot on shoulder, patch over one eye, drinking rum from a tankard. He scans the horizon with a huge brass telescope.

Hassan: "You cheap Factualist bitch! Go and never darken my rumpus room again!"

II

A.J. turns to the guests. "Cunts, pricks, fence straddlers, tonight I give you—that international-known impressario of blue movies and short-wave TV, the one, the only, The Great Slashtubitch!"

He points to a red velvet curtain sixty feet high. Lightning rends the curtain from top to bottom. The Great Slashtubitch stands revealed. His face is immense, immobile like a Chimu funeral urn. He wears full evening dress, blue cape and blue monocle. Huge grey eyes with tiny black pupils that seem to spit needles. (Only the Coordinate Factualist can meet his gaze.) When he is angered the charge of it will blow his monocle across the room. Many an ill-starred actor has felt the icy blast of Slashtubitch's displeasure: "Get out of my studio, you cheap four-flushing ham! Did you think to pass a counterfeit orgasm on me! THE GREAT SLASHTUBITCH! I could tell if you come by regard the beeg toe. Idiot! Mindless scum!! Insolent baggage!!! Go peddle thy ass and know that it takes sincerity and art, and devotion, to work for Slashtubitch. Not shoddy trickery, dubbed gasps, rubber turds and vials of milk concealed in the ear and shots of Yohimbine sneaked in the wings." (Yohimbine, derived from the bark of a tree growing in Central Africa, is the safest and most efficient aphrodisiac. It operates by dilating the blood vessels on the surface of the skin, particularly in the genital area.)

Slashtubitch ejects his monocle. It sails out of sight, returns like a boomerang into his eye. He pirouettes and disappears in a blue mist, cold as liquid air . . . fadeout. . . .

On Screen. Red Haired, green-eyed boy, white skin with a few freckles . . . kissing a thin brunette girl in slacks. Clothes and hair-do suggest existentialist bars of all the world cities. They are seated on low bed covered in white silk. The girl opens his pants with gentle fingers and pulls out his cock which is small and very hard.

A drop of lubricant gleams at its tip like a pearl. She caresses the crown gently: "Strip, Johnny." He takes off his clothes with swift sure movements and stands naked before her, his cock pulsing. She makes a motion for him to turn around and he pirouettes across the floor parodying a model, hand on hip. She takes off her shirt. Her breasts are high and small with erect nipples. She slips off her underpants. Her pubic hairs are black and shiny. He sits down beside her and reaches for her breast. She stops his hands.

"Darling, I want to rim you," she whispers.

"No. Not now."

"Please, I want to."

"Well, all right. I'll go wash my ass."

"No, I'll wash it."

"Aw shucks now, it ain't dirty."

"Yes it is. Come on now, Johnny boy."

She leads him into the bathroom. "All right, get down." He gets down on his knees and leans forward, with his chin on the bath mat. "Allah," he says. He looks back and grins at her. She washes his ass with soap and hot water sticking her finger up it.

"Does that hurt?"

"Nooooooooooo."

"Come along, baby." She leads the way into the bedroom. He lies down on his back and throws his legs back over his head, clasping elbows behind his knees. She kneel down and caress the backs of his thighs, his balls, running her fingers down the perennial divide. She push his cheeks apart, lean down and begin licking the anus, moving her head in a slow circle. She push at the sides of the asshole, licking deeper and deeper. He close his eyes and squirm. She lick up the perennial divide. His small, tight balls. . . . A great pearl stands out on the tip of his circumcized cock. Her mouth closes over the crown. She sucks rhythmically up and down, pausing on the up stroke and moving her head around in a circle. Her hand plays gently with his balls, slide down and middle finger up his ass. As she suck down toward the root of his cock she tickle his prostrate mockingly. He grin and fart. She is sucking his cock now in a frenzy. His body begins to contract, pulling up toward his chin. Each time the contraction is longer. "Wheeeeeeee!" the boy yell, every muscle tense, his whole body strain to empty through his cock. She drinks his jissom which fills her mouth in great hot spurts. He lets his feet flop back onto the bed. He arches his back and yawns.

Mary is strapping on a rubber penis: "Steely Dan III from

Yokohama," she says, caressing the shaft. Milk spurts across the room.

"Be sure that milk is pasteurized. Don't go giving me some kinda awful cow disease like anthrax or glanders or aftosa...."

"When I was a transvestite Liz in Chi used to work as an exterminator. Make advances to pretty boys for the thrill of being beaten as a man. Later I catch this one kid, overpower him with supersonic judo I learned from an old Lesbian Zen monk. I tie him up, strip off his clothes with a razor and fuck him with Steely Dan I. He is so relieved I don't castrate him literal he come all over my bedbug spray."

"He was torn in two by a bull dike. Most terrific vaginal grip I ever experienced. She could cave in a lead pipe. It was one of her parlor tricks."

"And Steely Dan II?"

"Chewed to bits by a famished candiru in the Upper Baboonsasshole. And don't say 'Wheeeeeeee!' this time."

"Why not? It's real boyish."

"Barefoot boy, check thy bullheads with the madame."

He looks at the ceiling, hands behind his head, cock pulsing. "So what shall I do? Can't shit with that dingus up me. I wonder is it possible to laugh and come at the same time? I recall, during the war, at the Jockey Club in Cairo, me and my asshole buddy, Lu, both gentlemen by act of Congress . . . nothing else could have done such a thing to either of us. . . . So we got laughing so hard we piss all over ourselves and the waiter say: 'You bloody hash-heads, get out of here!' I mean, if I can laugh the piss out of me I should be able to laugh out jissom. So tell me something real funny when I start coming. You can tell by certain premonitory quiverings of the prostate gland. . . ."

She puts on a record, metallic cocaine be-bop. She greases the dingus, shoves the boy's legs over his head and works it up his ass with a series of corkscrew movements of her fluid hips. She moves in a slow circle, revolving on the axis of the shaft. She rubs her hard nipples across his chest. She kisses him on the neck and chin and eyes. He runs his hands down her back to her buttocks, pulling her into his ass. She revolves faster, faster. His body jerks and writhes in convulsive spasms. "Hurry up, please," she says. "The milk is getting cold." He does not hear. She presses her mouth against his. Their faces run together. His sperm hits her breast with light, hot licks.

Mark is standing in the doorway. He wears a turtle-neck black sweater. Cold, handsome, narcissistic face. Green eyes and black hair. He looks at Johnny with a slight sneer, his head on one side, hands on his jacket pockets, a graceful hoodlum ballet. He jerk his head and Johnny walk ahead of him into the bedroom. Mary follow. "All right, boys," she says, sitting down naked on a pink silk dais overlooking the bed. "Get with it!"

Mark begin to undress with fluid movements, hip rolls, squirm out of his turtle-neck sweater revealing his beautiful white torso in a mocking belly dance. Johnny deadpan, face frozen, breath quick, lips dry, remove his clothes and drop them on the floor. Mark lets his shorts fall on one foot. He kick like a chorus-girl, sending the shorts across the room. Now he stand naked, his cock stiff, straining up and out. He run slow eyes over Johnny's body. He smile and lick his lips.

Mark drop on one knee, pulling Johnny across his back by one arm. He stand up and throw him six feet onto the bed. Johnny land on his back and bounce. Mark jump up and grab Johnny's ankles, throw his legs over his head. Mark's lips are drawn back in a tight snarl. "All right, Johnny boy." He contracts his body, slow and steady as an oiled machine, push his cock up Johnny's ass. Johnny give a great sigh, squirming in ecstasy. Mark hitches his hands behind Johnny's shoulders, pulling him down onto his cock which is buried to the hilt in Johnny's ass. Great whistles through his teeth. Johnny screams like a bird. Mark is rubbing his face against Johnny's, snarl gone, face innocent and boyish as his whole liquid being spurt into Johnny's quivering body.

A train roar through him whistle blowing ... boat whistle, fog-horn, sky rocket burst over oily lagoons ... penny arcade open into a maze of dirty pictures ... ceremonial cannon boom in the harbor ... a scream shoots down a white hospital corridor ... out along a wide dusty street between palm trees, whistles out across the desert like a bullet (vulture wings husk in the dry air), a thousand boys come at once in out-houses, bleak public school toilets, attics, basements, treehouses, Ferris wheels, deserted houses, limestone caves, rowboats, garages, barns, rubbly windy city outskirts behind mud walls (smell of dried excrement) ... black dust blowing over lean copper bodies ... ragged pants dropped to cracked bleeding bare feet ... (place where vultures fight over fish heads) ... by jungle lagoons, vicious fish snap at white sperm floating on black water, sand flies bite the copper ass, howler monkeys like wind in the trees (a land of great brown rivers where whole trees float, bright colored snakes in the branches, pensive lemurs watch the shore with sad eyes), a red plane traces arabesques in blue substance of sky, a rattlesnake strike, a cobra rear, spread, spit white venom, pearl and opal chips fall in a slow silent rain through air clear as glycerine. Time jump like a broken typewriter, the boys are old men, young hips quivering and twitching in boy-spasms go slack and flabby, draped over an outhouse seat, a park bench, a stone wall in Spanish sunlight, a sagging furnished room bed (outside red brick slum in clear winter sunlight) ... twitching and shivering in dirty underwear, probing for a vein in the junk-sick morning, in an Arab café muttering and slobbering—the Arabs whisper "Medjoub" and edge away—(a Medjoub is a special sort of religious Moslem lunatic ... often epileptic among other disorders). "The Moslems must have blood and jissom.... See, see where Christ's blood streams in the spermament," howls the the Medjoub.... He stand up screaming and black blood spurt solid from his last erection, a pale white statue standing there, as if he had stepped whole across the Great Fence, climbed it innocent and calm as a boy climb the fence to fish in the forbidden pond—in a few seconds he catch a huge catfish— The Old Man will rush out of a little black hut cursing, with a pitchfork and the boy run laughing across the Missouri field—he find a beautiful pink arrowhead and snatch it up as he runs with a flowing swoop of young bone and muscle—(his bones blend into the fields, he lies dead by the wooden fence a shotgun by his side, blood on frozen red clap seeps into the winter stubble of Georgia).... The catfish billows out behind him.... He come to the fence and throw the catfish over into blood-streaked grass ... the fish lies squirming and squawking—vaults the fence. He snatch up the catfish and disappear up a flint-studded red clay road between oaks and persimmons dropping red-brown leaves in a windy fall sunset, green and dripping in Summer dawn, black against a clear winter day ... the Old Man scream curses after him ... his teeth fly from his mouth and whistle over the boy's head, he strain forward, his neck-cords tight as steel hoops, black blood spurt in one solid piece over the fence and he fall a fleshless mummy by the fever grass. Thorns grow through his ribs, the windows break in his hut, dusty glass-slivers in black putty—rats run over the floor and boys jack off in the dark musty bedroom on summer afternoons and eat berries that grow from his body and bones, mouths smeared with purple-red juices....

The old junky has found a vein ... blood blossoms in the dropper like a Chinese flower ... he push home the heroin and the boy who jacked off fifty years ago shine immaculate through the ravaged flesh, fill the outhouse with the sweet nutty smell of young male lust....

How many years threaded on a needle of blood? Hands slack on lap he sit looking out at the winter dawn with the cancelled eyes of junk. The old queer squirm on a limestone bench in Chapultepec Park as Indian adolescents walk by, arms around each other's necks and ribs, straining his dying flesh to occupy young buttocks and thighs, tight balls and spurting cocks.

Mark and Johnny sit facing each other in a vibrating chair, Johnny impaled on Mark's cock.

"All set, Johnny?"

"Turn it on."

Mark flips the switch and the chair vibrate. . . . Mark tilt his head looking up at Johnny, his face remote, eyes cool and mocking on Johnny's face. . . . Johnny scream and whimper. . . . His face disintegrates as if melted from within. . . . Johnny scream like a mandrake, black out as his sperm spurt, slump against Mark's body an angel on the nod. Mark pat Johnny's shoulder absently. . . . Room like gymnasium. . . . The floor is foam rubber, covered in white silk. . . . One wall is glass. . . . The rising sun fills the room with pink light. Johnny is led in, hands tied, between Mary and Mark. Johnny sees the gallows and sags with a great "Ohhhhhhhhhhh!" his chin pulling down towards his cock, his legs bending at the knees. Sperm spurts, arching almost vertical in front of his face. Mark and Mary are suddenly impatient and hot. . . . They push Johnny forward onto the gallows platform covered with moldy jockstraps and sweat shirts. Mark is adjusting the noose.

"Well, here you go." Mark starts to push Johnny off the platform.

Mary: "No, let me." She locks her hands behind Johnny's buttocks, puts her forehead against him, smiling into his eyes she moves back, pulling him off the platform into space. . . . His face swells with blood. . . . Mark reaches up with one lithe movement and snaps Johnny's neck . . . sound like a stick broken in wet towels. A shudder runs down Johnny's body . . . one foot flutters like a trapped bird. . . . Mark has draped himself over a swing and mimics Johnny's twitches, closes his eyes and sticks his tongue out. . . . Johnny's cock springs up and Mary guides it up her cunt, writhing against him in a fluid belly dance, groaning and shrieking with delight . . . sweat pours down her body, hair hangs over her face in wet strands. "Cut him down, Mark," she screams. Mark reaches over with a snap knife and cuts the rope, catching Johnny as he falls, easing him onto his back with Mary still impaled and writhing. . . . She bites away Johnny's lips and nose and sucks out his eyes with a pop.... She tears off great hunks of cheek.... Now she lunches on his prick.... Mark walks over to her and she looks up from Johnny's half-eaten genitals, her face covered with blood, eyes phosphorescent.... Mark puts his foot on her shoulder and kicks her over on her back.... He leaps on her, fucking her insanely ... they roll from one end of the room to the other, pinwheel end-over-end and leap high in the air like great hooked fish.

"Let me hang you, Mark.... Let me hang you.... Please, Mark, let me hang you!"

"Sure baby." He pulls her brutally to her feet and pins her hands behind her.

"No, Mark!! No! No! No," she screams, shitting and pissing in terror as he drags her to the platform. He leaves her tied on the platform in a pile of old used condoms, while he adjusts the rope across the room ... and comes back carrying the noose on a silver tray. He jerks her to her feet and tightens the noose. He sticks his cock up her and waltzes around the platform and off into space swinging in a great arc.... "Wheeeeee!" he screams, turning into Johnny. Her neck snaps. A great fluid wave undulates through her body. Johnny drops to the floor and stands poised and alert like a young animal.

He leaps about the room. With a scream of longing that shatters the glass wall he leaps out into space. Masturbating end-over-end, three thousand feet down, his sperm floating beside him, he screams all the way against the shattering blue of the sky, the rising sun burning over his body like gasoline, down past great oaks and persimmons, swamp cypress and mahogany, to shatter in liquid relief in a ruined square paved with limestone. Weeds and vines grow between the stones, and rusty iron bolts three feet thick penetrate the white stone, stain it shit-brown of rust.

Johnny dowses Mary with gasoline from an obscene Chimu jar of white jade.... He anoints his own body.... They embrace, fall to the floor and roll under a great magnifying glass set in the roof ... burst into flame with a cry that shatters the glass wall, roll into space, fucking and screaming through the air, burst into blood and flames and soot on brown rocks under a desert sun. Johnny leaps about the room in agony. With a scream that shatters the glass wall he stands spreadeagle to the rising sun, blood spurting out his cock ... a white marble god, he plummets through epileptic explosions into the old Medjoub writhe in shit and rubbish by a mud wall under a sun that scar and grab the flesh into goose-pimples.... He is a boy sleeping against the mosque wall, ejaculates wet dreaming into a thousand cunts pink and smooth as sea shells, feeling the delight of prickly pubic hairs slide up his cock.

John and Mary in hotel room (music of East St Louis Toodleoo). Warm spring wind blows faded pink curtains in through open window.... Frogs croak in vacant lots where corn grows and boys catch little green garter snakes under broken limestone stelae stained with shit and threaded with rusty barbed wire....

(*Neon*—chlorophyll green, purple, orange—flashes on and off.)

Johnny extracts a candiru from Mary's cunt with his calipers.... He drops it into a bottle of mescal where it turns into a Maguey worm.... He gives her a douche of jungle bone-softener, her vaginal teeth flow out mixed with blood and cysts.... Her cunt shines fresh and sweet as spring grass.... Johnny licks Mary's cunt, slow at first, with rising excitement parts the lips and licks inside feeling the prickle of pubic hairs on his tumescent tongue.... Arms thrown back, breasts pointing straight up, Mary lies transfixed with neon nails.... Johnny moves up her body, his cock with a shining round opal of lubricant at the open slit, slides through her pubic hairs and enters her cunt to the hilt, drawn in by a suction of hungry flesh.... His face swells with blood, green lights burst behind his eyes and he falls with a scenic railway through screaming girls....

Damp hairs on the back of his balls dry to grass in the warm spring wind. High jungle valley, vines creep in the window. Johnny's cock swells, great rank buds burst out. A long tuber root creeps from Mary's cunt, feels for the earth. The bodies disintegrate in green explosions. The hut falls in ruins of broken stone. The boy is a limestone statue, a plant sprouting from his cock, lips parted in the half-smile of a junky on the nod.

The Beagle has stached the heroin in a lottery ticket.

One more shot—tomorrow the cure.

The way is long. Hard-ons and bring-downs are frequent.

It was a long time over the stony reg to the oasis of date palms where Arab boys shit in the well and rock 'n' roll across the sands of muscle beach eating hot-dogs and spitting out gold teeth in nuggets.

Toothless and strictly from the long hunger, ribs you could wash your filthy overalls on, that corrugate, they quaver down from the outrigger in Easter Island and stalk ashore on legs stiff and brittle as stilts ... they nod in club windows ... fallen into the fat of lack-need to sell a slim body.

The date palms have died of meet lack, the well filled with dried shit and mosaic of a thousand newspapers: "Russia denies ... The Home Secretary views with pathic alarm ... The trap was sprung at 12:02. At 12:30 the doctor went out to eat oysters, returned at 2:00 to clap the hanged man jovially on the back. 'What! Aren't you dead yet? Guess I'll have to pull your leg. Haw Haw! Can't let you choke at this rate—I'd get a warning from the President. And what a disgrace if the dead wagon cart you out alive. My balls would drop off with the shame of it and I apprenticed myself to an experienced ox. One two three pull.'"

The sail plane falls silent as erection, silent as greased glass broken by the young thief with old-women hands and cancelled eyes of junk.... In a noiseless explosion he penetrates the broken house, stepping over the greased crystals, a clock ticks loud in the kitchen, hot air ruffles his hair, his head disintegrates in a heavy duck load.... The Old Man flips out a red shell and pirouettes around his shotgun. "Aw, shucks, fellers, tweren't nothing.... Fish in the barrel.... Money in the bank ... round-heeled boy, one greased shot brain goose and he flop in an obscene position.... Can you hear me from where you are, boy?

"I was young myself once and heard the siren call of easy money and women and tight boy-ass and lands sake don't get my blood up I am subject to tell a tale make your cock stand up and yipe for the pink pearly way of young cunt or the lovely brown mucus-covered palpitating tune of the young boy-ass play your cock like a recorder ... and when you hit the prostate pearl sharp diamonds gather in the golden lad balls inexorable as a kidney stone.... Sorry I had to kill you.... The old grey mare ain't what she used to be.... Can't run down an audience ... got to *bring* down that house on the wing, run or sit.... Like an old lion took bad with cavities he need that amident toothpaste keep a feller biting fresh at all times.... Them old lions shit suet turn boyeater.... And who can blame them, boys being so sweet so cold so fair in St James Infirmary?? Now, son, don't you get rigor mortis on me. Show respect for the aging prick.... You may be a tedious old fuck yourself some day.... Oh, uh; I guess not.... You have, like Housman's barefoot shameless catamite The Congealed Shropshire Ingenue set your fleet foot on the silo of change.... But you can't kill those Shropshire boys ... been hanged so often he resist it like a gonococcus half castrate with pencillin rallies to a hideous strength and multiples geometric.... So leave us cast a vote for decent acquittal and put an end to those beastly exhibitions for which the sheriff levy a pound of flesh."

Sheriff: "I'll lower his pants for a pound, folks. Step right up. A serious and scientific exhibit concerning the locality of the Life Centre. This character has nine inches, ladies and gentlemen, measure them yourself inside. Only one pound, one queer three dollar bill to see a young boy come three times at least—I never demean myself to process a eunuch—*completely against his will*. When his neck snaps sharp, this character will shit-sure come to rhythmic attention and spurt it out all over you."

The boy stands on the trap shifting his weight from one leg to the other: "Gawd! What a boy hasta put up with in this business. Sure as shit some horrible old character get physical."

Trap falls, rope sings like wind in wire, neck snaps loud and clear as a Chinese gong.

The boy cuts himself down with a switch-blade, chases a screaming fag down the midway. The faggot dives through the glass of a penny arcade peep-show and rims a grinning Negro. Fadeout.

(Mary, Johnny and Mark take a bow with the ropes around their necks. They are not as young as they appear in the Blue Movies. . . . They look tired and petulant.)

THE COUNTY CLERK

The County Clerk has his office in a huge red brick building known as the Old Court House. Civil cases are, in fact, tried there, the proceeding inexorably dragging out until the contestants die or abandon litigation. This is due to the vast number or records pertaining to absolutely everything, all filed in the wrong place so that no one but the County Clerk and his staff of assistants can find them, and he often spends years in the search. In fact, he is still looking for material relative to a damage suit that was settled out of court in 1910. Large sections of the Old Court House have fallen in ruins, and others are highly dangerous owing to frequent cave-ins. The County Clerk assigns the more dangerous missions to his assistants, many of whom have lost their lives in the service. In 1912 two hundred and seven assistants were trapped in a collapse of the North-by-North-East wing.

When suit is brought against anyone in the Zone, his lawyers connive to have the case transferred to the Old Court House. Once this is done, the plaintiff has lost the case, so the only cases that actually go to trial in the Old Court House are those instigated by eccentrics and paranoids who want "a public hearing," which they rarely get since only the most desperate famine of news will bring a reporter to the Old Court House.

The Old Court House is located in the town of Pigeon Hole outside the urban zone. The inhabitants of this town and the surrounding area of swamps and heavy timber are people of such great stupidity and such barbarous practices that the Administration has seen fit to quarantine them in a reservation surrounded by a radio-active wall of iron bricks. In retaliation the citizens of Pigeon Hole plaster their town with signs: *"Urbanite Don't Let The Sun Set On You Here,"* an unnecessary injunction, since nothing but urgent business would take any urbanite to Pigeon Hole.

Lee's case is urgent. He has to file an immediate affidavit that he is suffering from bubonic plague to avoid eviction from the house he has occupied ten years without paying the rent. He exists in perpetual quarantine. So he packs his suitcase of affidavits and petitions and injunctions and certificates and takes a bus to the

Frontier. The Urbanite customs inspector waves him through: "I hope you've got an atom bomb in that suitcase."

Lee swallows a handful of tranquilizing pills and steps into the Pigeon Hole customs shed. The inspectors spend three hours pawing through his papers, consulting dusty books of regulations and duties from which they read incomprehensible and ominous excerpts ending with: "And as such is subject to fine and penalty under act 666." They look at him significantly.

They go through his papers with a magnifying glass.

"Sometimes they slip dirty limericks between the lines."

"Maybe he figures to sell them for toilet paper. Is this crap for your own personal use?"

"Yes."

"He says yes."

"And how do we know that?"

"I gotta affidavit."

"Wise guy. Take off your clothes."

"Yeah. Maybe he got dirty tattoos."

They paw over his body probing his ass for contraband and examine it for evidence of sodomy. They dunk his hair and send the water out to be analyzed. "Maybe he's got dope in his hair."

Finally, they impound his suitcase; and he staggers out of the shed with a fifty pound bale of documents.

A dozen or so Recordites sit on the Old Court House steps of rotten wood. They watch his approach with pale blue eyes, turning their heads slow on wrinkled necks (the wrinkles full of dust) to follow his body up the steps and through the door. Inside, dust hangs in the air like fog, sifting down from the ceiling, rising in clouds from the floor as he walks. He mounts a perilous staircase— condemned in 1929. Once his foot goes through, and the dry splinters tear into the flesh of his leg. The staircase ends in a painter's scaffold, attached with frayed rope and pullies to a beam almost invisible in dusty distance. He pulls himself up cautiously to a ferris wheel cabin. His weight sets in motion hydraulic machinery (sound of running water). The wheel moves smooth and silent to stop by a rusty iron balcony, worn through here and there like an old shoe sole. He walks down a long corridor lined with doors, most of them nailed or boarded shut. In one office, *Near East Exquisitries* on a green brass plaque, the Mugwump is catching termites with his long black tongue. The door of the County Clerk's office is open. The County Clerk sits inside gumming snuff, surrounded by six assistants. Lee stands in the doorway. The County Clerk goes on talking without looking up.

"I run into Ted Spigot the other day ... a good old boy, too. Not a finer man in the Zone than Ted Spigot.... Now it was a Friday I happen to remember because the Old Lady was down with the menstral cramps and I went to Doc Parker's drugstore on Dalton Street, just opposite Ma Green's Ethical Massage Parlor, where Jed's old livery stable used to be.... Now, Jed, I'll remember his second name directly, had a cast in the left eye and his wife came from some place out East, Algiers I believe it was, and after Jed died she married up again, and she married one of the Hoot boys, Clem Hoot if my memory serves, a good old boy too, now Hoot was around fifty-four fifty-five year old at the time.... So I says to Doc Parker: 'My old lady is down bad with the menstral cramps. Sell me two ounces of paregoric.'

"So Doc says, 'Well, Arch, you gotta sign the book. Name, address and date of purchase. It's the law.'

"So I asked Doc what the day was, and he said, 'Friday the 13th.'

"So I said, 'I guess I already had mine.'

" 'Well,' Doc says, 'there was a feller in here this morning. City feller. Dressed kinda flashy. So he's got him a RX for a mason jar of morphine.... Kinda funny looking prescription writ out on toilet paper.... And I told him straight out: "Mister, I suspect you to be a dope fiend." '

" ' "I got the ingrowing toe nails, Pop. I'm in agony," he says.'

" ' "Well," I says, "I gotta be careful. But so long as you got a legitimate condition and an RX from a certified bona feedy MD, I'm honored to serve you." '

" ' "That croaker's really certified," he say.... Well, I guess one hand didn't know what the other was doing when I give him a jar of Saniflush by error.... So I reckon he's had his too.'

" 'Just the thing to clean a man's blood.'

" 'You know, that very thing occurred to me. Should be a sight better than sulphur and molasses.... Now, Arch, don't think I'm nosey; but a man don't have no secrets from God and his druggist I always say.... Is you still humping the Old Gray Mare?'

" 'Why, Doc Parker ... I'll have you know I'm a family man and an Elder in the First Denominational Non-sextarian Church and I ain't had a piecea hoss ass since we was kids together.'

" 'Them was the days, Arch. Remember the time I got the goose grease mixed up with the mustard? Always was a one to grab the wrong jar, feller say. They could have heard you squealing over in

Cunt Lick County, just a squealing like a stoat with his stones cut off.'

" 'You're in the wrong hole, Doc. It was you took the mustard and me as had to wait till you cooled off.'

" 'Wistful thinking, Arch. I read about it one time inna magazine settin' in that green outhouse behind the station.... Now what I meant awhile back, Arch, you didn't rightly understand me.... I mean she ain't what she used to be what with all them carbuncles and cataracts and chilblains and haemorrhoids and aftosa.'

" 'Yas, Doc, Liz is right sickly. Never was the same after her eleventh miscarriaging.... There was something right strange about that. Doc Ferris he told me straight, he said: "Arch, 'tain't fitting you should see that critter." And he gives me a long look made my flesh crawl.... Well, you sure said it right, Doc. She ain't what she used to be. And your medicines don't seem to ease her none. In fact, she ain't been able to tell night from day since using them eye drops you sold her last month.... But, Doc, you oughtta know I wouldn't be humping Liz, the old cow, meaning no disrespect to the mother of my dead monsters. Not when I got that sweet little ol' fifteen year old thing.... You know that yaller girl used to work in Marylou's Hair Straightening and Skin Bleach Parlor over in Nigga town.'

" 'Getting that dark chicken meat, Arch? Gettin' that coon pone?'

" 'Gettin' it steady, Doc. Gettin' it steady. Well, feller say duty is goosing me. Gotta get back to the old crank case.'

" 'I'll bet she needs a grease job worst way.'

" 'Doc, she sure is a dry hole.... Well, thanks for the paregoric.'

" 'And thanks for the trade, Arch.... He he he ... Say, Archy boy, some night when you get caught short with a rusty load drop around and have a drink of Yohimbiny with me.'

" 'I'll do that, Doc, I sure will. It'll be just like old times.'

"So I went on back to my place and heated up some water and mixed up some paregoric and cloves and cinnamon and sassyfrass and give it to Liz, and it eased her some I reckon. Leastwise she let up aggravatin' me.... Well, later on I went down to Doc Parker's again to get me a rubber ... and just as I was leaving I run into Roy Bane, a good ol' boy too. There's not a finer man in this Zone than Roy Bane.... So he said to me he says, 'Arch, you see that ol' nigger over there in that vacant lot? Well, sure as shit and taxes, he comes there every night just as regular you can set your watch by him. See him behind them nettles? Every night round about eight thirty he goes over into that lot yonder and pulls himself off with steel wool.... Preachin' Nigger, they tell me.'

"So that's how I come to know the hour more or less on Friday the 13th and it couldn't have been more than twenty minutes half an hour after that, I'd took some Spanish Fly in Doc's store and it was jest beginning to work on me down by Grennel Bog on my way to Nigger town.... Well the bog makes a bend, used to be nigger shack there.... They burned that ol' nigger over in Cunt Lick. Nigger had the aftosa and it left him stone blind.... So this white girl down from Texarkana screeches out:

" 'Roy, that ol' nigger is looking at me so nasty. Land's sake I feel just dirty all over.'

" 'Now, Sweet Thing, don't you fret yourself. Me an' the boys will burn him.'

" 'Do it slow, Honey Face. Do it slow. He's give me a sick headache.'

"So they burned the nigger and that ol' boy took his wife and went back up to Texarkana without paying for the gasoline and old Whispering Lou runs the service station couldn't talk about nothing else all Fall: 'These city fellers come down here and burn a nigger and don't even settle up for the gasoline.'

"Well, Chester Hoot tore that nigger shack down and rebuilt it just back of his house up in Bled Valley. Covered up all the windows with black cloth, and what goes on in there ain't fittin' to speak of.... Now Chester he's got some right strange ways.... Well it was just where the nigger shack used to be, right across from the Old Brooks place floods out every Spring, only it wasn't the Brooks place then ... belonged to a feller name of Scranton. Now that piece of land was surveyed back in 1919.... I reckon you know the man did the job too.... Feller name of Hump Clarence used to witch out wells on the side.... Good ol' boy too, not a finer man in this Zone than Hump Clarence.... Well it was just around about in there I come on Ted Spigot ascrewin a mud puppy."

Lee cleared his throat. The Clerk looked up over his glasses. "Now if you'll take care, young feller, till I finish what I'm asaying, I'll tend to your business."

And he plunged into an anecdote about a nigra got the hydrophobia from a cow.

"So my pappy says to me: 'Finish up your chores, son, and let's go see the mad nigger....' They had that nigger chained to the bed,

and he was bawling like a cow.... I soon got enough of that ol'
nigger. Well, if you all will excuse me I got business in the Privy
Council. He he he!"

Lee listened in horror. The County Clerk often spent weeks in
the privy living on scorpions and Montgomery Ward catalogues.
On several occasions his assistants had forced the door and carried
him out in an advanced state of malnutrition. Lee decided to play
his last card.

"Mr Anker," he said, "I'm appealing to you as one Razor Back
to another," and he pulled out his Razor Back card, a memo of his
lush-rolling youth.

The Clerk looked at the card suspiciously: "You don't look like
a bone feed mast-fed Razor Back to me.... What you think about
the Jeeeeews....?"

"Well, Mr Anker, you know yourself all a Jew wants to do is
doodle a Christian girl.... One of these days we'll cut the rest of
it off."

"Well, you talk right sensible for a city feller.... Find out what
he wants and take care of him.... He's a good ol' boy."

THE FLASH

I

Disintoxication Notes. Paranoia of early withdrawal. . . . Everything looks blue. . . . Flesh dead, doughy, toneless.

Withdrawal Nightmares. A mirror-lined café. Empty. . . . Waiting for something. . . . A man appears in a side door. . . . A slight, short Arab dressed in a brown jellaba with gray beard and gray face . . . There is a pitcher of boiling acid in my hand. . . . Seized by a convulsion of urgency, I throw it in his face. . . .

Everyone looks like a drug addict. . . .

Take a little walk in the hospital patio. . . . In my absence someone has used my scissors, they are stained with some sticky, red brown gick. . . . No doubt that little bitch of a criada trimming her rag.

Horrible-looking Europeans clutter up the stairs, intercept the nurse when I need my medicine, empty piss into the basin when I am washing, occupy the toilet for hours on end—probably fishing for a finger stall of diamonds they have stashed up their asshole. . . .

In fact the whole clan of Europeans have moved in next to me. . . . The old mother is having an operation and her daughter move right in to see the old gash receive proper service. Strange visitors, presumably relatives . . . One of them wears as glasses those gadgets jewelers screw into their eyes to examine stones. . . . Probably a diamond-cutter on the skids . . . The man who loused up the Throckmorton Diamond and was drummed out of the industry. . . . All these jewelers standing around the Diamond in their frock coats, waiting on The Man. An error of one thousandth of an inch ruins the rock completely and they have to import this character special from Amsterdam to do the job. . . . So he reels in dead drunk with a huge air hammer and pounds the diamond to dust. . . .

I don't check these citizens. . . . Dope peddlers from Aleppo? . . . Slunk traffickers from Buenos Aires? Illegal diamond buyers from Johannesburg? . . . Slave traders from Somaliland? Collaborators at the very least. . . .

Continual dreams of junk: I am looking for a poppy field. . . . Moonshiners in black Stetsons direct me to a Near East café. . . . One of the waiters is a connection for Yugoslav opium. . . .

Buy a packet of heroin from a Malay Lesbian in white belted trenchcoat. . . . I cop the paper in Tibetan section of a museum. She keeps trying to steal it back.... I am looking for a place to fix....

The critical point of withdrawal is not the early phase of acute sickness, but the final step free from the medium of junk.... There is a nightmare interlude of cellular panic, life suspended between two ways of being.... At this point the longing for junk concentrates in a last, all-out yen, and seems to gain a dream power: circumstances put junk in your way.... You meet an old-time Schmecker, a larcenous hospital attendant, a writing croaker....

II

Habit Notes. Shooting Eukodol every two hours I have a place where I can slip my needle right into a vein, it stays open like a red, festering mouth, swollen and obscene, gathers a slow drop of blood and pus after the shot....

Eukodol is a chemical variation of codeine—dihydro-oxy-codeine.

This stuff comes on more like C than M.... When you shoot Coke in the mainline there is a rush of pure pleasure to the head.... Ten minutes later you want another shot ... The pleasure of morphine is in the viscera.... You listen down into yourself after a shot.... But intravenous C is electricity through the brain, activating cocaine pleasure connections.... There is no withdrawal syndrome with C. It is a need of the brain alone—a need without body and without feeling. Earthbound ghost need. The craving for C lasts only a few hours as long as the C channels are stimulated. Then you forget it. Eukodol is like a combination of junk and C. Trust the Germans to concoct some really evil shit. Eukodol like morphine is six times stronger than codeine. Heroin six times stronger than morphine. Dihydro-oxy-heroin should be six times stronger than heroin. Quite possible to develop a drug so habit-forming that one shot would cause lifelong addiction.

Habit Note continued: Picking up needle I reach spontaneously for the tie-up cord with my left hand. This I take as a sign I can hit the one useable vein in my left arm. (The movements of tying up are such that you normally tie up the arm with which you reach for the cord.) The needle slides in easily on the edge of a callus. I feel around. Suddenly a thin column of blood shoots up into the syringe, for a moment sharp and solid as a red cord.

The body knows what veins you can hit and conveys this knowledge in the spontaneous movements you make preparing to take a shot.... Sometimes the needle points like a dowzer's wand. Sometimes I must wait for the message. But when it comes I always hit blood.

A red orchid bloomed at the bottom of the dropper. He hesitated for a full second, then pressed the bulb, watching the liquid rush into the vein as if sucked by the silent thirst of his blood. There was an iridescent, thin coat of blood left in the dropper, and the white paper collar was soaked through with blood like a bandage. He reached over and filled the dropper with water. As he squirted the water out, the shot hit him in the stomach, a soft sweet blow.

Look down at my filthy trousers, haven't been changed in months.... The days glide by strung on a syringe with a long thread of blood.... I am forgetting sex and all sharp pleasures of the body—a grey, junk-bound ghost. The Spanish boys call me El Hombre Invisible—the Invisible Man....

Twenty push ups every morning. Use of junk removes fat, leaves muscle more or less intact. The addict seems to need less tissue.... Would it be possible to isolate the fat-removing molecule of junk?

More and more static at the Drug Store, mutterings of control like a telephone off the hook ... Spent all day until 8 P.M. to score for two boxes of Eukodol....

Running out of veins and out of money.

Keep going on the nod. Last night I woke up with someone squeezing my hand. It was my other hand.... Fall asleep reading and the words take on code significance.... Obsessed with codes.... Man contracts a series of diseases which spell out a code message....

Take a shot in front of D.L. Probing for a vein in my dirty bare foot.... Junkies have no shame.... They are impervious to the repugnance of others. It is doubtful if shame can exist in the absence of sexual libido.... The junky's shame disappears with his non-sexual sociability which is also dependent on libido.... The addict regards his body impersonally as an instrument to absorb the medium in which he lives, evaluates his tissue with the cold hands of a horse trader. "No use trying to hit there." Dead fish eyes flick over a ravaged vein.

Using a new type sleeping pill called Soneryl.... You don't feel sleepy.... You shift to sleep without transition, fall abruptly into the middle of a dream.... I have been years in a prison camp suffering from malnutrition....

The President is a junky but can't take it direct because of his position. So he gets fixed through me. . . . From time to time we make contact, and I recharge him. These contacts look, to the casual observer, like homosexual practices, but the actual excitement is not primarily sexual, and the climax is the separation when the recharge is completed. The erect penises are brought into contact—at least we used that method in the beginning, but contact points wear out like veins. Now I sometimes have to slip my penis under his left eyelid. Of course I can always fix him with an Osmosis Recharge, which corresponds to a skin shot, but that is admitting defeat. An OR will put the President in a bad mood for weeks, and might well precipitate an atomic shambles. And the President pays a high price for the Oblique Habit. He has sacrificed all control, and is dependent as an unborn child. The Oblique Addict suffers a whole spectrum of subjective horror, silent protoplasmic frenzy, hideous agony of the bones. Tensions build up, pure energy without emotional content finally tears through the body throwing him about like a man in contact with high tension wires. If his charge connection is cut off cold, the Oblique Addict falls into such violent electric convulsions that his bones shake loose, and he dies with the skeleton straining to climb out of his unendurable flesh and run in a straight line to the nearest cemetery.

The relation between the OA (Oblique Addict) and his RC (Recharge Connection) is so intense that they can only endure each other's company for brief and infrequent intervals—I mean aside from recharge meets, when all personal contact is eclipsed by the recharge process.

III

The Sailor touched the door gently, following patterns of painted oak in a slow twist, leaving faint, iridescent whorls of slime. His arm went through to the elbow. He pulled back an inside bolt and stood aside for the boy to enter.

Heavy, colorless smell of death filled the empty room.

"The trap hasn't been aired since the Exterminator fumigated for coke bugs," said the Sailor apologetically.

The boy's peeled senses darted about in frenzied exploration. Tenement flat, railroad flat vibrating with silent motion. Along one wall of the kitchen a metal trough—or was it metal, exactly?—ran into a sort of aquarium or tank half-filled with translucent green fluid. Moldy objects, worn out in unknown service, littered the floor: a jock-strap designed to protect some delicate organ of flat, fan-shape; multi-levelled trusses, supports and bandages; a large U-shaped yoke of porous pink stone; little lead tubes cut open at one end.

Currents of movement from the two bodies stirred stagnant odor pools; atrophied boy-smell of dusty locker rooms, swimming pool chlorine, dried semen. Other smells curled through pink convolutions, touching unknown doors.

The Sailor reached under the wash-stand and extracted a package in wrapping paper that shredded and fell from his fingers in yellow dust. He laid out dropper, needle and spoon on a table covered with dirty dishes. But no roach antennae felt for the crumbs of darkness.

"The Exterminator does a good job," said the Sailor. "Almost too good, sometimes."

He dipped into a square tin of yellow pyretheum powder and pulled out a flat package covered in red and gold Chinese paper.

"Like a firecracker package," the boy thought. At fourteen lost two fingers.... Fourth of July fireworks accident ... later, in the hospital, first silent proprietary touch of junk.

"They go off, here, kid." The Sailor put a hand to the back of his head. He camped obscenely as he opened the package, a complex arrangement of slots and overlays.

"Pure, one hundred per cent H. Scarcely a man is now alive ... and it's all yours."

"So what you want off me?"

"Time."

"I don't dig."

"I have something you want," his hand touched the package. He drifted away into the front room, his voice remote and blurred. "You have something I want ... five minutes here ... an hour someplace else ... two ... four ... eight ... Maybe I'm getting ahead of myself.... Every day die a little.... It takes up The Time...."

He moved back into the kitchen, his voice loud and clear. "Five years a piece. Nobody gives a better deal on the street." He put a finger on the dividing line below the boy's nose. "Right down the middle."

"Mister, I don't know what you're talking about."

"You will, baby ... in time."

"OK. So what do I do?"

"You accept?"

"Yeah, like ..." He glanced at the package. "Whatever ... I accept."

The boy felt a silent clunk fall through his flesh. The Sailor put a hand to the boy's eyes and pulled out a pink scrotal egg with one closed, pulsing eye. Black fur boiled inside translucent flesh of the egg.

The Sailor caressed the egg with nakedly inhuman hands— black-pink, thick, fibrous, long white tendrils sprouting from abbreviated finger tips. Death fear and Death weakness hit the boy, shutting off his breath, stopping his blood. He leaned against a wall that seemed to give slightly. He clicked back into junk focus.

The Sailor was cooking a shot. "When the roll is called up yonder we'll be there, right?" he said, feeling along the boy's vein, erasing goose-pimples with a gentle old woman finger. He slid the needle in. A red orchid bloomed at the bottom of the dropper. The Sailor pressed the bulb, watching the solution rush into the boy-vein, sucked by silent thirst of blood.

"Jesus!" said the boy. "I never been hit like that before!"

He lit a cigarette and looked around the kitchen, twitching in sugar need. "Aren't you taking off?" he asked.

"With that milk sugar shit? Junk is a one-way street. No U-turn. You can't go back no more."

IV

Sucking terror from needle scars, underwater scream mouthing numb nerve warnings of the yen to come, throbbing bite site of rabies . . .

"If God made anything better he kept it for himself," the Sailor used to say, his transmission slowed down with twenty goof balls.

(Pieces of murder fall slow as opal chips through glycerine.)

Watching you and humming over and over, "Johnny's So Long At The Fair."

Pushing in a small way to keep up our habit. . . .

"And *use* that alcohol," I say slamming a spirit lamp down on the table.

"You fucking can't—wait—hungry junkies all the time black up my spoons with matches. . . . That's all I need for pen Indef. the heat rumbles a black spoon in the trap. . . .

"I thought you was quitting. . . . Wouldn't feel right fucking up your cure.

"Takes a lot of guts to kick a habit, kid."

Looking for veins in the thawing flesh. Hour-Glass of junk spills its last black grains into the kidneys. . . .

"Heavily infected area," he muttered, shifting the tie up.

"Death was their Culture Hero," said my Old Lady looking up from the Mayan Codices.... "They got fire and speech and the corn seed from death.... Death turns into a maize seed."

The Ouab Days are upon us
   raw pealed winds of hate and mischance
      blew the shot.

"Get those fucking dirty pictures out of here," I told her. The Old Timer Schmecker supported himself on a chair back, juiced and goof-balled ... a disgrace to his blood.

"What are you one of these goof-ball artists?"

Yellow smells of skid row sherry and occluding liver drifted out of his clothes when he made the junky gesture throwing the hand out palm up to cope ...
      smell of chili houses an dank overcoats and atrophied testicles....

He looked at me through the tentative, ectoplasmic flesh of cure ... thirty pounds materialized in a month when you kick ... soft pink putty that fades at the first silent touch of junk.... I saw it happen ... ten pounds lost in ten minutes ... standing there with the syringe in one hand ... holding his pants up with the other.
      sharp reek of diseased metal.

Walking in a rubbish heap to the sky ... scattered gasoline fires ... smoke hangs black and solid as excrement in the motionless air ... smudging the white film of noon heat ... D.L. walks beside me ... a reflection of my toothless gums and hairless skull ... flesh smeared over the rotting phosphorescent bones consumed by slow cold fires.... He carries an open can of gasoline and the smell of gasoline envelopes him.... Coming over a hill of rusty iron we meet a group of Natives ... flat two-dimension faces of scavenger fish....

"Throw the gasoline on them and light it....

QUICK...

white flash ... mangled insect screams ...

I woke up with the taste of metal in my mouth back from the dead
      trailing the colorless death smell
      afterbirth of a withered grey monkey
      phantom twinges of amputation ...

"Taxi boys waiting for a pickup," Eduardo said and died of an overdose in Madrid....
      Powder trains burn back through pink convolutions of tumescent flesh ... set off flash bulbs of orgasm ... pin-point

photos of arrested motion ... smooth brown side twisted to light a cigarette. ...

He stood there in a 1920 straw hat somebody gave him ... soft mendicant words falling like dead birds in the dark street. ...

"No more ... No more ... No mas ..."

A heaving sea of air hammers in the purple brown dusk tainted with rotten metal smell of sewer gas ... young worker faces vibrating out of focus in yellow halos of carbide lanterns ... broken pipes exposed. ...

"They are rebuilding the City."

Lee nodded absently. ... "Yes ... Always ..."

Either way is a bad move to The East Wing. ...

If I knew I'd be glad to tell you. ...

"No good ... no bueno ... hustling himself. ..."

"No glot ... C'lom Fliday"

THE SOFT MACHINE

It was in Paris that Burroughs wrote *The Soft Machine* and *The Ticket That Exploded*, the two novels which finished the trilogy that he began with *The Naked Lunch*. The manuscript of *The Naked Lunch* itself was published there by Maurice Girodias of Olympia Press, brought to him by Burroughs' old friend Allen Ginsberg. It had previously appeared in partial serial form in the *Chicago Review*, which led to the expulsion of that periodical from the university which had until then financed it, and then in *Big Table*, which the former editors of the *Chicago Review* had founded for the purpose.

Living in a small hotel on the rue Git-le-Coeur on the Left Bank, Burroughs quietly continued to write while his reputation grew. The *Travellers Companion* series was notorious for making available unusual and daring work of literary quality which British and American publishers knew at the time would lead to prosecution if they attempted them. Olympia put their quality work into the *Travellers Companion* series while the purely commercial pornography that they also published appeared under the *Ophelia Press* imprint, which had a wider sale in Europe and helped to subsidize the former.

Girodias was in many ways a crusader as well as a daring publisher. Born a British subject, son of Jack Kahane from Manchester who founded the Obelisk Press in Paris in the late twenties, he was reading galley proofs of Henry Miller's novels for his father as a boy. The Obelisk imprint became part of *Editions de Chene*, which during the war passed into the possession of Stock. The young Kahane, half Jewish, survived the war by taking his Auvernian mother's name, which he has since retained, although his brother Eric, translator of Harold Pinter and other British writers into French, who did translations into English for Girodias during the fifties, kept his original name.

Girodias, having lost the rights to most of the novels of Henry Miller during the war, to the annoyance of them both, brought out English translations under the Olympia imprint of the Marquis de Sade, Jean Genet and Samuel Beckett (who was then writing his novels in French), also Beckett's last English novel, *Watt*; he also commissioned work from a group of British and Americans living in Paris, which included Alexander Trocchi, Christopher Logue, Norman Rubington, Terry Southern and Gregory Corso. His biggest commercial success was Vladimir Nabokov's *Lolita*, which later became a bestseller in America and Britain and made Girodias temporarily affluent. The money was partially spent on political publishing, because Girodias was by then attacking not only fiction writers irked by the censorship of the English-speaking countries, but controversial historical documents as well. The long-buried secret diaries of Roger Casement, the Irish patriot hanged by the British in 1917, were published by Girodias to the fury of the British Home Office, who would not previously admit their existence. The Home Office has ever since been his most implacable enemy.

Girodias instantly recognized that Burroughs was his ideal writer, a visionary whose books could arouse sexually as well as change the way we view the world, a genius *maudit* in the tradition of Sade, and he encouraged him to continue writing while he published *The Naked Lunch*, a book which, apart from its power as literature, had erotic appeal to heterosexuals as well as homosexuals. Burroughs, in his fleapit of a hotel room, saw few people and wrote steadily, constantly reworking and mixing the pages that came from his typewriter. *The Soft Machine*, in which he moved closer to science fiction, with a locale set in "a mythical area which bears some resemblance to South America and also to the Planet Venus"—according to the author—concerns "a struggle between controllers and those who are endeavouring to throw off control". While writing this book, Burroughs also developed other material, some of which was later diverted to *Nova Express*, published much later and not by Olympia. He also incorporated passages that had been removed, sometimes accidentally, from *The Naked Lunch*. Cut-up technique appears frequently, necessitating the use of dashes between some phrases. And characters we have met before and will meet again, the sailor, Clem Snide, Carl, Dr Benway, and Mr Bradly Mr Martin, emerge in the text. The final section given here is called "Dead Fingers Talk", a title that Burroughs later used for the volume that appeared under that name when he joined up sections of all three books of the trilogy to form a totally new text that could be acceptably published in Britain. This appeared in 1963 and sparked off the correspondence in *The Times Literary Supplement* to which reference has already been made and which enabled unexpurgated editions to appear in the more relaxed atmosphere of the sixties. This correspondence is now included as an appendix in the 1982 Calderbook reprint of *The Naked Lunch*. The chapter headings in this section and throughout the rest of the book are those of the author.

DEAD ON ARRIVAL

I was working the hole with the sailor and we did not do bad. Fifteen cents on an average night boosting the afternoons and short-timing the dawn we made out from the land of the free. But I was running out of veins. I went over to the counter for another cup of coffee ... in Joe's Lunch Room drinking coffee with a napkin under the cup which is said to be the mark of someone who does a lot of sitting in cafeterias and lunchrooms ... Waiting on the man ... "What can we do?" Nick said to me once in his dead junky whisper. "They know we'll wait...." Yes, they know we'll wait ...

There is a boy sitting at the counter thin-faced kid his eyes all pupil. I see he is hooked and sick. Familiar face maybe from the pool hall where I scored for tea sometime. Somewhere in gray strata of subways all-night cafeterias rooming house flesh. His eyes flickered the question. I nodded toward my booth. He carried his coffee over and sat down opposite me.

The croaker lives out Long Island ... light yen sleep waking up for stops. Change. Start. Everything sharp and clear. Antennae of TV suck the sky. The clock jumped the way time will after four P.M.

"The Man is three hours late. You got the bread?"

"I got three cents."

"Nothing less than a nickel. These double papers he claims." I looked at his face. Good looking. "Say kid I know an Old Auntie Croaker right for you like a Major ... Take the phone. I don't want him to rumble my voice."

About this time I meet this Italian tailor cum pusher I know from Lexington and he gives me a good buy on H ... At least it was good at first but all the time shorter and shorter ... "Short Count Tony" we call him ...

Out of junk in East St Louis sick dawn he threw himself across the washbasin pressing his stomach against the cool porcelain. I draped myself over his body laughing. His shorts dissolved in rectal mucus and carbolic soap, summer dawn smells from a vacant lot.

"I'll wait here ... Don't want him to rumble me ..."

Made it five times under the shower that day soapy bubbles of egg flesh seismic tremors split by fissure spurts of jissom ...

I made the street, everything sharp and clear like after rain. See

Sid in a booth reading a paper his face like yellow ivory in the sunlight. I handed him two nickels under the table. Pushing in a small way to keep up The Habit: INVADE. DAMAGE. OCCUPY. Young faces in blue alcohol flame.

"And use that alcohol. You fucking can't wait hungry junkies all the time black up my spoons. That's all I need for Pen Indef the fuzz rumbles a black spoon in my trap." The old junky spiel. Junk hooks falling.

"Shoot your way to freedom kid."

Trace a line of goose pimples up the thin young arm. Slide the needle in and push the bulb watching the junk hit him all over. Move right in with the shit and suck junk through all the hungry young cells.

There is a boy sitting like your body. I see he is a hook. I drape myself over him from the pool hall. Draped myself over his cafeteria and his shorts dissolved in strata of subways . . . and all house flesh . . . toward the booth . . . down opposite me . . . The Man I Italian tailor . . . I know bread. "Me a good buy on H."

"You're quitting? Well I hope you make it, kid. May I fall down and be paralyzed if I don't mean it . . . You gotta friend in me. A real friend and if."

Well the traffic builds up and boosters falling in with jackets shirts and ties, kids with a radio torn from the living car trailing tubes and wires, lush-workers flash rings and wrist watches falling in sick all hours. I had the janitor cooled, an old rummy, but it couldn't last with that crowd.

"Say you're looking great kid. Now do yourself a favor and stay off. I been getting some really great shit lately. Remember that brown shit sorta yellow like snuff cooks up brown and clear . . ."

Junky in east bath room . . . invisible and persistent dream body . . . familiar face maybe . . . scored for some time or body . . . in that grey smell of rectal mucus . . . night cafeterias and junky room dawn smells, three hours from Lexington made it five times . . . soapy egg flesh . . .

"These double papers he claims of withdrawal."

"Well I thought you was quitting . . ."

"I can't make it."

"*Imposible quitar eso.*"

Got up and fixed in the sick dawn flutes of Ramadan.

"*William tu tomas más medicina? . . . No me hágas casa, William.*"

Casbah house in the smell of dust and we made it . . . empty eukodal boxes stacked four feet along the walls ... dead on the surplus blankets ... girl screaming ... *vecinos* rush in ...

"What did she die of?"

"I don't know she just died."

Bill Gains in Mexico City room with his douche bag and his stash of codeine pills powdered in a bicarbonate can. "I'll just say I suffer from indigestion." coffee and blood spilled all over the place. cigarette holes in the pink blanket ... The Consul would give me no information other than place of burial in The American Cemetery.

"Broke? Have you no pride? Go to your Consul." He gave me an alarm clock ran for a year after his death.

Leif repatriated by the Danish. freight boat out of Casa for Copenhagen sank off England with all hands. Remember my medium of distant fingers?—

"What did she die of?"

"End."

"Some things I find myself."

The Sailor went wrong in the end. hanged to a cell door by his principals: "Some things I find myself doing I'll pack in is all."

Bread knife in the heart ... rub and die ... repatriated by a morphine script ... those out of Casa for Copenhagen on special yellow note ...

"All hands broke? Have you no pride?" Alarm clock ran for a year. "He just sit down on the curb and die." Esperanza told me on Niño Perdido and we cashed a morphine script. those Mexican Nar. scripts on special yellow bank-note paper ... like a thousand dollar bill ... or a Dishonorable Discharge from the US Army ... And fixed in the cubicle room you reach by climbing this ladder.

Yesterday call flutes of Ramadan: "*No me hágas casa.*"

Blood spill over shirts and light. the American trailing in form ... He went to Madrid. This frantic Cuban fruit finds Kiki with a *novia* and stabs him with a kitchen knife in the heart. (Girl screaming. Enter the nabors.)

"*Quédase con su medicina, William.*"

Half bottle of Fundador after half cure in the Jew Hospital. shots of demerol by candlelight. They turned off the lights and water. Paper-like dust we made it. Empty walls. Look anywhere. No good. *No bueno.*

He went to Madrid ... Alarm clock ran for yesterday ... "*No me hágas casa.*" Dead on arrival ... you might say at the Jew Hospital ... blood spilled over the American ... trailing lights and water ... The Sailor went so wrong somewhere in that grey flesh ... He just sit down on zero ... I nodded on Niño Perdido his coffee over three hours late ... They all went away and sent papers ... The Dead Man write for you like a major ... Enter *vecinos* ... Freight boat smell of rectal mucus went down off England with all dawn smell of distant fingers ... About this time I went to your Consul. He gave me a Mexican after his death ... Five times of dust we made it ... with soap bubbles of withdrawal crossed by a thousand junky nights ... Soon after the half maps came in by candlelight ... OCCUPY ... Junk lines falling ... Stay off ... Bill Gains in the Yellow Sickness ... Looking at dirty pictures casual as a ceiling fan short-timing the dawn we made it in the corn smell of rectal mucus and carbolic soap ... familiar face maybe from the vacant lot ... trailing tubes and wires ... "You fucking-can't-wait-hungry-junkies! ..." Burial in the American Cemetery. "*Quédase con su medicina* ..." On Niño Perdido the girl screaming ... They all went way through Casbah House ... "Couldn't you write me any better than that? Gone away ... You can look any place."

No good. *No Bueno.*

You wouldn't believe how hot things were when I left the States —I knew this one pusher wouldn't carry any shit on his person just shoot it in the line—Ten twenty grains over and above his own absorption according to the route he was servicing and piss it out in bottles for his customers so if the heat came up on them they cop out as degenerates—So Doc Benway assessed the situation and came up with this brain child—

"Once in the Upper Baboonasshole I was stung by a scorpion— the sensation is not dissimilar to a fix—Hummm."

So he imports this special breed of scorpions and feeds them on metal meal and the scorpions turned a phosphorescent blue color and sort of hummed. "Now we must find a worthy vessel," he said—So we flush out this old goof ball artist and put the scorpion to him and he turned sort of blue and you could see he was fixed right to metal—These scorpions could travel on a radar beam and service the clients after Doc copped for the bread—It was a good thing while it lasted and the heat couldn't touch us—However all these scorpion junkies began to glow in the dark and if they didn't score on the hour metamorphosed into scorpions straight away—So there was a spot of bother and we had to move on disguised as young junkies on the way to Lexington—Bill and Johnny we sorted out the names but they keep changing like one day I would wake up as Bill the next day as Johnny—So there we are in the train compartment shivering junk sick our eyes watering and burning.

EARLY ANSWER

Predated checks bounce all around us in green place by the ball park—Come and jack off—passport vending machines—Jimmy walked along North End Road—(Slow-motion horses pulling carts —boys streaked with coal dust)—a low-pressure area and the wind rising—Came to the World's End Pissoir and met a boy with wide shoulders, black eyes glinting under the street lights, a heavy silk scarf tucked into his red- and white-striped T-shirt—In the bedroom sitter the boy peeled off his clothes and sat down naked on the bed blowing cigarette smoke through his pubic hairs—His cock came up in the smoke—Switchblade eyes squinted, he watched with a smile wasn't exactly a smile as Jimmy folded his clothes—raw and peeled, naked now his cock pulsing—Jimmy picked up his key and put it in his mouth sucking the metal taste—The other sat smoking and silent—A slow drop of lubricant squeezed out the end of his cock glistening in light from the street—Shutters clattered in the rising wind—A rotten vegetable smell seeped through the dingy room, shadow cars moved across the rose wall paper—

K9 had an appointment at The Sheffield Arms Pub but the short wave faded out on the location—Somewhere to the left? or was it to the right?—On? Off? North End Road?—He walked through empty market booths, shutters clattering—Wind tore the cover off faces he passed raw and peeled—Came to World's End wind blowing through empty time pockets—No Sheffield Arms—Back to his room full of shadows—There he was sitting on the bed with the smile that wasn't exactly a smile—At the washbasin a boy was using his toothbrush—

"Who are these people?"

The boy turned from the washbasin. "You don't remember me?—Well we met in a way that is"—The toothbrush in his hand was streaked with blood.

Jimmy sat down on the bed his rectum tingling—The other picked up his scarf from a chair and ran it through his fingers looking at Jimmy with a cruel idiot smile—His hands closed on Jimmy's elbows twisting him over on his stomach down on the bed—The boy found a pajama cord and tied Jimmy's hands behind his back—Jimmy lay there gasping and sucked the key, tasting metal in his mouth—The other saddled Jimmy's Body—He spit on his hands and rubbed the spit on his cock—He placed his hands on Jimmy's ass cheeks and shoved them apart and dropped a gob of spit on the rectum—He slid the scarf under Jimmy's hips and pulled his body up onto his cock—Jimmy gasped and moved with it—The boy slid the scarf up along Jimmy's body to the neck—

He must have blacked out though he hadn't had much to drink at the pub—two so-called double brandies and two Barley wines—He was lying on a lumpy studio bed in a strange room—familiar too—in shoes and overcoat—someone else's overcoat—such a coat he would never have owned himself—a tweedy loose-fitting powder-blue coat—K9 ran to tight-fitting black Chesterfields which he usually bought second-hand in hock shops—He had very little money for clothes though he liked to dress in "banker drag" he called it—black suits—expensive ties and linen shirts—Here he was in such a coat as he would never voluntarily have owned or worn—someone else's room—bed sitter—cheap furniture suitcases open—K9 found two keys covered with dust on the mantel—Sat down convenient and sorted out his name—

"You never learned to use your Jimmy—slow with the right—there will be others behind him with the scarf—We met you know in a way that is in the smell of wine—You don't remember me?"

Taste of blood in his throat familiar too—and overcoat—someone else's—streaked with coal dust—The bed sitter boy as it always does folded his clothes—Lay there gasping fresh in today—

"Went into what might be called the comfortable and got myself a flat jewelry lying about wholesale side—Learned how to value them marketable commodities come level on average—well groceries —She started screaming for a respectable price—I was on the roof so I had to belt her—Find a time buyer before doing sessions—There's no choice if they start job for instance—Have to let it go cheap and start further scream along the line—one or two reliable thieves—Work was steady at the gate to meet me—early answer to use on anyone considering to interfere—Once in a while I had to put it about but usually what you might call a journeyman thief—It was done so modern and convenient—Sorted out punishment and reward lark—On, off? the bed down on his stomach is he? Ah there you are behind him with the scarf—Hands from 1910—There's no choice if took off his clothes—Have to let it go cheap and start naked."

Twisted the scarf tighter and tighter around Jimmy's neck— Jimmy gasped coughing and spitting, face swollen with blood—His spine tingled—Coarse black hair suddenly sprouted all over him. Canines tore through his gum with exquisite toothache pain—He kicked in bone wrenching spasms. Silver light popped in his eyes.

He decided to take the coat with him—Might pass someone on the stairs and they would think he was the tenant since the boy resembled him in build and features being younger of course but then people are not observant come level on average—Careful—

"Careful—Watch the exits—wait a bit—no good at this rate— Watch the waves and long counts—no use moving out—try one if you want to—all dies in convulsions screaming without a body— Know the answer?—arsenic two years: operation completed—We are arsenic and bleeding gums—Who? *Quién es?*—World's End loud and clear—so conjured up wide shoulders and black eyes glinting—shadow cars through the dingy room—My page deals the bedroom sitter out of suitcase here on the bed where you know me with cruel idiot smile as Jimmy's eyes pop out—Silk scarf moved up rubbing—Pubic hair sprouted all over him tearing the flesh like wire—Eyes squinted from a smell I always feel—Hot spit burned his rectum open—The warm muscle contracts—Kicked breathless coughing and spitting adolescent image blurred in film smoke— through the gums the fist in his face—taste of blood—His broken body spurted life in other flesh—identical erections kerosene lamp —electric hair sprouted in ass and genitals—taste of blood in the throat—Hot semen spurted idiot mambo—one boy naked in Panama—Who?—*Quién es?*—Compost heap stench where you know me from—a smell I always feel when his eyes pop out—

"Know the answer? arsenic two years: goof ball bum in 1910 Panama. They'll do it every time—Vampires is no good all possessed by overwhelming Minraud girl—"

"Are you sure they are not for protection?"

"Quite sure—nothing here but to borrow your body for a special purpose: ('Excellent—Proceed to the ice.')—in the blood arsenic and bleeding gums—They were addicted to this round of whatever visits of a special kind—An errand boy of such a taste took off his clothes—Indications enough naked now his cock healed scar tissue —Flesh juice vampires is no good—all sewage—sweet rotten smell of ice—no use of them better than they are—The whole thing tell you no good *no bueno* outright or partially."

"Reason for the change of food not wholly disinterested—The square fact is that judges like a chair—For many years he used Parker—Fed up with present food in the Homicide Act and others got the job—So think before time that abolition is coming anyway after that, all the Top Jobbies would like to strike a bargain in return for accepting the end of hanging—Generous? Nothing—I wasn't all that far from ebbing in position—"

"Having to move fast—Nail that Broker before they get to him—Doing him a favor any case—"

He found the Broker in a café off the Socco—heavy with massive muscled flesh and cropped grey hair—K9 stood in the shadow and tugged his mind screen—The Broker stood up and walked down an alley—K9 stepped out of the shadows in his new overcoat—

"Oh it's you—Everything all right?—"

K9 took off his hat respectfully and covered his gun with it—He had stuffed the hat with the Green Boy's heavy silk scarf—a crude silencer but there was nobody in the alley—It wasn't healthy to be within earshot when the Broker had business with anyone—He stood with the hat an inch from the Broker's mid section—He looked into the cold grey eyes—

"Everything is just fine," he said—

And pumped three Police Specials into the massive stomach hard as a Japanese wrestler—The Broker's mouth flew open sucking for breath that did not come—K9 gave him three more and stepped aside—The Broker folded, slid along a wall and flopped face up his eyes glazing over—Lee dropped the burning hat and scarf on a pile of excrement and walked out of the alley powder smoke drifting from his cheap European suit—He walked toward flesh of Spain and Piccadilly—

"Wind hand to the hilt—Fed up you understand until I die—Work we have to do and way got the job—End getting to know whose reports are now ended—'One more change,' he said, 'touching circumstance'—Have you still—Come back to the Spanish bait it's curtains under his blotter."

Who? *Quién es?*—Question is far away—In this hotel room you are writing whiffs of Spain—Boy stretches a leg—His cock flipped out in the kerosene lamp—sputter of burning insect wings—Heard the sea—tin shack over the mud flats—erogenous holes and pepper smells—

In the sun at noon shirt open as his pants dropped—lay on his stomach and produced a piece of soap—rubbed the soap in—He gasped and moved with it—whiffs of his feet in the warm summer afternoon—

Who? *Quién es?* It can only be the end of the world ahead loud and clear—

Kiki steps forward on faded photo—pants slipping down legs

with a wriggle stood naked spitting on his hands—Shot a bucket grinning—over the whispering tide flats youths in the act, pants down, bare feet in dog's excrement—Street smells of the world siphoned back red-and-white T-shirt to brown Johnny—that stale dawn smell of naked sleep under the ceiling fan—Shoved him over on his stomach kicking with slow pleasure—

"Hooded dead gibber in the turnstile—What used to be me is backward sound track—fossil orgasm kneeling in inane cooperation." wind through the pissoir—*J'aime ces types vicieux qu'ici montrent la bite*"—green place by the water pipe—dead leaves caught in pubic hairs—"Come and jack off—1929"—Woke in stale smell of vending machines—The boy with grey flannel pants stood there grinning a few inches in his hand—Shadow cars and wind through other flesh—came to World's End. Brief boy on screen revolving lips and pants and forgotten hands in countries of the world—

On the sea wall met a boy in red-and-white T-shirt under a circling albatross—"Me Brown Meester?"—warm rain on the iron roof—The boy peeled his stale underwear—Identical erection flipped out in kerosene lamp—The boy jumped on the bed, slapped his thighs: "I screw Johnny up ass? *Asi como perros*"—Rectums merging to idiot Mambo—one boy naked in Panama dawn wind—

In the hyacinths the Green Boys smile—Rotting music trailing vines and birdcalls through remote dreamy lands—The initiate awoke in that stale summer dawn smell, suitcases all open on a brass bed in Mexico—In the shower a Mexican about twenty, rectums naked, smell of carbolic soap and barrack toilets—

Trails my summer dawn wind in other flesh strung together on scar impressions of young Panama night—pictures exploded in the kerosene lamp—open shirt flapping in the pissoir—cock flipped out and up—water from his face—sex tingled in the boy's slender tight ass—

"You wanta screw me?"

"Breathe in, Johnny—Here goes—"

They was ripe for the plucking forgot way back yonder in the corn hole—lost in little scraps of delight and burning scrolls—through the open window trailing swamp smells and old newspapers— rectums naked in whiffs of raw meat—genital smells of the two bodies merge in shared meals and belches of institution cooking— spectral smell of empty condoms down along penny arcades and mirrors—Forgotten shadow actor walks beside you—mountain wind of Saturn in the morning sky—From the death trauma weary good-by then—orgasm addicts stacked in the attic like muttering burlap—

Odor rockets over oily lagoons—silver flakes fall through a maze of dirty pictures—windy city outskirts—Smell of empty condoms, excrement, black dust—ragged pants to the ankle—

Bone faces—place of nettles along adobe walls open shirts flapping—savanna and grass mud—The sun went—The mountain shadow touched ragged pants—whisper of dark street in faded Panama photo—"Muy got good one, Meester" smiles through the pissoir—Orgasm siphoned back street smells and a Mexican boy—Woke in the filtered green light, thistle shadows cutting stale underwear—

The three boys lay on the bank rubbing their stomachs against the warm sand—They stood up undressing to swim—Billy gasped as his pants dropped and his cock flipped out he hadn't realized it was that far up from the rubbing—They swam lazily letting the warm water move between their legs and Lloyd walked back to his pants and brought a piece of soap and they passed it back and forth laughing and rubbing each other and Billy ejaculated his thin brown stomach arched out of the water as the spurts shot up in the sunlight like tiny rockets—He sagged down into the water panting and lay there against the muddy bottom—

Under the old trestle trailing vines in the warm summer afternoon undressing to swim and rubbing their bellies—Lloyd rubbing his hand down further and further openly rubbing his crotch now and grinning as the other two watched and Billy looked at Jammy hesitantly and began to rub too and slowly Jammy did the same—They came into the water watching the white blobs drift away—The Mexican boy dropped his pants and his cock flipped out and he looked at Billy grinning—Billy turned and waded into the water and the Mexican followed him and turned him around feeling his crotch and shoved him down on his back in the shallow water, hitched his brown arms under Billy's knees and shoved them back against his chest—The Mexican held his knees with one arm and with the other hand dipped a piece of soap in the water and began rubbing it up and down Billy's ass—Billy shuddered and his body went limp letting it happen—The Mexican was rubbing soap on his own cock now with one hand—shiny black pubic hairs reflected sharp as wire—Slowly shoved his cock in—Billy gasped and moved with it—Spurts fell against his chest in the sunlight and he lay there in the water breathing sewage smells of the canal—

Billy squirmed up onto a muddy bank and took a handful of the

144

warm mud and packed it around his cock and Lloyd poured a bucket of water on the mud and Billy's cock flipped out jumping in the green filtered light under the old trestle—

Stale underwear of penny arcades slipping down legs, rectums feeling the warm sun, laughing and washing each other soapy hands in his crotch, pearly spasms stirring the warm water—whiff of dried jissom in the bandanna trailing sweet young breath through remote lands—soft globs on a brass bed in Mexico—naked—wet—carbolic soap—tight nuts—piece of soap in the locker room rubbing each other off to "My Blue Heaven"—grinning as the other two watched—

The Mexican dropped his pants with a wriggle and stood naked in the filtered green light, vines on his back—Rubbing his crotch now into Billy's ass—Billy moved with it, rectum wriggling cock inside rubbing—

Ali squirmed teeth bared grinning—His thin brown stomach hit the pallet—"You is coming, Johnny?"—Sunlight on the army blankets—rectum wriggling slow fuck on knees *así como perros*—orgasm crackled with electric afternoon—bodies stuck together in magnetic eddies—Squirming cock in his intestines, rectum wriggling felt the hot sperm deep in his body—

Shoved him over on his stomach kicking—The Mexican held his knees—Hand dipped a piece of soap—Shoved his cock in laughing —Bodies stuck together in the sunlight kicked whiffs of rectal mucus—laughing teeth and pepper smells—"You is feeling the hot quick Mexican kid naked Mambo to your toes Johnny ... dust in bare leg hairs tight brown nuts breech very hot ... How long you want us to fuck very nice Meester? Flesh diseased dirty pictures we fucking tired of fuck very nice Mister." Sad image of sickness at the attic window say something to you *"adios"* worn out film washed back in prep school clothes to distant closing dormitory fragments off the page stained toilet pictures blurred rotting pieces of "Freckle Leg" dormitory dawn dripping water on his face diseased voice so painful telling you "Sparks" is over New York. "Have I done the job here?" With a telescope you can watch our worn out film dim jerky far away shut a bureau drawer faded sepia smile from an old calendar falling leaves sun cold on a thin boy with freckles folded away in an old file now standing last review.

"Maze of dirty pictures and vending machine flesh whispers use of fraud on faded photo—IBM song yodels dime a dozen type overcoats—Not taking any adolescent on shit envelope in the bath cubicle—Come of your stale movies sings Danny Deever in drag—

Times lost or strayed long empty cemetery with a moldy pawn ticket—fading whisper down skid row to Market Street shows all kinds masturbation and self-abuse—Young boys need it special." silver paper in the wind distant 1920 wind and dust. He was looking at some thing a long time ago where the second hand book shop used to be just opposite the old cemetery.

"Who? *Quién es?—Hable, señor*—Talk loud and clear."

"We are all from the American women with a delicate lilt—I represent the lithe aloof young men of the breed charmingly—We are all empowered to make arrests and enough with just the right shade of show you."

"*Belt Her*—Find a time buyer before ports are now ended—These are rotten if they start job for instance—Blind bargain in return for accepting 'one more chance'—Generous?—Nothing—That far to the bait and it's curtains—Know what they meant if they start job for instance?"

"Dead young flesh in stale underwear vending sex words to magnetic Law 334—Indicates simple tape is served sir, through iron repetition—Ass and genitals tingling in 1929 jack-off spelt out broken wings of Icarus—Control system ousted from half the body whispers skin instructions to memory of melting ice—arca of Spain —channels ahead loud and clear—Line of the body fitted to other underwear and Kiki steps forward on faded photo—sad image dusted by the Panama night."

"So think before they can do any locks over the Chinese that abolition is war of the past—The end of hanging generous? Just the same position—Changed place of years in the end is just the same—Going to do?—Perhaps alone would you? All good things come to about that was that—"

Call through remote dawn of back yards and ash pits—plaintive ghost in the turnstile—Shadow cars and wind faces came to World's End—street light on soiled clothes dim jerky far away dawn in his eyes. Do you begin to see there is no boy there in the dark room? He was looking at something a long time ago. Changed place?—Same position—Sad image circulates through backward time—Clom Fliday."

CASE OF THE CELLULOID KALI

The name is Clem Snide—I am a Private Ass Hole—I will take on any job any identity any body—I will do anything difficult dangerous or downright dirty for a price—

The man opposite me didn't look like much—A thin grey man in a long coat that flickered like old film—He just happens to be the biggest operator in any time universe—

"I don't care myself you understand"—He watched the ash spiraling down from the end of his Havana—It hit the floor in a puff of grey dust—

"Just like that—Just time—Just time—Don't care myself if the whole fucking shithouse goes up in chunks—I've sat out novas before—I was born in a nova."

"Well Mr Martin, I guess that's what birth is you might say."

"I wouldn't say—Have to be moving along any case—The ticket that exploded posed little time—Point is they are trying to cross me up—small timers—still on the old evacuation plan—Know what the old evacuation plan is, Mr Snide?"

"Not in detail."

"The hanging gimmick—death in orgasm—gills—No bones and elementary nervous system—evacuation to the Drenched Lands—a bad deal on the level and it's not on the level with Sammy sitting in—small timers trying to cross me up—Me, Bradly-Martin, who invented the double-cross—Step right up—Now you see me now you don't—A few scores to settle before I travel—a few things to tidy up and that's where you come in—I want you to contact the Venus mob, the Vegetable People and spill the whole fucking compost heap through Times Square and Piccadilly—I'm not taking any rap for that green bitch—I'm going to rat on everybody and split this dead whistle stop planet wide open—I'm clean for once with the nova heat—like clean fall out—"

He faded in spiraling patterns of cigar smoke—There was a knock at the door—Registered letter from Antwerp—Ten thousand dollar check for film rights to a novel I hadn't written called *The Soft Ticket*—Letter from somebody I never heard of who is acting as my agent suggests I contact the Copenhagen office to discuss the Danish rights on my novel *Expense Account*—bar backed by pink shell—new Orleans jazz thin in the Northern night. A boy slid off a white silk bar stool and held out the hand: "Hello, I'm Johnny Yen, a friend of—well, just about everybody. I was more physical before my accident you can see from this interesting picture. Only the head was reduced to this jelly but like I say it the impression on my face was taken by the other man's eyes drive the car head-on it was and the Big Physician (he's very technical) rushed him off to a surgery and took out his eyes and made a quick impression and slapped it on me like a pancake before I started to dry out and curled around the edges. So now I'm back in harness you might say: and I have all of "you" that what I want from my audience is the last drop then bring me another. The place is hermetic. We think so blockade we thought nobody could get thru our flak thing. they thought. Switch Artist me. Oh, there goes my frequency. I'm on now . . ."

The lights dimmed and Johnny pranced out in goggles flickering Northern Lights wearing a jockstrap of undifferentiated tissue that must be in constant movement to avoid crystallization. A penis rose out of the jock and dissolved in pink light back to a clitoris, balls retract into cunt with a fluid plop. Three times he did this to wild *"Olés!"* from the audience. Drifted to the bar and ordered a heavy blue drink. D noted patches of white crystal formed along the scar lines on Johnny's copy face.

"Just like canals. Maybe I'm a Martian when the Crystals are down."

You will die there a screwdriver through the head. The thought like looking at me over steak and explain it all like that stay right here. She was also a Reichian analyst. Disappear more or less remain in acceptable form to you the face.

"We could go on cutting my cleavage act, but *genug basta assez* dice fall *hombre* long switch street . . . I had this terrible accident in a car a Bentley it was I think they're so nice that's what you pay for when you buy one it's yours and you can be sure nobody will pull it out from under our assets. Of course we don't have assholes here you understand somebody might go and get physical. So we are strictly from urine. And that narrows things to a fine line down the middle fifty feefty and what could be fairer than that my Uncle Eyetooth always says he committed fornication but I don't believe it me old heavy water junky like him . . . So anyhoo to get back to my accident in my Bentley once I get my thing in a Bentley it's mine already.

"So we had this terrible accident or rather he did. Oh dear what am I saying? It wasn't my first accident you understand yearly wounded or was it monthly Oh dear I must stay on that middle line . . .

"Survivor. Survivor. Not the first in my childhood. Three thousand years in show business and always keep my nose clean. Why I was a dancing boy for the Cannibal Trog Women in the Ice Age. remember? All that meat stacked up in the caves and the Blue Queen covered with limestone flesh creeps into your bones like cold grey honey . . . that's the way they keep them not dead but paralyzed with this awful stuff they cook down from vampire bats get in your hair Gertie always keep your hair way up inside with a vampire on premises bad to get in other alien premises. The Spanish have this word for it, something about props *ajeno* or something like that I know so am *ya la yo* mixa everything allup. They call me Puto the Cement Mixer, now isn't that cute? Some people think I'm just silly but I'm not silly at all . . . and this boyfriend told me I looked just like a shrew ears quivering hot and eager like burning leaves and those were his last words engraved on my back tape—along with a lot of other old memories that disgust me, you wouldn't believe the horrible routines I been involved through my profession of Survival Artist . . . and they think that's funny, but I don't laugh except real quick between words no time you understand laughing they could get at me doesn't keep them off like talking does, now watch—"

A flicker pause and the light shrank and the audience sound a vast muttering in Johnny's voice.

"You see"—Shadows moved back into nightclub seats and drank nightclub drinks and talked nightclub talk—"They'd just best is all. So I was this dancing boy for these dangerous old cunts paralyzed men and boys they dug special stacked right up to the ceiling like the pictures I saw of Belsen or one of those awful contracted places and I said they are at it again . . . I said the Old Army Game. I said 'Pass the buck.' Now you see it, now you don't . . . Paralyzed with this awful gook the Sapphire Goddess let out through this cold sore she always kept open on her lips, that is a hole in the limestone you understand she was like entirely covered with one of those stag rites . . . Real concentrated in there and irradiated to prevent an accident owing to some virus come lately wander in from Podunk Hepatitis . . . But I guess I'm talking too much about private things . . . But I know this big atomic professor, he's very technical too, says: 'There are no secrets any more, Pet,' when I was smooching around him for a quickie. My Uncle still gives me a sawski for a hot nuclear secret and ten years isn't hay, dahling, in these times when practically anybody is subject to wander in from the desert with a quit claim deed and snatch a girl's snatch right out from under her assets ... over really I should say but some of we boys are so sick we got this awful cunt instead of a decent human asshole disgust you to see it ... So I just say anything I hear on the old party line.

"I used to keep those old Cave Cunts at bay with my Impersonation Number where I play this American Mate Dance in Black Widow drag and I could make my face flap around you wouldn't believe it and the noises I made in uh orgasm when SHE ate me—I played both parts you unnerstand, imitated the Goddess Herself and turn right into stone for security ... And SHE couldn't give me enough juice running out of this hole was her only orifice and she was transported dais and all, die ass and all, by blind uniques with no balls, had to crawl under HER dais dressed in Centipede Suit of the Bearer which was put on them as a great honor and they was always fighting over matter of crawl protocol or protocrawl ... So all these boys stacked to the ceiling covered with limestone ... you understand they weren't dead any more than a fresh oyster is dead, but dead in the moment when the shell was cracked and they were eaten all quivering sweet and tasty. vitamins the right way ... eaten with little jeweled adzes jade and sapphires and chicken blood rubies all really magnificent. Of course I pinched everything I could latch onto with my prehensile piles I learned it boosting in Chi to pay the Luxury Tax on C. three thousand years in show business ... Later or was it earlier, the Mayan Calendar is all loused up you know ... I was a star Corn God inna Sacred Hanging Ceremony to fructify the Corn devised by this impresario who specializes in these far out bit parts which fit me like a condom, he says the cutest things. He's a doctor too. A big physician made my face over after 'the accident' collided with my Bentley head on ... the cops say they never see anything so intense and it is a special pass I must be carrying I wasn't completely obliterated.

"Oh there's my doctor made the face over after my accident. He calls me Pygmalion now, isn't that cute? You'll love him."

The doctor was sitting in a surgical chair of gleaming nickel. His soft boneless head was covered with grey green fuzz, the right side of his face an inch lower than the left side swollen smooth as a boil around a dead, cold undersea eye.

"Doctor, I want you to meet my friend Mister D the Agent, and he's a lovely fellow too."

("Some time he don't hardly hear what you saying. He's very technical.")

The doctor reached out his abbreviated fibrous fingers in which surgical instruments caught neon and cut Johnny's face into fragments of light.

"Jelly," the doctor said, liquid gurgles through his hardened purple gums. His tongue was split and the two sections curled over each other as he talked: "Life jelly. It sticks and grows on you like Johnny."

Little papules of tissue were embedded in the doctor's hands. The doctor pulled a scalpel out of Johnny's ear and trimmed the papules into an ash tray where they stirred slowly exuding a green juice.

"They say his prick didn't synchronize at all so he cut it off and made some kinda awful cunt between the two sides of him. He got a whole ward full of his 'fans' he call them already.

"When the wind is right you can hear them scream in Town Hall Square. And everybody says 'But this is interesting.'

"I was more *physical* before my *accident*, you can see from this interesting picture."

Lee looked from the picture to the face, saw the flickering phosphorescent scars—

"Yes," he said, "I know you—You're dead *nada* walking around visible."

So the boy is rebuilt and gives me the eye and there he is again walking around some day later across the street and "No dice" flickered across his face—The copy there is a different being, something ready to slip in—boys empty and banal as sunlight her way always—So he is exact replica is he not?—empty space of the original—

So I tailed the double to London and the Hook Von Holland and caught him out strangling a naked faggot in the bed sitter—I slip on the antibiotic hand cuffs and we adjourn to the Mandrake Club for an informative little chat—

"What do you get out of this?" I ask bluntly.

"A smell I always feel when their eyes pop out"—The boy looked at me his mouth a little open showing the whitest teeth this Private Eye ever saw—naval uniform buttoned in the wrong holes quilted with sea mist and powder smoke, smell of chlorine, rum and moldy jockstraps—and probably a narcotics agent is hiding in the spare stateroom that is always locked—There are the stairs to the attic

151

room he looked out of and his mother moving around—dead she was they say—dead—with such hair too—red.

"Where do you feel it?" I prodded.

"All over," he said, eyes empty and banal as sunlight—"Like hair sprouting all over me"—He squirmed and giggled and creamed in his dry goods—

"And after every job I get to see the movies—You know—" And he gave me the sign twisting his head to the left and up—

So I gave him the sign back and the words jumped in my throat all there like and ready the way they always do when I'm right "You make the pilgrimage?"

"Yes—The road to Rome."

I withdrew the antibiotics and left him there with that dreamy little-boy look twisting the napkin into a hangman's knot—On the bus from the air terminal a thin grey man sat down beside me—I offered him a cigarette and he said "Have one of mine," and I see he is throwing the tin on me—"Nova police—You are Mr Snide I believe." And he moved right in and shook me down looking at pictures, reading letters checking back on my time track.

"There's one of them," I heard some one say as he looked at a photo in my files.

"Hummm—yes—and here's another—Thank you Mr Snide—You have been most cooperative—"

I stopped off in Bologna to look up my old friend Green Tony thinking he could probably give me a line—up four flights in a tenement past the old bitch selling black-market cigarettes and cocaine cut with Saniflush, through a dirty brown curtain and there is Green Tony in a pad with Chinese jade all over and Etruscan cuspidors—He is sitting back with his leg thrown over an Egyptian throne smoking a cigarette in a carved emerald holder—He doesn't get up but he says: "Dick Tracy in the flesh," and motions to a Babylonian couch.

I told him what I was after and his face went a bright green with rage, "That stupid bitch—She bringa the heat on all of us—Nova heat—" He blew a cloud of smoke and it hung there solid in front of him—Then he wrote an address in the smoke—No. 88 Via di Nile, Roma."

This 88 Nile turned out to be one of those bar-soda fountains like they have in Rome—You are subject to find a maraschino cherry in your dry martini and right next to some citizen is sucking a banana split disgust you to see it—Well I am sitting there trying not to see it so I look down at the far end of the counter and dug a boy

very dark with kinky hair and something Abyssinian in his face—
Our eyes lock and I give him the sign—And he gives it right
back—So I spit the maraschino cherry in the bartender's face and
slip him a big tip and he says "*Rivideci* and bigger.*"

And I say "Up yours with a double strawberry phosphate."

The boy finishes his Pink Lady and follows me out and I take him
back to my trap and right away get into an argument with the clerk
about no visitors *stranezza* to the hotel—Enough garlic on his
breath to deter a covey of vampires—I shove a handful of lire into
his mouth "Go buy yourself some more gold teeth," I told him—

When this boy peeled off the dry goods he gives off a slow stink
like a thawing mummy—But his asshole sucked me right in all my
experience as a Private Eye never felt anything like it—In the flash
bulb of orgasm I see that fucking clerk has stuck his head through
the transom for a refill—Well expense account—The boy is lying
there on the bed spreading out like a jelly slow tremors running
through it and sighs and says: "Almost like the real thing isn't it?"

And I said "I need the time milking," and give him the sign so
heavy come near slipping a disk.

"I can see you're one of our own," he said warmly sucking
himself back into shape—"Dinner at eight"—He comes back at
eight in a souped up Ragazzi and we take off 160 per and scream
to stop in front of a villa I can see the Bentleys and Hispano Bear
Cats and Stutz Suisses and what not piled up and all the golden
youth of Europe is disembarking—"Leave your clothes in the
vestibule," the butler tells us and we walk in on a room full of people
all naked to a turn sitting around on silk stools and a bar with a pink
shell behind it—This cunt undulates forward and give me the sign
and holds out her hand "I am the the Contessa di Vile your hostess
for tonight"—She points to the boys at the bar with her cigarette
holder and their cocks jumped up one after the other—And I did
the polite thing too when my turn came—

So all the boys began chatting in unison "*The movies!—The
movies!*—We want *the movies!*—*" So she led the way into the
projection room which was filled with pink light seeping through
the walls and floor and ceiling—The boy was explaining to me that
these were actual films taken during the Abyssinian War and how
lucky I was to be there—Then the action starts—There on the
screen is a gallows and some young soldiers standing around with
prisoners in loincloths—The soldiers are dragging this kid up onto
the gallows and he biting and screaming and shitting himself and
his loincloth slips off and they shove him under the noose and one

of them tightens it around his neck standing there now mother naked—Then the trap fell and he drops kicking and yelping and you could hear his neck snap like a stick in a wet towel—He hangs there pulling his knees up to the chest and pumping out spurts of jissom and the audience coming right with him spurt for spurt—So the soldiers strip the loincloths off the others and they all got hard-ons waiting and watching—Got through a hundred of them more or less one at a time—Then they run the movie in slow motion slower and slower and you are coming slower and slower until it took an hour and then two hours and finally all the boys are standing there like statues getting their rocks off geologic—Meanwhile an angle comes dripping down and forms a stalactite in my brain and I slip back to the projection room and speed up the movie so the hanged boys are coming like machine guns—Half the guests explode straight-away from altered pressure chunks of limestone whistling through the air. The others are flopping around on the floor like beached idiots and the Contessa gasps out "Carbon dioxide for the love of Kali"—So somebody turned on the carbon dioxide tanks and I made it out of there in an aqualung—Next thing the nova heat moves in and bust the whole aquarium.

"Humm, yes, and here's another planet—"

The officer moved back dissolving most cooperative connections formed by the parasite—Self-righteous millions stabbed with rage.

"That bitch—She brings the heat three dimensional."

"The ugly cloud of smoke hung there solid female blighted continent—This turned out to be one of those association locks in Rome—I look down at the end—He quiets you, remember?—Finis. So I spit the planet from all the pictures and give him a place of residence with inflexible authority—Well, no terms—A hand has been taken—Your name fading looks like—Madison Avenue machine disconnected."

PRETEND AN INTEREST

Benway "camped" in the Board of Health. He rushed in anywhere brazenly impounding all junk. He was of course well-known but by adroit face rotation managed to piece out the odds, juggling five or six bureaus in the air thin and tenuous drifting-away cobwebs in a cold Spring wind under dead crab eyes of a doorman in green uniform carrying an ambiguous object composite of club, broom and toilet plunger, trailing a smell of ammonia and scrubwoman flesh. An undersea animal surfaced in his face, round disk mouth of cold grey gristle, purple rasp tongue moving in green saliva: "Soul Cracker," Benway decided. Species of carnivorous mollusk. Exists on Venus. It might not have bones. Time-switched the tracks through a field of little white flowers by the ruined signal tower. Sat down under a tree worn smooth by others sat there before. We remember the days as long procession of the Secret Police always everywhere in different form. In Guayaquil sat on the river bank and saw a big lizard cross the mud flats dotted with melon rind from passing canoes.

Carl's dugout turned slowly in the brown iridescent lagoon infested with sting ray, fresh water shark, arequipa, candirus, water boa, crocodile, electric eel, aquatic panther and other noxious creatures dreamed up by the lying explorers who infest bars marginal to the area.

"This inaccessible tribe, you dig, lives on phosphorescent metal paste they mine from the area. Transmute to gold straightaway and shit it out in nuggets. It's the great work."

Liver-sick gold eyes gold maps gold teeth over the *aguardiente* cooked on the Primus stove with canella and tea to cut the oil taste leaves silver sores in the mouth and throat.

"That was the year of the Rindpest when all the tourists died even the Scandinavians and we boys reduced to hawk the farter LWR—Local Wage Rate."

"No calcium in the area you understand. One blighter lost his entire skeleton and we had to carry him about in a canvas bathtub. A jaguar lapped him up in the end, largely for the salt I think."

Tin boys reduced to hawk the farter the substance and the strata —You know what that means? Carried the youth to dead water infested with consent—That was the year of The Clear—Local Wage Rate of Program Empty Body—

"Head Waters of the Baboon-asshole ... That's hanging vine country—"(The hanging vine flicked around the youth's neck molding to his skull bones in a spiraling tendril motion snapped his neck, he hangs now ejaculating as disk mouths lined with green hairs fasten to his rectum growing tendrils through his body dissolving his bones in liquid gurgles and plops into the green eating jelly.)

"This bad place you write, Meester. You win something like jellyfish."

They live in translucent jelly and converse in light flashes liquefying bones of the world and eating the jelly—boy chrysalis rotting in the sun—lazy undersea eyes on the nod over the rotting meat vegetable sleep—limestone dope out of shale and water ...

The youth is hanged fresh and bloody—Tall ceremony involves a scorpion head—lethal mating operation from the Purified Ones— No calcium in the area—Exists on Venus—It might not have bones —Ray moss of orgasm and death—Limestone God a mile away— Better than shouts: "Empty body!" Dead land here you understand waiting for some one marginal to the area.

"Deep in fucking drum country" (The naked Initiate is strapped with his back and buttocks fitted to a wooden drum. The drummer beats out orgasm message until the Initiate's flesh lights up with blue flame inside and the drum takes life and fucks the boy ((puffs of smoke across a clear blue sky ...)) The initiate awoke in other flesh the lookout different ... And he plopped into squares and patios on "Write me Meester.")

Puerto Joselito is located at the confluence of two strong brown rivers. The town is built over a vast mud flat crisscrossed by stagnant canals, the buildings on stilts joined by a maze of bridges and catwalks extend up from the mud flats into higher ground surrounded by tree columns and trailing lianas, the whole area presenting the sordid and dilapidated air of a declining frontier post or an abandoned carnival.

"The town of Puerto Joselito, dreary enough in its physical aspect, exudes a suffocating fog of smouldering rancid evil as if the town and inhabitants were slowly sinking in wastes and garbage. I found these people deep in the vilest superstitions and practices.

"Various forms of ritual execution are practiced here. These gooks have an aphrodisiac so powerful as to cause death in a total blood spasm leaving the empty body cold and white as marble. This substance is secreted by the Species Xiucutl Crustanus, a flying scorpion, during its lethal mating season in the course of which all male Xiucutl die maddened by the substance and will fly on any male creature infecting with its deadly sperm. In one ceremony the condemned are painted as gold, silver, copper and marble statues, then inoculated with Xiucutl sperm their convulsions are channeled by invisible control wires into exquisite ballets and freeze into garden fountains and park pedestals. And this is one of many ceremonies revolving on the Ceremonial Calendar kept by the Purified Ones and the Earth Mother.

"The Purified One selects a youth each month and he is walled into a crystal cubicle molded on cervical vertebrae. On the walls of the cubicle, sex programs are cut in cuneiforms and the walls revolve on silent hydraulic pressures. At the end of the month the youth is carried through the street on a flower float and ceremonially hanged in the limestone ball court, it being thought that all human dross passes from the Purified One to die in the youth at the moment of orgasm and death. Before the youth is hanged he must give his public consent, and if he cannot be brought to consent he hangs the Purified One and takes over his functions. The Purified Ones are officially immortal with monthly injections of youth substance." Quote Green-Baum Early Explorer.

Carl's outboard vibrated in a haze of rusty oil, bit a jagged piece out of the dugout canoe and sank, in iridescent brown water. Somewhere in the distance the muffled jelly sound of underwater dynamite: ("The natives are fishing"). howler monkeys like wind through leaves. The dugout twisted slowly and stopped, touching a ruined jetty. Carl got out with his Nordic rucksack and walked to the square on high ground. He felt a touch on his shoulder light as wind. A man in moldy grey police tunic and red flannel underwear one bare foot swollen and fibrous like old wood covered with white fungus, his eyes mahogany color flickered as the watcher moved in and out. He gasped out the word "Control" and slipped to the ground. A man in grey hospital pajamas eating handfuls of dirt and trailing green spit crawled over to Carl and pulled at his pants cuff. Another moves forward on brittle legs breaking little puffs of bone meal. His eyes lit up a stern glare went out in smell of burning metal. From all sides they came pawing hissing spitting: *"Papeles," "Documentes," "Passaport."*

"What is all this scandal?" The Comandante in clean khaki was standing on a platform overlooking the square. Above him was an elaborate multileveled building of bamboo. His shirt was open on a brown chest smooth as old ivory. A little pistol in red leather cover crawled slowly across his skin leaving an iridescent trail of slime.

"You must forgive my staff if they do not quite measure up to your German ideal of spit and polish . . . backward . . . uninstructed . . . each living all alone and cultivating his little virus patch . . . They have absolutely nothing to do and the solitude . . ." He tapped his forehead. His face melted and changed under the flickering arc lights.

"But there must be thirty of them about," said Carl.

The Comandante gave him a sharp look. "They are synchronized of course. They can not see or even infer each other so all think he is only police officer on post. Their lines you *sabe* never cross and some of them are already . . ."

"And some of them are already dead. This is awkward since they are not legally responsible. We try to bury them on time even if they retain intact protest reflex. Like Gonzalez the Earth Eater. We bury him three times." The Comandante held up three fingers sprouting long white tendrils. "Always he eat way out. And now if you will excuse me the soccer scores are coming in from the Capital. One must pretend an interest."

The Comandante had aged from remote crossroads of Time crawled into a metal locker and shut the door whimpering with fears, emerged in a moldy green jock-strap his body painted I-red, U-green. The Assistant flared out of a broom closet high on ammonia with a green goatee and marble face. He removed Carl's clothes in a series of locks and throws. Carl could feel his body move to the muscle orders. The Assistant put a pail over his head and screamed away into distant hammers.

The Comandante spread jelly over Carl's naked paralyzed body. The Comandante was molding a woman. Carl could feel his body draining into the woman mold. His genitals dissolving, tits swelling as the Comandante penetrated applying a few touches to face and hair—(Jissom across the mud wall in the dawn sound of barking dogs and running water—) Down there the Comandante going through his incantations around Carl's empty body. The body rose presenting an erection, masturbates in front of the Comandante. Penis flesh spreads through his body bursting in orgasm explosions granite cocks ejaculate lava under a black cloud boiling with monster crustaceans. Cold grey undersea eyes and hands touched Carl's body. The Comandante flipped him over with sucker hands and fastened his disk mouth to Carl's asshole. He was lying in a hammock of green hair, penis-flesh hammers bursting his body.

Hairs licked his rectum, spiraling tendrils scraping pleasure centers, Carl's body emptied in orgasm after orgasm, bones lit up green through flesh dissolved into the disk mouth with a fluid plop. He quivers red now in boneless spasms, pink waves through his body at touch of the green hairs.

The Comandante stripped Carl's body and smeared on green jelly nipples that pulled the flesh up and in. Carl's genitals wither to dry shit he sweeps clear with a little whisk broom to white flesh and black shiny pubic hairs. The Comandante parts the hairs and makes Incision with a little curved knife. Now he is modeling a face from the picture of his *novia* in the Capital.

"And now, how you say, 'the sound effects.'" He puts on a record of her voice, Carl's lips follow and the female substance breathed in the words.

"Oh love of my *alma!* Oh wind of morning!"

"Most distasteful thing I ever stand still for." Carl made words in the air without a throat, without a tongue. "I hope there is a *farmacia* in the area."

The Comandante looked at him with annoyance: "You could wait in the office please."

He came out putting on his tunic and strapping on a Luger.

"A drugstore? Yes I *creo*... Across the lagoon... I will call the guide."

Carl walked through a carnival city along canals where giant pink salamanders and goldfish stirred slowly, penny arcades, tattoo booths, massage parlors, side shows, blue movies, processions, floats, performers, pitchmen to the sky.

Puerto Joselito is located Dead Water. Inactive oil wells and mine shafts, strata of abandoned machinery and gutted boats, garbage of stranded operations and expeditions that died at this point of the dead land where sting rays bask in brown water and grey crabs walk the mud flats on brittle stilt legs. The town crops up from the mud flats to the silent temple of high jungle streams of clear water cut deep clefts in yellow clay and falling orchids endanger the traveler.

In a green savanna stand two vast penis figures in black stone, legs and arms vestigial, slow blue smoke rings pulsing from the stone heads. A limestone road winds through the pillars and into The City. A rack of rusty iron and concrete set in vacant lots and rubble, dotted with chemical gardens. A smell of junky hat and death about the town deadens and weight these sentences with "disgust you to see it." Carl walked through footpaths of a vast shanty town. A dry wind blows hot and cold down from Chimborazo a soiled post card in the prop blue sky. Crab men peer out of abandoned quarries and shag heaps some sort of vestigial eye growing cheek bone and a look about them as if they could take root and grow on anybody. Muttering addicts of the orgasm drug, boneless in the sun, gurgling throat gristle, heart pulsing slowly in transparent flesh eaten alive by the crab men.

Carl walked through the penis posts into a town of limestone huts. A ring of priests sat around the posts legs spread, erections pulsing to flicker light from their eyes. As he walked through the electric eyes his lips swelled and his lungs rubbed against the soft inner ribs. He walked over and touched one of the priests and a shock threw him across the road into a sewage ditch. Maize fields surrounded the town with stone figures of the Young Corn God erect penis spurting maize shoots looks down with young cruelty and innocent lips parted slightly terminal caress in the dropping eyes. The Young Corn God is led out and his robes of corn silk stripped from his body by lobster priests. A vine rope is attached to the stone penis of the Maize God. The boy's cock rises iridescent in the morning sun and you can see the other room from there by a mirror on the wardrobe . . . Well now, in the city a group of them came to this valley grow corn do a bit of hunting fishing in the river.

Carl walked a long row of living penis urns made from men whose penis has absorbed the body with vestigial arms and legs breathing through purple fungoid gills and dropping a slow metal excrement like melted solder forms a solid plaque under the urns stand about three feet high on rusty iron shelves wire mesh cubicles joined by catwalks and ladders a vast warehouse of living penis urns slowly transmuting to smooth red terra cotta. Others secrete from the head crystal pearls of lubricant that forms a shell of solid crystal over the red penis flesh.

A blast of golden horns: "The Druid priest emerges from the Sacred Grove, rotting bodies hang about him like Spanish moss. His eyes blue and cold as liquid air expand and contract eating light."

The boy sacrifice is chosen by erection acclaim. universal erection feeling for him until all pricks point to "Yes." Boy feels the "Yes" run through him and melt his bones to "Yes" stripped naked in the Sacred Grove shivering and twitching under the Hanging Tree green disk mouths sucking his last bone meal. He goes to the Tree naked on flower floats through the obsidian streets red stone buildings and copper pagodas of the Fish City stopping in Turkish Baths and sex rooms to make blue movies with youths.

The entire city is in heat during this ceremony, faces swollen with tumescent purple penis flesh. Lightning fucks flash on any street corner leave a smell of burning metal blue sparks up and down the spine. A vast bath-town of red clay cubicles over twisting geological orgasm with the green crab boys disk mouths' slow rasping tongues on spine centers twisting in the warm black ooze.

Noteworthy is the Glazing Ceremony when certain of the living urns are covered with terra cotta and baked in red brick ovens by the women who pull the soft red meat out with their penis forks and decorate house and garden with the empty urns. The urnings for the Glazing Ceremony are chosen each day by locker number from the public urn and numbers read out over the soft speaker inside the head. Helpless urns listening to the number call charge our soft terror-eating substance, our rich substance.

Now it is possible to beat the number before call by fixing the urn or after call by the retroactive fix which few are competent to practice. There is also a Ceremonial Massage in which the penis flesh is rubbed in orgasm after orgasm until Death in Centipede occurs. Death in Centipede is the severest sentence of the Insect Court and of course all urnings are awaiting sentence for various male crimes. *Pues*, every year a few experienced urnings beat the house and make Crystal Grade. When the crystal cover reaches a certain thickness the urning is exempt from ceremonial roll call and becomes immortal with nothing to do but slowly accrete a thicker cover in the Crystal Hall of Fame.

Few beat the house: a vast limestone bat. High mountain valley cut off by severest sentence of symbiotic cannibalism. So the game with one another.

"I dunno me. Only work here. Technical Sergeant."

"Throw it into wind Jack."

A pimp leans in through the Country Club window. "Visit the House of David boys and watch the girls eat shit. Makes a man feel good all over. Just tell the madam a personal friend of mine." He drops a cuneiform cylinder into the boy's hip pocket feeling his ass with lost tongue of the penis urn people in a high mountain valley of symbiotic cannibalism. The natives are blond and blue-eyed sex in occupation. It is unlawful to have orgasm alone and the inhabitants live in a hive of sex rooms and flickering blue movie cubicles. You can spot one on the cubicle skyline miles away. We all live in the blue image forever. The cubicles fade out in underground steam baths where lurk the Thurlings, malicious boys' spirits fugitive from the blue movie who mislead into underground rivers. (The traveler is eaten by aquatic centipedes and carnivorous underwater vines.)

Orgasm death spurts over the flower floats—Limestone God a mile away—Descent into penis flesh cut off by a group of them came to this game under the Hanging Tree—Insect legs under red Arctic night—He wore my clothes and terror—

The boy ejaculates blood over the flower floats. Slow vine rope drops him in a phallic fountain. wire mesh cubicles against the soft inner ribs. vast warehouse of penis and the shock threw him ten feet to smooth dirt and flak. God with erect penis spurting crystal young cruelty and foe solid. dazzling terminal caress in silent corridors of Corn God. erection feeling for descent in the morning sun feels the "Yes" from there by a mirror on you stripped naked. In the city a group of them came to this last bone meal under the Hanging Tree.

"Pretty familiar."

The Priests came through the Limestone Gates playing green flutes: translucent lobster men with wild blue eyes and shells of flexible copper. A soundless vibration in the spine touched center of erection and the natives moved toward the flute notes on a stiffening blood tube for the Centipede Rites. A stone penis body straddles the opening to the cave room of steam baths and sex cubicles and the green cab boys who go all the way on any line.

The Natives insert a grill of silver wires deep into the sinus where a crystal slowly forms. They strum the wires with insect hairs growing through flesh weaving cold cocaine sex frequencies.

From The Living God Cock flows a stream of lubricant into a limestone trough green with algae. The priests arrange the initiates into long dog-fuck lines molding them together with green jelly from the lubricant tanks. Now the Centipede skin is strapped on each body a segment and the centipede whips and cracks in electric spasms of pleasure throwing off segments kicking spasmodically uncontrolled diarrhea spurting orgasm after orgasm synchronized with the flicker lights. Carl is taken by the centipede legs and pulled into flesh jelly dissolving bones—Thick black hair sprouts through his tumescent flesh—He falls through a maze of penny arcades and dirty pictures, locker rooms, barracks, and prison flesh empty with the colorless smell of death—

Cold metal excrement on all the walls and benches, silver sky raining the metal word fallout—Sex sweat like iron in the mouth. Scores are coming in. Pretend an interest.

In a puppet booth the manipulator takes pictures of bored

insolent catatonics with eight-hour erections reading comics and chewing gum. The impresario is a bony Nordic with green fuzz on his chest and legs. "I get mine later with the pictures. I can't touch the performers. Wall of glass you know show you something interesting."

He pulls aside curtain: schoolboy room with a banner and pin-ups. on the bed naked boy puppet reading comics and chewing gum with a hypo.

Ghost your German. Spit penny arcades, tattoo booths, Nordic processions, human performers, trapeze artists. Whores of all sexes importune from scenic railways and ferris wheels where they rent cubicles, push up manhole covers in a puff of steam, pull at passing pant cuffs, careen out of the Tunnel of Love waving condoms of jissom. Old blind queens with dirty peep shows built into their eye sockets disguise themselves as penny arcades and feel for a young boy's throbbing cock with cold metal hands, sniff pensively at bicycle seats in Afghan Hound drag, Puerto Joselito is located through legs. Ghost slime sitting naked on tattoo booths, virus flesh of curse. suffocating town, this. Ways to bury explorer.

Old junky street cleaners push little red wagons sweeping up condoms and empty H caps, KY tubes, broken trusses and sex devices, kif garbage and confetti, moldy jockstraps and bloody Kotex, shit-stained color comics, dead kitten and afterbirths, jenshe babies of berdache and junky.

Everywhere the soft insidious voice of the Pitchman delayed action language lesson muttering under all your pillows "Shows all kinds masturbation and self-abuse. Young boys need it special."

DEAD FINGERS TALK

Glad to have you aboard reader, but remember there is only one captain of this subway—Do not thrust your cock out the train window or beckon lewdly with thy piles nor flush thy beat benny down the drain—(Benny is overcoat in antiquated Times Square argot)—It is forbidden to use the signal rope for frivolous hangings or to burn Nigras in the washroom before the other passengers have made their toilet—

Do not offend the office manager—He is subject to take back the keys of the shithouse—Always keep it locked so no sinister stranger sneak a shit and give all the kids in the office some horrible condition—And Mr Anker from accounting, his arms scarred like a junky from countless Wassermans, sprays plastic over it before he travails there—I stand on the Fifth Amendment, will not answer the question of the Senator from Wisconsin: "Are you or have you ever been a member of the male sex?"—They can't make Dicky whimper on the boys—Know how I take care of crooners?—Just listen to them—A word to the wise guy—I mean you gotta be careful of politics these days—Some old department get physical with you, kick him right in his coordinator—"Come see me tonight in my apartment under the school privy—Show you something interesting," said the janitor drooling green coca juice—

The city mutters in the distance pestilent breath of the cancerous librarian faint and intermittent on the warm Spring wind—

"Split is the wastings of the cup—Take it away," he said irritably —Black rocks and brown lagoons invade the world—There stands the deserted transmitter—Crystal tubes click on the message of retreat from the human hill and giant centipedes crawl in the ruined cities of our long home—Thermodynamics has won at a crawl—

"We were caught with our pants down," admits General Patterson. "They reamed the shit out of us."

Safest way to avoid these horrid perils is come over here and shack up with Scylla—Treat you right, kid—Candy and cigarettes—

Woke up in a Turkish Bath under a Johannesburg bidonville—

"Where am I you black bastards?"

"Why you junky white trash rim a shitting Nigger for an eyecup of paregoric?"

Dead bird—quail in the slipper—money in the bank—Past port and petal crowned with calm leaves she stands there across the river and under the trees—

Brains spilled in the cocktail lounge—The fat *macho* has burned down the Jai Lai bookie with his obsidian-handled .45—Shattering bloody blue of Mexico—Heart in the sun—Pantless corpses hang from telephone poles along the road to Monterrey—

Death rows the boy like sleeping marble down the Grand Canal out into a vast lagoon of souvenir post cards and bronze baby shoes—

"Just build a privy over me, boys," says the rustler to his bunk mates, and the sheriff nods in dark understanding Druid blood stirring in the winds of Panhandle—

Decayed corseted tenor sings Danny Deever in drag:

They have taken all his buttons off and cut his pants away
For he browned the colonel sleeping the man's ass is all agley
And he'll swing in 'arf a minute for sneaking shooting fey.

"Billy Budd must hang—All hands after to witness this exhibit."

Billy Budd gives up the ghost with a loud fart and the sail is rent from top to bottom—and the petty officers fall back confounded—"Billy" is a transvestite liz.

"There'll be a spot of bother about this," mutters The Master at Arms—The tars scream with rage at the cheating profile in the rising sun—

"Is she dead?"

"So who cares."

"Are we going to stand still for this?—The officers pull the switch on us," says young Hassan, ship's uncle—

"Gentlemen," says Captain Vere "I can not find words to castigate this foul and unnatural act whereby a boy's mother take over his body and infiltrate her horrible old substance right onto a decent boat and with bare tits hanging out, unfurls the nastiest colors of the spectroscope."

A hard-faced matron bandages the cunt of Radiant Jade—

"You see, dearie, the shock when your neck breaks has like an awful effect—You're already dead of course or at least unconscious or at least stunned—but—uh—well—you see—It's a *medical fact*—All your female insides is subject to spurt out your cunt the way it turned the last doctor to stone and we sold the results to Paraguay as a state of Bolivar."

"I have come to ascertain death not perform a hysterectomy," snapped the old auntie croaker munching a soggy crumpet with his grey teeth—A hanged man plummets through the ceiling of Lord Rivington's smart mews flat—Rivington rings the Home Secretary:

"I'd like to report a leak—"

"Everything is leaking—Can't stem it—*Sauve qui peut*," snaps the Home Secretary and flees the country disguised as an eccentric Lesbian abolitionist—

"We hear it was the other way around, doc," said the snide reporter with narrow shoulders and bad teeth—

The doctor's face crimsoned: "I wish to state that I have been acting physician at Dankmoor prison for thirty years man boy and bestial and always keep my nose clean—Never compromise myself to be alone with the hanged man—Always insist on the presence of my baboon assistant witness and staunch friend in any position."

Mr Gilly looks for his brindle-faced cow across the piney woods where armadillos, innocent of a cortex, frolic under the .22 of black Stetson and pale blue eyes.

"Lawd Lawd have you seen my brindle-faced cow?—Guess I'm taking up too much of your time—Must be busy doing *something* feller say—Good stand you got whatever it is—Maybe I'm asking too many questions—talking too much—You wouldn't have a rope would you?—A *hemp* rope? Don't know how I'd hold that old brindle-faced cow without a rope if I did come on her—"

Phantom riders—chili joints—saloons and the quick draw—hangings from horseback to the jeers of sporting women—black smoke on the hip in the Chink laundry—"No tickee no washee—Clom Fliday—"

Walking through the piney woods in the summer dawn, chiggers pinpoint the boy's groin with red dots—Smell of boy balls and iron cool in the mouth—

"Now I want you boys to wear shorts," said the sheriff, "Decent women with telescopes can see you—"

Whiff of dried jissom in a bandanna rises from the hotel drawer—Sweet young breath through the teeth, stomach hard as marble spurts it out in soft, white globs—Funny how a man comes back to something he left in a Peoria hotel drawer 1929—

1920 tunes drift into the locker room where two boys first time tea high jack off to "My Blue Heaven"—

In the attic of the big store on bolts of cloth we made it—

"Careful—don't spill—Don't rat on the boys."

The cellar is full of light—In two weeks the tadpoles hatch—I wonder whatever happened to Otto's boy who played the violin? A hard-faced boy patch over one eye parrot on shoulder says: "Dead men tell no tales or do they?"—He prods the skull with his cutlass and a crab scuttles out—The boy reaches down and picks up a scroll of hieroglyphs—"The map!—The map!"

The map turns to shitty toilet paper in his hands, blows across a vacant lot in East St Louis.

The boy pulls off the patch—The parrot flies away into the jungle—Cutlass turns to a machete—He is studying the map and swatting sand flies—

Junk yacks at our heels and predated checks bounce all around us in the Mayan ball court—

"Order in the court—You are accused of soliciting with prehensile piles—What have you to say in your defense?"

"Just cooling them off, judge—Raw and bleeding—Wouldn't you?"

"I want you to *smell* this bar stool," said the paranoid ex-Communist to the manic FBI agent—"Stink juice, and you may quote me has been applied by paid hoodlums constipated with Moscow goldwasser."

The man in a green suit—old English cut with two side vents and change pockets outside—will swindle the aging proprietress of a florist shop—"Old flub got a yen on for me—"

Carnival of splintered pink peppermint—"Oh Those Golden Slippers"—He sits up and looks into a cobra lamp—

"I am the Egyptian," he said looking all flat and silly.

And I said: "Really, Bradford, don't be tiresome—"

Under the limestone cave I met a man with Medusa's head in a hatbox and said "Be careful" to the customs inspector, freezed his hand forever an inch from the false bottom—

Will the gentle reader get up off his limestones and pick up the phone?—Cause of death: completely uninteresting.

They cowboyed him in the steam room—Is this Cherry Ass Gio? The Towel Boy or Mother Gillig Old Auntie of Westminster Place? Only dead fingers talk in braille—

Second run cotton trace the bones of a fix—

But is all back seat dreaming since the hitchhiker with the chewed thumb and he said: "If decided?—Could I ride with you chaps?"— (Heard about the death later in a Copenhagen bar—Told a story about crayfish and chased it with a Jew joke out behind the fear of what I tell him we all know here.) So it jumped in my throat and was all there like and ready when we were sitting under the pretties, star pretties you understand, not like me talking at all I used to talk differently. Who did?—Paris?

"Mr Bradly Mr Martin, Johnny Yenshe, Yves Martin."

Martin he calls himself but once in the London YMCA on Tottenham Court (never made out there)—Once on Dean Street in Soho—No it wasn't Dean Street that was someone else looked like Bradly—It was on some back time street, silent pockets of Mexico City—(half orange with red pepper in the sun)—and the weakness hit me and I leaned against a wall and the white spot never washed out of my glen plaid coat—Carried that wall with me to a town in Ecuador can't remember the name, remember the towns all around but not that one where time slipped on the beach—sand winds across the blood—half a cup of water and Martin looked at the guide or was it the other, the Aussie, the Canadian, the South African who is sometimes there when the water is given out and always there when the water gives out—and gave him half his own water ration with gambler fingers could switch water if he wanted to—On the street once Cavesbury Close I think it was somebody called him Uncle Charles in English and he didn't want to know the man walked away dragging one leg—

Mr Bradly Mr Martin, slotless fade-out of distant fingers in the sick morning—I told him you on tracks—couldn't reach me with the knife—couldn't switch iron—and zero time to stop—couldn't make turnstile—bad shape from death Mr Shannon no cept pay of distant fingers spilling old photo—at me with the knife and fell over the white subway—on tracks I told—The shallow water came in with the tide of washed condoms and sick sharks fed on sewage—only food for this village—swamp delta to the green sky that does not change—I—We—They—sit quietly where you made this dream—"*Finnies nous attendons une bonne chance*"—(Footnote: Last words in the diary of Yves Martin who presumably died of thirst in the Egyptian desert with three companions—Just who died is uncertain since one member of the party has not been found alive or dead and identity of the missing person is dubious—The bodies were decomposed when found, and identification was based on documents. But it seems the party was given to exchange of identifications, and even to writing in each others' diaries—Other members of the expedition were Mr Shannon, Mr Armstrong, Monsieur Pillou, Ahmed Akid the guide—)

As the series is soon ending are these experiments really necessary?

THE TICKET THAT EXPLODED

The imagery that characterizes this, the last novel of the trilogy is very different and much of the time more visually poetic than the writing in Burroughs' other novels. Creatures from Venus, especially a species of Fish Boys, swimming in their own environment and copulating innocently, Green Boys and Insect people, all belong to a world of subliminal reverie and dream, and they alternate with characters from our own and other planets, intent on control or on rejecting that control. Episodes from the drug scene recur frequently and his cut-up and fold-in technique is found everywhere. This was the period in the early sixties of his greatest absorption in literary experiment. *The Ticket That Exploded* is in many ways the most far-out of his major novels: later he would retreat from mechanical experiment and try to return closer to the atmosphere of *The Naked Lunch*, partly for commercial reasons and partly because his interest in experimenting with the accidental juxtaposition of word and incident had diminished.

Significant is the exterior matter, much of it from popular American culture of the 'forties and earlier, for instance the popular songs in 'Do You Love Me' (page 179), which he has cut into his own material to startling effect. Familiar nostalgia becomes part of a new look at sexuality, the link between fantasy, Tin Pan Alley and sex as practised. The science fiction interplanetary incidents can be read largely as metaphors for the spread of disease in modern society, much of it man-made, and the increasing control of the state over our lives. The abstract nature of the text increases the power of the prophecy, which is Orwellian both in its grim satiric humour and the accuracy of its prediction.

IN A STRANGE BED

Lykin was the first to awake—He could not remember where he was—Slowly his blue eyes blurred with exhaustion registered glowing red rocks and metallic shrubs with silver leaves that surrounded the little pool where he lay—The ghastly night flooded back into his memory—Controls of their space craft had suddenly blanked out by the intervention of an invisible alien force like an icy draught through the cabin—Not only the mechanical controls had been put out of action but their nerve centers had been paralyzed—He and Bradly the Co-pilot had sat helpless in their pressure seats for two hours while the invading force guided their ship in a sickening spiral through the poisonous cloud belts of an unknown planet—Lykin and Bradly had blacked out when they landed—How had they gotten out of the ship?—He stood up and tripped over the sleeping form of his companion naked except for the skin-tight transparent space suit that clung to his muscular body—He decided to have a quick look at the terrain before waking Bradly—He was at the bottom of a gully surrounded by red rocks of some translucent substance—He climbed out of the gully and found himself on a plateau—A fantastic landscape of multicolored rock carved like statues of molten blue lava interspaced with stalagmites of a pearly white intensity he had never experienced in his previous explorations—The sky was like a green ocean—There were four suns on the horizon around the plateau, each sun of a different color—Blue, green, red, and one (much larger than the others) a brilliant silver—The air was of a tingling clarity that seemed to support his body so that movements were incredibly precise and easily performed—He turned and started back down the gully toward the pool—He felt a click in his brain like a crystal flare and heard a silver voice: "Come stranger"—Bradly was accustomed to telepathic phenomena but this voice was unusually clear and immediate—He climbed over a large rock and saw the pool—His friend was still asleep—Beside him sat an amphibious green fish boy shimmering with water from the pool—The creature pulsed with translucent green light that flooded through the flesh in eddies—The head was a pointed dome that sprang from a slender neck on either side of which protruded gills like sensitive spongy wings—The creature was covered by a membranous substance with a network of transparent veins—The body surface was in constant motion like slow water dripping down a statue—The face was almost flat but with lips and nose sharply and beautifully delineated and huge liquid eyes above the high ridged cheekbones the delicate structure of which shone through transparent skin—The being was sitting in a cross-legged position and from its thighs jutted small silver fins of fine gauze—The slender sinuous legs ended in webbed flippers—Between the legs Lykin could see the genitals half aroused in curiosity as the fish boy stroked the head of his sleeping companion and touched the space suit with tentative jabs of its long green fingers—Lykin moved cautiously so as not to frighten the creature back into the pool—The fish boy turned and looked at him with a shy dreamy smile—An electric shiver ran up his spine and burst in crystal fish syllables: "Approach stranger—Have no fear" —The creature's mouth had not moved—Lykin moved forward with excitement tingling through his body and knelt beside the water boy who extended a dripping hand and lightly clasped his shoulder—A thrill ran through him from the contact—Underwater memory bubbles burst in his brain—He was in the alien medium, squirming in crystal rock pools and basking on edges of limestone fanned by giant ferns in the sound of dripping water—Swimming through ruined cities with the water creature twisting in slow swirls of orgasm, shooting out explosions of colored bubbles to the surface, trailing blue streamers—

Ali woke in a strange bed to find the proprietor standing over him, "Who the fuck are you and what are you doing in my apartment?" Ali flashed back to the suburban cocktail party—music from the '20s—old women doing the Charleston—and the Irishman with iron-grey hair who looked like a con cop from vaudeville—

"Easy way and a tough way to do things, kid—i can put you up for the night in this apartment—The owner is out of town and i don't *think* he'll be back before tomorrow night—"

"But Mr O'Brien said—"

"Tell O'Brien he can stay in his own precinct—This happens to be my apartment—Put on your dry goods and cut—"

Ali dressed hastily—Tucking his shirt he slipped out into the American suburb—The streets were empty and clean like after a heavy rain—At an intersection of cracked concrete boys turned slow circles on roller skates under a half-moon in the morning sky, swept by storms of color as the sun rose—Ali felt his steps lighter and lighter—He floated away on eddies of blue and green—He alighted in the clear atmosphere of a green land where every blade of grass shone as if framed in crystal—The gravity pull was light so his feet barely touched the ground as he ran along clear streams of water under dripping trees—came to a city of worn marble streets and copper domes—In the lobby of a luxury hotel page boys in elaborate uniforms assessed his financial status with experienced eyes—On the wall was a little sign:

The Nature of Begging

Need?——Lack-

Want?——Need-

Life?——Death-

Ali walked out into the main square—fish smells and dead eyes in doorways—obscene gestures of proposition—In a dark side street off the square Ali found what looked like an old chemist's shop with jars of colored liquid in the window—A little black man, body bent by a fibrous tumor came forward to meet him with a chirp of interrogation—He was wearing double lens glasses that slid down on his nose—Ali drew out the plastic bag he carried with the flattened grey membrane inside—The shopkeeper took it in smooth black fingers and held it up to the light—He gave a little chirping call and his assistant came in from shadow recesses of the shop—It was some creature like a large grasshopper with a body that changed color as he walked past the jars—The eyes were crystal lens—His penis, which was held in upright position by a long silver cord extending into the abdomen, moved in flash erections to currents of color—He held the membrane in adzes and grafting tools that fitted into his fibrous finger stumps—As he looked his body pulsed a brilliant green—The shopkeeper nodded and brought out a jar about two feet high full of a heavy white fluid—The assistant opened the envelope with a little curved knife and dropped the membrane into the jar—As Ali watched the membrane stirred like a Japanese flower and blossomed into a tiny green newt with human head—The creature opened black liquid eyes for a few seconds then curled into foetal sleep and sank to the bottom of the jar—The shopkeeper covered the jar with a cloth and put it on a dark shelf—He smiled and drew a map on the counter—Starting from the shop a dotted line led to a system of canals, a pump, two penises in orgasm, closed eyes of sleep five times—Then the dotted line led back to the shop—He looked at Ali to be sure he understood—Ali nodded and walked on the dotted line—The marble streets ended in mud—He could see a system of canals with thatched huts and gardens and tanks tended by little black men with fibrous tumors and moles from which sprouted green hairs—They looked up from their work and flashed quick smiles—A heavy smell of compost heaps and rotten ponds filled the air—As he passed over a bridge a green newt boy surfaced in a canal smiled and masturbated quickly ejaculating an iridescent fluid that glinted in the clear light—He twisted with a mocking laugh and dove out of sight in the black water—Ali walked along the canal and found himself in a maze of pumps and locks and could not find how he got there or the way out—At the bottom of this maze a man in green tattered uniform motioned him to come down pointing to an iron stairway that led out on a wooden ramp—The man stood waiting at the end of the ramp—Ali walked toward him smiling like a dog—"i am a stranger here—i am sorry if—i do not know your laws"—The guard was smiling too—a slow familiar smile like: "Perhaps you don't go into the prison if"—flashed back to customs shed in South America —Ali bent over a chair feeling quick pants of the young policeman on his naked back—The carbine leaning against one wall sharp and clear in the flash bulb of orgasm—"So"—he thought "things are not different here"—

The man led him to a shed—Inside was a pallet on the floor—Clothing hung from wooden pegs—In another room he could see levers and wheels obviously controlling the pumps and locks—The man flicked Ali's clothes—He undressed slowly dropping his pants with a wriggling motion as his cock flipped out and up—The man stood naked in green light that filtered into the shed from overhanging vines and fruit trees—He picked Ali up in his arms and kissed him—His breath had a vegetable smell slightly rotten like tropical fruit—He carried Ali to the pallet and shoved his knees up to his ears—From a shelf he took a little jar of what looked like frogs' eggs and gave off an odor of moldy proteins—He rubbed the eggs into Ali's ass—Ali could feel something coming alive in his rectum and wriggling down into his testicles—The man slid his cock in—Ali squirmed teeth bared wriggling feelers caressing his penis rubbing around nerves at the tip—The man caught his ejaculation in the jar—Tiny green frogs with sucker paws stirred in the sperm—

He stayed for five nights with the man sleeping on the pallet and eating meals of fruit from the garden and helping with the wheels and levers—At the end of five days the man gave him the jar of eggs and he went back to the shop and gave the eggs to the shopkeeper—

The shopkeeper smiled and took the other jar down from the shelf—The green newt boy, still curled in sleep, had grown until it filled the jar—The shopkeeper drew a map on the counter dotted line to a hut in the canal system—And Ali walked out carrying the jar along the line to a hut where an old man greeted him—Ali uncovered the jar—The man clapped his hands softly and made a little clucking noise—He showed Ali a series of tanks behind his hut like an elaborate cesspool, one tank draining into another—In the tanks were green newt boys in various stages and the last tank opened out into black water of the canal—The man emptied the jar into the first tank—Ali turned to walk away and felt the man's hand on his shoulder, led him back into the hut—He measured Ali's neck like a tailor and selected from a shelf two dried gills which he fitted carefully and gave to Ali in a plastic envelope—He motioned to the sky—He made a choking sound and pointed to the bag—

Ali began hustling around the square where the nobles cruised in the evening—dark street life of a place forgotten—The city was swept by waves of giant carnivorous land crabs and Ali learned to hide himself when he heard their snapping claws like radio static—Explosions of time film was another danger in the city—One evening in the square he heard a rumble like muffled thunder—Everyone running for the canals and shouting "the Studio went up"—A cloud of red nitrous fumes settled on the city—Ali, gasping and choking, remembered and reached for his plastic bag—He put the gills around his neck and dove into a wellhead carved to resemble a stone rectum—As he fell deep into the green water he could feel the gills cut into his neck—A sudden sharp taste of blood and he was breathing and swimming along an underground passage —He could see light ahead and came out into one of the open canals—

Ali woke in a strange bed—As you listen fill in with him "Who the fuck are you and what are you doing in my image track?" Ali was wide awake now and clicked "out of here." female impersonators, music back to the '20s, suburban pool halls and vaudeville voice of a grey-haired Irishman who turned over a steady stream of "easy way and a tough way to do time"—Meanwhile i had forgotten the owner in this apartment—scent of memory pictures—people gone —back tomorrow night—

"But Mr O'Brien said"—

"Tell O'Brien to stay in his own precinct—This happens to be my dawn wind in other flesh"—

Ali dressed hastily and slipped out—Board members, look, the streets are empty—Young faces melted the law, turned slow circles on roller skates—Nova Police look at the wired color sunrise—

Errand boy floating on eddies of red and green alighted in slow-motion flashes of clear atmosphere—The gravity pull was lighter—does not know the frequency of junk—marble streets and copper domes—Darkened eyes of page boys in elaborate physical skin put his financial status out in the streets—East St Louis music on chirping call—His genitals were voices out into other dressing rooms—long silver thread that extended in flash erections back and forth—switch to office of a garage—sharp desire held the membrane—

"Yes you have grafting tools—Without you i on pavement"—

The shopkeeper nodded good bye—translucent white fade-out—Sticky office spattered light on naked knives—from his face newsreels of riots moving in fast—Ali round the Board—

"What's this Japanese flower blossomed into sinking ship? You trying source of human head on screen?"

Boneless mummy curled into foetal tank—The shopkeeper covered—fade-out at dawn—Hurry up—Hands put it on a dark shelf—He smile and twist brain—starting with the shop a dotted corpse last round—the gate from two cocks orgasm—men smoking on the end of the line—sleep five times—then the dotted line—

"We been subliminated in doorways," looked at Ali to be sure he understood, "Beside you wind voices on dotted line trailed system of canals—not think the Doctor on stage"—

They looked up from their work—empty all hate faces—vapor trails writing the sky—Some boy surfaced in the canal—Iridescent harbor glinted in the stellar light—mocking laugh of absent tenants—ghost riots along the canal and found himself in a garage—Stood naked—good bye of hydraulic pumps spattered on his face—out at the bottom interrogate substance of green uniform was motioning "want it"—tentative empty flesh of KY and rectal mucus?—End of the ramp man stood waiting—gate from human form—"We been subliminated like a dog—stranger face sucked in other apparatus"—"sorry if"—

The man was smiling, flapping vapor like rusty swamp smell—flicker back to a custom shed in South America—("First we must write the ticket")—Feeling the quick pants of mummy—goosed his ass—carbine leaning against one wall—burning orgasm—wind voices beside masturbating pallet on the floor—

"Out of here, female impersonators"—

Wooden pegs in another room forgotten memory controlling the structure of his Scandinavian outhouse skin—The man flicked Ali's clothes—Prisoner pants with wriggling movement stood naked now in green mummy flesh, hanging vines and deflated skin—Death kissed him—His breath talked to the switchblade—He dropped Ali on the last parasite from the shelf before newsreels shut off—Looked like frog eggs—He was shoving the eggs—Poo Poo snickered, coming alive in his rectum like green neon—Into the prostate his slow fingers—Ali squirmed his teeth bared—The man caught his spurts like a pack of cards—He stayed for five nights in the tarnished office eating meals of fruit from color vapor—At the end of five days newsreels of riot move in fast—The eggs went back to boneless mummy— Ghost keeper smiled and fade-out at dawn—Hands of light fell apart in corpse—last jar—The shopkeeper drew a map in absent bodies—empty the canal area—Ali twisted through open shirt—He found his way to their ship in the harbor—The man travel on newsreels—Exquisite screen penis spurted again—corpse tanks— end of the line and last jar—led the Doctor on stage—Sex phantoms emptied the jars into afternoon image track—He turned to walk away and suffused the hut—people gone—Diarrhea exploded down from a shelf—

"Ali hanged after being milked, see?" made a choking noise and pointed—orgasm of a place forgotten—Corpses hang from gallows —"Land crabs"—He dissolved in smoke and crumpled cloth—

"All right, Doctor—Indications enough—i told you i would come—healed scars—The Studio went up—a cloud of nitrous Big Fix"—Ali gasped and choked and reached courage to pass without doing pictures around his neck—He could feel suddenly shut-off taste of blood and all the Garden of Delights—He could see sex scenes in the open canals of time—

DO YOU LOVE ME?

The young monk led Bradly to a cubicle—On a stone table was a tape recorder—The monk switched on the recorder and sounds of lovemaking filled the room—The monk took off his robe and stood naked with an erection—He danced around the table caressing a shadowy figure out of the air above the recorder—A tentative shape flickering in and out of focus to the sound track—The figure floated free of the recorder and followed the monk to a pallet on the floor—He went through a pantomime of pleading with the phantom who sat on the bed with legs crossed and arms folded—Finally the phantom nodded reluctant consent and the monk twisted through a parody of lovemaking as the tape speeded up: "Oh darling i love you oh oh deeper oh oh fuck the shit out of me oh darling do it again"—Bradly rolled on the floor, a vibrating air hammer of laughter shaking flesh from the bones—Scalding urine spurted from his penis—The Other Half swirled in the air above him screaming, face contorted in suffocation as he laughed the sex words from throat gristle in bloody crystal blobs—His bones were shaking, vibrated to neon—Waves of laughter through his rectum and prostate and testicles giggling out spurts of semen as he rolled with his knees up to his chin—

All the tunes and sound effects of *"Love"* spit from the recorder permutating sex whine of a sick picture planet: Do you love me?—But i exploded in cosmic laughter—Old acquaintance be forgot?—Oh darling, just a photograph?—Mary i love you i do do you know i love you through?—On my knees i hoped you'd love me too—I would run till i feel the thrill of long ago—Now my inspiration but it won't last and we'll be just a photograph—i've forgotten you then? i can't sleep, Blue Eyes, if i don't have you—Do i love her? i love you i love you many splendored thing—Can't even eat—Jelly on my mind back home—'Twas good bye deep in the true love—We'll never meet again, darling, in my fashion—Yes eyes ever shining that made me my way—Always it's a long trip to Tipperary—Tell Laura i love my blue heaven—Get up woman up off your big fat earth out into cosmic space with all your diamond rings—Do you do you do you love me?—Lovey lovey dovey brought to mind? What? Do you love me with a banjo?—Please don't be angry—i

wonder who—If i had learned to love you every time i felt blue—
But someone took you out of the stardust of the skies—Your charms
travel to remind me of you—together again—forgotten you eat—
Don't know how i'll make it baby—blue eyes the color of—Do you
love me? Love is *para olvidar*—Tell Laura oh jelly love you—i
can't—Got you under my skin on my mind—But i'll always be true
to my blue heaven—Love Mary?—Fuck the shit out of me—Get up
off your big fat rusty-dusty—It's a long way to go, St Louis woman
—prospect of red mesas out to space—Do you love me?—Do you
love void and scenic railways back home?? And do you love me with
a banjo permutated through do you love me?—i wonder who
permutated the structure every time i felt blue—But that was ferris
wheels clicking in the stardust of the sky—on perilous tracks—i had
a dog his name was Bill aworking clouds of *Me*—Tearing his insides
apart—Need a helping hand?—understanding out of date—Find
someone else at this time of day? Torch cutting through the eats?—

Don't know how i'll make it, baby—Electric fingers removed
"*Love*"—Do you love me?—Love is red sheets of pain hung oh oh
baby oh jelly—The guide slipped off his jelly—I've got you under
my skin pulsing red light—Clouds of *Me* always be true to you—
Hula hoops of color formed always be true to you darling in my
Bradly—Weak and torn i'll hurry to my blue heaven as i sank in
suffocation panic of rusty St Louis woman—With just a photograph, Mary, you know i love you through sperm—Contraction
turnstile hoped you'd love me too—Orgasm floated arms still i feel
the thrill of slow movement but it won't last—i've forgotten you
then?—i love you i love you and bones tearing his insides apart for
the ants to eat—Jelly jelly jelly shifting color orgasm back home—
Scratching shower of sperm that made cover of the board books—
It's a long way to Tipperary—soft luminous spurts to my blue
heaven—Pieces of cloud drifted through all the tunes from blue—
Exploded in cosmic laughter of cable cars . . . Me?—Oh, darling, i
love you in constant motion—i love you i do—You led Bradly into
a cubicle on my knees—love floating in a slow vertigo of you—
perilous tracks where wind whistled long ago—i can't sleep, baby,
skin pulling loose if i don't have you—a peg like many splendored
thing—i've got you deep in the guides body enclosed darling in *my*
fashion—yes cool hands on his naked flesh my way—evening intestines of the other—Tell Laura i love her sucked through pearly
genital woman off your big fat shower of sperm—Diamond rings
spurt out of you—Should be brought to mind—Ejaculated bodies
without a cover—

I learned to love you, pale adolescents—Someone took you out of the creature charms—We'll travel weak and torn by pain together—Silver films in the blood *para olvidar*—Tell Laura black fish movement of food love you—i can't sleep reflected in obsidian penis—Follow the swallow and released dream flesh in Isle of Capri—The truth in sunlight, Mary—memory riding the wind— It's a long way to go—someone walking—mountain wind—

Do i love you?—Crumpled cloth body ahoy—But remember the red open shirt flapping wind from you so true—Do you love me?— Vapor trails writing all the things you are—The great wind revolving what you could have—Indications in the harbor muttering blackbird—bye bye—Who's sorry now?—This time of day vultures in the street—'Twas good bye on vacant lots—weeds growing through broken road—smell of healed and half-healed scars—all the little things you used to do on a bicycle built for little time so i'll say: "You on sidewalk"—if you were the only girl in green neon, your voices muttering in the dog rotation—Dollar baby, how cute can you be in desolate underbrush? You were meant for me? Battered phonograph talk-face—I'm just a vagabond pass without —Can play the game as well as you, darling—train whistle open shirt flapping the cat and the fiddle—i am biologic from a long way to go—Nights are long with the St Louis suburb—Music seems to whisper Louise Mary on the pissoirs—i had a dog his name was Bill—(In other flesh open shirt flapping) on the railroad—He went away—Many names murmur—Someone walking—won't be two— i'm half crazy all for the love of *"Good Night"*—Shadow voices belong to me—Found a million acoustic qualities couldn't reach in a five-and-ten-cent store—Naked boy on association line but you'll find someone else this time of day—

The levanto dances who's sorry now?—Hy diddle diddle the cat and the fiddle—Long way to Tipperary—fading khaki pants— Since you went away i see that moon hit the road into space—Do you love me Waltzing Matilda rock around railroad back home? lovey lovey dovey St Louis Women after hours—Do you love me with a banjo permutated Dead Man Blues?—If you don't i wonder who permutated the structure—Everybody love my baby—Lover man, that was ferris wheels clicking in a loverly bunch—solitude through the cables—turkey in the straw—

"BAR MAID WATCH THE EATS!!"—

Don't Know how i'll make it—one meat ball—Pull my daisy ding-dong love—Do you love me, love sheets?—Everybody's gonna have religion oh baby oh jelly—The guide slipped Paul

under my skin pulsing red light—pallet on the floor darling Bradly
—weak and torn sank in bones and shit of rusty St Louis woman—
when the saints go marching through all the popular tunes waiting
for the sunrise in cosmic laughter of cable cars—the Sheik of Araby
in constant motion—Blue moon—Margie—ice cream on my knees
—Love floating in perilous tracks—

Do you love me, Nancy of the laughing sex words?—Still i feel
the thrill of your charms vibrated to neon—giggling out all the little
things you used to do—'Twas good bye on the line of Bradly's
naked body—love skin on a bicycle built for two—like a deflated
balloon—Your cool hands on his naked dollars, baby—You were
meant for me sucked through pearly genital face—Still i feel the
thrill of you spurting out through the orgasm seems to whisper:
"Louise, Mary, swamp mud"—In the blood little things you used
to do—recorder jack-off—Substitute mine—Bye Bye body halves
—i'm half crazy all for the love of color circuits—Do i love you in
throat gristle? Ship ahoy but remember the red river body explode
sex words to color—Do you love me?—Take a simple tape from all
the things you are—Moanin' low my sweet 8276 all the time—
Who's sorry now in the underwater street? 'Twas good bye on color
bicycle built for response in the other nervous system—

I'm just a vagabond of the board books—written in can play the
game as well as you—(That is color written the two compete)—Do
i love you? i wonder—loose? if i don't have to? a peg like every time
i felt blue? It's a long way through channels—Who's sorry now?
chartered that memory street—Bye Bye—bodies empty—ash from
falling tracks—Sweet man is going to go—Keep raining the throat
designed to water—Remember every little thing you used to do—
fish smell and dead—Know the answer? vacant lot the world and
i were the only boy—jelly jelly in the stardust of the sky—i've got
you deep inside of me enclosed darling in my fashion—Yes, baby,
electric fingers removed flesh my way—Sheets of pain hung oh
baby oh i love her sucked through pearly jelly—i've got you under
big fat scratching clouds of me—Always be true to your diamond
rings—Tell Laura black slow movement but it won't last—i've
forgotten you then? Decay breathing? Black lust tearing his insides
apart for ants? Love Mary?—The rose of memory shifting color
orgasms back home—Good bye—It's a long way to go—Someone
walking—Won't be two—

OPERATION REWRITE

The "Other Half" is the word. The "Other Half" is an organism. Word is an organism. The presence of the "Other Half" a separate organism attached to your nervous system on an air line of words can now be demonstrated experimentally. One of the most common "hallucinations" of subjects during sense withdrawal is the feeling of another body sprawled through the subject's body at an angle .. yes quite an angle it is the "Other Half" worked quite some years on a symbiotic basis. From symbiosis to parasitism is a short step. The word is now a virus. The flu virus may once have been a healthy lung cell. It is now a parasitic organism that invades and damages the lungs. The word may once have been a healthy neutral cell. It is now a parasitic organism that invades and damages the central nervous system. Modern man has lost the option of silence. Try halting your sub-vocal speech. Try to achieve even ten seconds of inner silence. You will encounter a resisting organism that *forces you to talk*. That organism is the word. In the beginning was the word. In the beginning of what exactly? The earliest artifacts date back about ten thousand years give a little take a little and "recorded"—(or prerecorded) history about seven thousand years. The human race is said to have been on set for 500,000 years. That leaves 490,000 years unaccounted for. Modern man has advanced from the stone ax to nuclear weapons in ten thousand years. This may well have happened before. Mr Brion Gysin suggests that a nuclear disaster in what is now the Gobi desert wiped out all traces of a civilization that made such a disaster possible. Perhaps their nuclear weapons did not operate on the same principle as the ones we have now. Perhaps they had no contact with the word organism. Perhaps the word itself is recent about ten thousand years old. What we call history is the history of the word. In the beginning of *that* history was the word.

The realization that something as familiar to you as the movement of your intestines the sound of your breathing the beating of your heart is also alien and hostile does make one feel a bit insecure at first. Remember that you can separate yourself from the "Other Half" from the word. The word is spliced in with the sound of your intestines and breathing with the beating of your heart. The first step is to record the sounds of your body and start splicing them in yourself. Splice in your body sounds with the body sounds of your best friend and see how familiar he gets. Splice your body sounds in with air hammers. Blast jolt vibrate the "Other Half" right out into the street. Splice your body sounds in with anybody or anything. Start a tapeworm club and exchange body sound tapes. Feel right out into your nabor's intestines and help him digest his food. *Communication must become total and conscious before we can stop it.*

"The Venusian invasion was known as 'Operation Other Half,' that is, a parasitic invasion of the sexual area taking advantage, as all invasion plans must, of an already existing fucked-up situation ('My God what a mess.' The District Supervisor reminded himself that it was forbidden not only to express contempt for the natives but even to entertain such feelings. Bulletin 2323 is quite explicit on this point. Still he was unable to expunge a residual distaste for protoplasmic life deriving no doubt from his mineral origins. His mission was educational ... the natives were to be scanned out of patterns laid down by the infamous 5th Colonists. Soon after his arrival he decided that he was confronting not only an outrageous case of colonial mismanagement but attempted nova as well. Reluctantly he called in the Nova Police. The Mission still functioned in a state of siege. Armed with nuclear weapons the 5th Colonists were determined to resist alterations. It had been necessary to issue weapons to his personnel. There were of course incidents .. casualties ... A young clerk in the Cultural Department declared himself the Angel of Death and had to be removed to a rest home. The DS was contemplating the risky expedient of a 'miracle' and the miracle he contemplated was *silence*. Few things are worse than a 'miracle' that doesn't come off. He had of course put in an application to the Home Office underlining the urgency of his case contingent on the lengths to which the desperate 5th Colonists might reasonably be expected to go. Higher command had been vague and distant. He had no definite assurance that the necessary equipment would arrive in time. Would he have 3D in time?)—The human organism is literally consisting of two halves from the beginning word and all human sex is this unsanitary arrangement whereby two entities attempt to occupy the same three-dimensional coordinate points giving rise to the sordid latrine brawls which have characterized a planet based on 'the Word,' that is, on separate flesh engaged in endless sexual conflict—The Venusian Boy-Girls under Johnny Yen took over the Other Half, imposing a sexual blockade on the planet—(It will be readily understandable that a program of systematic frustration was necessary in order to sell this crock of sewage as Immortality, the Garden of Delights, and *love*—)

"When the Board of Health intervened with inflexible authority, 'Operation Other Half' was referred to the Rewrite Department where the original engineering flaw of course came to light and the Venusian invasion was seen to be an inevitable correlate of the separation flesh gimmick—At this point a tremendous scream went up from the Venusians agitating to retain the flesh gimmick in some form—They were all terminal flesh addicts of course, motivated by pornographic torture films, and the entire Rewrite and Blueprint Departments were that disgusted ready to pull the switch out of hand to 'It Never Happened'—'Unless these jokers stay out of the Rewrite room'—

"The Other Half was only one aspect of Operation Rewrite— Heavy metal addicts picketed the Rewrite Office, exploding in protest—Control addicts prowled the streets trying to influence waiters, lavatory attendants, *clochards*, and were to be seen on every corner of the city hypnotizing chickens—A few rich control addicts were able to surround themselves with latahs and sat on the terraces of expensive cafés with remote cruel smiles unaware i wrote last cigarette—

"My God what a mess—Just keep all these jokers out of the Rewrite Room is all"—

So let us start with one average, stupid, representative case: Johnny Yen the Other Half, errand boy from the death trauma— Now look i'm going to say it and i'm going to say it slow—Death *is* orgasm *is* rebirth *is* death in orgasm *is* their unsanitary Venusian gimmick *is* the whole birth death cycle of action—You got it?—Now do you understand who Johnny Yen is? The Boy-Girl Other Half strip tease God of sexual frustration—Errand boy from the death trauma—His immortality depends on the mortality of others—The same is true of *all* addicts—Mr Martin, for example, is a heavy metal addict—His life line is the human junky—The life line of control addicts is the control word—That is these so-called Gods can only live without three-dimensional coordinate points by forcing three-dimensional bodies on others—Their existence is pure vampirism—They are utterly unfit to be officers—Either they accept a rewrite job or they are all broken down to lavatory attendants, irrevocably committed to the toilet—

All right, back to the case of Johnny Yen—one of many such errand boys—Green Boy-Girls from the terminal sewers of

Venus—So write back to the streets, Johnny, back to Ali God of Street Boys and Hustlers—Write out of the sewers of Venus to neon streets of Saturn—Alternatively Johnny Yen can be written back to a green fish boy—There are always alternative solutions—Nothing is true—Everything is permitted—

"*No hassan i sabbah—we want flesh—we want junk—we want power—*"

"That did it—Dial *police*"—

Note: Hassan i Sabbah, the 'Old Man of the Mountain', was historically Hassan III (1157–1221), also known as Hasan ibn Suffah founder of the Shi'ite sect of the Assassins, a fanatical Moslem sect, dedicated to ideological murder and total control of men and minds, not unlike the Ayatollah Khomeini in modern times. His best remembered dictum, 'Nothing is true, everything is permissible', appealed strongly to Burroughs and might well have come out of 1984.

COMBAT TROOPS IN THE AREA

As the shot of apomorphine cut through poisons of Minraud he felt a tingling burning numbness—his body coming out of deep freeze in the Ovens—Then viscera exploded in vomit—The mold of his body cracked and he stepped free—a slender green creature, his hands ended in black claws covered with fine magnetic wires that extended up the inner arm to the elbow—He was wearing a gas mask to breathe carbon dioxide of enemy planet—antennae ears tuned to all voices of the city, each voice classified on a silent switchboard—green disk eyes with pupils of a pale electric blue—body of a hard green substance like flexible jade—back brain and spine burned with blue sparks as messages crackled in and out—

"Shift body halves—Vibrate flesh—Cut tourists"—

The instructions were filed on transparent sheets waiting sound formation as he slid them into mind screens of the planet—He put on his broken body like an overcoat—Silent and purposeful under regulating center of the back brain, he went into a bar and stood at the pinball machine, his hard green core sinking into the other players writing the resistance message with magnetic wires—The machine clicked and tilted in his hands, electric purpose cutting association lines—Enemy plans exploded in a burst of rapid calculations—Vast insect calculating machine of the enemy flashed the warning—

"Combat troops in the area"—

Combat troops to fight the Insect People of Minraud for control of this planet—Crab guards gathered around the machine, sliding forward to feel with white-hot claws for the human spots of weakness opened up by The Green Boy of the Divide Line—The crab guard was not finding the spots—He pressed closer breathing the dry heat of Minraud, while flying scorpion men sank stingers into empty flesh, injecting the oven poison—Too late the crab guard saw the jade body and the disk eyes pounding deep into his nerve centers—The eyes converged in a single beam forcing the guard back like a fire hose—The pressure suddenly shut off as the eyes vibrated in air hammer synchronization—pounded the guard to writhing fragments—

The Scorpion Electricals buzzed away screaming—His converging eye beams exploded them in the air and they fell in a shower of blue sparks—He was standing over the green boy spitting words into his nervous system—

"Show me your controller—quickly or i kill"—

The green boy nodded—An old woman appeared on screen spitting phosphorescent hate, screaming for her shattered guard— the Lord of Time surrounded by files and calculating machines, word and image bank of a picture planet—It was over in a few stuttering seconds—Under vibrating pounding eyebeams that cut flesh and bone with electric needles her image blurred and exploded in a burst of nitrous film smoke—where she had stood a vast low-pressure area—winds of the earth through archives of Time as film and newspapers shredded to dust in a tornado of years and centuries—

"Word falling—Photo falling—Time falling—Break through in Grey Room"—Combat troops antennae crackling static orders poured inflexible violence along the middle line of body—took the planet in a few seconds cutting virus troops with stuttering light guns—galactic shock troops who never colonize—clicking tilting through pinball machines of the earth—lighting up the Board Books and dictating message of total resistance—

"Shift linguals—Cut word lines—Vibrate tourists—Free doorways—Pinball led streets—Word falling—Photo falling— Break through in Grey Room—Towers, open fire"—

Electric static orders poured through nerve circuits in stuttering seconds—

"Body halves off—appropriate instrument pinball color circuits—Sex words exploded in photo flash—Nitrous fumes drift from pinball machines and penny arcades of the world—Photo falling—Break through in grey room—Click, tilt, vibrate green goo planet—Towers, open fire—Explode word lines of the earth— Combat troops show board books and dictate out symbol language of virus enemy—Fight, controlled body prisoners—Cut all tape— Vibrate board books with precise shared meals—scraps—remains of 'Love' from picture planet—Get up off your rotting combos lit up by a woman—Word falling—Free doorways—Television mind destroyed—Break through in Grey Room—'Love' is falling—Sex word is falling—Break photograph—Shift body halves—Board books flashed idiot Mambo on 'their dogs'—with pale adolescents of love from Venus—Static orders pour in now—Venus camera writing all the things you are—Planet in 'Love' is a wind U turn back—Isn't time left—Partisans showing board books in Times

Square in Piccadilly—Tune and sound effects vibrating sex whine along the middle line of body—Explode substitute planet—Static learned every board book symbol with inflexible violence—color writing you out of star dust—took board books written in prisoner bodies—cutting all tape—Love Mary?—picture planet—Its combos lit up a woman—'Love' falling—Flesh falling—Photo falling—Image falling"—

Controllers of the Green Troops moved in now—Light-years in eyes that write character of biologic alteration—Vampires fall to dust—Crumpled cloth bodies on the glass and metal streets—The Venusians are relegated to terminal sewage deltas—The Uranians back to the heavy cold mist of mineral silence—Dry heat and insect forms close round the people of Mercury—Consequences and alternatives flash on off—Accept Rewrite or return to conditions you intended to impose on this colony—No appeal from eyes that see light-years in advance—Explode substitute giving orders—Green metal antennae crackling static in the transient hotels—cutting virus troops with static noises—Galactic shock troops break through moving in fast on music poured through nerve circuits—stuttering distant events—In a few seconds body halves off from St Louis—Ghost writing shows board books—Vibrate dead nitrous film streets—Fight, controlled body prisoners—Cut flute through board books—Scraps to go, doctor—cleaving new planet—Get up, please—Television mind destroyed—Love is falling from this paper punching holes in photograph—Shift body halves in the womb—a long way from St Louis—total resistance—cobblestone language with inflexible violence—Combat troops clicked the fair—a Barnum Bailey world—Word falling—Time falling—The fade-out—Good bye parasite invasion with weakness of dual structure, as the shot of apomorphine exploded the mold of their claws in vomit—Insect People Of Minraud preparing exact copy of scorpions crawling over his face—preparing exact copy of Bradly's body molded in two halves—Green boy slips the mold on during sex scene—Remember strange bed? mold heated up to 10,000 Fahrenheit—His street boy senses clicked an oven in transient flesh—Call in the Old Doctor—heavy twilight—A cigarette deal?—Kiki stepped forward—

"True? I can't feel it"—

"Yes, smiling"—

The man was only a face—Sex tingled in the shadow of street cafés—On the bed felt his cock stiffen—open fly—stroked it with gentle hands—Healed scars still pulsing in empty flesh of KY and

189

rectal mucus—flicker ghost only a few years older than Kiki—
Outskirts of the city, masturbated under thin pants—orgasms of
memory fingers—Blue twilight fell on his Scandinavian skin—
shadow beside him, KY on his slow fingers—As you listen fill in
with a pull—teeth ground together the image track—Muscles relax
and contract—Kicked his feet in the air—steady stream of drum
music in his head—forgotten scent of pubic hairs in other flesh with
loud snores—

"Without you i on pavement—Saw a giant crab snapping—Help
me—Sinking ship—You trying Ali God of Street Boys on screen?—
So we turn over knife wind voices covered—From the radio inter-
stellar sirocco"—

The room was full of white pillow flakes blowing out from a
conical insect nest of plaster—Scorpions crawled from the nest
snapping their claws—He felt the conical nests attached to his
side—white scorpions crawling over his face—He woke up screaming: "Take them off me—Take them off me"—

The dream still shuddered in milky dawn light—Kiki lay naked
in a strange bed—His street boy senses clicked back: standing in a
doorway his collar turned up against the cold Spring wind that
whistled down from the mountains—The man stopped under a
blue arc light in the heavy twilight—He put a cigarette to his mouth,
tapped his pockets, and turned his hands out—Kiki stepped
forward with his lighter extended smiling—The man was only a few
years older than Kiki—thin face hidden by the shadow of his
hat—They had sandwiches and beer at a booth where a kerosene
lamp flickered in the mountain wind—The man called a cab that
seemed to leave the ground on a long ride through rubbly outskirts
of the city—It was a neighborhood of large houses with gardens—
In the apartment Kiki sat down on the bed and felt his cock stiffen
under thin pants as the man stroked it with gentle abstract fingers—
Blue twilight fell through the room—He could only see a shadow
beside him—Kiki took the man's hand and closed the fist and
shoved a finger in and out—

"I fuck you?"—

"Si"—

The man put on a tape of Arab drum music—Kiki had been a
week in the cold streets dodging the police who were everywhere
checking papers after the manner of their species—He dropped his
worn pants and stood naked—His cock slid out of the foreskin
pulsing—As he sat down again on the bed a drop of lubricant
squeezed out and glistened in the faint bluish light—The man sat

down beside him and kissed him feeling his cock—Kiki pushed the man back on the bed—He found a tube of KY on the night table—On his knees above the dark shadowy figure he rubbed the KY on his cock—He put his hands under the man's knees and shoved them up to the ears and rubbed the KY into the man's ass with a slow circular pull—Teeth ground together as Kiki slid his cock in feeling the muscle relax and contract in spasmodic milking movements—The man kicked his feet in the air—"*Juntos*" said Kiki—He began to count and at the count of ten they came together—Kiki fell into a light sleep the drum music in his head—He woke up to find the man lighting a candle—"Cigarette?"—The man brought a package of cigarettes and lay down beside him—Kiki blew the smoke down through his pubic hairs and said "Abracadabra" as his cock rose out of the smoke—He rolled the man over, then pulled him up onto his knees and fucked him to the music—He draped himself over the man's back with loud snores—He was in fact very tired after the street, yawned as he crawled under the covers and snuggled against the man's back—

The man was not in bed beside him but seated at a table crumpled forward his head sunk into the collar of a heavy silk dressing gown—A muffled sound like muttering cloth drifted from the crumpled form—Kiki got out of bed naked and touched the man's shoulder—There was nothing there but cloth that fell in a heap on the floor leaking grey dust—Kiki found the man's wallet and slipped out the large bills—The man's clothes were too large so he put on his own clothes and went out shutting the door softly—He listened for a moment then stepped quickly down the stairs—In the doorway he stumbled over a pile of rags that smelled of urine and pulque—empty streets and from radios in empty houses a twanging sound of sirens that rose and fell vibrating the windows—The air was full of luminous grey flakes falling softly on crumpled cloth bodies—The street led to an open square—He could see people running now suddenly collapse to a heap of clothes—The grey flakes were falling heavier, falling through all the buildings of the city—Cold fear touched his street boy senses—A vista of phosphorescent slag heaps opened before him—

On the smoldering metal he saw a giant crab claws snapping—A voice in Kiki's head said "Stand aside" as Ali God of Street Boys from the neon cities of Saturn moved in—Dodging from side to side over the snapping claws his plasma knife tore a great rent in the crab's body that leaked black rusty oil—Ali doubled back from above and behind hitting the crab at the base of its brain—The claws flew off—The eyes went out—There was nothing but a smear of oil on the pavement—

"This way—To the Towers"—Ali pointed to an office building that dominated the square—Kiki ran toward the building covered now by tower fire—Hands pulled him into a doorway—On the roof of the building was a battery of radios and movie cameras that vibrated to static—A green creature with metal claw hands was giving orders to a group of partisans who manned the gun tower—From the radio poured a metallic staccato voice—

"Photo falling—Word Falling—Break through in Grey Room—Towers, open fire"—

Totally green troops in the area, K9—You are assigned to organize combat divisions at the Venusian Front—appalling conditions—total weapons—Without inoculation and training your troops will be paralyzed by enemy virus and drugs—then cut to pieces in the pain-pleasure signal switch—The enemy uses a vast mechanical brain to dictate the use and rotation of weapons—Precise information from virus invasion marks areas of weakness in the host and automatically brings into effect the weapons and methods of attack calculated always of course with alternate moves—They can turn on total pain of the Ovens—This is done by film and brain wave recordings mangled down to a form of concrete music—A twanging sound very much like positive feedback correlated with the Blazing Photo from Hiroshima and Nagasaki—They can switch on electric pleasure leading to death in orgasm—(The noose is a weapon—The weapon of Kali)—They can alternate pain and pleasure at supersonic speed like a speed up tough and con cop routine—

You are to infiltrate, sabotage and cut communications—Once machine lines are cut the enemy is helpless—They depend on elaborate installations difficult to move or conceal—encephalographic and calculating machines film and TV studios, batteries of tape recorders—Remember you do not have to organize similar installations but merely to put enemy installations out of action or take them over—A camera and two tape recorders can cut the lines laid down by a fully equipped film studio—The ovens and the orgasm death tune in can be blocked with large doses of apomorphine which breaks the circuit of positive feedback—But do not rely too heavily on this protection agent—They are moving to block apomorphine by correlation with nausea gas that is by increasing the nausea potential—And always remember that you are operating under conditions of guerrilla war—Never attempt to hold a position

under massive counterattack—"Enemy advance we retreat"—
Where?—The operation of retreat on this level involves shifting
three-dimensional coordinate points that is time travel on association lines—Like this:

sunlight through the dusty window and sat down on the sofa the
pearly drops of the basement workshop .. "You're pearling."
flaking plaster .. you finish me John's face grey and whispy spurts
of semen across off ".. long ago boy a soft blue flame in the dusty
floor the static still in image speed of light his eyes as he bent over
his ears rose shadows on the ten years the pool hall the crystal radio
set young flesh .." John is it true on Market St Bill leaned touching
dials and "if we were ten light-years away we across the table and
wires with gentle precise fingers could see ourselves here John
goosed him with "I'm trying to fix it so we can both ten years from
now? a cue and he collapsed listen at once." "Yes it's true." "Well
couldn't we across the table laughing .. he was opening a headphone on the bench travel in time?" they had not seen much with
a screwdriver .. "It's more complicated than you think." of each
other in the two heads so close John's "well time is past ten years
.. Bill had been fluffy blond hair brushed Bill's getting dressed and
away at school and later forehead. undressed eating sleeping not the
Eastern University. John had "Here hold this phone to your ear"
actions but the words became a legendary figure Do you hear
anything?" "What we say about what we living by gambling .. he
used "yes static." do. Would there be any time if systems for dice
and horses based on "Good" John cupped the other phone we
didn't say a mathematical theories .. to his ear. anything?" "Maybe
not. Maybe that St Louis summer night outside smell the two boys
at poised listening coal gas the moon red and out through the dusty
window first step" smoky .. they walked through empty across
back yards and ash pits .. "Yes if you could learn park frogs
croaking" "John the tinkling metal music of space to listen and not
lived in a loft over a Bill felt a prickle in his lips talk" .. over the
hills and speak-easy reached by that spread to the groin. far away
.. sunlight through outside wooden stairs .. sunlight through the
dusty window of the basement workshop John's face grey whispy a
soft blue flame in his eyes as he bent over the crystal radio set
touching dials and wires with gentle precise fingers.

"I'm trying to fix it so we can both listen at once."

He was opening a headphone on the bench with a screwdriver the
two heads so close John's fluffy blond hair brushed Bill's forehead.

"Here hold this phone to your ear. Do you hear anything?"

"Yes static."

"Good."

John cupped the other phone to his ear. The two boys sat poised listening out through the dusty window across back yards and ash pits the tinkling metal music of space. Bill felt a prickle in his lips that spread to the groin. He shifted on the wooden stool.

"John what is static exactly?"

"I've told you ten times. What's the use in my talking when you don't listen?"

"I hear music" .. faint intermittent 'Smiles.' Bill moving in time to the music brushed John's knee .. "Let's do it shall we?"

"All right."

John put the headphones down on the bench. There was a storage room next to the work shop. Bill opened the door with a key. He was the only one who had this key. smell of musty furniture .. smears of phosphorous paste on the walls .. Bill turned on a lamp a parchment shade with painted roses .. chairs upside down on a desk a leather sofa cracked and shiny. The boys stripped to their socks and sat down on the sofa.

"You're pearling."

spurts of semen across the dusty floor static still in his ears rose shadows on young flesh ..

"John is it true if we were ten light-years away we could see ourselves here ten years from now?"

"Yes it's true."

"Well couldn't we travel in time?"

"It's more complicated than you think."

"Well time is getting dressed and undressed eating sleeping not the actions but the *words* .. What we *say* about what we do. Would there be any time if we didn't say anything?"

"Maybe not. Maybe that would be the first step .. yes if we could learn to listen and not talk."

Over the hills and far away sunlight through the dusty window a soft blue flame in his eyes as he bent over .. his ears rose shadows on the crystal radio set .. He shifted on the wood the dusty window .. "Come up for a while" he said .. stool semen on the sofa a soft blue flame in "All right" Bill felt a tightening "John what is static exactly?" his eyes as he bent over in his stomach .. it was a room "I've told you ten times what his ears rose shadows on with rose wallpaper use of my saying anything. the crystal radio set partitioned off like a stage set when you don't listen?" .. "I'm trying to fix it so we can both .. Bill saw a work 'I hear music' ten years from

now listen at once" he was bench tools and radio faint intermittent
'Smiles' .. opening travel in time sets from the light John Bill
moving in time to the with a screwdriver" hold this turned on ..
the music brushed John's knee. phone to your ear the words do you
door he had painted Bill turned to John smiling hear anything? ..
we didn't say to his ear a number like "Let's do it shall we?"
anything maybe not maybe the two hotel door No. "All right" boys
poised listening out through 18 .. "Sit down" John took out a John
put down the headphones on the dusty window would cigarette
from a box on the bench. be the first step across back yards and ash
pits the night table there was storage room next to the yes if you
could it was rolled in brown workshop. Bill opened learn the tinkling metal music of space paper .. "What is it?" the door with a key
.. "That static gave me a hard-on." "Marijuana .. ever try it" "No"
he was the only one who had like something touched me he lit the
cigarette and the key. The smell and he brought his finger up ..
passed to Bill "Take it all musty furniture smears in three jerks
sitting with their the way down and hold phosphorous paste on the
walls arms around each other's that's right .." Bill Bill turned on
a lamp parchment shoulders looking down at feet a prickling in his
shade with painted roses the stiffening flesh flower smell lips .. the
wallpaper chairs upside down on a desk of young hard-ons "Let's
see who can seemed to glow leather sofa cracked and shiny shoot
the farthest" then he was laughing the boys stripped to their socks
they stood up Bill hit the wall until he doubled "I'm trying to fix
it so we can both ten years from now listen at once." opening travel
in time with a screwdriver "Hold this phone to your ear. the words
Do you hear anything?" We didn't say to his ear anything maybe
not maybe the two boys poised listening out through the dusty
window would be the first step across back yards and ash pits yes
if you could learn the tinkling metal music of space "That static
gave me a hard-on like something touched me" he brought his
finger up in three jerks sitting with arms around each other's
shoulders looking down at the stiffening flesh flower smell of young
hard-ons.

"Let's see who can shoot the farthest."

They stood up. Bill hit the wall .. the pearly drops .. flaking
plaster ..

"you finish me off" ...

long ago boy image .. speed of light .. ten years .. the pool hall
on Market St .. Bill leaned across the table for a shot and John
goosed him with a cue he collapsed across the table laughing. They

had not seen much of each other in the past ten years. Bill had been away at school and later at an Eastern University. John had become a legendary figure around town who lived by gambling he used a system for dice and horses based on a mathematical theory which accounted for the only constant factor in gambling: winning and losing comes in streaks. So double up when you are winning and fold up when you are losing .. St Louis summer night outside the pool hall smell of coal gas the moon red they walked through an empty park frogs croaking John lived over a speak-easy by the river .. a loft reached by outside wooden stairs.

"Come up for a while," he said.

"All right." Bill felt a tightening in his stomach. A room with rose wallpaper had been partitioned off from the loft like a stage set. As John turned on the light Bill saw a work bench tools and radio sets in the loft. On the door to the bedroom John had painted a number like a hotel door No 18 ..

"Sit down" .. John took a cigarette from a box on the night table. It was rolled in brown paper.

"What is it?"

"Marijuana. Ever try it?"

"No" .. John lit the cigarette and passed it to Bill. "Take it all the way down and hold it .. That's right .."

Bill felt a prickling in his lips. The wallpaper seemed to glow. Then he was laughing doubled over on the bed laughing until it hurt his ribs laughing. "My God I've pissed in my pants."

(Recollect in the officers' club Calcutta Mike and me was high on Ganja laughed till we pissed all over ourselves and the steward said "You bloody hash heads get out of here.")

He stood up his grey flannel pants stained down the left leg sharp odor of urine in the hot St Louis night.

"Take them off I can lend you a pair."

Bill kicked off his moccasins. Hands on his belt he hesitated.

"John I uh .."

"Well so what?"

"All right." Bill dropped his pants and shorts.

"Your dick is getting hard ... Sit here." John patted the bed beside him.

Bill tossed his shirt onto a chair. He stretched his legs out and knocked his feet together.

John tossed his shirt onto the floor by the window. He stood up and dropped his pants. He was wearing red shorts. He pulled his shorts down scraping erection and dropped the shorts over the lamp testing the heat with his hands. "All right," he decided his gentle precise fingers on Bill's shoulder fold sweet etcetera to bed—EE Cummings if my memory serves and what have I my friend to give you? Monkey bones of eddie and bill? John's shirt in the dawn light? .. dawn sleep .. smell of later morning in the room? Sad old human papers I carry .. empty magic of young nights .. Now listen .. ugh .. the dust the bribe .. (precise finger touching dead old path) .. was a window .. you .. ten-year-old face of laughter .. was a window of laughter shook the valley .. sunlight in his eyes for an instant Johnny's figure shone to your sudden "do it" .. stain on the sheets .. smell of young nights ..

NOVA EXPRESS

Nova Express really belongs to the trilogy, but the politics of publishing have, especially from the British point of view, isolated it from the others. It incorporates much material written at the same time as the earlier novels, which was put together with matter written after 1963 when Olympia Press was running into serious difficulties, partly because of the activities of British Customs and the French police who were urged by the former to harass this inconvenient publisher, and partly because Maurice Girodias had also set himself up as a restaurateur, where he rapidly lost the profits of *Lolita*. *Nova Express* was commissioned by Grove Press in New York who, because of a dispute with Calder & Boyars, publishers in Britain of the trilogy, sold it to Jonathan Cape who, being associated with more traditional fiction, were not successful with it.

Nova Express is in fact closer to traditional fiction with an interplanetary cops-and-robbers plot. Burroughs himself, in an interview with Allen Ginsberg, has called it the novel where he makes the clearest statement of his views and intentions. Burroughs visualizes invaders from Venus who wish first to enslave the planet—ours—and then exterminate us, pointing out that this is most easily accomplished by destroying our gods, as we destroyed the gods of the American Indians. But he also comments that the Christian god, the "Baptist vision of Jesus", is itself a means of control, and has become spiritually empty, not part of a culture that can strengthen us against take-over from without. As with Rousseau, there is inherently present in Burroughs' work a romantic historicism that yearns for an ideal past, a Garden of Eden where man was once free and innocent and did naturally all those things that today are called sinful, immoral or illegal.

LAST WORDS

Listen to my last words anywhere. Listen to my last words any world. Listen all you boards syndicates and governments of the earth. And you powers behind what filth deals consummated in what lavatory to take what is not yours. To sell the ground from unborn feet forever—

"Don't let them see us. Don't tell them what we are doing—"

Are these the words of the all-powerful boards and syndicates of the earth?

"For God's sake don't let that Coca-Cola thing out—"

"Not The Cancer Deal with The Venusians—"

"Not The Green Deal—Don't show them that—"

"Not The Orgasm Death—"

"*Not the ovens—*"

Listen: I call you all. Show your cards all players. Pay it all pay it all pay it *all* back. Play it all pay it all play it *all* back. For all to see. In Times Square. In Piccadilly.

"Premature. Premature. Give us a little more time."

Time for what? More lies? Premature? Premature for who? I say to all these words are not premature. These words may be too late. Minutes to go. Minutes to foe goal—

"Top Secret—Classified—For The Board—The Elite—The Initiates—"

Are these the words of the all-powerful boards and syndicates of the earth? These are the words of liars cowards collaborators traitors. Liars who want time for more lies. Cowards who can not face your "dogs" your "gooks" your "errand boys" your "human animals" with the truth. Collaborators with Insect People with Vegetable People. With any people anywhere who offer you a body forever. To shit forever. For this you have sold out your sons. Sold the ground from unborn feet forever. Traitors to all souls everywhere. You want the name of Hassan i Sabbah on your filth deeds to sell out the unborn?

What scared you all into time? Into body? Into shit? I will tell you: "*the word.*" Alien Word "*the.*" "*The*" *word* of Alien Enemy imprisons "*thee*" in Time. In Body. In Shit. Prisoner, come out. The great skies are open. I Hassan i Sabbah *rub out the word forever*.

If you I cancel all your words forever. And the words of Hassan i Sabbah as also cancel. Cross all your skies see the silent writing of Brion Gysin Hassan i Sabbah: drew September 17, 1899 over New York.

PRISONERS, COME OUT

"Don't listen to Hassan i Sabbah," they will tell you. "He wants to take your body and all pleasures of the body away from you. Listen to us. We are serving The Garden of Delights Immortality Cosmic Consciousness The Best Ever In Drug Kicks. And *love love love* in slop buckets. How does that sound to you boys? Better than Hassan i Sabbah and his cold windy bodiless rock? Right?"

At the immediate risk of finding myself the most unpopular character of all fiction—and history is fiction—I must say this:

"Bring together state of news—Inquire onward from state to doer—Who monopolized Immortality? Who monopolized Cosmic Consciousness? Who monopolized Love Sex and Dream? Who monopolized Life Time and Fortune? Who took from you what is yours? Now they will give it all back? Did they ever give anything away for nothing? Did they ever give any more than they had to give? Did they not always take back what they gave when possible and it always was? *Listen:* Their Garden Of Delights is a terminal sewer—I have been at some pains to map this area of terminal sewage in the so called pornographic sections of *Naked Lunch* and *Soft Machine*—Their Immortality Cosmic Consciousness and Love is second-run grade-B shit—Their drugs are poison designed to beam in Orgasm Death and Nova Ovens—Stay out of the Garden Of Delights—It is a man-eating trap that ends in green goo— Throw back their ersatz Immortality—It will fall apart before you can get out of The Big Store—Flush their drug kicks down the drain—*They are poisoning and monopolizing the hallucinogen drugs— learn to make it without any chemical corn*—All that they offer is a screen to cover retreat from the colony they have so disgracefully mismanaged. To cover travel arrangements so they will never have to pay the constituents they have betrayed and sold out. Once these arrangements are complete they will blow the place up behind them.

"And what does my program of total austerity and total resistance offer *you?* I offer you nothing. I am not a politician. These are conditions of total emergency. And these are my instructions for total emergency if carried out *now* could avert the total disaster *now* on tracks:

"*Peoples of the earth, you have all been poisoned.* Convert all available stocks of morphine to apomorphine. Chemists, work round the clock on variation and synthesis of the apomorphine formulae. Apomorphine is the only agent that can disintoxicate you and cut the enemy beam off your line. Apomorphine and silence. I order total resistance directed against this conspiracy to pay off peoples of the earth in ersatz bullshit. I order total resistance directed against The Nova Conspiracy and all those engaged in it.

"The purpose of my writing is to expose and arrest Nova Criminals. In *Naked Lunch, Soft Machine* and *Nova Express* I show who they are and what they are doing and what they will do if they are not arrested. Minutes to go. Souls rotten from their orgasm drugs, flesh shuddering from their nova ovens, prisoners of the earth to *come out.* With your help we can occupy The Reality Studio and retake their universe of Fear Death and Monopoly—

"(Signed) INSPECTOR J. LEE, NOVA POLICE"

Post Script Of The Regulator: I would like to sound a word of warning—To speak is to lie—To live is to collaborate—Anybody is a coward when faced by the nova ovens—There are degrees of lying collaboration and cowardice—That is to say degrees of intoxication—It is precisely a question of *regulation*—The enemy is not man is not woman—The enemy exists only where no life is and moves always to push life into extreme untenable positions—You can cut the enemy off your line by the judicious use of apomorphine and silence—*Use the sanity drug apomorphine.*

"Apomorphine is made from morphine but its physiological action is quite different. Morphine depresses front brain. Apomorphine stimulates the back brain. acts on the hypothalamus to regulate the percentage of various constituents in the blood serum and so normalize the constitution of the blood." I quote from *Anxiety and Its Treatment* by Doctor John Yerbury Dent.

PRY YOURSELF LOOSE AND LISTEN

I was traveling with The Intolerable Kid on The Nova Lark—We were on the nod after a rumble in The Crab Galaxy involving this two-way time stock; when you come to the end of a biologic film just run it back and start over—Nobody knows the difference—

Like nobody there before the film.* So they start to run it back and the projector blew up and we lammed out of there on the blast— Holed up in those cool blue mountains the liquid air in our spines listening to a little high-fi junk note fixes you right to metal and you nod out a thousand years.† Just.

* Postulate a biologic film running from the beginning to the end, from zero to zero as all biologic film run in any time universe—Call this film X1 and postulate further that there can only be one film with the quality X1 in any given time universe. X1 is the film and performers—X2 is the audience who are all trying to get into the film—Nobody is permitted to leave the biologic theater which in this case is the human body—Because if anybody did leave the theater he would be looking at a different film Y and Film X1 and audience X2 would then cease to exist by mathematical definition—In 1960 with the publication of *Minutes To Go*, Martin's stale movie was greeted by an unprecedented chorus of boos and a concerted walkout—"We seen this five times already and not standing still for another twilight of your tired Gods."

· Since junk *is* image the effects of junk can easily be produced and concentrated in a sound and image track—Like this: Take a sick junky—Throw blue light on his so-called face or dye it blue or dye the junk blue it don't make no difference and now give him a shot and photograph the blue miracle as life pours back into that walking corpse—That will give you the image track of junk—Now project the blue change onto your own face if you want The Big Fix. The sound track is even easier—I quote from *Newsweek*, March 4, 1963 Science section: "Every substance has a characteristic set of resonant frequencies at which it vibrates or oscillates."—So you record the frequency of junk as it hits the junk-sick brain cells—

"What's that?—Brain waves are 32 or under and can't be heard? Well speed them up, God damn it—And instead of one junky concentrate me a thousand— Let there be Lexington and call a nice Jew in to run it—"

Doctor Wilhelm Reich has isolated and concentrated a unit that he calls "the orgone"—Orgones, according to W. Reich, are the units of life—They have been photographed and the color is blue—So junk sops up the orgones and that's why they need all these young junkies—They have more orgones and give higher yield of the blue concentrate on which Martin and his boys can nod out a thousand years—Martin is stealing *your orgones.*—You going to stand still for this shit?

CHINESE LAUNDRY

When young Sutherland asked me to procure him a commission with the nova police, I jokingly answered: "Bring in Winkhorst, technician and chemist for The Lazarus Pharmaceutical Company, and we will discuss the matter."

"Is this Winkhorst a nova criminal?"

"No just a technical sergeant wanted for interrogation."

I was thinking of course that he knew nothing of the methods by which such people are brought in for interrogation—It is a precision operation—First we send out a series of agents—(usually in the guise of journalists)—to contact Winkhorst and expose him to a battery of stimulus units—The contact agents talk and record the response on all levels to the word units while a photographer takes pictures—This material is passed along to The Art Department—Writers write "Winkhorst," painters paint "Winkhorst," a method actor *becomes* "Winkhorst," and then "Winkhorst" will answer our questions—The processing of Winkhorst was already under way—

Some days later there was a knock at my door—Young Sutherland was standing there and next to him a man with coat collar turned up so only the eyes were visible spitting indignant protest—I noticed that the overcoat sleeves were empty.

"I have him in a strait jacket," said Sutherland propelling the man into my room—"This is Winkhorst."

I saw that the collar was turned up to conceal a gag—"But—You misunderstood me—Not on this level—I mean really—"

"You said bring in Winkhorst didn't you?"

I was thinking fast: "All right—Take off the gag and the strait jacket."

"But he'll scream the fuzz in—"

"No he won't."

As he removed the strait jacket I was reminded of an old dream picture—This process is known as retroactive dreaming—Performed with precision and authority becomes accomplished fact—If Winkhorst did start screaming no one would hear him—Far side of the world's mirror moving into my past—Wall of glass you know—Winkhorst made no attempt to scream—Iron cool he sat down—I asked Sutherland to leave us promising to put his application through channels—

"I have come to ask settlement for a laundry bill," Winkhorst said.

"What laundry do you represent?"

"The Chinese laundry."

"The bill will be paid through channels—As you know nothing is more complicated and time consuming than processing requisition orders for so-called 'personal expenses'—And you know also that it is strictly forbidden to offer currency in settlement."

"I was empowered to ask a settlement—Beyond that I know nothing—And now may I ask why I have been summoned?"

"Let's not say summoned—Let us just say invited—It's more humane that way you see—Actually we are taking an opinion poll in regard to someone with whom I believe you have a long and close association, namely Mr Winkhorst of The Lazarus Pharmaceutical Company—We are interviewing friends, relatives, coworkers to predict his chances for reelection as captain of the chemical executive softball team—You must of course realize the importance of this matter in view of the company motto 'Always play *soft* ball' is it not?—Now just to give the interview life let us pretend that you are yourself Winkhorst and I will put the questions directly ketch?—Very well Mr Winkhorst, let's not waste time—We know that you are the chemist responsible for synthesizing the new hallucinogen drugs many of which have not yet been released even for experimental purposes—We know also that you have effected certain molecular alterations in the known hallucinogens that are being freely distributed in many quarters—Precisely how are these alterations effected?—Please do not be deterred from making a complete statement by my obvious lack of technical knowledge—That is not my job—Your answers will be recorded and turned over to the Technical Department for processing."

"The process is known as stress deformation—It is done or was done with a cyclotron—For example the mescaline molecule is exposed to cyclotron stress so that the energy field is deformed and some molecules are activated on fissionable level—Mescaline so processed will be liable to produce, in the human subject—(known as 'canine preparations')—uh unpleasant and dangerous symptoms and in particular 'the heat syndrome' which is a reflection of nuclear fission—Subjects complain they are on fire, confined in a suffocating furnace, white hot bees swarming in the body—The hot bees are of course the deformed mescaline molecules—I am putting it simply of course—"

"There are other procedures?"

"Of course but always it is a question of deformation or association on a molecular level—Another procedure consists in exposing the mescaline molecule to certain virus cultures—The virus as you know is a very small particle and can be precisely associated on molecular chains—This association gives an additional tune-in with anybody who has suffered from a virus infection such as hepatitis for example—Much easier to produce the heat syndrome in such a preparation."

"Can this process be reversed? That is can you decontaminate a compound once the deformation has been effected?"

"Not so easy—It would be simpler to recall our stock from the distributors and replace it."

"And now I would like to ask you if there could be benign associations—Could you for example associate mescaline with apomorphine on a molecular level?"

"First we would have to synthesize the apomorphine formulae—As you know it is forbidden to do this."

"And for very good reason is it not, Winkhorst?"

"Yes—Apomorphine combats parasite invasion by stimulating the regulatory centers to normalize metabolism—A powerful variation of this drug could deactivate all verbal units and blanket the earth in silence, disconnecting the entire heat syndrome."

"You could do this, Mr Winkhorst?"

"It would not be easy—certain technical details and so little time—" He held up his thumb and forefinger a quarter inch apart.

"Difficult but not impossible, Mr Winkhorst?"

"Of course not—If I receive the order—This is unlikely in view of certain facts known to both of us."

"You refer to the scheduled nova date?"

"Of course."

"You are convinced that this is inevitable, Mr Winkhorst?'

"I have seen the formulae—I do not believe in miracles."

"Of what do these formulae consist, Mr Winkhorst?"

"It is a question of disposal—What is known as Uranium and this applies to all such raw material is actually a form of excrement—The disposal problem of radioactive waste in any time universe is ultimately insoluble."

"But if we disintegrate verbal units, that is vaporize the containers, then the explosion could not take place in effect would never have existed—"

"Perhaps—I am a chemist not a prophet—It is considered

axiomatic that the nova formulae can not be broken, that the process is irreversible once set in motion—All energy and appropriations is now being channeled into escape plans—If you are interested I am empowered to make an offer of evacuation—on a time level of course."

"And in return?"

"You will simply send back a report that there is no evidence of nova activity on planet earth."

"What you are offering me is a precarious aqualung existence in somebody else's stale movie—Such people made a wide U turn back to the '20s—Besides the whole thing is ridiculous—Like I send back word from Mercury: 'The climate is cool and bracing—The natives are soo friendly'—or 'On Uranus one is conscious of a lightness in the limbs and an exhilarating sense of freedom'—So Doctor Benway snapped, 'You will simply send back spitting notice on your dirty nova activity—It is ridiculous like when the egg cracks the climate is cool and bracing'—or 'Uranus is mushrooming freedom'—This is the old splintered pink carnival 1917—Sad little irrigation ditch—Where else if they have date twisting paralyzed in the blue movies?—You are offering me aqualung scraps—precarious flesh—soiled movie, rag on cock—Intestinal street boy smells through the outhouse.' "

"I am empowered to make the offer not assess in validity."

"The offer is declined—The so-called officers on this planet have panicked and are rushing the first life boat in drag—Such behavior is unbecoming an officer and these people have been relieved of a command they evidently experienced as an intolerable burden in any case—In all my experience as a police officer I have never seen such a downright stupid conspiracy—The nova mob operating here are stumble bums who couldn't even crash our police line-up anywhere else—"

This is the old needling technique to lure a criminal out into the open—Three thousand years with the force and it still works—Winkhorst was fading out in hot spirals of the crab nebula—I experienced a moment of panic—walked slowly to the tape recorder—

"Now if you would be so kind, Mr Winkhorst, I would like you to listen to this music and give me your reaction—We are using it in a commercial on the apomorphine program—Now if you would listen to this music and give me advantage—We are thinking of sullen strect boys for this spot—"

I put on some Gnaova drum music and turned around both guns

blazing—Silver needles under tons focus come level on average had opened up still as good as he used to be pounding stabbing to the drum beats—The scorpion controller was on screen blue eyes white hot spitting from the molten core of a planet where lead melts at noon his body half concealed by the portico of a Mayan temple—A stink of torture chambers and burning flesh filled the room— Prisoners staked out under the white hot skies of Minraud eaten alive by metal ants—I kept distance surrounding him with pounding stabbing light blasts seventy tons to the square inch—The orders loud and clear now: "Blast—Pound—Strafe—Stab—*Kill*" —The screen opened out—I could see Mayan codices and Egyptian hieroglyphs—Prisoners screaming in the ovens broken down to insect forms—Life-sized portrait of a pantless corpse hanged to a telegraph pole ejaculating under a white hot sky—Stink of torture when the egg cracks—always to insect forms—Staked out spines gathering mushroom ants—Eyes pop out naked hanged to a telegraph pole of adolescent image—

The music shifted to Pan Pipes and I moved away to remote mountain villages where blue mist swirled through the slate houses—Place of the vine people under eternal moonlight— Pressure removed—Seventy tons to the square inch suddenly moved out—From a calm grey distance I saw the scorpion controller explode in the low pressure area—Great winds whipping across a black plain scattered the codices and hieroglyphs to rubbish heaps of the earth—(A Mexican boy whistling Mambo, drops his pants by a mud wall and wipes his ass with a page from the Madrid codex) Place of the dust people who live in sand storms riding the wind—*Wind wind wind* through dusty offices and archives—Wind through the board rooms and torture banks of time—

("A great calm shrouds the green place of the vine people.")

INFLEXIBLE AUTHORITY

When I handed in my report to The District Supervisor he read it through with a narrow smile—"They have distracted you with a war film and given false information as usual—You are inexperienced of course—Total green troops in the area—However your unauthorized action will enable us to cut some corners—Now come along and we will get the real facts—"

The police patrol pounded into the home office of Lazarus & Co—

"And now Mr Winkhorst and you gentlemen of the board, let's

have the real story and quickly or would you rather talk to the partisans?"

"You dumb hicks."

"The information and quickly—We have no time to waste with such as you."

The DS stood there translucent silver sending a solid blast of inflexible authority.

"All right—We'll talk—The cyclotron processes image—It's the microfilm principle—smaller and smaller, more and more images in less space pounded down under the cyclotron to crystal image meal—We can take the whole fucking planet out that way up our ass in a finger stall—Image of both of us good as he used to be—A *stall* you dig—Just old showmen packing our ermines you might say—"

"Enough of that show—Continue please with your statement."

"Sure, sure, but you see now why we had to laugh till we pissed watching those dumb rubes playing around with photomontage— Like charging a regiment of tanks with a defective slingshot."

"For the last time out of me—Continue with your statement."

"Sure, sure, but you see now why we had such lookout on these dumb rubes playing around with a splintered carnival—Charging a regiment of tanks with a defective sanitarium 1917—Never could keep his gas—Just an old trouper is all"—(He goes into a song and dance routine dancing off stage—An 1890 cop picks him up in the wings and brings back a ventriloquist dummy.)

"This, gentlemen, is a death dwarf—As you can see manipulated by remote control—Compliments of Mr & Mrs D."

"Give me a shot," says the dwarf. "And I'll tell you something interesting."

Hydraulic metal hands proffer a tray of phosphorescent meal yellow brown in color like pulverized amber—The dwarf takes out a hypo from a silver case and shoots a pinch of the meal in the main line.

"Images—millions of images—That's what I eat—Cyclotron shit—Ever try kicking *that* habit with apomorphine?—Now I got all the images of sex acts and torture ever took place anywhere and I can just blast it out and control you gooks right down to the molecule—I got orgasms—I got screams—I got all the images any hick poet ever shit out—My Power's coming—My Power's coming —My Power's coming—" He goes into a faith healer routine rolling his eyes and frothing at the mouth—"And I got millions and millions and millions of images of Me, Me, Me, meee." (He nods out—He snaps back into focus screaming and spitting at Uranian Willy.) "You hick—You rat—Called the fuzz on me—All right—(Nods out)—I'm finished but you're still a lousy fink—"

"Address your remarks to me," said the DS.

"All right you hick sheriffs—I'll cook you all down to decorticated canine preparations—You'll never get the apomorphine formulae in time—Never! Never! Never!"—(Caustic white hot saliva drips from his teeth—A smell of phosphorous fills the room)—"Human dogs"—He collapses sobbing—"Don't mind if I take another shot do you?"

"Of course not—After giving information you will be disintoxicated."

"Disintoxicated he says—My God look at me."

"Good sir to the purpose."

"Shit—Uranian shit—That's what my human dogs eat—And I like to rub their nose in it—Beauty—Poetry—Space—What good is all that to me? If I don't get the image fix I'm in the ovens—You understand?—All the pain and hate images come loose—You understand *that* you dumb hick? I'm finished but your eyes still pop out—Naked candy of adolescent image Panama—*Who* look out different?—Cook you all down to decorticated mandrake—"

"Don't you think, Mr D, it is in your interest to facilitate our work with the apomorphine formulae?"

"It wouldn't touch me—Not with the habit I got—"

"How do you know?—Have you tried?"

"Of course not—If I allowed anyone to develop the formulae he would be *out* you understand?—And it only takes one out to kick over my hypo tray."

"After all you don't have much choice Mr D."

Again the image snapped back fading now and flickering like an old film—

"I still have the Board Room Reports—I can split the planet wide open tomorrow—And you, you little rat, you'll end up on ice in the ovens—Baked Alaska we call it—Nothing like a Baked Alaska to hold me vegetable—Always plenty wise guys waiting on the Baked Alaska." The dwarf's eyes sputtered blue sparks—A reek of burning flesh billowed through the room—

"I still mushroom planet wide open for jolly—Any hick poet shit out pleasures—Come closer and see my pictures—Show you something interesting—Come closer and watch them flop around in soiled linen—The Garden Boys both of us good as we used to be—Sweet pictures start coming in the hanged man knees up to the chin—You know—Beauty bare and still as good—Cock stand up spurting whitewash—Ever try his crotch when the egg cracks?— Now I got all the images in backward time—Rusty black pants— Delicate gooks in the locker room rubbing each other—I got screams—I *watched*—Burning heavens, idiot—Don't mind if I take another shot—Jimmy Sheffield is still as good as he used to be— Flesh the room in pink carnival—"

A young agent turned away vomiting; "Police work is not pleasant on any level," said the DS. He turned to Winkhorst: "This special breed spitting notice on your dirty pharmaceuticals— Level—"

"Well some of my information was advantage—It *is* done with a cyclotron—But like this—Say I want to heat up the mescaline formula what I do is put the blazing photo from Hiroshima and Nagasaki under my cyclotron and shade the heat meal in with mescaline—Indetectible—It's all so simple and magnificent really—Beauty bare and all that—Or say I want 'The Drenched Lands' on the boy what I do is put the image from his cock under the cyclotron spurting whitewash in the white hot skies of Minraud."

The death dwarf opens one eye—"Hey, copper, come here—Got something else to tell you—Might as well rat—Everyone does it here the man says—You know about niggers? Why darkies were born?—Travel flesh we call it—Transports better—Tell you something else—" He nods out.

"And the apomorphine formula, Mr Winkhorst?"

"Apomorphine is no word and no image—It is of course misleading to speak of a silence virus or an apomorphine virus since apomorphine is anti-virus—The uh apomorphine preparations must be raised in a culture containing sublethal quantities of pain and pleasure cyclotron concentrates—Sub-virus stimulates anti-virus special group—When immunity has been established in the surviving preparations—and many will not survive—we have the formulae necessary to defeat the virus powers—It is simply a question of putting through an inoculation program in the very limited time that remains—Word begets image and image *is* virus— Our facilities are at your disposal gentlemen and I am at your disposal—Technical sergeant I can work for anybody—These officers don't even know what button to push." He glares at the dwarf who is on the nod, hands turning to vines—

"I'm not taking any rap for a decorticated turnip—And you just let me tell you how much all the kids in the office and the laboratory hate you stinking heavy metal assed cunt sucking board bastards."

Technical Deposition of the Virus Power. "Gentlemen, it was first suggested that we take our own image and examine how it could be made more portable. We found that simple binary coding systems were enough to contain the entire image however they required a large amount of storage space until it was found that the binary information could be written at the molecular level, and our entire image could be contained within a grain of sand. However it was found that these information molecules were not dead matter but exhibited a capacity for life which is found elsewhere in the form of virus.. Our virus infects the human and creates our image in him.

"We first took our image and put it into code. A technical code developed by the information theorists. This code was written at the molecular level to save space, when it was found that the image material was not dead matter, but exhibited the same life cycle as the virus. This virus released upon the world would infect the entire population and turn them into our replicas, it was not safe to release the virus until we could be sure that the last groups to go replica would not notice. To this end we invented variety in many forms, variety that is of information content in a molecule, which, *enfin*, is always a permutation of the existing material. Information speeded up, slowed down, permutated, changed at random by radiating the virus material with high energy rays from cyclotrons, in short we have created an infinity of variety at the information level, sufficient to keep so-called scientists busy for ever exploring the 'richness of nature.'

"It was important all this time that the possibility of a human ever conceiving of being without a body should not arise. Remember that the variety we invented was permutation of the electromagnetic structure of matter energy interactions which are not the raw material of nonbody experience."

The basic nova mechanism is very simple: Always create as many insoluble conflicts as possible and always aggravate existing conflicts—This is done by dumping life forms with incompatible conditions of existence on the same planet—There is of course nothing "wrong" about any given life form since "wrong" only has reference to conflicts with other life forms—The point is these forms should not be on the same planet—Their conditions of life are basically incompatible in present time form and it is precisely the work of the Nova Mob to see that they remain in present time form, to create and aggravate the conflicts that lead to the explosion of a planet that is to nova—At any given time recording devices fix the nature of absolute need and dictate the use of total weapons—Like this: Take two opposed pressure groups—Record the most violent and threatening statements of group one with regard to group two and play back to group two—Record the answer and take it back to group one—Back and forth between opposed pressure groups—This process is known as "feed back"—You can see it operating in any bar room quarrel—In any quarrel for that matter—Manipulated on a global scale feeds back nuclear war and nova—These conflicts are deliberately created and aggravated by nova criminals—The Nova Mob: "Sammy The Butcher," "Green Tony," "Iron Claws," "The Brown Artist," "Jacky Blue Note," "Limestone John," "Izzy The Push," "Hamburger Mary," "Paddy The Sting," "The Subliminal Kid," "The Blue Dinosaur," and "Mr & Mrs D," also known as Mr Bradly Mr Martin" also known as "The Ugly Spirit" thought to be the leader of the mob—The Nova Mob—In all my experience as a police officer I have never seen such total fear and degradation on any planet—We intend to arrest these criminals and turn them over to the Biological Department for the indicated alterations—

Now you may well ask whether we can straighten out this mess to the satisfaction of any life forms involved and my answer is this—Your earth case must be processed by the Biologic Courts—admittedly in a deplorable condition at this time—No sooner set up than immediately corrupted so that they convene every day in a different location like floating dice games, constantly swept away by stampeding forms all idiotically glorifying their stupid ways of life—(most of them quite unworkable of course) attempting to seduce the judges into Venusian sex practices, drug the court officials, and intimidate the entire audience chambers with the threat of nova—In all my experience as a police officer I have never seen such total fear of the indicated alterations on any planet—A thankless job you see and we only do it so it won't have to be done some place else under even more difficult circumstances—

The success of the nova mob depended on a blockade of the planet that allowed them to operate with impunity—This blockade was broken by partisan activity directed from the planet Saturn that cut the control lines of word and image laid down by the nova mob—So we moved in our agents and started to work keeping always in close touch with the partisans—The selection of local personnel posed a most difficult problem—Frankly we found that most existing police agencies were hopelessly corrupt—the nova mob had seen to that—Paradoxically some of our best agents were recruited from the ranks of those who are called criminals on this planet—In many instances we had to use agents inexperienced in police work—There were of course casualties and fuck ups—You must understand that an undercover agent witnesses the most execrable cruelties while he waits helpless to intervene—sometimes for many years—before he can make a definitive arrest—So it is no wonder that green officers occasionally slip control when they finally do move in for the arrest—This condition, known as "arrest fever," can upset an entire operation—In one recent case, our man in Tangier suffered an attack of "arrest fever" and detained everyone on his view screen including some of our own undercover men—He was transferred to paper work in another area—

Let me explain *how* we make an arrest—nova criminals are not three-dimensional organisms—(though they are quite definite organisms as we shall see) but they need three-dimensional human agents to operate—The point at which the criminal controller intersects a three-dimensional human agent is known as "a coordinate point"—And if there is one thing that carries over from one human host to another and establishes identity of the controller it is *habit:* idiosyncrasies, vices, food preferences—(we were able to trace Hamburger Mary through her fondness for peanut butter) a gesture, a certain smile, a special look, that is to say the *style* of the controller—A chain smoker will always operate through chain smokers, an addict through addicts—Now a single controller can operate through thousands of human agents, but he must have a line of coordinate points—Some move on junk lines through addicts of the earth, others move on lines of certain sexual practices and so forth—It is only when we can block the controller out of all coordinate points available to him and flush him out from host cover that we can make a definitive arrest—Otherwise the criminal escapes to other coordinates—

We picked up our first coordinate points in London.

Fade out to a shabby hotel near Earl's Court in London. One of our agents is posing as a writer. He has written a so-called pornographic novel called Naked Lunch in which The Orgasm Death Gimmick is described. That was the bait. And they walked right in. A quick knock at the door and there It was. A green boy/girl from the sewage deltas of Venus. The colorless vampire creatures from a land of grass without mirrors. The agent shuddered in a light fever. "Arrest Fever." The Green Boy mistook this emotion as a tribute to his personal attractions preened himself and strutted round the room. This organism is only dangerous when directed by The Insect Brain Of Minraud. That night the agent sent in his report:

"Controller is woman—Probably Italian—Picked up a villa

216

outside Florence—And a Broker operating in the same area—Concentrate patrols—Contact local partisans—Expect to encounter Venusian weapons—"

In the months that followed we turned up more and more coordinate points. We put a round-the-clock shadow on The Green Boy and traced all incoming and outgoing calls. We picked up The Broker's Other Half in Tangier.

A Broker is someone who arranges criminal jobs:

"Get that writer—that scientist—this artist—He is too close—Bribe—Con—Intimidate—Take over his coordinate points—"

And the Broker finds someone to do the job like: "Call 'Izzy The Push,' this is a defenestration bit—Call 'Green Tony,' he will fall for the sweet con—As a last resort call 'Sammy The Butcher' and warm up The Ovens—This is a special case—"

All Brokers have three-dimensional underworld contacts and rely on The Nova Guards to block shadows and screen their operations. But when we located The Other Half in Tangier we were able to monitor the calls that went back and forth between them.

At this point we got a real break in the form of a defector from The Nova Mob: Uranian Willy The Heavy Metal Kid. Now known as "Willy The Fink" to his former associates. Willy had long been put on the "unreliable" list and marked for "Total Disposal In The Ovens." But he provided himself with a stash of apomorphine so escaped and contacted our Tangier agent. Fade out.

Paralyzed on this green land the "cycle of action"—The cycle of last door—Shut off "Mr Bradly Mr Apparent Because We Believe It"—Into air—You are yourself "Mr Bradly Mr Other Identities"—Action is an apparency creating and aggravating conflict—Total war of the past—I have said the "basic pre-clear identities" are now ended—Wind spirits melted "reality need" dictates use of throat bones—"Real is real" do get your heavy summons and are melted—Through all the streets time for him be able to not know his past walls and windows people and sky—Complete intentions falling—Look around here—no more flesh scripts dispense Mr—Heard your summons—Melted "Mr Bradly Mr Martin"

MELTED INTO AIR

Fade out muttering: "There's a lover on every corner cross the wounded galaxies"—

Distant fingers get hung up on one—"Oh, what'll we do?"

Slowly fading—I told him you on tracks—All over for sure—I'm absolutely prophesized in a dream grabbing Yuri by the shirt and throwing last words answer his Yugoslavian knife—I pick up Shannon Yves Martin may not refuse vision—Everybody's watching—But I continue the diary—"Mr Bradly Mr Martin?"—You are his eyes—I see suddenly Mr Beiles Mr Corso Mr Burroughs presence on earth is all a joke—And I think: "Funny—melted into air"—Lost flakes fall that were his shadow: This book—No good junky identity fading out—

"Smoke is all, boy—Dont intersect—I think now I go home and it's five times—Had enough slow metal fires—Form has been inconstant—Last electrician to tap on the bloody dream"—

"I see dark information from him on the floor—He pull out—Keep all Board Room Reports—Waiting chair to bash everybody—Couldn't reach tumescent daydream in Madrid—Flash a jester angel who stood there in 1910 straw words—Realize that this too is bad move—No good—No bueno—Young angel elevated among the subterraneans—Yes, he heard your summons—Nodded absently—"

"And I go home having lost—Yes, blind may not refuse vision to this book—"

CLOM FLIDAY

I have said the basic techniques of nova are very simple consist in creating and aggravating conflicts—"No riots like injustice directed between enemies"—At any given time recorders fix nature of absolute need and dictate the use of total weapons—Like this: Collect and record violent Anti-Semitic statements—Now play back to Jews who are after Belsen—Record what they say and play it back to the Anti-Semites—Clip clap—You got it?—Want more? Record white supremacy statements—Play to Negroes—Play back answer—Now The Women and The Men—No riots like injustice directed between "enemies"—At any given time position of recorders fixes nature of absolute need—And dictates the use of total weapons—So leave the recorders running and get your heavy metal ass in a space ship—Did it—Nothing here now but the recordings—Shut the whole thing right off—*Silence*—When you answer the machine you provide it with more recordings to be played back to your "enemies" keep the whole nova machine running—The Chinese character for "enemy" means to be similar to or to answer—Don't answer the machine—Shut it off—

"The Subliminal Kid" took over the streets of the world—Cruise cars and revolving turrets telescope movie lenses and recorders sweeping up sound and image of the city around and around faster and faster cars racing through all the streets of image record, take, play back, project on walls and windows people and sky—And slow moving turrets on slow cars and wagons slower and slower record take, play back, project slow motion street scene—Now fast—Now slow—slower—*Stop*—Shut off—No More—My writing arm is paralyzed—No more junk scripts, no more word scripts, no more flesh scripts—He all went away—No good—No bueno—Couldn't reach flesh—No glot—Clom Fliday—Through invisible door— Adios Meester William, Mr Bradley, Mr Martin—

I have said the basic techniques creating and aggravating conflict officers—At any given time dictate total war of the past—Changed place of years in the end is just the same—I have said the basic techniques of Nova reports are now ended—Wind spirits melted between "enemies"—Dead absolute need dictates use of throat bones—On this green land recorders get your heavy summons and are melted—Nothing here now but the recordings may not refuse vision in setting forth—*Silence*—Don't answer—That hospital melted into air—The great wind revolving turrets towers palaces— Insubstantial sound and image flakes fall—Through all the streets time for him to forbear—Blest be he on walls and windows people and sky—On every part of your dust falling softly—falling in the dark mutinous "No more"—My writing arm is paralyzed on this green land—Dead Hand, No more flesh scripts—Last door—Shut off Mr Bradly Mr—He heard your summons—Melted into air— You are yourself "Mr Bradly Mr Martin—" all the living and the dead—You are yourself—There be—

Well that's about the closest way I know to tell you and papers rustling across city desks . . . fresh southerly winds a long time ago.

September 17, 1899 over New York

THE WILD BOYS

The Wild Boys first appeared in 1969 and, although episodic like all Burroughs' work, it has a greater unity of subject-matter than any book written up to that date. There appears to be an inner conflict in the way Burroughs writes about a gang of latter-day Bacchantes who storm through the novel; they are both the villains and the heroes. But it contains all the usual ingredients, erotic, humorous, warning and self-mocking. Its subtitle "A Book of the Dead", emphasizes the necrophilia which becomes more emphatic as the author equates the dead hand of the drug scene with a world moving rapidly to self-destruction. This episode is the central one of the novel.

Burroughs has always been interested in the technology of weaponry, and here he gives full rein to his imagination on the subject, with Bosch-like devices entering the armoury of the Wild Boys. Later in the boy pirate passages of *Cities of the Red Night* (not included in this volume), he was to give considerable space to describing the development of eighteenth-century gunnery. Here and elsewhere a strong misogynist, anti-female, anti-matriarchal bias is evident, leading to an imagined world where birth needs no female participation.

"They have incredible stamina. A pack of wild boys can cover fifty miles a day. A handful of dates and a lump of brown sugar washed down with a cup of water keep them moving like that. The noise they make just before they charge ... well I've seen it shatter a greenhouse fifty yards away. Let me show you what a wild-boy charge is like." He led the way into the projection room. "These are actual films of course but I have arranged them in narrative sequence. As you know I was with one of the first expeditionary forces sent out against the wild boys. Later I joined them. Seen the charges from both sides. Well here's one of my first films."

The Colonel reins in his horse. It is a bad spot. Steep hills slope down to a narrow dry river bed. He scans the hillsides carefully through his field glasses. The hills slope up to black mesas streaked with iron ore.

"Since our arrival in the territory the regiment had been feted by the local population who told us how glad they were the brave English soldiers had come to free them from the wild boys. The women and children pelted us with flowers in the street. It reeked of treachery but we were blinded by the terrible Bor Bor they were putting in our food and drink. Bor Bor is the drug of female illusion and it is said that he who takes Bor Bor cannot see a wild boy until it is too late.

"The regiment is well into the valley. It is a still hot afternoon with sullen electricity in the air. And suddenly there they are on both sides of us against the black mesas. The valley echos to their terrible charge cry a hissing outblast of breath like a vast WHOOO? ... Their eyes light up inside like a cat's and their hair stands on end. And they charge down the slope with incredible speed leaping from side to side. We open up with everything we have and they still keep coming. They aren't human at all more like vicious little ghosts. They carry eighteen-inch bowie knives with knuckle-duster handles pouring into the river bed above and below us leaping down swinging their knives in the air. When one is killed a body is dragged aside and another takes his place. The regiment formed a square and it lasted about thirty seconds.

"I had prudently stashed my assets in a dry well where peering out through thistles I observed the carnage. I saw the Colonel empty his revolver and go down under ten wild boys. A moment later they tossed his bleeding head into the air and started a ball game. Just at dusk the wild boys got up and padded away. They left the bodies stripped to the skin many with the genitals cut off. The wild boys make little pouches from human testicles in which they carry their hashish and *khat*. The setting sun bathed the torn bodies in a pink glow. I walked happily about munching a chicken sandwich stopping now and again to observe an interesting cadaver.

"There are many groups scattered over a wide area from the outskirts of Tangier to the Blue Desert of Silence ... glider boys with bows and laser guns, rollerskate boys—blue jockstraps and steel helmets, eighteen-inch bowie knives—naked blowgun boys long hair down their backs a kris at the thigh, slingshot boys, knife throwers, bowmen, bare-hand fighters, shaman boys who ride the wind and those who have control over snakes and dogs, boys skilled in bone-pointing and Juju magic who can stab the enemy reflected in a gourd of water, boys who call the locusts and the fleas, desert boys shy as little sand foxes, dream boys who see each other's dreams and the silent boys of the Blue Desert. Each group developed special skills and knowledge until it evolved into humanoid subspecies. One of the more spectacular units is the dreaded Warrior Ants made up of boys who have lost both hands in battle. They wear aluminum bikinis and sandals and tight steel helmets. They are attended by musicians and dancing boys, medical and electronic attendants who carry the weapons that are screwed into their stumps, buckle them into their bikinis, lace their sandals wash and anoint their bodies with a musk of genitals, roses, carbolic soap, gardenias, jasmine, oil of cloves, ambergris and rectal mucus. This overpowering odor is the first warning of their presence. The smaller boys are equipped with razor-sharp pincers that can snip off a finger or sever a leg tendon. And they click their claws as they charge. The taller boys have long double-edged knives that can cut a scarf in the air screwed into both stumps."

On the screen the old regiment same canyon same Colonel. The Colonel sniffs uneasily. His horse rears and neighs. Suddenly there is a blast of silver light reflected from helmets knives and sandals. They hit the regiment like a whirlwind the ground ants cutting tendons, the shock troops slashing with both arms wade through the regiment heads floating in the air behind them. It is all over in a few seconds. Of the regiment there are no survivors. The wild boys take no prisoners. The first to receive attention were those so seriously wounded they could not live.

The Colonel paused and filled his kif pipe. He seemed to be looking at something far away and long ago and I flinched for I was a snippy Fulbright queen at the time dreading some distastefully intimate *experience* involving the amorous ghost of an Arab boy. What a bore he is with his tacky old Lawrence sets faithful native youths dying in his arms.

"As I have told you the first wild-boy tribes were fugitive survivors from the terror of Colonel Arachnid ben Driss. These boys in their early- and mid-teens had been swept into a whirlwind of riots, burning screams, machine guns and lifted out of time. Migrants of ape in gasoline crack of history. Officials denied that any repressive measures had followed nonexistent riots.

"'There is no Colonel Arachnid in the Moroccan Army' said a spokesman for the Ministry of the Interior.

"No witnesses could be found who had noticed anything out of the ordinary other than the hottest August in many years. The gasoline boys and Colonel Arachnid were hallucinated by a drunken Reuters man who became temporarily deranged when his house-boy deserted him for an English pastry cook. I was myself the Reuters man as you may have gathered."

Here are the boys cooking over campfires ... quiet valley by a stream calm young faces washed in the dawn before creation. The old phallic Gods of Greece and the assassins of Alamout still linger in the Moroccan hills like sad pilots waiting to pick up survivors. The piper's tune drifts down a St Louis street with the autumn leaves.

On screen an old book with gilt edges. Written in golden script *The Wild Boys*. A cold spring wind ruffles the pages.

Weather boys with clouds and rainbows and Northern lights in their eyes study the sky.

Glider boys ride a blue flash sunset on wings of pink and rose and gold laser guns shooting arrows of light. Roller-skate boys turn slow circles in ruined suburbs China-blue half-moon in the morning sky.

Blue evening shadows in the old skating rink, smell of empty locker rooms and moldy jockstraps. A circle of boys sit on a gym mat hands clasped around the knees. The boys are naked except for blue steel helmets. Eyes move in a slow circle from crotch to crotch, silent, intent, they converge on one boy a thin dark youth his face spattered with adolescent pimples. He is getting stiff. He steps to the center of the circle and turns around three times. He sits down knees up facing the empty space in the circle where he sat. He pivots slowly looking at each boy in turn. His eyes lock with one boy. A fluid click a drop of lubricant squeezes out the tip of his phallus. He lies back his head on a leather cushion. The boy selected kneels in front of the other studying his genitals. He presses the tip open and looks at it through a lens of lubricant. He twists the tight nuts gently runs a slow precise finger up and down the shaft drawing lubricant along the divide line feeling for sensitive spots in the tip. The boy who is being masturbated rocks back hugging knees against his chest. The circle of boys sits silent lips parted watching faces calmed to razor sharpness. The boy quivers transparent suffused with blue light the pearly glands and delicate coral tracings of his backbone exposed.

A naked boy on perilous wings soars over a blue chasm. The air is full of wings ... gliders launched from skis and sleds and skates, flying bicycles, sky-blue gliders with painted birds, an air schooner billowing white sails stabilized by autogiros. Boys climb in the rigging and wave from fragile decks.

Boy on a bicycle with autogiro wings sails off a precipice and floats slowly down into a valley of cobblestone streets and deep-blue canals. In a golf course sand pit hissing snake boys twist in slow copulations guarded by a ring of cobras.

The legend of the wild boys spread and boys from all over the world ran away to join them. Wild boys appeared in the mountains of Mexico, the jungles of South American and Southeastern Asia. Bandit country, guerrilla country, is wild-boy country. The wild boys exchange drugs, weapons, skills on a world-wide network. Some wild-boy tribes travel constantly taking the best cannabis seeds to the Amazon and bringing back cuttings of the Yage vine for the jungles of Southern Asia and Central Africa. Exchange of spells and potions. A common language based on variable transliteration of a simplified hieroglyphic script is spoken and written by the wild boys. In remote dream rest areas the boys fashion these glyphs from wood, metal, stone and pottery. Each boy makes his own picture set. Sea chest in an attic room, blue wallpaper ship scenes, copies of *Adventure* and *Amazing Stories*, a .22 pump-action rifle on the wall. A boy opens the chest and takes out the words one by one ... The erect phallus which means in wild-boy script as it does in Egyptian to stand before or in the presence of, to confront to regard attentively ... a phallic statue of ebony with star sapphire eyes a tiny opal set in the tip of the phallus ... two wooden statues face each other in a yellow oak rocking chair. The boy statues are covered with human skin tanned in ambergris, carbolic soap, rose petals, rectal mucus, smoked in hashish and burning leaves ... a yellow-haired boy straddles a copper-skinned Mexican, feet braced muscles carved in orgasm ... an alabaster boy lights up blue inside, piper boy with a music box, roller-skate boy of blue slate with a bowie knife in his hand, a post card world of streams, freckled boy, blue outhouses covered with morning glory- and rose vines where the boys jack off on July afternoons shimmers in a Gysin painting ... little peep shows ... flickering silver titles ... others with colors and odors and raw naked flesh ... tight nuts crinkle to autumn leaves ... blue chasms ... a flight of birds. These word objects travel on the trade routes from hand to hand. The wild boys see, touch, taste, smell the words. Shrunken head of a CIA man ... a little twisted sentry his face cyanide blue ...

(A highly placed narcotics official tells a grim President: "The wild-boy thing is a cult based on drugs, depravity and violence more dangerous than the hydrogen bomb.")

At a long work bench in the skating rink boys tinker with tiny jet engines for their skates. They forge and grind eighteen-inch bowie knives bolting on handles of ebony and the ironwoods of South America that must be worked with metal tools ...

The roller-skate boys swerve down a wide palm-lined avenue into a screaming blizzard of machine-gun bullets, sun glinting on their knives and helmets, lips parted eyes blazing. They slice through a patrol snatching guns in the air.

Jungle work bench under a thatched roof ... a ten-foot blowgun with telescopic sights operated by compressed air ... tiny blowguns with darts no bigger than a mosquito sting tipped with serum jaundice and strange fevers ...

In houseboats, basements, tents, tree houses, caves, and lofts the wild boys fashion their weapons ... a short double-edged knife

bolted to a strong spring whipped back and forth slices to the bone
... kris with a battery vibrator in the handle ... karate sticks ... a
knob of ironwood protrudes between the first and second fingers
and from each end of the fist ... loaded gloves and knuckle-dusters
... crossbows and guns powered by thick rubber sliced from an
inner tube. These guns shoot a lead slug fed in from a magazine
above the launching carriage. Quite accurate up to twenty yards ...
a cyanide injector shaped like a pistol. The needle is unscrewed
from the end of the barrel, the pistol cocked by drawing back a
spring attached to the plunger. A sponge soaked in cyanide solution
is inserted, the needle screwed back in place. When the trigger
releases the spring a massive dose of cyanide is squeezed into the
flesh causing instant death. When not in use the needle is capped
by a Buck Rogers Death Ray ... cyanide darts and knives with
hollow perforated blades ... a flintlock pistol loaded with crushed
glass and cyanide crystals ...

Cat boys fashion claws sewn into heavy leather gloves that are
strapped around the wrist and forearm, the incurving hollow claws
packed with cyanide paste. The boys in green jockstraps wait in a
tree for the jungle patrol. They leap down on the soldiers, deadly
claws slashing, digging in. Boys collect the weapons from twisted
blue hands. They wash off blood and poison in a stream and pass
around a kif pipe.

Snake boys in fish-skin jockstraps wade out of the bay. Each boy
has a venomous speckled sea snake coiled around his arm. They
move through scrub and palm to an electric fence that surrounds
the officer's club. Through flowering shrubs Americans can be
seen in the swimming pool blowing and puffing. The boys extend
their arms through the fence index finger extended. The snakes
drop off and glide toward the swimming pool.

A jungle patrol in Angola ... suddenly black mambas streak down
from trees on both sides of their path mouths open fangs striking
necks and arms lashing up from the ground. Mamba boys black as
obsidian with mamba-skin jockstraps and kris glide forward.

Five naked boys release cobras above a police post. As the snakes
glide down the boys move their heads from side to side. Phalluses
sway and stiffen. The boys snap their heads forward mouths open
and ejaculate. Strangled cries from the police box. Faces impassive
the boys wait until their erections subside.

Boys sweep a cloud of bubonic fleas like a net with tiny black knots
into an enemy camp.

A baby- and semen black market flourished in the corrupt border cities, and we recruited male infants from birth. You could take your boy friend's sperm to market, contact a broker who would arrange to inseminate medically inspected females. Nine months later the male crop was taken to one of the remote peaceful communes behind the front lines. A whole generation arose that had never seen a woman's face nor heard a woman's voice. In clandestine clinics fugitive technicians experimented with test-tube babies and cuttings. Brad and Greg got out just under a "terminate with extreme prejudice" order ... And here is their clinic in the Marshan Tangier. Laughing, comparing a line of boys jack off into test tubes ...

Here is a boy on his way to the cutting room. Brad and Greg explain they are going to take a cutting from the rectum very small and quite painless and the more excited he is when they take the cutting better chance there is that the cutting will *make* ... They arrange him on a table with his knees up rubber slings behind the knees to keep him spread and turn an orgone funnel on his ass and genitals. Then Brad slips a vibrating cutting tube up him. These are in hard rubber and plastic perforated with pinpoint holes. Inside is a rotary knife operated from the handle. When the ring expands it forces bits of the lining through the holes which are then clipped off by the knife.

Brad switches on the vibrator. The boy's pubic hairs crackle with blue sparks, tight nuts pop egg-blue worlds in air ... Some boys red out rose-red delicate sea-shell pinks come rainbows and Northern lights ... Here are fifty boys in one ward room, bent over hands on knees, on all fours, legs up. Greg throws the master switch. The boys writhe and squirm, leap about like lemurs, eyes blazing blue chasms, semen pulsing sparks of light. Little phantom figures dance on their bodies, slide up and down their pulsing cocks, and ride the cutting tubes ...

Little boy without a navel in a 1920 classroom. He places an apple on the teacher's desk

"I am giving you back your apple teacher."

He walks over to the blackboard and rubs out the word MOTHER. Flanked by Brad and Greg he steps to the front of the stage and takes a bow to an audience of cheering boys eating peanuts and jacking off.

Now the cuttings are no longer needed. The boys create offspring known as Zimbus. Brad and Greg have retired to a remote YMCA. Zimbus are created after a battle when the forces of evil are in retreat ...

The first to receive attention were those so seriously wounded that they could not live ... A red-haired boy who had been shot through the liver was quickly stripped of bikini and sandals and propped up in a sitting position. Since they believe that the spirit leaves through the back of the head a recumbent position is considered unfavorable. The pack stood around the dying boy in a circle and a technician deftly removed the helmet. I saw then that the helmet was an intricate piece of electronic equipment. The technician took an eighteen-inch cylinder from a leather carrying case. The cylinder is made up of alternate layers of thin iron and human skin taken from the genitals of slain enemies. In the center of the cylinder is an iron tube which protrudes slightly from one end. The tube was brought within a few inches of the boy's wound. This has the effect of reducing pain or expediting the healing of a curable wound. Pain-killing drugs are never used since the cell-blanketing effect impedes departure of the spirit. Now a yoke was fitted over the boy's shoulders and what looked like a diving helmet was placed over his head. This helmet covered with leather on the outside is in two pieces one piece covering the front of the head the other the back. The technician made an adjustment and suddenly the back section shot back to the end of the yoke where it was caught and held by metal catches. Two sections are of magnetized iron inside the technician adjusting the direction of magnetic flow so that by a repelling action the two sections spring apart pushing the spirit out the back of the head. The flow is then reversed so that the two sections are pulling towards each other but held apart. This pulls the spirit out. A luminous haze like heat waves was quite visibly draining out the boy's head. The dancing boys who had gathered in a circle around the dying boy began playing their flutes a haunting melody of Pan pipes train whistles and lonely sidings as the haze shot up into the afternoon sky. The body went limp and the boy was dead. I saw this process repeated a number of times. When the dying had been separated from their bodies by this device those with curable wounds were treated. The cylinder was brought within an inch of the wound and moved up and down. I witnessed the miracle of almost immediate healing. A boy with a great gash in his thigh was soon hobbling about the wound looking as if it had been received some weeks before. The firearms were divided among the dancing boys and attendants. The boys busied themselves skinning the genitals of the slain soldiers pegging the skins out and rubbing in pastes and unguents for curing. They butchered the young soldiers removing the heart and liver and bones for food and carted the cadavers some distance from the camp. These chores accomplished the boys spread out rugs and lit hashish pipes. The warriors were stripped by their attendants massaged and rubbed with musk. The setting sun bathed their lean bodies in a red glow as the boys gave way to an orgy of lust. Two boys would take their place in the center of a rug and copulate to drums surrounded by a circle of silent naked onlookers. I observed fifteen or twenty of these circles, copulating couples standing, kneeling, on all fours, faces rapt and empty. The odor of semen and rectal mucus filled the air. When one couple finished another would take its place. No words were spoken only the shuddering gasps and the pounding drums. A yellow haze hovered over the quivering bodies as the frenzied flesh dissolved in light. I noticed that a large blue tent had been set up and that certain boys designated by the attendants retired to this tent and took no part in the orgy. As the sun sank the exhausted boys slept in naked heaps. The moon rose and boys began to stir and light fires. Here and there hashish pipes glowed. The smell of cooking meat drifted through the air as the boys roasted the livers and hearts of the slain soldiers and made broth from the bones. Desert thistles shone silver in the moonlight. The boys formed a circle in a natural amphitheater that sloped down to a platform of sand. On this platform they spread a round blue rug about eight feet in diameter. The four directions were indicated on this rug by arrows and its position was checked against a compass. The rug looked like a map crisscrossed with white lines and shaded in striations of blue from the lightest egg blue to blue black. The musicians formed an inner circle around the rug playing on their flutes the haunting tune that had sped the dying on their way. Now one of the boys who had taken no part in the recent orgy stepped forward onto the rug. He stood there naked sniffing quivering head thrown back scanning the night sky. He stepped to the North and beckoned with both hands. He repeated the same gesture to the South East and West. I noticed that he had a tiny blue copy of the rug tattooed on each buttock. He knelt in the center of the rug studying the lines and patterns looking from the rug to his genitals. His phallus began to stir and stiffen. He leaned back until his face was turned to the sky. Slowly he raised both hands palms up and his hands drew a blue mist from the rug. He turned his hands over palms down and slowly lowered them pulling blue down from the sky. A pool of color swirled about his thighs. The mist ran into a vague shape as the color shifted from blue to pearly grey pink and finally red. A red being was now visible in front of the boy's body lying on his back knees up transparent thighs on either side of his flanks. The boy knelt there studying the red shape his eyes molding the body of a red-haired boy. Slowly he placed his hands behind knees that gave at his touch and moved them up to trembling ears of red smoke. A red boy was lying there buttocks spread the rectum a quivering rose that seemed to breathe, the body clearly outlined but still transparent. Slowly the boy penetrated the phantom body I could see his penis inside the other and as he moved in and out the soft red gelatin clung to his penis thighs and buttocks young skin taking shape legs in the air kicking spasmodically a red face on the rug lips parted the body always more solid. The boy leaned forward and fastened his lips to the other mouth spurting sperm inside and suddenly the red boy was solid buttocks quivering against the boy's groin as they breathed in and out of each other's lungs locked together the red body solid from the buttocks and penis to the twitching feet. They remained there quivering for thirty seconds. A red mist steamed off the red boy's body. I could see freckles and leg hairs. Slowly the boy withdrew his mouth. A red-haired boy lay there breathing deeply eyes closed. The boy withdrew his penis, straightened the red knees and lay the newborn Zimbu on his back. Now two attendants stepped forward with a litter of soft leather. Carefully they lifted the Zimbu onto the litter and carried him to the blue tent.

Another boy stepped onto the rug. He stood in the center of the rug and leaned forward hands on knees his eyes following the lines and patterns. His penis stiffened. He stood upright and walked to the four directions lifting his hands each time and saying one word I did not catch. A little wind sprang up that stirred the boy's pubic hairs and played over his body. He began to dance to the flutes and drums and as he danced a blue will-o'-the-wisp took shape in front of him shifting from one side of the rug to the other. The boy spread out his hands. The will-o'-the-wisp tried to dodge past but he caught it and brought his arms together pulling the blue shape against him. The color shifted from blue to pearly grey streaked with brown. His hands were stroking a naked flank and caressing a penis out of the air buttocks flattened against his body as he moved in fluid gyrations lips parted teeth bared. A brown body solid now ejaculated in shuddering gasps sperm hitting the rug left white streaks and spots that soaked into the crisscross of white lines. The boy held the Zimbu up pressing his chest in and out with his own breathing quivering to the blue tattoo. The Zimbu shud-

233

dered and ejaculated again. He hung limp in the other's arms. The attendants stepped forward with another litter. The Zimbu was carried away to the blue tent.

A boy with Mongoloid features steps onto the rug playing a flute to the four directions. As he plays phantom figures swirl around him taking shape out of moonlight, campfires and shadows. He kneels in the center of the rug playing his flute faster and faster. The shape of a boy on hands and knees is forming in front of him. He puts down his flute. His hands mold and knead the body in front of him pulling it against him with stroking movements that penetrate the pearly grey shape caressing it inside. The body shudders and quivers against him as he forms the buttocks around his penis stroking silver genitals out of the moonlight grey then pink and finally red the mouth parted in a gasp shuddering genitals out of the moon's haze a pale blond boy spurting thighs and buttocks and young skin. The flute player kneels there arms wrapped tightly around the Zimbu's chest breathing deeply until the Zimbu breathes with his own breathing quivering to the blue tattoo. The attendants step forward and carry the pale blond Zimbu to the blue tent.

A tall boy black as ebony steps onto the rug. He scans the sky. He walks around the rug three times. He walks back to the center of the rug. He brings both hands down and shakes his head. The music stops. The boys drift away.

It was explained to me that the ceremony I had just witnessed was performed after a battle in case any of the boys who had just been killed wished to return and that those who had lost their hands might wish to do since the body is born whole. However most of the spirits would have gone to the Blue Desert of Silence. They might want to return later and the wild boys made periodic expeditions to the Blue Desert. The Zimbus sleep in the blue tent. Picture in an old book with gilt edges. The picture is framed with roses intertwined ... two bodies stuck together pale wraith of a blond boy lips parted full moon a circle of boys in silver helmets naked knees up. Under the picture in gold letters. Birth of a Zimbu. Boy with a flute charming a body out of the air. I turn the page. Boy with Mongoloid features is standing on a circular rug. He looks down at his stiffening phallus. A little wind stirs his pubic hairs. Buttocks tight curving inward at the bottom of the two craters a round blue tattoo miniature of the rug on which he stands. I turn the page. A boy is dancing will-o'-the-wisp dodges in front of him. I turn the page. Will-o'-the-wisp in his arms gathering outline luminous blue eyes trembling buttocks flattened against his body holding the Zimbu tight against his chest. His breathing serves as the Zimbu's lungs until his breathing is his own quivering to the blue tattoo children of lonely sidings, roses, afternoon sky. I turn the pages. Dawn shirt framed in roses dawn wind between his legs distant lips.

EXTERMINATOR!

Exterminator! is really a collection of short stories and texts, some of which appeared in little magazines between 1966 and 1974, when the whole collection was published in book form. The title story is partly autobiographical because Burroughs worked for a while for a company of "exterminators", the American name for fumigators whose principal job is to get rid of cockroaches. Some of the episodes are really experimental work in progress, which often reads like poetry, as in 'Cold Lost Marbles'. 'The Teacher' uses material that interleaves with a film script that was commissioned from Burroughs about Dutch Schulz, a notorious American gangster of the prohibition era who was gunned down by rivals in a restaurant in the thirties. It gave him a golden opportunity to indulge his interest in that turbulent period of his youth.

"EXTERMINATOR!"

"You need the service?"

During the war I worked for A. J. Cohen Exterminators ground floor office dead-end street by the river. An old Jew with cold grey fish eyes and a cigar was the oldest of four brothers. Marv was the youngest wore windbreakers had three kids. There was a smooth well-dressed college trained brother. The fourth brother burly and muscular looked like an old time hoofer could bellow a leather lunged "Mammy" and you hope he won't do it. Every night at closing time these two brothers would get in a heated argument from nowhere I could see the older brother would take the cigar out of his mouth and move across the floor with short sliding steps advancing on the vaudeville brother.

"You vant I should spit right in your face!? You vant!? You vant? You vant!?"

The vaudeville brother would retreat shadowboxing presences invisible to my goyish eyes which I took to be potent Jewish Mammas conjured up by the elder brother. On many occasions I witnessed this ritual open mouthed hoping the old cigar would let fly one day but he never did. A few minutes later they would be talking quietly and checking the work slips as the exterminators fell in.

On the other hand the old brother never argued with his exterminators. "That's why I have a cigar" he said the cigar being for him a source of magical calm.

I used my own car a black Ford V8 and worked alone carrying my bedbug spray, pyrethrum powder, bellows and bulbs of fluoride up and down stairs.

"Exterminator! You need the service?"

A fat smiling Chinese rationed out the pyrethrum powder—it was hard to get during the war—and cautioned us to use fluoride whenever possible. Personally I prefer a pyrethrum job to a fluoride. With the pyrethrum you kill the roaches right there in front of God and the client whereas this starch and fluoride you leave it around and back a few days later a southern defense worker told me "They eat it and run around here fat as hawgs."

From a great distance I see a cool remote naborhood blue windy day in April sun cold on your exterminator there climbing the grey wooden outside stairs.

"Exterminator lady. You need the service?"

"Well come in young man and have a cup of tea. That wind has a bite to it."

"It does that, mam, cuts me like a knife and I'm not well you know/cough/."

"You put me in mind of my brother Michael Fenny."

"He passed away?"

"It was a long time ago April day like this sun cold on a thin boy with freckles through that door like yourself. I made him a cup of hot tea. When I brought it to him he was gone." She gestured to the empty blue sky "Cold tea sitting right where you are sitting now." I decide this old witch deserves a pyrethrum job no matter what the fat Chinese allows. I lean forward discreetly.

"Is it roaches Mrs Murphy?"

"It is that from those Jews downstairs."

"Or is it the hunkys next door Mrs Murphy?"

She shrugs "Sure and an irish cockroach is as bad as another."

"You make a nice cup of tea Mrs Murphy ... Sure I'll be taking care of your roaches ... Oh don't be telling me where they are ... You see I *know* Mrs Murphy ... experienced along these lines ... And I don't mind telling you Mrs Murphy I *like* my work and take pride in it."

"Well the city exterminating people were around and left some white powder draws roaches the way whiskey will draw a priest."

"They are a cheap outfit Mrs Murphy. What they left was fluoride. The roaches build up a tolerance and become addicted. They can be dangerous if the fluoride is suddenly withdrawn ... Ah just here it is ..."

I have spotted a brown crack by the kitchen sink put my bellows in and blow a load of the precious yellow powder. As if they had heard the last trumpet the roaches stream out and flop in convulsions on the floor.

"Well I never!" says Mrs Murphy and turns me back as I advance for the *coup de grâce* ... "Don't shoot them again. Just let them die."

When it is all over she sweeps up a dustpan full of roaches into the wood stove and makes me another cup of tea.

When it comes to bedbugs there is a board of health regulation against spraying beds and that of course is just where the bugs are in most cases now an old wood house with bedbugs back in the wood for generations only thing is to fumigate ... So here is Mamma with a glass of sweet wine her beds back and ready ...

I look at her over the syrupy red wine ... "Lady we don't spray no beds. Board of health regulations you know."

"Ach so the wine is not enough?"

She comes back with a crumpled dollar. So I go to work ... bedbugs great red clusters of them in the ticking of the mattresses. I mix a little formaldehyde with my kerosene in the spray it's more sanitary that way and if you tangle with some pimp in one of the Negro whorehouses we service a face full of formaldehyde keeps the boy in line. Now you'll often find these old Jewish grandmas in a back room like their bugs and we have to force the door with the younger generation smooth college trained Jew there could turn into a narcotics agent while you wait.

"All right grandma, open up! The exterminator is here."

She is screaming in Yiddish no bugs are there we force our way in I turn the bed back ... my God thousands of them fat and red with grandma and when I put the spray to them she moans like the Gestapo is murdering her nubile daughter engaged to a dentist.

And there are whole backward families with bedbugs don't want to let the exterminator in.

"We'll slap a board of health summons on them if we have to" said the college trained brother ... "I'll go along with you on this one. Get in the car."

They didn't want to let us in but he was smooth and firm. They gave way muttering like sullen troops cowed by the brass. Well he told me what to do and I did it. When he was settled at the wheel of his car cool grey and removed he said "Just plain ordinary sons of bitches. That's all they are."

TB sanitarium on the outskirts of town ... cool blue basements fluoride dust drifting streaks of phosphorous paste on the walls ... grey smell of institution cooking ... heavy dark glass front door ... Funny thing I never saw any patients there but I don't ask questions. Do my job and go a man who works for his living ... Remember this janitor who broke into tears because I said shit in front of his wife it wasn't me actually said it was Wagner who was dyspeptic and thin with knobby wrists and stringy yellow hair ... and the fumigation jobs under the table I did on my day off ...

Young Jewish matron there "Let's not talk about the company. The company makes too much money anyway. I'll get you a drink of whiskey." Well I have come up from the sweet wine circuit. So I arrange a sulphur job with her five Abes and it takes me about two hours you have to tape up all the windows and the door and leave the fumes in there 24 hours studying the good work.

One time me and the smooth brother went out on a special fumigation job ... "This man is sort of a crank ... been out here a number of times ... claims he has rats under the house ... We'll have to put on a show for him."

Well he hauls out one of those tin pump guns loaded with cyanide dust and I am subject to crawl under the house through spider webs and broken glass to find the rat holes and squirt the cyanide to them.

"Watch yourself under there" said the cool brother. "If you don't come out in ten minutes I'm coming in after you."

I liked the cafeteria basement jobs long grey basement you can't see the end of it white dust drifting as I trace arabesques of fluoride on the wall.

We serviced an old theatrical hotel rooms with rose wallpaper photograph albums ... "Yes that's me there on the left."

The boss has a trick he does every now and again assembles his staff and eats arsenic been in that office breathing the powder in so long the arsenic just brings an embalmer's flush to his smooth grey cheek. And he has a pet rat he knocked all its teeth out feeds it on milk the rat is now very tame and affectionate. I stuck the job nine months. It was my record on any job. Left the old grey Jew there with his cigar the fat Chinese pouring my pyrethrum powder back into the barrel. All the brothers shook hands. A distant cry echoes down cobblestone streets through all the grey basements up the outside stairs to a windy blue sky.

"Exterminator!"

DAVY JONES

"Young boys need it special."

An adolescent stands with his fly sticking out and pimples explode all over his face.

Here is Audrey at 14 fear and uncertainty written across his face that most people instinctively dislike and distrust. He looks like a sheep-killing dog with sheep blood all over his face wagging his tail at the same time ready to snap or take to his heels. On Saturdays he would go down to the courthouse and sit in on trials the smell of stale sweat and cigar smoke brings it all back how Audrey quailed under the cold eyes of cigar-smoking detectives.

Audrey has slunk into the courtroom and forgot to take off his hat.

"TAKE OFF YOUR HAT."

He sits down shattered as was his usual condition. He turned and looked to his right. Sitting on the second bench ahead of him was a black man one elbow over the back of the bench. Audrey stared at the man who could easily have seen him out of the corner of his eye. If he was aware of Audrey's scrutiny he gave no sign. What held Audrey open mouthed was the immediate knowledge that this man was not moving *inside* not moving one fraction of an inch for anybody and his physical immobility accumulated a power that Audrey could feel like an electrical force field. And now a case was called.

"DAVY JONES."

A boy of about 15 escorted by a bored cop stood in front of the judge. Looking back I see something like a stage with a suggestion of curtains. As his name is called Davy Jones walks in from the left. He is 15 powerfully built and tall completely relaxed and sure of himself he stands in front of the judge with an insolent smile. Audrey realized that the *boy was fearless*. He licked his lips and started to get a hard-on.

"I'm not guilty" said the boy saucily.

The judge moved back. He shied back his fat flesh retreating. "You *are* guilty. You've been *found* guilty and I'm sentencing you to 5 years in Boonville."

BOONVILLE ... Audrey buttoned his coat to cover his crotch.

He remembered a newspaper story about boys held in the city prison awaiting transfer to the reformatory at Boonville, Missouri ... complaints of "loathsome actions of the boys performed at the dormitory windows in plain sight of passers-by." ... He saw himself in a cell with Davy Jones ...

"I'm not guilty" the boy said again smiling openly contemptuous.

"Any relatives in the courtroom?" the judge asked.

The black man spoke from the bench ... "I'm the boy's father. He's not the type to do that." He did not move or change his position. His voice fell in the court-room as flatly insulting as hard black knuckles across the judge's face.

The judge blinked and moved back ... "He *is* the type ... He's been found guilty of armed robbery ..."

"He's not the type."

Audrey realized that the judge was afraid of this man. The judge and the bailiffs as well. Nobody told him to stand up or address the court as your honor.

Years later in New Orleans while in jail on narcotics charges he met another black of the same quality. He was known as Clutch because of a deformed hand. He was skeleton thin composed cool and aloof with the other prisoners. And insolent to the narcs.

"Old monkey climbing up on your back boy?" said a narc clapping him jovially on the back.

"I don't know what you're talking about now" said Clutch coldly.

The narc dropped his hand and turned away coughing. Why did they take it from him? Because they were afraid of him. Davy Jones father and son and Clutch destroy the whole white world.

THE TEACHER

Vista of riots and burning cities cuts to a remote muted board room. Faces of wealth and power sipping ice water. A padded door flies open in a blast of riot sound effects Audrey Carsons in a light black suit and grey fedora dances into the board room with Charlie Workman and Jimmy the Shrew.

"I'm the Sheik of Araby ..."

He shatters a pitcher of ice water on the table grabs the chairman by the tie holding the jagged shards inches from his face.

"Or else belongs to me ..."

The board members disappear in a silver flash. Weary old voice drifts from a tape recorder.

"Smeared with the blood of old movies we hope to last?"

"The song is ended ..."

Audrey points to the night sky over St Louis Missouri the old broken point of origin. A cluster of stars winks out.

"Dead stars. We went out long ago."

"But the melody lingers on ..."

Darkness falls on beer drops and Harlem streets.

"Now you and the song are gone ..."

"Or else come and took over."

"But the melody lingers on ..."

Public school classroom 1920s. Albert Stern as the teacher is calling the roll.

"Arthur Flegenheimer ..."

Camera pans through corridors and dining room grey sugar greasy black cutlery.

"Arthur Flegenheimer ..."

Camera tracks through washrooms and toilets.

Come and jack off ... June 17, 1922.

Phallic shadows on a distant wall.

"Arthur Flegenheimer ..."

The teacher writes Absent by his name.

The screen darkens into the hiss of a gas oven and hospital sound effects.

Newspaper picture of the waxen corpse of Albert Stern looking like the little man on a wedding cake.

GANG "KILLER" A SUICIDE IN RAGS.

Newspaper picture of Dutch Schultz on deathbed.

DUTCH SCHULTZ DEAD.

On the day that Dutch Schultz died the winning number was 00. His number was up.

Harlem basement cabaret ... music ... lights ... a faggot prances out in a pea-green suit and grey fedora.

ARTIST

"COME IN WITH THE DUTCHMAN
COME IN WITH THE DUTCHMAN
COME IN WITH THE DUTCHMAN
OR ELSE"

He clutches his chest and does a split pratfall. The hat flies off his head on spring. He zips his legs together and catches the hat.

"COME IN WITH THE DUTCHMAN
COME IN WITH THE DUTCHMAN
COME IN WITH THE DUTCHMAN
OR ELSE"

He smashes a bag of ketchup against his face, grabs his crotch and bends forward wiggling his ass like a randy dog.

CLUB 400 ... Chauffeur-driven limousines guests in evening dress bowed in by the obsequious snarling doorman.

"Good evening Mr Poindexter ..."

"BEAT IT YOU FUCKING BUM."

A moving van stops in front of the 400 and a pack of yelping screaming faggots leap out led by the ARTIST. They buzz by the doorman one snatches his hat and fill the club screeching, camping, snatching tablecloths curtains and drapes for impersonation acts. The ARTIST jumps up onto the bar and does The Strip Polka.

"TAKE IT OFF TAKE IT OFF
SCREAM THE GIRLS FROM THE REAR"

Women is helped into her mink coat by hat-check girl. She preens herself then sniffs and stiffens and looks down. Her coat is in rags streaming red and orange fumes blobs of smoking fur fall to the floor. She screams like a baby.

Cry of new-born baby ... a door opens ... Doctor Stern thin, tubercular, sad stands in the doorway.

"You can come in now Mr Flegenheimer ... a fine boy ... where can I wash my hands?"

Dutch washing his hands in the lavatory of THE PALACE CHOP HOUSE. The door opens behind him. Sound and smell of frying steak.

Hospital sound effects hospital room. Dutch in bed two detectives and a police stenographer with clipboard.

1ST DETECTIVE
"Who shot you?"
DUTCH
"I don't know sir honestly I don't. I went to the toilet. I was in the toilet and when I reached the (a word not clear) the boy came at me."

Police stenographer writes this down.

2ND DETECTIVE
"What boy?"

Dutch as youth in street crap game. He has thrown a seven but the dice are still moving as a boy snatches them up.

BOY
"THEY'RE MY DICE."
DUTCH
"How much did you have in the pot?"
BOY
"Not a nickle."

Dutch kicks him in the mouth knocking out his front teeth. Flash of the boy's shocked bleeding face.

Cut back to the teacher calling the roll in Public School 12 1922.

TEACHER
"Arthur Flegenheimer ..."

Dutch clutches his side in the lavatory of THE PALACE CHOP HOUSE.

DUTCH
"OH MAMA MAMA I BEEN SHOT THROUGH THE LIVER."
1ST DETECTIVE
"Don't holler."
DUTCH
"Mother is the best bet and don't let Satan draw you too fast."
2ND DETECTIVE
"Now what are we sitting here for?"

DUTCH
"In the olden days they waited and they waited."
IST DETECTIVE
"Don't get wise."

Hospital room some hours later. There is only one detective in the room and he is dozing in a chair. Grey immobile the SCRIBE looks down at his clipboard pencil poised waiting. Dutch speaks in the voice of Albert Stern.

ALBERT STERN
"Please let me get in and eat."

Police stenographer writes this down. Detective wakes up.

DETECTIVE
"Who shot you?"
DUTCH
"The boss himself."

THE SILVER CORD an exclusive night club. The proprietor is seen unhooking the famous silver rope to admit favored clients. Albert Stern in a filthy evening jacket pocked with cigarette burns his pants held up by a length of rope runs towards the silver cord the doorman ten feet behind him.

ALBERT STERN
"PLEASE LET ME GET IN AND EAT."

Behind the doorman is a flying wedge of panhandlers. They burst through the cord ripping it from the hook.

DUTCH
"Oh mama mama DON'T TEAR DON'T RIP ..."
IST DETECTIVE
"Control yourself."

They pour into the dining room. The waiters try to oust them but they are like sacks of mendicant concrete clutching at the guests with filthy fingers, snatching food and drinks from the tables, urinating on the floor.

Death pees with decayed fingers. The Dutchman washes his hands.

A flashy overexpensive night spot. Officious waiters with a flourish deposit dishes with a silver cover on tables.

WAITER 1
"Voilà le *Lapin Chasseur* ..."

He lifts the cover to reveal the bloated corpse of a huge rat showing its yellow teeth in a pile of garbage.

WAITER 2
"Voilà le *Faisan Suprême* ..."

Lifts cover to reveal a buzzard cooked in sewage.

WAITER 3
"Voilà les *Fruits de Mer* ..."

Lifts cover to reveal a live horseshoe crab on its back in used condoms shit-stained newspapers and bloody Kotex.
     The guests scream gag cover their faces with napkins.
     Room in OLD HARMONY HOTEL upstate New York red curtains and carpets turn-of-the-century décor DEATH OF STONEWALL JACKSON on the wall.
     "That picture's awful dusty ..."
     Dixie Davis is reading *Collier's* magazine. Martin Krompier looks at the ceiling. They are both very bored with the argument between Dutch and Jules Martin.

DUTCH
"I don't want harmony. I want harmony. Oh mama mama who give it to him?"
1ST DETECTIVE
"Who give it to *you* Dutch?"

Dutch pours a drink and shoves his face within inches of Martin's.

DUTCH
"So Jules Judas Martin thought the Dutchman was through did he? Thought he could put his big greasy mitt in for forty thousand clams did he?"
JULES MARTIN
"Look Dutch we don't owe a nickle ..."
DUTCH
"Cut that out we don't owe a nickle ..."
JULES MARTIN
"SAY LIST ..."
DUTCH
"Shut up you gotta big mouth ..."

As he says this Dutch flips a .38 from his waistband shoves the barrel right into Martin's mouth and pulls the trigger. Jules Martin falls to the floor screaming moaning spitting blood and smoke.

In the hospital room doctor is filing the end off morphine ampoule and filling syringe.

1ST DETECTIVE
"Can't you give him something that will get him to talk doctor?"
DOCTOR
"Talk to *who*? The man is delirious ..."
DUTCH
"Oh and then he clips me ... Come on cut that out we don't owe a nickle ..."
JULES MARTIN
"SAY LIST ..."
1ST DETECTIVE
"WHAT are you? a ventriloquist?"
2ND DETECTIVE
"Control yourself."

Dixie Davis snatches up his coat and briefcase and flounces to the door. With his hand on the brass doorknob he turns around.

DIXIE DAVIS
"To do a thing like that right in front of me Arthur ... After all I'm a professional man ..."

He opens the door. Hotel porter walks by whistling "Home Sweet Home" down the empty corridor.

DUTCH
"A boy has never wept or dashed a thousand Kim."
1ST DETECTIVE
"That takes the rag off the bush."

The SCRIBE writes boys running and beckoning from playgrounds and bridges. A skull-faced porter turns around. The number on his cap is 23.

TEACHER
"Arthur Flegenheimer ..."
2ND DETECTIVE
"Was it the boss shot you?"
1ST DETECTIVE
(Wheedling and obscene) "Come on Dutch who shot you?"

2ND DETECTIVE
(Tough and peremptory) "Come on Dutch who shot you?"

Campaign poster of the DA his mustache bristling ominously dissolves to 12 men seated at long table. Background shots vaguely seen are taken from other sets in the film. This is the board room, the hospital room. Dutch's office, THE PALACE CHOP HOUSE. At one end of the table sits an old Don with dark glasses. At the other end sits Lepke Buchalter the JUDGE doe-eyed and enigmatic. He is the nominal chairman but the old Don is obviously in control.

OLD DON
"Kick him upstairs into a governor . . ."
ANASTASIA
"Or President even . . ."
MEMBER 3
"DAs come and go . . ."
GURRAH
"Why wait? I say hit him . . ."
MEMBER 5
"We can ride this out. I say forget him . . ."
LUCKY LUCIANO
"This is 1935 not 1925. Time to pack in the cowboy act."
MEMBER 8
"Brings on my ulcers to think about it."
MEMBER 9
"Undecided."
DUTCH
"I say he's got to be hit on the head. We gotta make an example."
JUDGE
"An example of what Mr Flegenheimer? There seems to be a difference of opinion. We will put it to a vote . . . for or against?" . . . (He glances at the old Don) . . . "My vote is against."
OLD DON
(Shakes his head and smiles) "Against."
ANASTASIA
(He lifts his hands and turns them out) . . . "It's a natural It's beautiful . . . but . . ."
(He drops his hands palm down on the table)
"Against."
LUCKY LUCIANO
"Against."

252

MEMBER 8
"Against it from the beginning."
MEMBER 9
"I'm against it."
MEMBER 5
"Against."
DUTCH
"Wait a minute here . . ."
JUDGE
"You are outvoted Mr Flegenheimer."
DUTCH
"He's gotta go. If no one else is gonna do it I'm gonna hit him myself."

The old Don smiles . . . hospital sound effects . . . voice of nurse echoes down the hall . . .

NURSE
"Quarter grain GOM . . ."

Car in Holland Tunnel. Piggy is at the wheel his round pale face smooth and bland. The hulking snarling strangler Mendy Weiss sits on the jump seat. In the back seat are Charlie The Bug Workman and Jimmy the Shrew. Workman is a cool casual killer in a tailor-made twilight blue suit and grey fedora pale face cold metallic grey eyes. The Shrew is in the tight pea-green suit and grey fedora smooth poreless red skin tight over the cheekbones lips parted from long yellow teeth the color of old ivory. The tunnel lights ring their heads with an orange halo.

ARTIST
"COME IN WITH THE DUTCHMAN
COME IN WITH THE DUTCHMAN
COME IN WITH THE DUTCHMAN"

Back room of THE PALACE CHOP HOUSE. Dutch is sitting at a table with Lulu Rosencrantz, Abe Landau and Otto Daba Berman. Beer mugs on the table cigar smoking in an ashtray. Aba Daba is working adding machine and writing figures down on ledger paper.

DUTCH
"HEY WONG."

Chinese cook appears in upper panel of green door leading to the kitchen.

"Steak medium with French fries."

The cook nods and disappears.
Press conference the Police Commissioner behind his desk.

REPORTER
"Any line on the Dutch Schultz shoot-down Commissioner?"
COMMISSIONER
"We have. At least one of the gunmen has been positively identified as Albert Stern."
REPORTER
"Who's this Albert Stern?"
COMMISSIONER
"Because of his spectacles and his mild appearance he is known as the Teacher. Wild Boy would be a better name for him. A hophead gunman top trigger for the Big Six he is probably one of the most dangerous killers alive today."

Hospital room. Detectives are drinking coffee from paper cups.

DUTCH
"Come on open the soap duckets."

Sound of frying fat.
Flash of city after nuclear attack ... rubble ... heat waves ... a gang of boys carrying shards and bars of blistered metal ... faces of hatred evil and despair streaked with coal dust.

DUTCH
"THE CHIMNEY SWEEPS TAKE TO THE SWORD ..."
2nd DETECTIVE
"The doctor wants you to lie quiet."
Porter whistles "Home Sweet Home" down the corridor of OLD HARMONY HOTEL.
Color shot of advertisement circa 1910 shows blown-up soup tin. Written on it in rainbow letters RAINBOW JACK'S FRENCH CANADIAN BEAN SOUP. Picture on can shows mountain lake and rainbow red-haired lumberjack holds up the can with the picture on it.

DUTCH
"French Canadian Bean Soup . . ."

Bare room of Albert Stern. He is lying by the open gas oven. Hiss of escaping gas mixes with hospital sound effects.

DUTCH
"I want to pay. Let them leave me alone."

Teacher calling the roll in Public School 12. This shot rapidly darkens.

TEACHER
"Arthur Flegenheimer.
Arthur Flegenheimer."

A last despairing cry from darkness.

"ARTHUR FLEGENHEIMER . . ."

Darkness on screen. Silence on screen.

OLD MOVIE

In the noon streets three men sitting on ash cans. One of the men looked up and saw Agent 23. Electric hate crackled between them. In a panic 23 tried to pull his eyes back. He could not do so. He held one point and felt the pilot land. Something cracked in his head like a red egg and the ground swayed beneath him then he could feel it pouring out his eyes. A crowd was gathering quick and silent eyes blazing hate. 23 ran toward them up the narrow street moving his head from side to side burning a path through charred flesh and shredded brains running very light on his feet up the steep stone street toward the skies of Marrakech the whole film tilted now the stones moving in waves under his feet a blaze of blue and he was stabbing two black holes in the blue sky smoking with a sound like falling mountains the sky ripped open and he was through the film barrier. Standing naked in front of a wash-stand copper luster basin the film jumped and shifted music across the golf course he was a caddy it seems looking for lost balls by the pond flickering silver buttocks in the dark room fading flickering all from an old movie that will give at his touch.

COLD LOST MARBLES

my ice skates on a wall
luster of stumps washes his lavender horizon
he's got a handsome face of a lousy kid
rooming houses dirty fingers
whistled in the shadow
"Wait for me at the detour."
river . . . snow . . . someone vague faded in a mirror
filigree of trade winds
cold white as lace circling the pepper trees
the film is finished
memory died when their photos weather worn points of
polluted water under the trees in the mist shadow of
boys by the daybreak in the peony fields cold lost
marbles in the room carnations three ampoules of
morphine little blue-eyed twilight grins between his
legs yellow fingers blue stars erect boys of sleep
have frozen dreams for I am a teenager pass it on
flesh and bones withheld too long yes sir *oui oui*
craps last map . . . lake . . . a canoe . . . rose tornado in
the harvest brass echo tropical jeers from Panama
City night fences dead fingers you in your own body
around and maybe a boy skin spreads to something
else on Long Island the dogs are quiet.

THE THIRD MIND

The Third Mind was written jointly by William Burroughs and Brion Gysin, the American artist and photographer who was for many years a close friend of the author. It would perhaps be more accurate to call the volume a record of their work together. Nowhere else is Burroughs so clear about his method of working. The introduction to this *Reader* has already covered the salient points, but it is interesting to read Burroughs' own self-analyses either in recorded interviews or written self-exposition. *The Third Mind* is the synthesis of two other minds into a superior mind and represents at the same time the result achieved when different literary material is put together to end up with an independent new text. The poem "Minutes to Go" by Brion Gysin first appeared in a volume published by the English Bookshop in Paris, then run by Gaite Frogé, an enthusiastic French lady whose bookshop also had an art gallery in the basement and was a centre and meeting place for the English-speaking writers and artists who lived in Paris in the fifties and early sixties. "Minutes to Go" contained poetry and experimental prose by Burroughs, Gysin and Sinclair Beiles, the latter a South African engaged in theatrical happenings before that term became fashionable.

MINUTES TO GO

the hallucinated have come to tell you that yr utilities
are being shut off   dreams monitored   thought directed
sex is shutting down everywhere   you are being sent

all words are taped   agents everywhere
marking down the live ones   to exterminate

they are turning out the lights

no   they are not evil   nor the devil   but men
on a mission   with a spot of work to do

this   dear friends   they intend to do on you

you have been offered a choice   between liberty and
freedom   and   No!   you cannot have both

the next step   is everyone into space   but it has been
a long dull wait   since the last tower of babel
that first derisive visit of the   paraclete

let's not hear that noise again   and again
that may well be   the last word   anywhere

this is not the beginning   in the beginning was the word
the word has been in for a too   long time
you in the word and   the word in you

we are out
you are in

we have come to let you out

here and now we will show you   what you can do
with and to
the word
the words
any word
all the words

Pick a book   any book   cut it up
cut up

prose
poems
newspapers
magazines
the bible
the koran
the book of moroni
lao-tzu
confucius
the bhagavad gita
anything
letters
business correspondence
ads
all the words

slice down the middle   dice into sections
according to taste
chop in some bible   pour on some Madison Avenue
prose
shuffle like cards   toss like confetti
taste it like piping hot   alphabet soup

pass yr friends' letters   yr office carbons
through any such sieve   as you may find or invent

you will soon see   just what they really are
saying   this is the terminal method for
finding the truth

piece together a masterpiece   a week
use better materials   more highly charged words

there is no longer a need   to drum up a season of
geniuses   be your own agent   until we deliver
the machine   in commercially reasonable quantities

we wish to announce   that while we esteem
this to be truly   the American Way
we have no commitments   with any government
groups

the writing machine   is for everybody
do it yourself   until the machine comes
here is the system   according to us

B.G.

INTERVIEW WITH WILLIAM S. BURROUGHS*

BURROUGHS: I don't know about where fiction ordinarily directs itself, but I am quite deliberately addressing myself to the whole area of what we call dreams. Precisely what is a dream? A certain juxtaposition of word and image. I've recently done a lot of experiments with scrapbooks. I'll read in the newspaper something that reminds me of or has relation to something I've written. I'll cut out the picture or article and paste it in a scrapbook beside the words from my book. Or I'll be walking down the street and I'll suddenly see a scene from my book and I'll photograph it and put it in a scrapbook. I've found that when preparing a page, I'll almost invariably dream that night something relating to this juxtaposition of word and image. In other words, I've been interested in precisely how word and image get around on very, very complex association lines. I do a lot of exercises in what I call time travel, in taking coordinates, such as what I photographed on the train, what I was thinking about at the time, what I was reading and what I wrote; all of this to see how completely I can project myself back to that one point in time.

INTERVIEWER: In *Nova Express* you indicate that silence is a desirable state.

BURROUGHS: The *most* desirable state. In one sense a special use of words and pictures can conduce silence. The scrapbooks and time travel are exercises to expand consciousness, to teach me to think in association blocks rather than words. I've recently spent a little time studying hieroglyph systems, both the Egyptian and the Mayan. A whole block of associations—boonf!—like that! Words—at least the way we use them—can stand in the way of what I call nonbody experience. It's time we thought about leaving the body behind.

INTERVIEWER: Marshall McLuhan said that you believed heroin was needed to turn the human body into an environment that includes the universe. But from what you've told me, you're not at all interested in turning the body into an environment.

* Extracted from the1966 interview by Conrad Knickerbocker in *Paris Review*; reprinted in *Writers at Work*, 3rd Series (New York, 1967).

BURROUGHS: No, junk narrows consciousness. The only benefit to me as a writer (aside from putting me into contact with the whole carny world) came to me after I went off it. What I want to do is to learn to see more of what's out there, to look outside, to achieve as far as possible a complete awareness of surroundings. Beckett wants to go inward. First he was in a bottle and now he is in the mud. I am aimed in the other direction: outward.

INTERVIEWER: Have you been able to think for any length of time in images, with the inner voice silent?

BURROUGHS: I'm becoming more proficient at it, partly through my work with scrapbooks and translating the connections between words and images. Try this: Carefully memorize the meaning of a passage, then read it; you'll find you can actually read it without the words' making any sound whatever in the mind's ear. Extraordinary experience, and one that will carry over into dreams. When you start thinking in images, without words, you're well on the way.

INTERVIEWER: Why is the wordless state so desirable?

BURROUGHS: I think it's the evolutionary trend. I think that words are an around-the-world, ox-cart way of doing things, awkward instruments, and they will be laid aside eventually, probably sooner than we think. This is something that will happen in the space age. Most serious writers refuse to make themselves available to the things that technology is doing. I've never been able to understand this sort of fear. Many of them are afraid of tape recorders and the idea of using any mechanical means for literary purposes seems to them some sort of a sacrilege. This is one objection to the cut-ups. There's been a lot of that, a sort of superstitious reverence for the word: My God, they say, you can't cut up these words. Why *can't* I? I find it much easier to get interest in the cut-ups from people who are not writers—doctors, lawyers, or engineers, any open-minded, fairly intelligent person—than from those who are.

INTERVIEWER: How did you become interested in the cut-up technique?

BURROUGHS: A friend, Brion Gysin, an American poet and painter, who has lived in Europe for thirty years, was, as far as I know, the first to create cut-ups. His cut-up poem, "Minutes to Go," was broadcast by the BBC and later published in a pamphlet. I was in Paris in the summer of 1960; this was after the publication there of *Naked Lunch*. I became interested in the possibilities of this technique, and I began experimenting myself. Of course, when you think of it, "The Waste Land" was the first great cut-up collage, and Tristan Tzara had done a bit along the same lines. Dos Passos used the same idea in "The Camera Eye" sequences in *USA*. I felt I had been working toward the same goal; thus it was a major revelation to me when I actually saw it being done.

INTERVIEWER: What do cut-ups offer the reader that conventional narrative doesn't?

BURROUGHS: Any narrative passage or any passage, say, of poetic images is subject to any number of variations, all of which may be interesting and valid in their own right. A page of Rimbaud cut up and rearranged will give you quite new images. Rimbaud images—real Rimbaud images—but new ones.

INTERVIEWER: You deplore the accumulation of images and at the same time you seem to be looking for new ones.

BURROUGHS: Yes, it's part of the paradox of anyone who is working with word and image, and after all, that is what a writer is still doing. Painter too. Cut-ups establish new connections between images, and one's range of vision consequently expands.

INTERVIEWER: Instead of going to the trouble of working with scissors and all those pieces of paper, couldn't you obtain the same effect by simply free-associating at the typewriter?

BURROUGHS: One's mind can't cover it that way. Now, for example, if I wanted to make a cut-up of this [*picking up a copy of the* Nation], there are many ways I could do it. I could read cross-column; I could say: "Today's men's nerves surround us. Each technological extension gone outside is electrical involves an act of collective environment. The human nervous environment system itself can be reprogrammed with all its private and social values because it is content. He programs logically as readily as any radio net is swallowed by the new environment. The sensory order." You find it often makes quite as much sense as the original. You learn to leave out words and to make connections. [*Gesturing*] Suppose I should cut this down the middle here, and put this up here. Your mind simply could not manage it. It's like trying to keep so many chess moves in mind, you just couldn't do it. The mental mechanisms of repression and selection are also operating against you.

INTERVIEWER: You believe that an audience can be eventually trained to respond to cut-ups?

BURROUGHS: Of course, because cut-ups make explicit a psycho-sensory process that is going on all the time anyway. Somebody is reading a newspaper, and his eye follows the column in the proper Aristotelian manner, one idea and sentence at a time. But subliminally he is reading the columns on either side and is aware of the person sitting next to him. That's a cut-up. I was sitting in a lunchroom in New York having my doughnuts and coffee. I was thinking that one *does* feel a little boxed in in New York, like living in a series of boxes. I looked out the window and there was a great big Yale truck. That's cut-up—a juxtaposition of what's happening outside and what you're thinking of. I make this a practice when I walk down the street. I'll say, When I got to here I saw that sign, I was thinking this, and when I return to the house I'll type these up. Some of this material I use and some I don't. I have literally thousands of pages of notes here, raw, and I keep a diary as well. In a sense it's traveling in time.

Most people don't see what's going on around them. That's my principal message to writers: For Godsake, keep your *eyes* open. Notice what's going on around you. I mean, I walk down the street with friends. I ask, "Did you see him, that person who just walked by?" No, they didn't notice him. I had a very pleasant time on the train coming out here. I haven't traveled on trains in years. I found there were no drawing rooms. I got a bedroom so I could set up my typewriter and look out the window. I was taking photos, too. I also noticed all the signs and what I was thinking at the time, you see. And I got some extraordinary juxtapositions. For example, a friend of mine has a loft apartment in New York. He said, "Every time we go out of the house and come back, if we leave the bathroom door open, there's a rat in the house." I look out the window, there's Able Pest Control.

INTERVIEWER: The one flaw in the cut-up argument seems to lie in the linguistic base on which we operate, the straight declarative sentence. It's going to take a great deal to change that.

BURROUGHS: Yes, it is unfortunately one of the great errors of Western thought, the whole either-or proposition. You remember Korzybski and his idea of non-Aristotelian logic. Either-or thinking just is not accurate thinking. That's not the way things occur, and I feel the Aristotelian construct is one of the great shackles of Western civilization. Cut-ups are a movement toward breaking this down. I should imagine it would be much easier to find acceptance of the cut-ups from, possibly, the Chinese, because you see already there are many ways that they can read any given ideograph. It's already cut up.

INTERVIEWER: What will happen to the straight plot in fiction?

BURROUGHS: Plot has always had the definite function of stage direction, of getting the characters from here to there, and that will continue, but the new techniques, such as cut-up, will involve much more of the total capacity of the observer. It enriches the whole aesthetic experience, extends it.

INTERVIEWER: *Nova Express* is a cut-up of many writers?

BURROUGHS: Joyce is in there. Shakespeare, Rimbaud, some writers that people haven't heard about, someone named Jack Stern. There's Kerouac. I don't know, when you start making these fold-ins and cut-ups you lose track. Genet, of course, is someone I admire very much. But what he's doing is classical French prose. He's not a verbal innovator. Also Kafka, Eliot, and one of my favorites is Joseph Conrad. My story "They Just Fade Away" is a fold-in (instead of cutting, you fold) from *Lord Jim*. In fact, it's almost a retelling of the *Lord Jim* story. My Stein is the same Stein as in *Lord Jim*. Richard Hughes is another favorite of mine. And Graham Greene. For exercise, when I make a trip, such as from Tangier to Gibraltar, I will record this in three columns in a notebook I always take with me. One column will contain simply an account of the trip, what happened: I arrived at the air terminal, what was said by the clerks, what I overheard on the plane, what hotel I checked into. The next column presents my memories: that is, what I was thinking of at the time, the memories that were activated by my encounters. And the third column, which I call my reading column, gives quotations from any book that I take with me. I have practically a whole novel alone on my trips to Gibraltar. Besides Graham Greene, I've used other books. I used *The Wonderful Country* by Tom Lea on one trip. Let's see ... and Eliot's *The Cocktail Party*; *In Hazard* by Richard Hughes. For example, I'm reading *The Wonderful Country* and the hero is just crossing the frontier into Mexico. Well, just at this point I come to the Spanish frontier, so I note that down in the margin. Or I'm on a boat or a train and I'm reading *The Quiet American*; I look around and see if there's a quiet American aboard. Sure enough, there's a quiet sort of young American with a crew cut, drinking a bottle of beer. It's extraordinary, if you really keep your eyes open. I was reading Raymond Chandler, and one of his characters was an albino gunman. My God, if there wasn't an albino in the room. He wasn't a gunman.

Who else? Wait a minute, I'll just check my coordinate books to see if there's anyone I've forgotten—Conrad, Richard Hughes, science fiction, quite a bit of science fiction. Eric Frank Russell has written some very, very interesting books. Here's one, *The Star*

Virus; I doubt if you've heard of it. He develops a concept here of what he calls Deadliners, who have this strange sort of seedy look. I read this when I was in Gibraltar, and I began to find Deadliners all over the place. The story of a fish pond in it, and quite a flower garden. My father was always very interested in gardening.

INTERVIEWER: In view of all this, what will happen to fiction in the next twenty-five years?

BURROUGHS: In the first place, I think there's going to be more and more merging of art and science. Scientists are already studying the creative process, and I think the whole line between art and science will break down and that scientists, I hope, will become more creative and writers more scientific. And I see no reason why the artistic world can't absolutely merge with Madison Avenue. Pop art is a move in that direction. Why can't we have advertisements with beautiful words and beautiful images? Already some of the very beautiful color photography appears in whiskey ads, I notice. Science will also discover for us how association blocks actually form.

INTERVIEWER: Do you think this will destroy the magic?

BURROUGHS: Not at all. I would say it would enhance it.

INTERVIEWER: Have you done anything with computers?

BURROUGHS: I've not done anything, but I've seen some of the computer poetry. I can take one of those computer poems and then try to find correlatives of it—that is, pictures to go with it; it's quite possible.

INTERVIEWER: Does the fact that it comes from a machine diminish its value to you?

BURROUGHS: I think that any artistic product must stand or fall on what's there.

INTERVIEWER: Therefore, you're not upset by the fact that a chimpanzee can do an abstract painting?

BURROUGHS: If he does a good one, no. People say to me, "Oh this is all very good, but you got it by cutting up." I say that has nothing to do with it, how I got it. What is any writing but a cut-up? Somebody has to program the machine; somebody has to *do* the cutting up. Remember that I first made selections. Out of hundreds of possible sentences that I might have used, I chose one.

THE CUT-UP METHOD OF BRION GYSIN

At a surrealist rally in the 1920s Tristan Tzara the man from nowhere proposed to create a poem on the spot by pulling words out of a hat. A riot ensued wrecked the theater. André Breton expelled Tristan Tzara from the movement and grounded the cut-ups on the Freudian couch.

In the summer of 1959 Brion Gysin painter and writer cut newspaper articles into sections and rearranged the sections *at random*. "Minutes to Go" resulted from this initial cut-up experiment. "Minutes to Go" contains unedited unchanged cut-ups emerging as quite coherent and meaningful prose.

The cut-up method brings to writers the collage, which has been used by painters for fifty years. And used by the moving and still camera. In fact all street shots from movie or still cameras are by the unpredictable factors of passersby and juxtaposition cut-ups. And photographers will tell you that often their best shots are accidents . . . writers will tell you the same. The best writing seems to be done almost by accident by writers until the cut-up method was made explicit—all writing is in fact cut-ups; I will return to this point—had no way to produce the accident of spontaneity. You cannot *will* spontaneity. But you can introduce the unpredictable spontaneous factor with a pair of scissors.

The method is simple. Here is one way to do it. Take a page. Like this page. Now cut down the middle and across the middle. You have four sections: 1   2   3   4 . . . one two three four. Now rearrange the sections placing section four with section one and section two with section three. And you have a new page. Sometimes it says much the same thing. Sometimes something quite different—cutting up political speeches is an interesting exercise—in any case you will find that it says something and something quite definite. Take any poet or writer you fancy. Here, say, or poems you have read over many times. The words have lost meaning and life through years of repetition. Now take the poem and type out selected passages. Fill a page with excerpts. Now cut the page. You have a new poem. As many poems as you like. As many Shakespeare Rimbaud poems as you like. Tristan Tzara said: "Poetry is for everyone." And André Breton called him a cop and expelled

him from the movement. Say it again: "Poetry is for everyone."
Poetry is a place and it is free to all cut up Rimbaud and you are
in Rimbaud's place. Here is a Rimbaud poem cut up.

"Visit of memories. Only your dance and your voice house. On the
suburban air improbable desertions . . . all harmonic pine for strife.
   "The great skies are open. Candor of vapor and tent spitting
blood laugh and drunken penance.
   "Promenade of wine perfume opens slow bottle.
   "The great skies are open. Supreme bugle burning flesh children
to mist."

Cut-ups are for everyone. Anybody can make cut-ups. It is experimental in the sense of being *something to do*. Right here write now.
Not something to talk and argue about. Greek philosophers
assumed logically that an object twice as heavy as another object
would fall twice as fast. It did not occur to them to push the two
objects off the table and see how they fall. Cut the words and see
how they fall. Shakespeare Rimbaud live in their words. Cut the
word lines and you will hear their voices. Cut-ups often come
through as code messages with special meaning for the cutter.
Table tapping? Perhaps. Certainly an improvement on the usual
deplorable performance of contacted poets through a medium.
Rimbaud announces himself, to be followed by some excruciatingly bad poetry. Cut Rimbaud's words and you are assured of
good poetry at least if not personal appearance.
   All writing is in fact cut-ups. A collage of words read heard
overheard. What else? Use of scissors renders the process explicit
and subject to extension and variation. Clear classical prose can be
composed entirely of rearranged cut-ups. Cutting and rearranging
a page of written words introduces a new dimension into writing
enabling the writer to turn images in cinematic variation. Images
shift sense under the scissors smell images to sound sight to sound
sound to kinesthetic. This is where Rimbaud was going with his
color of vowels. And his "systematic derangement of the senses."
The place of mescaline hallucination: seeing colors tasting sounds
smelling forms.
   The cut-ups can be applied to other fields than writing. Dr
Neumann in his *Theory of Games and Economic Behavior* introduces the cut-up method of random action into game and military
strategy: assume that the worst has happened and act accordingly.
If your strategy is at some point determined . . . by random factor

your opponent will gain no advantage from knowing your strategy since he cannot predict the move. The cut-up method could be used to advantage in processing scientific data. How many discoveries have been made by accident? We cannot produce accidents to order. The cut-ups could add new dimension to films. Cut gambling scene in with a thousand gambling scenes all times and places. Cut back. Cut streets of the world. Cut and rearrange the word and image in films. There is no reason to accept a second-rate product when you can have the best. And the best is there for all. "Poetry is for everyone" ...

Now here are the preceding two paragraphs cut into four sections and rearranged:

ALL WRITING IS IN FACT CUT-UPS OF GAMES AND ECONOMIC BEHAVIOR OVERHEARD? WHAT ELSE? ASSUME THAT THE WORST HAS HAPPENED EXPLICIT AND SUBJECT TO STRATEGY IS AT SOME POINT CLASSICAL PROSE. CUTTING AND REARRANGING FACTOR YOUR OPPONENT WILL GAIN INTRODUCES A NEW DIMENSION YOUR STRATEGY. HOW MANY DISCOVERIES SOUND TO KINESTHETIC? WE CAN NOW PRODUCE ACCIDENT TO HIS COLOR OF VOWELS. AND NEW DIMENSION TO FILMS CUT THE SENSES. THE PLACE OF SAND. GAMBLING SCENES ALL TIMES COLORS TASTING SOUNDS SMELL STREETS OF THE WORLD. WHEN YOU CAN HAVE THE BEST ALL: "POETRY IS FOR EVERYONE" DR NEUMANN IN A COLLAGE OF WORDS READ HEARD INTRODUCED THE CUT-UP SCISSORS RENDERS THE PROCESS GAME AND MILITARY STRATEGY, VARIATION CLEAR AND ACT ACCORDINGLY. IF YOU POSED ENTIRELY OF REARRANGED CUT DETERMINED BY RANDOM A PAGE OF WRITTEN WORDS NO ADVANTAGE FROM KNOWING INTO WRITER PREDICT THE MOVE. THE CUT VARIATION IMAGES SHIFT SENSE ADVANTAGE IN PROCESSING TO SOUND SIGHT TO SOUND. HAVE BEEN MADE BY ACCIDENT IS WHERE RIMBAUD WAS GOING WITH ORDER THE CUT-UPS COULD "SYSTEMATIC DERANGEMENT" OF THE GAMBLING SCENE IN WITH A TEA HALLUCINATION: SEEING AND PLACES. CUT BACK. CUT FORMS. REARRANGE THE WORD AND IMAGE TO OTHER FIELDS THAN WRITING.

CUT-UPS: A PROJECT FOR DISASTROUS SUCCESS—BY BRION GYSIN

William Burroughs and I first went into techniques of writing, together, back in room #15 of the Beat Hotel during the cold Paris spring of 1958. *Naked Lunch* manuscript of every age and condition floated around the hermetically sealed room as Burroughs, thrashing about in an ectoplasmic cloud of smoke, ranted through the gargantuan roles of Doc Benway, A. J., Clem & Jody and hundreds of others he never had time to ram through the typewriter. "Am I an octopus?" he used to whine as he shuffled through shoals of typescript with all tentacles waving in the undersea atmosphere.

It looked, in those days, as though *Naked Lunch*, named so long before its birth by Kerouac, might never see the light of day outside room #15. The appearance of extracts was only hors d'oeuvres laid out on "Big Table." A pal, back in New York, was said to be willing to edit to conformist standards more fragments, which their author had scattered from Texas to Tangier, Venice, Paris; Mexico, too, probably. There was said to be a whole suitcaseful in a Tangier bar or in some junky's villa—anyway, it never got printed and where is it now?

"The cut-up method was used in (on?) *Naked Lunch* without the author's full awareness of the method he was using. The final form of *Naked Lunch* and the juxtaposition of sections were determined by the order in which material went—at random—to the printer," he writes in "The Cut-Up Method of Brion Gysin" in *A Casebook on the Beats*.

Well, those were troublous times. Sinclair Beiles flipped in and out with scraps of galley proof even as more packets of old manuscript flowed out into the space Burroughs was trying to clear out in order to kick his habit right there, as soon as the book was out of the room. The raw material of *Naked Lunch* overwhelmed us. Showers of fading snapshots fell through the air: Old Bull's Texas farm, the Upper Reaches of the Amazon ("Yage country, man. See the old *brujo*."); Tangier and the Mayan Codices ("Ain't it almost too horrible. Dig what they really up to and you wig."); shots of boys from every time and place. Burroughs was more intent on Scotch-taping his photos together into one great continuum on the wall, where scenes faded and slipped into one another, than occupied with editing the monster manuscript. ("Am I the Collier brothers?") When he found himself in front of the wrecked typewriter, he hammered out new stuff. There were already dozens of variants and, if something seemed missing, slices of earlier writing slid silently into place alongside later routines because none of the pages was numbered.

What to do with all this? Stick it on the wall along with the photographs and see what it looks like. Here, just stick these two pages together and cut down the middle. Stick it all together, end to end, and send it back like a big roll of music for a pianola. It's just material, after all. There is nothing sacred about words.

"Word falling. Photo falling. Breakthrough in grey room."

Naked Lunch appeared and Burroughs disappeared. He kicked his habit with apomorphine and flew off to London to see Dr Dent, who had first turned him on to the cure.

While cutting a mount for a drawing in room #15, I sliced through a pile of newspapers with my Stanley blade and thought of what I had said to Burroughs some six months earlier about the necessity for turning painters' techniques directly into writing. I picked up the raw words and began to piece together texts that later appeared as "First Cut-Ups" in "Minutes to Go." At the time I thought them hilariously funny and hysterically meaningful. I laughed so hard my neighbors thought I'd flipped. I hope you may discover this unusual pleasure for yourselves—this short-lived but unique intoxication. Cut up this page you are reading and see what happens. See what I say as well as hear it.

I can tell you nothing you do not know. I can show you nothing you have not seen. Anything I may say about Cut-Ups must sound like special pleading unless you try it for yourself. You cannot cut up in your head any more than I can paint in my head. Whatever you do in your head bears the prerecorded pattern of your head. Cut through that pattern and all patterns if you want something new. Take a letter you have written or a letter written to you. Cut the page into four or into three columns—any way you may choose. Shuffle the pieces and put them together at random. Cut through the word lines to hear a new voice off the page. A dialogue often breaks out. "It" speaks. Herrigel describes such an experience in *Zen in the Art of Archery* when "It" shot the arrow.

This took Herrigel six years to achieve and demanded his complete submission to a "Master," who said to him in farewell: "Even if broad seas lie between us, I shall always be with you when you practice what you have learned." Creepy? Very. That is how the Masters get around and stay around. To hell with all monopolies. As Burroughs wrote me on a card for the New Year, 1960: "Blitzkrieg the citadel of enlightenment!" Painters first suggested the means were at hand more than fifty years ago. About the time they got horses off the streets and planes in the sky, we freed ourselves from the animals and got the machine on our hands.

The means are our machines. The prime agents of the explosive force, Nova, are factors of geometric progression to the Count Down and we better catch up on their methods, but quick. I do not mean atomic piles—Hands off! I do not mean spaceships—mere Iron Lungs. I mean machines in the hands of anybody can push a button. Take your own tape recorder. I can tell you nothing you do not know. I can show you nothing you have not seen. Record your very own voice on a length of tape. Better read something you consider important. Allen Ginsberg says, in his blurb for *Soft Machine* by Burroughs: ". . . Methods which would be vain unless the author had something to cut up to start with . . ." In other words, you need words. I made my "Poem of Poems" on the tape recorder; cutting the sonnets of Shakespeare, *Anabasis* by St John Perse in the Eliot translation, and fragments of Huxley on mescaline into the Song of Songs. As Burroughs, later, had occasion to answer Spender: "It all depends on the results."

The Divine Tautology came up at me off a page one day: I AM THAT I AM, and I saw that it was lopsided. I switched the last two words to get better architectural balance around the big THAT. There was a little click as I read from right to left and then permutated the other end. AM I THAT AM I? "It" asked a question. My ear ran away down the first one hundred and twenty simple permutations and I heard, I think, what Newton said he heard: a sort of wild pealing inside my head, like an ether experience, and I fell down.

Burroughs looked grave. "Unfortunately, the means are at hand for disastrous success," he finished the quote from his New Year's card when he heard the first permutated poems speak up for themselves out of the tape recorder. "Come, come!" I protested, laughing. "Surely this is, at last, the 'artless art' the Zen-zooters are pushing. You can't call *me* the author of those poems, now, can you? I merely undid the word combination, like the letter lock on a piece of good luggage, and the poem made itself."

Who reads a newspaper can answer the conundrum of the Ages:

What are we here for? Man is here to go. But it will take more than the resources of energy in matter to keep him up there as long as he insists on being that animal, Man. "Am I THAT? Am I? Am I? Am I? ..." If I ask that I am more than THAT. Kick that Man Habit, Man. The Biological Film, now showing on Earth, can and must be rewritten. It is a lousy movie to be withdrawn Now from the dimensional screen and sent back to Rewrite. If, indeed: In the Beginning was the Word, then, the next step is: Rub out the Word.

I was helped by the BBC, who broadcast my poem "Minutes to Go." I took my tape experiments to them in London and the BBC loaned me their experimental studio with all its machines and technicians for three days. We put together a program that was later broadcast but the most interesting material remained unfinished. "Unusual sights leak out," the cut-ups had announced one day, and unusual sounds, too. Back in our Beat Hotel, Burroughs and I went on making the machines talk for themselves and broadcast Rimbaud's "disordering of the senses" through the walls.

The Exterminator, on which we collaborated, appeared at this time. In it are some Permutated Poems, faced by a page of symbols that are immediately legible as are, in a fashion, the drawings that follow. Who runs may read my drawing. Run faster to read better. I will show you this again when I make a picture with the words as they come back to me out of the tape recorder. After all, if you could look at the magnetic particles inside this plastic tape, you would see that my voice has translated them into a series of repetitive patterns. Word symbols turn back into visual symbols—tilted back and forth through this "me," my very own machine. Every thing, at that moment, is one. I am the artist when I am open. When I am closed I am Brion Gysin.

Science is near enough ready to tell me who *he* is for me to be much less interested than formerly in him. I could not care less about his so-called talent or lack of it. Brion Gysin is a drag. I am not interested; I am his soul. Yet, as long as he is one with matter in hand, I am bound to a vital interest in the pattern of his activities and patterns of the matter in which he is so desperately involved. Science and Art are two branches of the same investigation. Within the last fifty years both Science and Painting have overhauled their concept of Matter. Sand on the canvas; $e = mc^2$.

One of the easy ways the human mind, probably owing to its structure, can best conceive Space is in the limitless projection of a multidimensional grid through which progressive movement can be plotted, an infinite variety of form conceived, etc. It makes, in fact, a space picture rather like a cellular scaffolding—the bright jungle gym of Mathematics; an exercise for controlling matter and knowing space.

Now, Magic calls itself The Other Method and, as my limited education permitted no venture through maths, and as Brion Gysin had led me into a maze of Moroccan adventures, I had to content myself with what he stewed in for eight years after the war: Moorish fleshpots and the misery of the Moors. Magic is practiced more assiduously than hygiene in Morocco, though ecstatic dancing to music of the secret brotherhoods is, there, a form of psychic hygiene. You know your music when you hear it one day. You fall into line and dance until you pay the piper.

My own music was the wild flutes of the hill tribe Ahl Serif. Their secret, guarded even from them, was that they were still performing the Rites of Pan under their ragged cloak of Islam. Westermark first recognized their patron, Bou Jeloud, the Father of Skins, to be Pan, the little goat god of panic with his pipes. From an account of their dances, he gathered they must still be running the Roman Lupercalia, which had attached itself to the principal Muslim feast of the lunar year to survive.

I went into business with these people; opening a restaurant with Pan music in Tangier, called the Thousand and One Nights. It was well named, for some unforeseen, complex, cataclysmic catastrophe occurred every night.

Burroughs was in Tangier, practicing to be El Hombre Invisible and doing little writing, I believe, in those days. He spent his month staring at the toe of his shoe in an underground room of the Casbah, filled with thousands of empty Eukudol boxes. On remittance day or in the company of visiting Venetians like Alan Ansen (now in exile), he would materialize at my restaurant. "That Gysin's probably a Swiss innkeeper with a phony 'von' to his name," he used to snarl, "but I dig his pigeon pie and dancing boys the greatest." He really needed the couscous in those days: he was thin, very thin.

I fell out of business, not over money but magic. My Swiss banker never objected to items marked MAGIC that appeared in the bookkeeping done by his bank. He just raised an eyebrow and asked: "Are you running an ethnographic museum, perhaps?" In a way, I kept some notes and drawings, meaning to write a recipe book of magic. My Pan people were furious when they found out. They poisoned my food twice and then, apparently, resorted to more efficacious means to get rid of me.

During a routine kitchen check, I called for a ladder to see if a ventilator had truly been oiled. There was the Mare's Nest under my nose: a treasure trove for an ethnographer, I suppose. Seven round, speckled pebbles; seven big seeds in their pods; seven shards of mirror surrounded a small square paper packet, barely dusted over with soot. The charm stuck together with goo, probably made of newts' eyes, menstrual blood, pubic hair and chewing gum. Inside was the text, written in rusty ink from right to left across the square of paper, which had then been turned on its side and written over again to form the cabalistic grid. The invocation, when I got it hazily made out, called on the Jinn of the Hearth: "May Massa Brahim [Brion] leave this house as the smoke leaves this fire, never to return ..."

Several days later, on January 5, 1958, I lost the business over a signature given to a friendly American couple who "wanted to help me out." I was out with the shirt on my back.

I barely made it to London, where I sold my pictures of the Sahara and then crossed to Paris, which I have lived in off and on for the last thirty years. Ran into grey-green Burroughs in the Place St Michel. "Wanna score?" For the first time in all the years I had known him, I really scored with him.

Hamri and I had first met him in the hired gallery of the Rembrandt Hotel in Tangier in 1954 when he wheeled into our exhibition, arms and legs flailing, talking a mile a minute. We found he looked very Occidental, more Private Eye than Inspector Lee: he trailed long vines of *Bannisteria Caapi* from the Upper Amazon after him and old Mexican bullfight posters fluttered out from under his long trench coat instead of a shirt. An odd blue light often flashed around under the brim of his hat. Hamri and I decided, rather smugly, that we could not afford to know him because he was too Spanish. Obviously he would soon pick up with Manolo, Pepe, Kiki ... whereas; "Henrique! Joselito!" Burroughs whinnied—sort of South American boy-cries, for all we knew.

I cannot say I saw Burroughs clear during the restaurant days that followed. Caught a glimpse of him glimmering rapidly along through the shadows from one *farmacia* to the next, hugging a bottle of paregoric. I close my eyes and see him in winter, cold silver blue, rain dripping from the points of his hat and his nose.

Willie the Rat scuttles over the purple sheen of wet pavements, sniffing. Burroughs slices through the crowd in the Socco Chico, his raincoat glinting like the underbelly of a shark. He dashes at Kiki with a raised knife of rain-glitter running off his chop-finger hand. Burroughs lives chez Tony Dutch. He pokes a long, quivering nose out of calle Cristianos, picking up on: Is Kiki around? He plucks Kiki out of the Mar Chica with his glittering eye. When you squint up your eyes at him, he turns into Coleridge, De Quincey, Poe, Baudelaire and Gide . . . Now, wherefore stoppest thou me?

Hamri and me we waggle our beards—everything just like we always say. Meester Weeli-yam. (*Weeli, weeli!* What Arab women cry in alarm. Hamri's joke.) Meester Weeli-yam lives in a room Hamri and I know well, and we can imagine him down there, or so we thought, but we never could, really, because we never went to see him in all the years and really could never have imagined the celestial number of empty Eukudol boxes he had stacked up; we never knew. We never heard Kiki say: "*Quédase con su medicina,* Meester William," and shut the door to go away and be killed by just such another knife. But that was in another country and the boy is dead.

So, when Meester Weeli-yam show in St Michel, I pause; hearing Paul Bowles: "I really don't know; they're all so taken up with madness and drugs. I don't get it. But you'd like Burroughs if only you'd get to know him." We make a meet. He lives in "Heart'sease Street," rue Git le Coeur, where I lived 1938–39. But "Must hurry to my doctor—yes, my analyst; recommended by a rich junky friend with whom I goofed on my apomorphine cure with Dr Dent, unfortunately." Later, I make it up to room #15. Where are the alumni of room #15 today?

Naked Lunch served at all hours in a dark, airless, transitional room full of transformations and metamorphoses. Kafka's cockroach fled in terror. Seeing and hearing new. Burroughs bought a stainless-steel dowsing ball from a magic shop and hung it up for decoration. We learned to scry. He was tossing back whole boxes of Eubispasmes to keep his habit up but his nose clean until he could kick *Naked Lunch.* Then, the All-time Home Cure with Mr Summerface in attendance. The All-time Grizzlies out of Bill, too. Horror bears in all disguise. Cosmic Hoods. Agents rampant. Bone-cracking crustaceans. Mister Ugly Spirit. "Ah feel Ah'm about to give birth to some horrible critter," he moaned in front of the pulsing mirror. "Ah don't feel rightly hooman!" Like the Old Man of the Sea, he dissolved into all the scaly-green monsters of legend, right there in a puddle of ectoplasm, there on his bed.

Later, much later: "I suppose, Brion, you know the story about the two great magicians who had a meet to prove who's tops? First one goes through his scary-faces routine and settles back, real confident: 'Now, *you* show Me.' The second magician leans over and whispers: 'Boo!' "

I look around at the pictures, which he was the first to dig: "See the Silent Writing of Brion Gysin, Hassan-i-Sabbah, across all skies!" I write across the picture space from right to left and, then, I turn the space and write across that again to make a multi-dimensional grid with the script I picked up from the Pan people. Who runs may read. I have, I think, paid the pipers in full. Within the bright scaffolding appears a world of Little Folk, swinging in their flowering-ink jungle gym, exercising control of matter and knowing space. Writing is fifty years behind painting. Painters have been doing this sort of magic for years. They sprung words on canvas before World War I. Surely, this is the "artless art." You can't call *me* the author of these images come trooping out of the colors, now can you? Catch up on your writing: make with the words.

I roll you out a bright, new cellular framework of Space and, in it, I write your Script anew. Light writes in Space. Art is the tail of a comet. The comet is Light. We aim to rewrite this Show and there is no part in it for Hope. Cut-Ups are Machine Age knife-magic, revealing Pandora's box to be the downright nasty Stone Age gimmick it is. Cut through what you are reading. Cut this page now. But copies—after all, we are in Proliferation, too—to do cut-ups and fold-ins until we can deliver the Reality Machine in commercially reasonable quantities.

FOLD-INS

In my writing I am acting as a map maker, an explorer of psychic areas, to use the phrase of Mr Alexander Trocchi, as a cosmonaut of inner space, and I see no point in exploring areas that have already been thoroughly surveyed—A Russian scientist has said: "We will travel not only in space but in time as well—" That is to travel in space is to travel in time—If writers are to travel in space time and explore areas opened by the space age, I think they must develop techniques quite as new and definite as the techniques of physical space travel—Certainly if writing is to have a future it must at least catch up with the past in painting, music and film—Mr Lawrence Durrell has led the way in developing a new form of writing with time and space shifts as we see events from different viewpoints and realize that so seen they are literally not the same events, and that the old concepts of time and reality are no longer valid—Brion Gysin, an American painter living in Paris, has used what he calls "the cut-up method" to place at the disposal of writers the collage used in painting for fifty years—Pages of text are cut and rearranged to form new combinations of word and image—In writing my last two novels, *Nova Express* and *The Ticket That Exploded*, I have used an extension of the cut-up method I call "the fold-in method"—A page of text—my own or someone else's—is folded down the middle and placed on another page—The composite text is then read across half one text and half the other—The fold-in method extends to writing the flashback used in films, enabling the writer to move backward and forward on his time track—For example I take page one and fold it into page one hundred—I insert the resulting composite as page ten—When the reader reads page ten he is flashing forward in time to page one hundred and back in time to page one—the *déjà vu* phenomenon can so be produced to order—This method is of course used in music, where we are continually moved backward and forward on the time track by repetition and rearrangements of musical themes—

In using the fold-in method I edit, delete and rearrange as in any other method of composition—I have frequently had the experience of writing some pages of straight narrative text which were then folded in with other pages and found that the fold-ins were clearer and more comprehensible than the original texts—Perfectly clear narrative prose can be produced using the fold-in method—Best results are usually obtained by placing pages dealing with similar subjects in juxtaposition—

What does any writer do but choose, edit and rearrange material at his disposal?—The fold-in method gives the writer literally infinite extension of choice—Take for example a page of Rimbaud folded into a page of St John Perse—(two poets who have much in common)—From two pages an infinite number of combinations and images are possible—The method could also lead to a collaboration between writers on an unprecedented scale to produce works that were the composite effort of any number of writers living and dead—This happens in fact as soon as any writer starts using the fold-in method—I have made and used fold-ins from Shakespeare, Rimbaud, from newspapers, magazines, conversations and letters so that the novels I have written using this method are in fact composites of many writers—

I would like to emphasize that this is a technique and like any technique will, of course, be useful to some writers and not to others—In any case a matter for experimentation not argument—The conferring writers have been accused by the press of not paying sufficient attention to the question of human survival—In *Nova Express* (reference is to an exploding planet) and *The Ticket That Exploded*, I am primarily concerned with the question of survival—with nova conspiracies, nova criminals, and nova police—A new mythology is possible in the space age where we will again have heroes and villains with respect to intentions toward this planet—

NOTES ON THESE PAGES

To show "the fold-in method" in operation I have taken the two texts I read at The Writers' Conference and folded them into newspaper articles on The Conference, The Conference Folder, typed out selections from various writers, some of who were present and some of whom were not, to form a composite of many writers living and dead: Shakespeare, Samuel Beckett, T. S. Eliot, F. Scott Fitzgerald, William Golding, Alexander Trocchi, Norman Mailer, Colin MacInnes, Hugh MacDiarmid.

Mr Bradly Mr Martin, in my mythology, is a God that failed, a God of Conflict in two parts so created to keep a tired old show on the road, The God of Arbitrary Power and Restraint, Of Prison and

Pressure, who needs subordinates, who needs what he calls "his human dogs" while treating them with the contempt a con man feels for his victims—But remember the con man needs the Mark— The Mark does not need the con man—Mr Bradly Mr Martin needs his "dogs" his "errand boys" his "human animals"—He needs them because he is literally blind. They do not need him. In my mythological system he is overthrown in a revolution of his "dogs"—"Dogs that were his eyes shut off Mr Bradly Mr Martin."

"The ticket that exploded posed little time so I'll say good night."

bath cubicle . . . lapping water over the concrete floor . . . pants slide . . . twisting thighs . . . penny arcades of an old dream . . . played the flute, shirt flapping down the cool path . . . on the 30th of July a distant room left no address . . . sleep breath . . . pale dawn wallpaper . . . faded morning . . . a place forgotten . . . a young man is dust and shredded memories naked empty a ding-dong bell . . . what in St Louis after September? . . . curtains . . . red light . . . blue eyes in the tarnished mirror pale fingers fading from ruined suburbs . . . fingers light and cold pulled up his pants . . . dark pipes call #23 . . . you touched from frayed jacket masturbated under thin pants . . . cracked pavements . . . sharp fish smells and dead eyes in doorways . . . soccer scores . . . the rotting kingdom . . . ghost hands at the paneless café . . .

"Like good-by, Johnny. On the 30th of July death left no address."

outskirts of the city . . . bare legs hairs . . . lunar fingers light and cold . . . distant music under the slate roof . . . soccer scores . . . the street blew rain . . . dawn shadow . . .

"Like good-by, Johnny."

cold blue room . . . distant music on the wind . . . tarnished mirror in the bath cubicle young face lapping water . . . red light . . . felt his pants slide . . . twisting thighs . . . street dust on bare leg hairs . . . open shirt . . . city sounds under the slate roof . . . played the flute with fingers fading . . . the street blew rain . . . pale smell of dawn in the door . . . played the flute with fingers light and cold . . . dark pipes left no address . . . sleep breath under the slate roof . . . silence ebbing from rose wallpaper . . . outskirts of the city masturbated under thin pants ten-year-old keeping watch . . . outside East St Louis . . . cracked pavement . . . sharp scent of weeds . . . faded khaki pants . . . soccer scores . . . the driver shrugged . . . violence roared past the Café de France . . . he dressed hastily shirt flapping . . .

"Like good-by, Johnny."

wind through the curtains ... bare iron frame of a dusty bed ....
in the tarnished mirror dead eyes of an old dream and the dreamer
gone at dawn shirt ... takes his way toward the sea breath of the
trade winds on his face open shirt flapping ... cool path from
ruined suburbs ... stale memories ... excrement mixed with
flowers ... fly full of dust pulled up his pants ... birdcalls ...
lapping water ... a distant cool room ... leg hairs rub rose wallpaper ... pale dawn shirt in the door ... sharp smell of weeds ...
you touched frayed jacket ... mufflers ... small pistols ... quick
fires from bits of driftwood ... fish smells and dead eyes in doorways ... a place forgotten ... the ancient rotting kingdom ... ghost
hands at paneless windows ... dust and shredded memories of war
and death ... petrified statues in a vast charred plain ...

in a rubbish heap to the sky Metal chess determined gasoline
fires and smoke in motionless air—Smudge two speeds—DSL
walks "here" beside me on extension lead from hairless skull—
Flesh-smeared recorder consumed by slow metal fires—Dog-proof
room important for our "oxygen" lines—Group respective recorder layout—"Throw the gasoline on them" determined the life
form we invaded: insect screams—I woke up with "marked for
invasion" recording set to run for as long as phantom "cruelties"
are playing back while waiting to pick up Eduardo's "corrupt"
speed and volume variation Madrid—Tape recorder banks tumescent flesh—Our mikes planning speaker stood there in 1910 straw
word—Either way is a bad move to The Biologic Stairway—The
whole thing tell you—No good—*No bueno* outright or partially—
The next state walking in a rubbish heap to Form A—Form A
directs sound channels heat—White flash mangled down to a form
of music—Life Form A as follows was alien focus—Broken pipes
refuse "oxygen"—Form A parasitic wind identity fading out—
"Word falling—Photo falling" flesh-smeared counterorders—
determined by last Electrician—Alien mucus cough language
learned to keep all Board Room Reports waiting sound formations
—Alien mucus tumescent code train on Madrid—Convert in
"dirty pictures S"—simple repetition—Whole could be used as
model for a bad move—Better than shouts: "No good—*No
bueno*"—

CITIES OF THE RED NIGHT

Cities of the Red Night is William Burroughs' most recent publication, and his longest novel to date, which appeared in 1981 first in the United States and shortly afterwards in Britain, receiving the best reviews on publication of any of his novels. It signalled his ultimate and belated recognition by the literary establishments of both London and New York where, in spite of having become a household name to the generation of the sixties and to all booksellers, and even with his immense European reputation, he was still regarded with considerable suspicion. It is nearer to a conventional novel than any of his earlier work, while the hangings, sodomy and other controversial subject-matter have obviously ceased to shock. Although *Cities* is episodic, most of the interweaving plots continue thoughout the book, so that the eighteenth-century adventures of Captain Mission, put into fictional form through the diaries, notebooks and descriptions of a pirate ship and its crew of libertarian and randy adolescents alternate with the quest of Clem Snide, private investigator or "private asshole", signalling his lack of brightness, who is sent to find a missing boy, Jerry; the latter turns out to have died in a ceremony of ritual magic in Athens, but the search continues. And there are many other plots, as for instance the scouting party of Yen Lee in Tibet, and the journey of Farnsworth, a British district health officer in Waghdas, an opium addict, whose dying delirium may be the subject of the whole novel. Not only do the episodes and the characters—in spite of different time scales and historical periods—overlap, merge and transmute each other, as the author with his earlier books cuts up and folds in his own and other work, but the concept of time travel, as derived from the theories of J. W. Dunne, on which much of the work of J. B. Priestley is also based, is given full expression in this book.

These extracts are mostly from two sections of the book, Clem Snide's search for Jerry Green, and the descriptions of the Cities of the Red Night, a manuscript within a manuscript, which is given to Clem Snide when, his search for one missing person having faded into another not unrelated search, Lola La Chata enlightens him about the fate of John Everson, the second missing person. The manuscript helps to explain the Burroughs version of history, the prescence of a fever that through death and orgasm (usually by hanging) enables *karma* to take place, the reincarnation of the dead by fusion with the living.

The other main plot, interleaved with Clem Snide's quest, is the story of the boy pirates fighting the Spanish two centuries earlier, based on Captain Mission's story. But that is not given here; in fact it is a whole novel on its own that the reader will find in the complete book, published by *Picador* simultaneously with this Reader.

All that remains to be said is that to readers of William Burroughs, *Cities of the Red Night* is above all highly enjoyable, offering little in the way of experimental writing or intellectual difficulty, while at the same time opening the mind to a bewildering series of historical, sociological and mystical ideas. It is never clear here, or for that matter elsewhere in Mr Burroughs' work, exactly when he has his tongue in his cheek in expounding theories of lost civilizations, ESP, international conspiracy or para-psychology, but as a writer he knows how to catch the interest and hold it. The hardcover edition was illustrated with Pieter Brueghel's *Triumph of the Dead*, which reveals a landscape where the horrors of war are portrayed both realistically and symbolically on the same canvas: this is exactly what Burroughs does in fictional terms. He has emerged finally as a great storyteller as well as a great moralist of unconventional hue. Although he is still writing, and further novels and collections of essays will appear in the future, *Cities of the Red Night* succeeds in rounding off a remarkable literary career, which was founded in the degradation of his own drug addiction, and has managed to use all the horrors of his personal experience and of a clear-sighted but jaundiced observation of the real world, together with a synthesis of reading, thought, experiment and imagination, so that the period of maturity that began with *The Naked Lunch* and ends for the time being with *Cities of the Red Night* has given American writing its outstanding voice of the post-war period.

THE HEALTH OFFICER

September 13, 1923.

Farnsworth, the District Health Officer, was a man so grudging in what he asked of life that every win was a loss; yet he was not without a certain plodding persistence of effort and effectiveness in his limited area. The current emergency posed by the floods and the attendant cholera epidemic, while it did not spur him to any unusual activity, left him unruffled.

Every morning at sunrise, he bundled his greasy maps—which he studied at breakfast while he licked butter off his fingers—into his battered Land-Rover and set out to inspect his district, stopping here and there to order more sandbags for the levees (knowing his orders would be disregarded, as they generally were unless the Commissioner happened to be with him). He ordered three bystanders, presumably relatives, to transport a cholera case to the district hospital at Waghdas and left three opium pills and instructions for preparing rice water. They nodded, and he drove on, having done what he could.

The emergency hospital at Waghdas was installed in an empty army barracks left over from the war. It was understaffed and overcrowded, mostly by patients who lived near enough and were still strong enough to walk. The treatment for cholera was simple: each patient was assigned to a straw pallet on arrival and given a gallon of rice water and half a gram of opium. If he was still alive twelve hours later, the dose of opium was repeated. The survival rate was about twenty percent. Pallets of the dead were washed in carbolic solution and left in the sun to dry. The attendants were mostly Chinese who had taken the job because they were allowed to smoke the opium and feed the ash to the patients. The smell of cooking rice, opium smoke, excrement, and carbolic permeated the hospital and the area around it for several hundred yards.

At ten o'clock the Health Officer entered the hospital. He requisitioned more carbolic and opium, sent off another request for a doctor, which he expected and hoped would be ignored. He felt that a doctor fussing around the hospital would only make matters worse; he might even object to the opium dosage as too high, or attempt to interfere with the opium smoking of the attendants. The

Health Officer had very little use for doctors. They simply complicated things to make themselves important.

After spending half an hour in the hospital, he drove to Ghadis to see the Commissioner, who invited him to lunch. He accepted without enthusiasm, declining a gin before lunch and a beer with lunch. He picked at the rice and fish, and ate a small plate of stewed fruit. He was trying to persuade the Commissioner to assign some convicts to work on the levees.

"Sorry, old boy, not enough soldiers to guard them."

"Well, it's a serious situation."

"Daresay."

Farnsworth did not press the point. He simply did what he could and let it go at that. Newcomers to the district wondered what kept him going at all. Old-timers like the Commissioner knew. For the Health Officer had a sustaining vice. Every morning at sunrise, he brewed a pot of strong tea and washed down a gram of opium. When he returned from his rounds in the evening, he repeated the dose and gave it time to take effect before he prepared his evening meal of stewed fruit and wheat bread. He had no permanent houseboy, since he feared a boy might steal his opium. Twice a week he had a boy in to clean the bungalow, and then he locked his opium up in an old rusty safe where he kept his reports. He had been taking opium for five years and had stabilized his dosage after the first year and never increased it, nor gone on to injections of morphine. This was not due to strength of character, but simply to the fact that he felt he owed himself very little, and that was what he allotted himself.

Driving back to find the sandbags not there, the cholera patient dead, and his three relatives droopy-eyed from the opium pills he had left, he felt neither anger nor exasperation, only the slight lack that had increased in the last hour of his drive, so that he stepped harder on the accelerator. Arriving at his bungalow, he washed down an opium pill with bottled water and lit the kerosene stove for his tea. He carried the tea onto the porch and by the time he had finished the second cup, he was feeling the opium wash through the back of his neck and down his withered thighs. He could have passed for fifty; actually he was twenty-eight. He sat there for half an hour looking at the muddy river and the low hills covered with scrub. There was a mutter of thunder, and as he cooked his evening meal the first drops of rain fell on the rusty galvanized iron roof.

He awoke to the unaccustomed sound of lapping water. Hastily he pulled on his pants and stepped onto the porch. Rain was still falling, and the water had risen during the night to a level of twelve inches under the bungalow and a few inches below the hubcaps of his Land-Rover. He washed down an opium pill and put the water on the stove for his tea. Then he dusted off an alligator-skin Gladstone bag and started packing, opening drawers and compartments in the safe. He packed clothes, reports, a compass, a sheath knife, a .45 Webley revolver and a box of shells, matches, and a mess kit. He filled his canteen with bottled water and wrapped a loaf of bread in paper. Pouring his tea, the water rising under his feet, he experienced a tension in the groin, a surge of adolescent lust that was stronger for being inexplicable and inappropriate. His medical supplies and opium he packed in a separate bag, and as an added precaution, a slab of opium the size of a cigarette package, wrapped in heavy tinfoil, went into his side coat pocket. By the time he had finished packing, his pants were sticking out at the fly. The opium would soon take care of that.

He stepped from the porch into the Land-Rover. The motor caught, and he headed for high ground above the flood. The route he took was seldom used and several times he had to cut trees out of the road with an ax. Towards sundown, he reached the medical mission of Father Dupré. This was out of his district, and he had met the priest only once before.

Father Dupré, a thin red faced man with a halo of white hair, greeted him politely but without enthusiasm. He brightened somewhat when Farnsworth brought out his medical supplies and went with him to the dispensary and hospital, which was simply a large hut screened-in at the sides. The Health Officer passed out opium pills to all the patients.

"No matter what is wrong with them, they will feel better shortly."

The priest nodded absently as he led the way back to the house. Farnsworth had swallowed his opium pill with water from his canteen, and it was beginning to take effect as he sat down on the porch. The priest was looking at him with a hostility he was trying hard to conceal. Farnsworth wondered what exactly was wrong. The priest fidgeted and cleared his throat. He said abruptly in a strained voice, "Would you care for a drink?"

"Thank you, no. I never touch it."

Relief flooded the priest's face with a beneficent glow. "Something else then?"

"I'd love some tea."

"Of course. I'll have the boy make it."

The priest came back with a bottle of whiskey, a glass, and a soda siphon. Farnsworth surmised that he kept his whiskey under lock and key somewhere out of the reach of his boys. The priest poured himself a generous four fingers and shot in a dash of soda. He took a long drink and beamed at his guest. Farnsworth decided that the moment was propitious to ask a favor, while the good father was still relieved at not having to share his dwindling supply of whiskey, and before he had overindulged.

"I want to get through to Ghadis if possible. I suppose it's hopeless by road, even if I had enough petrol?"

The priest got a map and spread it out on the table. "Absolutely out of the question. This whole area is flooded. Only possibility is by boat to here . . . from there it's forty miles downriver to Ghadis. I could lend you a boat with a boy and outboard, but there's no petrol here. . . ."

"I think I have enough petrol for that, considering its all downstream."

"You'll run into logjams—may take hours to cut through . . . figure how long it could take you at the longest, and then double it . . . my boy only knows the route as far as here. Now this stretch here is very dangerous . . . the river narrows quite suddenly, no noise you understand, and no warning . . . advise you to take the canoe out and carry it down to here . . . take one extra day, but well worth it at this time of year. Of course you *might* get through—but if anything goes wrong . . . the current, you understand . . . even a strong swimmer . . ."

The following day at dawn, Farnsworth's belongings and the supplies for the trip were loaded into the dugout canoe. The boy, Ali, was a smoky black with sharp features, clearly a mixture of Arab and Negro stock. He was about eighteen, with beautiful teeth and a quick shy smile. The priest waved from the jetty as the boat swung into midstream. Farnsworth sat back lazily, watching the water and the jungle slide past. There was not much sign of life. A few birds and monkeys. Once three alligators wallowing in a mudbank slid into the water, showing their teeth in depraved smiles. Several times logjams had to be cleared with an ax.

At sundown they made camp on a gravel bank. Farnsworth put water on for tea while Ali walked to the end of the bank and dropped a hook baited with a worm into a deep clear pool. By the time the water was boiling, he was back with an eighteen-inch fish. As Ali cleaned the fish and cut it into sections, Farnsworth washed down his opium pill. He offered one to Ali, who examined it, sniffed at it, smiled, and shook his head.

"Chinese boy ..." He leaned over holding an imaginary opium pipe to a lamp. He drew the smoke in and let his eyes droop. "No get—" He put his hands on his stomach and rocked back and forth.

By the afternoon of the second day the stream had widened considerably. Towards sundown Farnsworth took an opium pill and dozed off. Suddenly he was wide awake with a start, and he reached for the map. This was the stretch that Father Dupré had warned him about. He turned towards Ali, but Ali knew already. He was steering for shore.

The silent rush of the current swept the boat broadside, and the rudder wire snapped like a bowstring. The boat twisted out of control, swept towards a logjam. A splintering crash, and Farnsworth was underwater, struggling desperately against the current. He felt a stab of pain as a branch ripped through his coat and along his side.

He came to on the bank. Ali was pushing water out of his lungs. He sat up breathing heavily and coughing. His coat was in tatters, oozing blood. He felt for the pocket, and looked at his empty hand. The opium was gone. He had sustained a superficial scratch down the left hip and across the buttock. They had salvaged nothing except the short machete that Ali wore in a sheath at his belt, and Farnsworth's hunting knife.

Farnsworth drew a map in the sand to approximate their position. He calculated the distance to one of the large tributaries to be about forty miles. Once there, they could fashion a raft and drift downstream to Ghadis, where of course ... the words of Father Dupré played back in his mind: "Figure the longest time it could take you and then double it ..."

Darkness was falling, and they had to stay there for the night, even though he was losing precious travel time. He knew that in seventy-two hours at the outside he would be immobilized for lack of opium. At daybreak they set out heading north. Progress was slow; the undergrowth had to be cut step by step. There were swamps and streams in the way, and from time to time deep gorges that necessitated long detours. The unaccustomed exertion knocked the opium out of his system, and by nightfall he was already feverish and shivering.

By morning he was barely able to walk, but managed to stagger along for a few miles. The next day he was convulsed by stomach cramps and they barely covered a mile. The third day he could not move. Ali massaged his legs, which were knotted with cramps, and brought him water and fruit. He lay there unable to move for four days and four nights.

Occasionally he dozed off and woke up screaming from nightmares. These often took the form of attacks by centipedes and scorpions of strange sizes and shapes, moving with great speed, that would suddenly rush at him. Another recurrent nightmare was set in the market of a Near Eastern city. The place was at first unknown to him but more familiar with each step he took, as if some hideous jigsaw of memory were slowly falling into place: the stalls all empty of food and merchandise, the smell of hunger and death, the greenish glow and a strange smoky sun, sulfurous blazing hate in faces that turned to look at him as he passed. Now they were all pointing at him and shouting a word he could not understand.

On the eighth day he was able to walk again. He was still racked with stomach cramps and diarrhea, but the leg cramps were almost gone. On the tenth day he felt distinctly better and stronger, and was able to eat a fish. On the fourteenth day they reached a sandbank by a wide clear river. This was not the tributary they were looking for, but would certainly lead into it. Ali had saved a piece of carbolic soap in a tin box, and they stripped off their tattered clothes and waded into the cool water. Farnsworth washed off the dirt and sweat and smell of his sickness. Ali was rubbing soap on his back and Farnsworth felt a sudden rush of blood to the crotch. Trying to hide his erection, he waded ashore with his back to Ali, who followed laughing and splashing water to wash the soap off.

Farnsworth lay down on his shirt and pants and fell into a wordless vacuum, feeling the sun on his back and the faint ache of the healing scratch. He saw Ali sitting naked above him, Ali's hands massaging his back, moving down to the buttocks. Something was surfacing in his body, drifting up from remote depths of memory, and he saw as if projected on a screen a strange incident from his adolescence. He was in the British Museum at the age of fourteen, standing in front of a glass case. He was alone in the room. In the case was the figure, about two feet long, of a reclining man. The man was naked, the right knee flexed, holding the body a few inches off the ground, the penis exposed. The hands were extended in front of the man palms down, and the face was reptile or animal, something between an alligator and a jaguar.

The boy was looking at the thighs and buttocks and genitals, breathing through his teeth. He was getting stiff and lubricating, his pants sticking out at the fly. He was squeezing into the figure, a dream tension gathering in his crotch, squeezing and stretching, a strange smell unlike anything he had ever smelled before but familiar as smell itself, a naked man lying by a wide clear river—the twisted figure. Silver spots boiled in front of his eyes and he ejaculated.

Ali's hands parted his buttocks, he spit on his rectum—his body opening and the figure entering him in a silent rush, flexing his right knee, stretching his jaw forward into a snout, his head flattening, his brain squeezing out the smell from inside ... a hoarse hissing sound was forced from his lips and light popped in his eyes as his body boiled and twisted out scalding spurts.

Stage with a jungle backdrop. Frogs croak and birds call from recorder. Farnsworth as an adolescent is lying facedown on sand. Ali is fucking him and he squirms with a slow wallowing movement showing his teeth in a depraved smile. The lights dim for a few seconds. When the lights come up Farnsworth is wearing an alligator suit that leaves his ass bare and Ali is still fucking him. As Ali and Farnsworth slide offstage Farnsworth lifts one webbed finger to the audience while a Marine band plays "Semper Fl." Offstage splash.

THE RESCUE

A sepia etching onscreen. Written at the bottom in gold lettering: "The Hanging of Captain Strobe the Gentleman Pirate. Panama City; May 13, 1702." In the center of the square in front of a courthouse Captain Strobe stands on a gallows platform with a noose around his neck. He is a slender handsome youth of twenty-five in eighteenth-century costume, his blond hair tied in a knot at the back of his head. He looks disdainfully down at the crowd. A line of soldiers stands in front of the gallows.

The etching slowly comes alive, giving off a damp heat, a smell of weeds and mud flats and sewage. Vultures roost on the old courthouse of flaking yellow stucco. The gypsy hangman—thin, effeminate-looking, with greasy crinkled hair and glistening eyes—stands by the gallows with a twisted smirk on his face. The crowd is silent, mouths open, waiting.

At a signal from an officer, a soldier steps forward with an ax and knocks the support from under the platform. Strobe falls and hangs there, his feet a few inches above the limestone paving which is cracked here and there, weeds and vines growing through. Five minutes pass in silence. Vultures wheel overhead. On Strobe's face is a strange smile. A yellow-green aura surrounds his body.

The silence is shattered by an explosion. Chunks of masonry rain down on the square. The blast swings Strobe's body in a long arc, his feet brushing the weeds. The soldiers rush offstage, leaving only six men to guard the gallows. The crowd surges forward, pulling out knives, cutlasses, and pistols. The soldiers are disarmed. A lithe boy who looks like a Malay shows white teeth and bright red gums as he throws a knife. The knife catches the hangman in the throat just above the collarbone. He falls squawking and spitting blood like a stricken bird. Captain Strobe is cut down and borne to a waiting carriage.

The carriage careens into a side street. Inside the cart the boy loosens the noose and presses air in and out of Strobe's lungs. Strobe opens his eyes and writhes in agony from the pricklings and shootings as his circulation returns. The boy gives him a vial of black liquid.

"Drink this, Captain."

In a few minutes the laudanum takes effect and Strobe is able to walk as they leave the cart. The boy leads the way along a jungle path to a fishing boat moored at a pier on the outskirts of the city. Two younger boys are in the boat. The boat is cast off and the sail set. Captain Strobe collapses on a pallet in the cabin. The boy helps him undress and covers him with a cotton blanket.

Strobe lay back with closed eyes. He had not slept since his capture three days ago. The opium and the movement of the boat spread a pleasant languor through his body. Pictures drifted in front of his eyes....

A vast ruined stone building with square marble columns in a green underwater light ... a luminous green haze, thicker and darker at ground level, shading up to light greens and yellows ... deep blue canals and red brick buildings ... sunlight on water ... a boy standing on a beach naked with dusky rose genitals ... red night sky over a desert city ... clusters of violet light raining down on sandstone steps and bursting with a musky smell of ozone ... strange words in his throat, a taste of blood and metal ... a white ship sailing across a gleaming empty sky dusted with stars ... singing fish in a ruined garden ... a strange pistol in his hand that shoots blue sparks ... beautiful diseased faces in red light, all looking at something he cannot see....

He awoke with a throbbing erection and a sore throat, his brain curiously blank and factual. He accepted his rescue as he had been prepared to accept his death. He knew exactly where he was: some forty miles south of Panama City. He could see the low coastline of mangrove swamps laced with inlets, the shark fins, the stagnant seawater.

THE PRIVATE ASSHOLE

The name is Clem Williamson Snide. I am a private asshole.

As a private investigator I run into more death than the law allows. I mean the law of averages. There I am outside the hotel room waiting for the corespondent to reach a crescendo of amorous noises. I always find that if you walk in just as he goes off he won't have time to disengage himself and take a swing at you. When me and the house dick open the door with a passkey, the smell of shit and bitter almonds blows us back into the hall. Seems they both took a cyanide capsule and fucked until the capsules dissolved. A real messy love death.

Another time I am working on a routine case of industrial sabotage when the factory burns down killing twenty-three people. These things happen. I am a man of the world. Going to and fro and walking up and down in it.

Death smells. I mean it has a special smell, over and above the smell of cyanide, carrion, blood, cordite or burnt flesh. It's like opium. Once you smell it you never forget. I can walk down a street and get a whiff of opium smoke and I know someone is kicking the gong around.

I got a whiff of death as soon as Mr Green walked into my office. You can't always tell whose death it is. Could be Green, his wife, or the missing son he wants me to find. Last letter from the island of Spetsai two months ago. After a month with no word the family made inquiries by long-distance phone.

"The embassy wasn't at all helpful," said Mr Green.

I nodded. I knew just how unhelpful they could be.

"They referred us to the Greek police. Fortunately, we found a man there who speaks English."

"That could be Colonel Dimitri."

"Yes. You know him?"

I nodded, waiting for him to continue.

"He checked and could find no record that Jerry had left the country, and no hotel records after Spetsai."

"He could be visiting someone."

"I'm sure he would write."

"You feel then that this is not just an instance of neglect on his part, or perhaps a lost letter? ... That happens in the Greek islands...."

"Both Mrs Green and I are convinced that something is wrong."

"Very well, Mr Green, there is the question of my fee: a hundred dollars a day plus expenses and a thousand-dollar retainer. If I work on a case two days and spend two hundred dollars, I refund six hundred to the client. If I have to leave the country, the retainer is two thousand. Are these terms satisfactory?"

"Yes."

"Very good. I'll start right here in New York. Sometimes I have been able to provide the client with the missing person's address after a few hours' work. He may have written to a friend."

"That's easy. He left his address book. Asked me to mail it to him care of American Express in Athens." He passed me the book.

"Excellent."

Now, on a missing-person case I want to know everything the client can tell me about the missing person, no matter how seemingly unimportant and irrelevant. I want to know preferences in food, clothes, colors, reading, entertainment, use of drugs and alcohol, what cigarette brand he smokes, medical history. I have a questionnaire printed with five pages of questions. I got it out of the filing cabinet and passed it to him.

"Will you please fill out this questionnaire and bring it back here day after tomorrow. That will give me time to check out the local addresses."

"I've called most of them," he said curtly, expecting me to take the next plane for Athens.

"Of course. But friends of an MP—missing person—are not always honest with the family. Besides, I daresay some of them have moved or had their phones disconnected. Right?" He nodded. I·put my hands on the questionnaire. "Some of these questions may seem irrelevant but they all add up. I found a missing person once from knowing that he could wriggle his ears. I've noticed that you are left-handed. Is your son also left-handed?"

"Yes, he is."

"You can skip that question. Do you have a picture of him with you?"

He handed me a photo. Jerry was a beautiful kid. Slender, red hair, green eyes far apart, a wide mouth. Sexy and kinky-looking.

"Mr Green, I want all the photos of him you can find. If I use any I'll have copies made and return the originals. If he did any painting, sketching, or writing I'd like to see that too. If he sang or played an instrument I want recordings. In fact, any recordings of his voice. And please bring if possible some article of clothing that hasn't been dry-cleaned since he wore it."

"It's true then that you use uh psychic methods?"

"I use any methods that help me to find the missing person. If I can locate him in my own mind that makes it easier to locate him outside it."

"My wife is into psychic things. That's why I came to you. She has an intuition that something has happened to him and she says only a psychic can find him."

That makes two of us, I thought. He wrote me a check for a thousand dollars. We shook hands.

I went right to work. Jim, my assistant, was out of town on an industrial-espionage case—he specializes in electronics. So I was on my own. Ordinarily I don't carry iron on an MP case, but this one smelled of danger. I put on my snub-nosed .38 in a shoulder holster. Then I unlocked a drawer and put three joints of the best Colombian, laced with hash, into my pocket. Nothing like a joint to break the ice and stir the memory. I also took a deck of heroin. It buys more than money sometimes.

Most of the addresses were in the SoHo area. That meant lofts, and that often means the front door is locked. So I started with an address on Sixth Steet.

She opened the door right away, but she kept the chain on. Her pupils were dilated, her eyes running, and she was snuffling, waiting for the Man. She looked at me with hatred.

I smiled. "Expecting someone else?"

"You a cop?"

"No. I'm a private investigator hired by the family to find Jerry Green. You knew him."

"Look, I don't have to talk to you."

"No, you don't have to. But you might want to." I showed her the deck of heroin. She undid the chain.

The place was filthy—dishes stacked in a sink, cockroaches running over them. The bathtub was in the kitchen and hadn't been used for a long time. I sat down gingerly in a chair with the springs showing. I held the deck in my hand where she could see it. "You got any pictures of him?"

She looked at me and she looked at the heroin. She rummaged in a drawer, and tossed two pictures onto a coffee table that wobbled. "Those should be worth something."

They were. One showed Jerry in drag, and he made a beautiful girl. The other showed him standing up naked with a hard-on. "Was he gay?"

"Sure. He liked getting fucked by Puerto Ricans and having his picture took."

"He pay you?"

"Sure, twenty bucks. He kept most of the pictures."

"Where'd he get the money?"

"I don't know."

She was lying. I went into my regular spiel. "Now look, I'm not a cop. I'm a private investigator paid by his family. I'm paid to find him, that's all. He's been missing for two months." I started to put the heroin back into my pocket and that did it.

"He was pushing C."

I tossed the deck onto the coffee table. She locked the door behind me.

Later that evening, over a joint, I interviewed a nice young gay couple, who simply *adored* Jerry.

"Such a sweet boy . . ."

"So understanding . . ."

"Understanding?"

"About gay people. He even marched with us. . . ."

"And look at the postcard he sent us from Athens." It was a museum postcard showing a statue of a nude youth found at Kouros. "Wasn't that cute of him?"

Very cute, I thought.

I interviewed his steady girl friend, who told me he was all mixed up.

"He had to get away from his mother's influence and find himself. We talked it all over."

I interviewed everyone I could find in the address book. I talked to waiters and bartenders all over the SoHo area: Jerry was a nice boy . . . polite . . . poised . . . a bit reserved. None of them had an inkling of his double life as a coke pusher and homosexual transvestite. I see I am going to need some more heroin on this one. That's easy. I know some narco boys who owe me a favor. It takes an ounce and a ticket to San Francisco to buy some names from the junky chick.

Seek and you shall find. I nearly found an ice pick in my

stomach. Knock and it shall be opened unto you. Often it wasn't opened unto me. But I finally found the somebody who: a twenty-year-old Puerto Rican kid named Kiki, very handsome and quite fond of Jerry in his way. Psychic too, and into Macambo magic. He told me Jerry had the mark of death on him.

"What was his source for the coke?"

His face closed over. "I don't know."

"Can't blame you for not knowing. May I suggest to you that his source was a federal narc?"

His deadpan went deader. "I didn't tell you anything."

"Did he hear voices? Voices giving him orders?"

"I guess he did. He was controlled by something."

I gave him my card. "If you ever need anything let me know."

Mr Green showed up the next morning with a stack of photos. The questionnaire I had given him had been neatly filled out on a typewriter. He also brought a folio of sketches and a green knitted scarf. The scarf reeked of death.

I glanced at the questionnaire. Born April 18, 1951, in Little America, Wyoming. "Admiral Byrd welcomes you aboard the Deep Freeze Special." I looked through the photos: Jerry as a baby ... Jerry on a horse ... Jerry with a wide sunlit grin holding up a string of trout ... graduation pictures ... Jerry as the Toff in the high school play *A Night at an Inn*. They all looked exactly as they should look. Like he was playing the part expected of him. There were about fifty recent photos, all looking like Jerry.

Take fifty photos of anyone. There will be some photos where the face is so different you can hardly recognize the subject. I mean most people have many faces. Jerry had *one*. Don Juan says anyone who always looks like the same person isn't a person. He is a person impersonator.

I looked at Jerry's sketches. Good drawing, no talent. Empty and banal as sunlight. There were also a few poems, so bad I couldn't read them. Needless to say, I didn't tell Mr Green what I had found out about Jerry's sex and drug habits. I just told him that no one I had talked to had heard from Jerry since his disappearance, and that I was ready to leave for Athens at once if he still wanted to retain me. Money changed hands.

At the Athens Hilton I got Dimitri on the phone and told him I was looking for the Green boy.

"Ah yes ... we get so many of these cases ... our time and resources are limited."

"I understand. But I've got a bad feeling about this one. He had some kinky habits."

"S-M?"

"Sort of ... and underworld connections...." I didn't want to mention C over the phone.

"If I find anything out I'll let you know."

"Thanks. I'm going out to Spetsai tomorrow to have a look around. Be back on Thursday...."

I called Skouras in Spetsai. He's the tourist agent there. He owns or leases villas and rents out apartments during the season. He organizes tours. He owns the discotheque. He is the first man any traveler to Spetsai sees, and the last, since he is also the agent for transport.

"Yes, I know about it. Had a call from Dimitri. Glad to help any way I can. You need a room?"

"If possible I'd like the room he had."

"You can have any room you want ... the season is over."

For once the hovercraft was working. I was in luck. The hovercraft takes an hour and the boat takes six.

Yes, Skouras remembered Jerry. Jerry arrived with some young people he'd met on the boat—two Germans with rucksacks and a Swedish girl with her English boyfriend. They stayed at one of Skouras's villas on the beach—the end villa, where the road curves out along the sea wall. I knew the place. I'd stayed there once three years earlier in 1970.

"Anything special about the others?"

"Nothing. Looked like thousands of other young people who swarm over the islands every summer. They stayed a week. The others went on to Lesbos. Jerry went back to Athens alone."

Where did they eat? Where did they take coffee? Skouras knew. He knows everything that goes on in Spetsai.

"Go to the discotheque?"

"Every night. The boy Jerry was a good dancer."

"Anybody in the villa now?"

"Just the caretaker and his wife."

He gave me the keys. I noticed a worn copy of *The Magus* by John Fowles. As soon as anyone walks into his office, Skouras knows whether he should lend him the book. He has his orders. Last time I was there he lent me the book and I read it. Even rode out on a horse to look at the house of the Magus and fell off the horse on the way back. I pointed to the book. "By any chance ..."

He smiled. "Yes. I lent him the book and he returned it when he left. Said he found it most interesting."

"Could I borrow it again?"

"Of course."

The villa stood a hundred feet from the beach. The apartment was on the second floor—three bedrooms off a hall, kitchen and bathroom at the end of the hall, balcony along one side of the building. There was a musty smell, dank and chilly, blinds down. I pulled up the blinds in all three bedrooms and selected the middle one, where I had stayed before. Two beds, two chairs, coat hangers on nails in the wall.

I switched on an electric heater and took my recorder out of its case. This is a very special recorder designed and assembled by my assistant, Jim, and what it won't pick up isn't there. It is also specially designed for cut-ins and overlays, and you can switch from Record to Playback without stopping the machine.

I recorded a few minutes in all three rooms. I recorded the toilet flushing and the shower running. I recorded the water running in the kitchen sink, the rattle of dishes, and the opening and closing and hum of the refrigerator. I recorded on the balcony. Now I lay down on the bed and read some selections from *The Magus* into the recorder.

I will explain exactly how these recordings are made. I want an hour of Spetsai: an hour of places where my MP has been and the sounds he has heard. But not in sequence. I don't start at the beginning of the tape and record to the end. I spin the tape back and forth, cutting in at random so that *The Magus* may be cut off in the middle of a word by a flushing toilet, or *The Magus* may cut into sea sounds. It's a sort of *I Ching* or table-tapping procedure. How random is it actually? Don Juan says that nothing is random to a man of knowledge: everything he sees or hears is there just at that time waiting to be seen and heard.

I get out my camera and take pictures of the three rooms, the bathroom, and the kitchen. I take pictures from the balcony. I put the machine back in the case and go outside, recording around the villa and taking pictures at the same time: pictures of the villa; a picture of the black cat that belongs to the caretaker; pictures of the beach, which is empty now except for a party of hardy Swedes.

I have lunch in a little restaurant on the beach where Jerry and his friends used to eat. Mineral water and a salad. The proprietor remembers me and we shake hands. Coffee at the waterfront café where Jerry and his friends took coffee. Record. Take pictures. I cover the post office, the two kiosks that sell imported cigarettes and newspapers. The one place I don't record is in Skouras's office. He wouldn't like that. I can hear him loud and clear: "I'm a landlord and not a detective. I don't want your MP in my office. He's bad news."

I go back to the villa by a different route, covering the bicycle rental agency. It is now three o'clock. A time when Jerry would most likely be in his room reading. I read some more of *The Magus* into the recorder with flushing toilets, running water, my footsteps in the hall, blinds being raised and lowered. I listen to what I have on tape, with special attention to the cut-ins. I take a walk along the sea wall and play the tape back to the sea and the wind.

Dinner in a restaurant where Jerry and his friends ate the night they arrived. This restaurant is recommended by Skouras. I take my time with several ouzos before a dinner of red snapper and Greek salad, washed down with retsina. After dinner I go out to the discotheque to record some of the music Jerry danced to. The scene is really dead. A German countess is dancing with some local youths.

Next day there was a wind and the hovercraft was grounded. I took the noon boat and after six hours was back in my room at the Hilton.

I took out a bottle of Johny Walker Black Label duty-free scotch and ordered a soda siphon and ice from Hilton room service. I put Jerry's graduation picture in a silver frame on the desk, assembled the questionnaire, and put the tape recorder with an hour of Spetsai beside it. The waiter came in with the ice and soda siphon.

"Is that your son, sir?"

I said yes because it was the easy thing to say. I poured myself a small drink and lit a Senior Service. I started thinking out loud, cutting into the tape. . . .

"Suspected to be involved in some capacity: Marty Blum, a small-time operator with big-time connections. Was in Athens at or about the time young Jerry disappeared.

"Helen and Van—also in Athens at the time. Van was trying to get a permit to run a disintoxication clinic on one of the islands. He didn't get it. Left Athens for Tangier. Left Tangier for New York. Trouble at immigration. Thought to be in Toronto." What did I know about these two birds? Plenty. "Doctor Van: age, fifty-seven; nationality, Canadian. Dope-pushing and abortions sidelines and front for his real specialty, which is transplant operations. Helen, his assistant: age, sixty; nationality, Australian. Masseuse, abortionist, suspected jewel thief and murderess."

The Countess Minsky Stahlinhof de Gulpa, known as Minny to her friends and sycophants: a heavy woman like a cold fish under tons of gray shale. "White Russian and Italian descent. Stratospherically wealthy, near the billion mark. The source of her wealth: manipulation of commodity prices. She moves into a poor country like Morocco and buys up basic commodities like sugar, kerosene, and cooking oil, holds them off the market in her warehouses, then puts them back on the market at a higher price. The Countess has squeezed her vast wealth out of the poorest people. She has other interests than money. She is a very big operator indeed. She owns immense estates in Chile and Peru and has some secret laboratories there. She has employed biochemists and virologists. Indication: genetic experiments and biologic weapons."

And what of the Countess de Vile? "De Vile: very wealthy but not Gulpa's strata. A depraved, passionate and capricious woman, evil as Circe. Extensive underworld and police contacts. On close terms with Mafia dons and police chiefs in Italy, New York, Morocco, and South America. A frequent visitor at the Countess de Gulpa's South American retreat. Several unsolved missing-person cases, involving boys of Jerry's age, point to the South American laboratories as terminal."

I glanced through the questionnaire. "Medical history: scarlet fever at the age of four." Now, scarlet fever is a rarity since the introduction of antibiotics. "Could there have been a misdiagnosis?"

All this I was feeding into the recorder in pieces, and a lot more. An article I had just finished reading when Mr Green came into my office. This was an article on head transplants performed on monkeys, the Sunday *Times*, December 9, 1973. I now took it out of a file and read parts of it into the recorder. "Monkey heads transplanted onto monkey bodies can now survive for about a week. The drawing above portrays controversial operation. 'Technically a human head transplant is possible,' Dr White says, 'but scientifically there would be no point.'"

My first meeting with Mr Green: the smell of death, and something shifty about him. From talking to Jerry's friends, I found out that this was a family trait. They all described him as hard to figure or hard to pin down. Finally I turned on the TV. I played the tape back at low volume while I watched an Italian western with Greek subtitles, keeping my attention on the screen so I was subconsciously hearing the tape. They were hanging a rustler from horseback when the phone rang.

It was Dimitri. "Well, Snide, I think we have found your missing person . . . unfortunately."

"You mean dead?"

"Yes. Embalmed, in fact." He paused. "And without his head."

"*What?*"

"Yes. Head severed at the shoulders."

"Fingerprints check?"

"Yes."

I waited for the rest of it.

"Cause of death is uncertain. Some congestion in the lungs. May have been strangulation. The body was found in a trunk."

"Who found it?"

"I did. I happened to be down at the port double-checking the possibility that the boy may have left by freighter, and I saw a trunk being carried aboard a ship with Panamanian registry. Well, something about the way they were carrying it . . . the disposition of the weight, you understand. I had the trunk returned to customs and opened. The uh the method of embalming . . . unusual to say the least. The body was perfectly preserved but no embalming fluid had been used. It was also completely nude."

"Can I have a look?"

"Of course. . . ."

The Greek doctor had studied at Harvard and he spoke perfect English. Various internal organs were laid out on a white shelf. The body, or what was left of it, was in a fetal position.

"Considering that this boy has been dead at least a month, the internal organs are in a remarkable state of preservation," said the doctor.

I looked at the body. Pubic, rectal and leg hairs were bright red. However, he was redder than he should have been. I pointed to some red blotches around the nipples, crotch, thighs and buttocks. "What's that? Looks like some kind of rash."

"I was wondering about that. . . . Of course it could have been an

allergy. Redheads are particularly liable to allergic reactions, but—"
He paused. "It looks like scarlet fever."

"We are checking all hospitals and private clinics for scarlet fever admissions," Dimitri put in, ". . . or any other condition that could produce such a rash."

I turned to the doctor. "Doctor, would you say that the amputation was a professional job?"

"Definitely."

"All questionable doctors and clinics will be checked," said Dimitri.

The preservative seemed to be wearing off, and the body gave off a sweet musky smell that turned me quite sick. I could see Dimitri was feeling it too, and so was the doctor.

"Can I see the trunk?"

The trunk was built like an icebox: a layer of cork, and the inside lined with thin steel.

"The steel is magnetized," Dimitri told me. "Look." He took out his car keys and they stuck to the side of the trunk.

"Could this have had any preservative effect?"

"The doctor says no."

Dimitri drove me back to the Hilton. "Well, it looks like your case is closed, Mr Snide."

"I guess so . . . any chance of keeping this out of the papers?"

"Yes. This is not America. Besides, a thing like this, you understand . . ."

"Bad for the tourist business."

"Well, yes."

I had a call to make to the next of kin. "Afraid I have some bad news for you, Mr Green."

"Yes?"

"Well, the boy has been found."

"Dead, you mean?"

"I'm sorry, Mr Green. . . ."

"Was he murdered?"

"What makes you say that?"

"It's my wife. She's sort of, well, psychic. She had a dream."

"I see. Well, yes, it looks like murder. We're keeping it out of the papers, because publicity would impede the investigation at this point."

"I want to retain you again, Mr Snide. To find the murderer of my son."

"Everything is being done, Mr Green. The Greek police are quite efficient."

"We have more confidence in you."

"I'm returning to New York in a few days. I'll contact you as soon as I arrive."

The trail was a month old at least. I was fairly sure the murderer or murderers were no longer in Greece. No point in staying on. But there was something else to check out on the way back.

FEVER SPOOR

I stop over in London. There is somebody I want to see there, if I can find him without too much trouble. Could save me a side trip to Tangier.

I find him in a gay bar called the Amigo. He is nattily dressed, with a well-kept beard and shifty eyes. The Arabs say he has the eyes of a thief. But he has a rich wife and doesn't need to steal.

"Well," he says. "The private eye.... Business or pleasure?"

I look around. "Only business would bring me here." I show him Jerry's picture. "He was in Tangier last summer, I believe."

He looks at the picture. "Sure, I remember him. A cock-teaser."

"Missing-person case. Remember who he was with?"

"Some hippie kids."

The description sounds like the kids Jerry was with in Spetsai. Props. "Did he go anywhere else?"

"Marrakesh, I think."

I am about to finish my drink and leave.

"Oh, you remember Peter Winkler who used to run the English Pub? Did you know he was dead?"

I haven't heard, but I am not much interested. "So? Who or what killed him?"

"Scarlet fever."

I nearly spill my drink. "Look, people don't die of scarlet fever now. In fact, they rarely get it."

"He was living out on the mountain ... the Hamilton summer house. It's quite isolated, you know. Seems he was alone and the phone was out of order. He tried to walk to the next house down the road and collapsed. They took him to the English hospital."

"That would finish anyone off. And I suppose Doc Peterson was in attendance? Made the diagnosis and signed the death certificate?"

"Who else? He's the only doctor there. But what are you so stirred up about? I never thought you and Winkler were very close."

I cool it. "We weren't. It's just that I started out to be a doctor and I don't like to see a case botched."

"I wouldn't say he botched it. Shot him full of pen strep. Seems he was too far gone to respond."

"Yeah. Pen strep is right for scarlet fever. He must have been practically dead on arrival."

"Oh, not quite. He was in the hospital about twenty-four hours."

I don't say any more. I've said too much already. Looks like I'll have to make that side trip to Tangier.

I checked into the Rembrandt and took a taxi to the Marshan. It was 3:00 P.M. when I rang the doctor's bell. He was a long time coming to the door, and was not pleased to see me.

"I'm sorry to disturb you during the siesta hour, Doctor, but I'm only in town for a short stay and it's rather important. . . ."

He was not altogether mollified but he led me into his office.

"Doctor Peterson, I have been retained by the heirs of Peter Winkler to investigate the circumstances of his death. The fact that he was found unconscious by the side of a road has led them to speculate that there might be some question of accidental death. That would mean double indemnity on the insurance."

"No question whatsoever. There wasn't a mark on him—except for the rash, that is. Well, his pockets were turned inside out, but what do you expect in a place like this?"

"You're quite sure that he died of scarlet fever?"

"Quite sure. A classical case. I think that the fever may have caused brain damage and that is why he didn't respond to antibiotics. Cerebral hemorrhage may have been a contributory cause. . . ."

"There was bleeding?"

"Yes . . . from the nose and mouth."

"And this couldn't have been a concussion?"

"Absolutely no sign of concussion."

"Was he delirious at any time?"

"Yes. For some hours."

"Did he say anything? Anything that might indicate he had been attacked?"

"It was gibberish in some foreign language. I administered morphine to quiet him."

"I'm sure you did the right thing, Doctor, and I will report to his heirs that there is nothing to support a claim of accidental death. That is your considered opinion?"

"It is. He died of scarlet fever and/or complications attendant on scarlet fever."

I thanked him and left. I had some more questions, but I was sure he couldn't or wouldn't answer them. I went back to the hotel and did some work with the recorder.

At seven o'clock I walked over to the English Pub. There was a young Arab behind the bar whom I recognized as one of Peter's boyfriends. Evidently he had inherited the business. I showed him Jerry's picture.

"Oh yes. Mister Jerry. Peter like him very much. Give him free drinks. He never make out though. Boy just lead him on."

I asked about Peter's death.

"Very sad. Peter alone in house. Tell me he want to rest few days."

"Did he seem sick?"

"Not sick. He just look tired. Mister Jerry gone to Marrakesh and I think Peter a little sad."

I could have checked hospitals in Marrakesh for scarlet fever cases, but I knew already what I needed to know. I knew why Peter hadn't responded to antibiotics. He didn't have scarlet fever. He had a virus infection.

ARE YOU IN SALT

Back in New York I call the Greens from my loft. I've put $5,000 worth of security into this space. The windows are shatterproof glass with rolling bars. The door is two inches of solid steel from an old bank vault. It gives you a safe feeling, like being in Switzerland.

Mr Green can see me right away. He gives an address on Spring Street. Middle-class loft ... big modern kitchen ... Siamese cat ... plants. Mrs Green is a beautiful woman, red hair, green eyes, a faraway dreamy look. I notice *Journeys out of the Body, Psychic Discoveries Behind the Iron Curtain*, the Castaneda books. Mr Green mixes me a Chivas Regal.

I clarify my position.... "Private investigator ... no authority to make an arrest ... I can only pass evidence along to the local police.... Frankly, in this case I can't hold out much hope of obtaining an arrest, let alone a conviction."

"We still want to retain you."

"Why, exactly?"

"We want to know the truth," said Mrs Green. "Whether the killers can be brought to trial or not."

I pull out the questionnaire with Jerry's medical history. "It says here that Jerry had scarlet fever at the age of four."

"Yes. We were living in Saint Louis at the time," said Mrs Green.

"Who was the doctor?"

"Old Doctor Greenbaum. He lived next door."

"Is he still alive?"

"No, he died ten years ago."

"And he made the diagnosis?"

"Yes."

"Would you say that he was a competent diagnostician?"

"Not really," said Mr Green. "But why is this important?"

"Jerry apparently had an attack of scarlet fever or something similar shortly before he was killed." I turned to Mrs Green. "Do you remember the details? How the illness started?"

"Why yes. It was a Thursday and he had taken a ride with an English governess we had then. When he got back he was shivering and feverish and he had a rash. I thought it was measles and called

Doctor Greenbaum. He said it wasn't a measles rash, that it was probably a light case of scarlet fever. He prescribed Aureomycin and the fever went away in a few days."

"Was Jerry delirious at any time during this illness?"

"Yes, as a matter of fact he was. He seemed quite frightened and talked about 'animals in the wall.'"

"Do you remember what animals, Mrs Green?"

"He mentioned a giraffe and a kangaroo."

"Do you remember anything else?"

"... Yes," she said after a pause. "There was a strange smell in the room ... sort of a musky smell ... like a *zoo*."

"Did Doctor Greenbaum comment on this odor?"

"No, I think he had a cold at the time."

"Did you notice it, Mr Green?"

"Well, yes, it was on the sheets and blankets when we sent them to the cleaners.... Exactly how was Jerry killed, Mr Snide?"

"A massive overdose of heroin."

"He wasn't—"

"No, he wasn't an addict, and the Greek police are convinced the heroin was not self-administered."

"Do you have any idea why he would have been murdered?"

"I'm not at all sure, Mr Green. It could have been a case of mistaken identity."

When I got to the office the next day my assistant, Jim Brady, was already there, having come straight from the airport. He is very slim, six feet, 135 pounds, black Irish. Actually he is twenty-eight but he looks eighteen, and often has to show his ID card to be served in a bar. He handed me a packet from Athens: a photograph, and a message from Dimitri typed on yellow paper in telegraph style:

HAVE FOUND VILLA WHERE JERRY GREEN WAS KILLED STOP ON MAINLAND FORTY MILES FROM ATHENS STOP HEAD STILL MISSING STOP VILLA RENTED THROUGH LONDON TRAVEL AGENCY STOP FALSE NAMES STOP

DIMITRI

The photo showed a bare high-ceiling room with exposed beams. There was a heavy iron lantern-hook in one beam. Dimitri had circled this hook in white ink and had written under it: "Traces of rope fiber."

"A Mr Everson called," said Jim. "His son is missing. I made an appointment."

"Where is he missing?"

"In Mexico. A Mayan archaeologist. Missing six weeks. I sent Mr Everson the questionnaire and asked him for pictures of the boy."

"Good." I had no special feeling about this case, but it was taking me in the direction I wanted to go.

Back at the loft we decide to try some sex magic. According to psychic dogma, sex itself is incidental and should be subordinated to the intent of the ritual. But I don't believe in rules. What happens, happens.

The altar is set up for an Egyptian rite timed for sunset, which is in ten minutes. It is a slab of white marble about three feet square. We mark out the cardinal points. A hyacinth in a pot for earth: North. A red candle for fire: South. An alabaster bowl of water for water: East. A glyph in gold on white parchment for air: West. We then put up the glyphs for the rite, in gold on white parchment, on the west wall, since this is the sundown rite and we are facing west. Also we place on the altar a bowl of water, a bowl of milk, an incense burner, some rose essence, and a sprig of mint.

All set, we strip down to sky clothes and we are both stiff before we can get our clothes off. I pick up an ivory wand and draw a circle around our bodies while we both intone translations of the rite, reading from the glyphs on the wall.

"Let the Shining Ones not have power over me." Jim reads it like the Catholic litany and we are both laughing.

"I have purified myself."

We dip water from the bowl and touch our foreheads.

"I have anointed myself with unguents."

We dip the special ointment out of an alabaster jar, touching foreheads, insides of the wrists, and the base of the spine, since the rite will have a sexual climax.

"I bring to you perfume and incense."

We add more incense, a few drops of rose oil, and a pinch of benzoin to the burner.

We pay homage to the four cardinal points as we invoke Set instead of Khentamentiu, since this is in some sense a black ritual. It is now exactly the hour of sunset, and we pay homage to Tem, since Ra, in his setting, takes that name. We make lustrations with water and milk to the cardinal points, dipping a mint sprig into the bowls as we invoke the shining elementals. It is time now for the ritual climax, in which the gods possess our bodies and the magical intention is projected in the moment of orgasm and visualized as an outpouring of liquid gold.

"My phallus is that of Amsu."

I bend over and Jim rubs the ointment up my ass and slides his cock in. A roaring sound in my ears as pictures and tapes swirl in my brain. Shadowy figures rise beyond the candlelight: the goddess Ix Tab, patroness of those who hang themselves ... a vista of gallows and burning cities from Bosch ... Set ... Osiris ... smell of the sea ... Jerry hanging naked from the beam. A sweet rotten red musky metal smell swirls round our bodies palpable as a haze, and as I start to ejaculate, the room gets lighter. At first I think the candles have flared up and then I see Jerry standing there naked, his body radiating light. There is a skeleton grin on his face, which fades to the enigmatic smile on the statues of archaic Greek youths and then he changes into Dimitri, with a quizzical amused expression.

So we send the Shining Ones home and go to bed.

"Why do you think the head was cut off?" asks Jim.

"Obvious reason: to obscure the cause of death in case the body was found. But they didn't figure on the body being found. There was some special purpose they had in mind, to use both the head and the body." Drawings of transplanted monkey heads flash in front of my eyes.

"Where do you think the head is now?"

"In New York."

HORSE HATTOCK TO RIDE TO RIDE

Next day when we got to the office there was a telegram from Dimitri:

HAVE SUSPECT IN CUSTODY WHO WITNESSED DEATH OF JERRY GREEN STOP WIRE IF WISH TO INTERVIEW SUSPECT

We took the next plane to Athens and checked into the Hilton Dimitri sent a car for us.

Jim was a bit stiff when they shook hands in Dimitri's air-conditioned office ... wall-to-wall blue carpet, a desk, leather-covered chairs, a picture of the Parthenon on the wall, everything neat and impersonal as a room in the Hilton.

Dimitri raised one eyebrow. "I infer you disapprove of our politics, Mr Brady. For myself I disapprove of any politics. Please understand that I stand to gain nothing from this investigation. My political superiors want the whole thing dropped ... a few degenerate foreigners ... it's bad for the tourist business."

Jim blushed sulkily and looked at his shoes and turned one foot sideways.

"What about this witness you got?" I asked.

Dimitri leaned back in his chair behind the desk and put the tips of his fingers together. "Ah yes—Adam North, the perfect witness. Survived his perfection because he was in custody. On the morning that the Green boy was killed, September eighteenth, young North was arrested with a quarter-ounce of heroin in his possession. When I saw the laboratory report I ordered him placed in isolation. The heroin he had been buying from street pushers was about ten percent. This was almost one hundred percent. It would have killed him in a matter of seconds."

"Well, if they would kill him to shut him up about something, why let him know about it in the first place?" Jim asked.

"A searching question. You see, he was a sort of camera from which a film could be withdrawn and developed. But first the bare bones, later the meat. Adam North had been approached by someone fitting"—Dimitri glanced at me—"your description of Marty Blum, and offered a quarter-ounce of heroin plus a thousand-dollar bonus to be paid in two installments to witness a magical ritual involving a simulated execution. He was suspicious."

Dimitri turned on a tape recorder. "Why *me*?" said a stupid, surly young voice. It went on.

"So this character from a comic strip says I am a perfect. 'A perfect *what*?' I ask him. 'A perfect witness,' he tells me. He has five C-notes in his hand. 'Well, all right,' I say. 'But there is a condition,' he says. 'You must promise to refrain from heroin or any other drug for three days prior to the ceremony. You have to be in a pure condition.' 'Promise on my scout's honor.' I told him and he lays the bread on me. 'But one more thing,' he says. He gives me a color picture of a kid with red hair who looks sorta like me. 'This is the subject. You will concentrate on this picture for the next three days.' So I tell him 'Sure' and split. And would you believe it, with five hundred cools in my pocket I can't score for shit nowhere no way. So when the chauffeur comes to pick me up in a Daimler I am sick as a dog."

Dimitri shut off the tape recorder. "He was driven to a villa outside of Athens where he witnessed a bizarre ceremony culminating in the hanging of the Green boy. Back in Athens he was given the quarter-ounce of heroin. He was on his way back to his girl friend's apartment when the arrest was made."

"It still doesn't make any sense," Jim said. "They drag him in as a witness, God knows why, then knock him off to shut him up."

"They did not intend to *shut* him up. They intended to *open* him and extract the film. Adam North was a perfect witness. He is Jerry's age, born on the same day, and resembles him enough to be a twin brother. You are acquainted with the symptoms of heroin withdrawal ... the painful intensity of impressions, light fever, spontaneous orgasms ... a sensitized film. And a heroin overdose is the easiest of deaths, so the pictures registered on the sensitized withdrawal film come off without distortion in a heroin OD."

"I see," said Jim.

"It's all here on the tape, but I think you would like to see this boy. He is, I should tell you, retarded."

As we were going down in the elevator, Dimitri continued. "There is reason to suspect a latent psychosis, masked by his addiction."

"Is he receiving any medication?" I asked.

"Yes—methadone, orally. I don't want his disorder to surface here."

"You mean he could become a public charge?" I asked.

"More than that—he could become a sanitary hazard."

We saw Adam North in one of the interrogation rooms, under fluorescent lights. A table, a tape recorder, four chairs. He was a handsome blond kid with green eyes. The resemblance to Jerry was remarkable. However, while Jerry was described as very bright and quick, this boy had a slack, vacuous, stupid look about him, sleepy and sullen like a lizard resentfully aroused from hibernation. Dimitri explained that we were investigators hired by Jerry's family, and we had a few questions. The boy looked down at the table in front of him and said nothing.

"This man who offered you the quarter-ounce of H. You'd seen him before?" I asked.

"Yeah. When I first came here he steered me to a score. I figure he is creaming off a percentage."

"What did he look like?"

"Gray face, pockmarks, stocky medium build, fancy purple vest and a watch chain. Like he stepped out of the 1890s. Didn't seem to feel the heat."

"Anything else?"

"Funny smell about him, like something rotten in a refrigerator."

"Please describe the ritual you witnessed," I said.

"Allow me," interrupted Dimitri. He looked at the boy and said, "Ganymede" and snapped his fingers. The boy shivered and closed his eyes, breathing deeply. When he spoke, his voice was altered beyond recognition. I had the impression he was translating the words from another tongue, a language of giggles and turkey gobbles and coos and purrs and whimpers and trills.

"Ganymede Hotel . . . shutters closed . . . naked on the bed . . . Jerry's picture . . . it's coming alive . . . gets me hot to look at it . . . I know he's in a room just like this . . . waiting . . . there's a smell in the room, *his* smell . . . I can smell what's going to happen . . . naked with animal masks . . . demon masks . . . I'm naked but I don't have a mask. We are standing on a stage . . . translucent noose . . . it's squirming like a snake . . . Jerry is led in naked by a twin sister . . . can't hardly tell them apart. There's a red haze over everything, and the *smell*—" The kid whimpered and squirmed and rubbed his crotch. "She's tying his hands behind him with a red scarf . . . she's got the noose around his neck . . . It's *growing* into him . . . his cock is coming up and he gets red all over right down to his toenails—we

317

call it a red-on...." Adam giggled. "The platform falls out from under him and he's hanging there kicking. He goes off three times in a row. His twin sister is catching the seed in a bottle. It's going to *grow*...." The boy opened his eyes and looked uncertainly at Dimitri, who shook his head in mild reproof.

"You still think all this happened, Adam?"

"Well, sure, Doctor, I remember it."

"You remember dreams too. Your story has been checked and found to be without factual foundation. This was hardly necessary since you have been under constant surveillance since your arrival in Athens. The heroin you were taking has been analyzed. It contains certain impurities which can cause a temporary psychosis with just such bizarre hallucination as you describe. We were looking for the wholesalers who were distributing this poisonous heroin. We have them now. The case is closed. I advise you to forget all about it. You will be released tomorrow. The consulate has arranged for you to work your way home on a freighter."

The boy was led away by a white-coated attendant.

"What about the other witnesses, who wore masks?" I asked Dimitri.

"I surmised that they would be eligible for immediate disposal. A charter plane for London leaving Athens the day after the ritual murder crashed in Yugoslavia. There were no survivors. I checked the passenger list with my police contacts in England. Seven of the passengers belonged to a Druid cult suspected of robbing graves and performing black-magic rituals with animal sacrifices. One of the animals allegedly sacrificed was a horse. Such an act is considerably more shocking to the British sensibility than human sacrifice."

"They sacrificed a *horse*?"

"It's an old Scythian practice. A naked youth mounts the horse, slits its throat and rides it to the ground. Dangerous, I'm told. Rather like your American rodeos."

"What about the twin sister who hanged him?" Jim demanded.

Dimitri opened a file. " 'She' is a transvestite, Arn West born Arnold Atkins at Newcastle upon Tyne. A topflight ultraexpensive assassin specializing in sexual techniques and poisons. His consultation fee to listen to a proposition is a hundred thousand dollars, nonrefundable. Known as the Popper, the Blue Octopus, the Siren Cloak.

"And now, would you gentlemen care to join me for dinner? I

would like to hear from you, Mr Snide, the complete story and not a version edited for the so limited police mentality."

Dimitri's house was near the American Embassy. It was not the sort of house you would expect a police official on a modest salary to own. It took up almost half a block. The grounds were surrounded by high walls, with six feet of barbed wire on top. The door looked like a bank vault.

Dimitri led the way down a hall with a red-tiled floor into a book-lined room. French doors opened onto a patio about seventy feet long and forty feet wide. I could see a pool, trees and flowers. Jim and I sat down and Dimitri mixed drinks. I glanced at the books: magic, demonology, a number of medical books, a shelf of Egyptology and books on the Mayans and Aztecs.

I told Dimitri what I knew and what I suspected. It took about half an hour. After I had finished, he sat for some time in silence, looking down into his drink.

"Well, Mr Snide," he said at last. "It would seem that your case is closed. The killers are dead."

"But they were only—"

"Exactly: Servants. Dupes. Hired killers, paid off with a special form of death. You will recognize the rite as the Egyptian sunset rite dedicated to Set. A sacrifice involving both sex and death is the most potent projection of magical intention. The participants did not know that one of the intentions they were projecting was their own death in a plane crash."

"Any evidence of sabotage?"

"No. But there was not much left of the plane. The crash occurred outside Zagreb. Pilot was off course and flying low. It looks like pilot error. There are, of course, techniques for producing such errors.... You are still intending to continue on this case? To find the higher-ups? And why exactly?"

"Look, Colonel, this didn't start with the Green case. These people are old enemies."

"Do not be in a hurry to dispose of old enemies. What would you do without them? Look at it this way: You are retained to find a killer. You turn up a hired assassin. You are not satisfied. You want to find the man who hired him. You find another servant. You are not satisfied. You find another servant, and another, right up to Mr or Mrs Big—who turns out to be yet another servant ... a servant of forces and powers you cannot reach. Where do you stop? Where do you draw the line?"

He had a point.

He went on: "Let us consider what has happened here. A boy has been hanged for ritual and magical purposes. Is this so startling? . . . You have read *The Bog People*?"

I nodded.

"Well, a modest consumption of one nude hanging a year during the spring festivals . . . such festivals, within reason, could serve as a safety valve. . . . After all, worse things happen every day. Certainly this is a minor matter compared with Hiroshima, Vietnam, mass pollution, droughts, famines . . . you have to take a broad general view of things."

"It might not be within reason at all. It might become pandemic."

"Yes . . . the Aztecs got rather out of hand. But you are referring to your virus theory. Shall we call it 'Virus B-23'? The 'Hanging Fever'? And you are extrapolating from two cases which may not be connected. Peter Winkler may have died from something altogether different. I know you do not want to entertain such a possibility, but suppose that such an epidemic does occur?" He paused. "How old was Winkler?"

"In his early fifties."

"So. Jerry was a carrier of the illness. He did not die of it directly. Winkler, who was thirty years older, died in a few days. Well . . . there are those who think a selective pestilence is the most humane solution to overpopulation and the attendant impasses of pollution, inflation, and exhaustion of natural resources. A plague that kills the old and leaves the young, minus a reasonable percentage . . . one might be tempted to let such an epidemic run its course even if one had the power to stop it."

"Colonel, I have a hunch that what we might find in the South American laboratories would make the story we heard from Adam North sound like a mild Gothic romance for old ladies and children."

"Exactly what I am getting at, Mr Snide. There are risks not worth taking. There are things better left unseen and unknown."

"But somebody has to see and know them eventually. Otherwise there is no protection."

"That somebody who has to see and know may not be you. Think of your own life, and that of your assistant. You may not be called upon to act in this matter."

"You have a point."

"He sure does," said Jim.

"Mr Snide, do you consider Hiroshima a crime?"

"Yes."

"Were you ever tempted to go after the higher-ups?"

"No. It wasn't my business."

"The same considerations may apply here. There is, however, one thing you can do: find the head and exorcise it. I have already done this with the body. Mr Green agreed to burial here in the American cemetery."

He walked across the room to a locked cabinet and returned with an amulet: runic lettering on what looked like parchment in an iron locket. "Not parchment—human skin . . ." he told me. "The ceremony is quite simple: the head is placed in a magic circle on which you have marked the cardinal points. You repeat three times: 'Back to water. Back to fire. Back to air. Back to earth.' You then touch the crown of the head, the forehead, and the spot behind the right ear, in this case—he was left-handed—with the amulet."

There was a knock at the door, and a middle-aged Greek woman with a mustache wheeled in the dinner of red mullet and Greek salad. After dinner and brandy we got up to take our leave.

"I have said you may not be called upon to act. On the other hand, you may be called upon. You will know if this happens, and you will need help. I can give you a contact in Mexico City . . . 18 Callejón de la Esperanza."

"Got it," said Jim.

"My driver will take you back to the Hilton."

"Nightcap?"

"No," Jim said. "I've got a headache. I'm going up to the room."

"I'll check the bar. See you very shortly." I had seen someone I knew from the American Embassy. Probably CIA. I could feel that he wanted to talk to me.

He looked up when I walked in, nodded and asked me to join him. He was young, thin, sandy-haired, glasses . . . refined and rather academic-looking. He signaled the waiter and I ordered a beer.

After the waiter had brought the beer and gone back to the bar, the man leaned forward, speaking in a low precise voice.

"Shocking thing about the Green boy." He tried to look concerned and sympathetic but his eyes were cold and probing. I would have to be very careful not to tell him anything he didn't already know.

"Yes, isn't it."

"I understand it was uh well, a sex murder." He tried to look embarrassed and a bit salacious. He looked about as embarrassed and salacious as a shark. He was cold and fishy like the Countess de Gulpa. I remembered that he was rich.

"Something like that."

"It must have been terrible for the family. You didn't tell them the truth?"

Watch yourself, Clem.... "I'm not sure I know the truth. The story I actually told them is of course a confidential matter...."

"Of course. Professional ethics." Without a trace of overt irony, he managed to convey a vast icy contempt for me and my profession. I just nodded. He went on. "Strange chap, Dimitri."

"He seems very efficient."

"Very. It doesn't always pay to be too efficient."

"The Chinese say it is well to make a mistake now and then."

"Did you know that Dimitri has resigned?"

"He didn't say so...."

"He was the object of professional jealousy. Career men resent someone with independent means who doesn't really need the job. I should know." He smiled ruefully, trying to look boyish.

"Well, perhaps you can avoid the error of overefficiency."

He let that roll off him. "I suppose these hippies go in for all sorts of strange far-out sex cults...."

"I have found their sex practices to be on the whole rather boringly ordinary...."

"You've read *Future Shock*, haven't you?"

"Skipped through it."

"It's worth looking at carefully."

"I found *The Biological Time Bomb* more interesting."

He ignored this. "Dimitri's dabbling in magic hasn't done him any good either ... career-wise, I mean."

"Magic? That seems out of character."

I could tell he knew I had just been to Dimitri's house for dinner. He was hoping I would tell him something about the house: books, decorations.... Which meant he had never been there. A slight spasm of exasperation passed over his face like a seismic tremor. His face went dead and smooth as a marble mask, and he said slowly: "Isn't your assistant awfully young for the kind of work you're doing?"

"Aren't you a bit young for the kind of work you're doing?"

He decided to laugh. "Well, youth at the helm. Have another beer?"

322

"No thanks. Got an early plane to catch." I stood up. "Well, good night, Skipper."

He decided not to laugh. He just nodded silently. As I walked out of the bar I knew that he deliberately was not looking after me.

No doubt about it. I had been warned in no uncertain terms to lay off and stay out, and I didn't like it—especially coming at a time when I had about decided to lay off and stay out. And I didn't like having Jim threatened by a snot-nosed CIA punk. The Mafia couldn't have been much cruder.

"Your assistant very young man. You looka the book called *Future Shock* maybe?"

When I got to the room I found the door open. As I stepped in I caught a whiff of the fever smell—the rank animal smell of Jerry's naked headless body. Jim was lying on the bed covered by a sheet up to his waist. As I looked at him I felt a prickling up the back of my neck. I was looking at Jerry's face, which wore a wolfish grin, his eyes sputtering green fire.

QUIÉN ES?

We flew back with a three-hour stopover at Orly. I had decided what I was going to do. I was going to refund Mr Green's retainer, minus travel expenses, and tell him the actual killers were dead in a plane crash. The Greek police consider the case closed. Nothing further I can do.

Back in my New York loft I called the Greens. "This is Clem Snide calling. I'd like to speak to Mr Green, please."

A woman's voice sounded guarded: "What is it in reference to, please?"

"I am a private investigator retained by Mr Green."

"Well, I'm afraid you can't speak to him. You see, Mr and Mrs Green are dead."

"Dead?"

"Yes. They were killed last night in a car crash. This is Mrs Green's sister." She sounded pretty cool about it.

"I'm terribly sorry...." I was thinking about what Dimitri had said. The "Adepts" who had hanged Jerry did not know what magical intentions they were projecting. They did not know to whom they were aspeak ... plane crash ... car crash ...

I didn't want to think about the Green case anymore, but it stuck to me like the fever smell. What had Dimitri called it? B-23, the Hanging Fever.

Death is enforced separation from the body. Orgasm is identification with the body. So death in the moment of orgasm literally *embodies* death. It would also yield an earth-bound spirit—an incubus dedicated to reproducing that particular form of death.

I took a Nembutal and finally slept.

Someone was murdered in this room a long time ago. How long ago ...
the empty safe ... the bloody pipe threader? His partner must have done
it. They never caught him. Easy to disappear in those days, when a silver
dollar bought a good meal and piece of ass. Smell of dust and old fear in the
room. Someone is at the back door. Quién es? *The hall is dark.*

It's Marty come to call ... gaslight now on the yellow pockmarked
face, the cold gray eyes, the brilliantined black hair, the coat with fur
trimming at the collar, the purple waistcoat beneath....

"We had a hard time finding you." His drunken driver there can hardly stand up. "Wore himself out getting here, he did."

"He made a few stops along the way."

"Come along to the Metropole and have some bubbly. It's my treat."

Now Broadway's full of guys who think they're mighty wise, just because they know a thing or two

"No thanks."

"What do you mean, no thanks? We had a long way to find you."

You can see them every day, strolling up and down Broadway, boasting of the wonders they can do

"I'm expecting someone from the Palace."

"Your old pals aren't good enough anymore? Is that it?"

"I don't remember we were exactly pals, Marty."

There are con men and drifters, Murphy men and grifters, and they all hang around the Metropole

"Let me in, Dalford. I've come a long way."

"All right, but ..."

But their names would be mud, like a chump playing stud, if they lost that old ace down in the hole

"Nice place you got here. Plenty of room. You could put the Metropole in here if it came to that...." He is sitting on the bed now.

They'll tell you of trips that they're going to take, from Florida up to the old North Pole

"Look, Marty ..."

I wake up. Jim is covered with white foam. I can't wake him. "Jamie! ... Jamie! ..." Cold white foam.

I wake up. Jim is standing with a pipe threader in his hand, looking towards the back door.... "I thought someone was in the room."

I got up and dressed and went into the kitchen to make breakfast. It tasted disgusting. The Everson questionnaire and pictures had arrived, and I looked through them as I drank coffee. The pictures were quite ordinary. The Everson boy looked like the clean-cut American Boy. I wondered why he had taken up such an esoteric subject as Mayan archaeology.

Jim came in and asked if he could take the day off. He does that occasionally, has an apartment of his own in the East Village. After he left, I sat down and went carefully through the Everson case: the boy had been in Mexico City doing some research in the library preparatory to a dig in Yucatán. In his last letter he said he was leaving for Progreso in a few days and would write from there.

After two weeks, his family was worried. They waited another week then called the US Embassy in Mexico City. A man checked his address, and the landlady said he had packed and left almost three weeks ago. A police check of hotel registration in Progreso turned up nothing. It had now been about six weeks with no word.

Several possibilities had occurred to me: He may have gone on some alternate dig. Postal service in rural Mexico is practically nonexistent. Probably there was no more involved than two or three lost letters. I was inclined to favor some such simple explanation. I had no special feelings about this case and felt sure I could locate young Everson without much difficulty. I decided to knock off and take in a porn flick.

It was good, as porn flicks go—beautiful kids on screen—but I couldn't understand why they had so much trouble coming. And all the shots were stylized. Every time a kid came all over a stomach or an ass, he rubbed the jism around like tapioca.

I left in the middle of a protracted fuck, and walked down Third Avenue to the Tin Palace for a drink.

There was a hippie with a ratty black beard at one end of the bar and I could smell Marty on him—that cold gray smell of the time traveler. I'd seen him around before. The name is Howard Benson. Small-time pusher, pot and C and occasional O. Lives somewhere in the neighborhood. He caught my eye, drank up and hurried out.

I gave him a few seconds' start and tailed him to a loft building on Greene Street. I waited outside until his light went on, picked the front-door lock and went in. I had an Identikit picture of Marty with me that Jim drew. It looks like a photo. I was going to show it to this Howard and say it was a picture of a murder suspect, and see what I could surprise or bluff out of him.

His loft was on the third floor. I knocked loud and long. No answer. I could feel somebody inside. *"Police!"* I shouted. "Open the door or we'll break it down!" Still no answer. Well, that would keep the neighbors out of the hall.

It took me about two minutes to get the door open. I walked in. There was somebody there, all right. Howard Benson was lying on his face in a pool of blood. The murder weapon was there too: a bloody pipe threader that had smashed in the back of his head.

I took a quick look around. There was a filthy pile of bedding in one corner and a phone beside it, some tools, dusty windows, a splintery floor. Benson was lying in front of an old-fashioned safe which was open. A dead gray smell hung in that loft like a fog. Marty was there.

The whole scene was like something out of the 1890s. I bent down and sniffed at the open safe. Faint but unmistakable, the fever smell. I got a nail. It stuck to the sides of the safe. The walls were magnetized. Jerry's head had been in that safe.

Quickly I drew a circle around the safe, seeing the head as clearly as I could inside. I repeated the words and touched the absent head three times with the amulet that Dimitri had given me. A tingle ran up my arm.

Half an hour later, I was sitting in O'Brien's office. His boss, Captain Graywood, was also there. Graywood was a blond man with thick glasses and a blank expression.

"You want the whole story, then?"

"That's the general idea."

I told them most of it, what I knew about Marty, and showed them the picture. I told them about Dimitri finding the body and about Adam North's story. Captain Graywood never changed his expression. Once or twice O'Brien turned into his brother, the priest. When I had finished he took a deep breath.

"Quite a story, Clem. We've had cases like that ... and worse things too: torture, castration ... cases that don't get into the papers or into the courts."

Captain Graywood said, "So it is your theory that the head was brought here as a potent magical object?"

"Yes."

"And you are convinced that the head was in that safe?"

"Yes."

"And why do you think the body was addressed to South America?"

"I don't know the answer to that."

"Ecuador is headhunter country, isn't it?"

"Yes."

"It is logical to assume then that someone planned to reunite the head and the body in South America."

"I think so."

"You haven't told us everything."

"I've told you what I *know*."

"This Marty ... Dimitri's men never saw him?"

"No."

"But you could see him?"

"Yes."

"We can't arrest a ghost," said O'Brien.

"Well, if he can make himself solid enough to beat someone's brains out with a pipe wrench, you might be able to.... Question of being there at the right time."

EVEN THE COCKROACHES

The Cucaracha, where Kiki worked as a waiter, had "La Cucaracha" on the jukebox. It's a basement restaurant, with a small bar and a few tables. It was 11.00 P.M. and the place was empty. I hadn't seen Kiki since I interviewed him on the Green case. Looking very handsome in a worn dinner jacket, he was leaning against the bar, talking to the bargirl. She does a striptease act uptown on weekends which is a thing to see.

Because old Pancho shakes the dirt out

I shook hands with Kiki, ordered a margarita, and sat down, and right on cue a cockroach crawled across the table. When Kiki brought the margarita I pointed to the cockroach and said, "He's getting his marijuana and getting it steady."

"*Si*," said Kiki absently, and brushed the cockroach away with his towel.

I looked around and saw there was one other diner by the door. I hadn't noticed him when I came in. He was sitting alone and reading a book called *Thin Air* about a top-secret navy project to make a battleship and all the sailors on it disappear. It was supposed to confuse the enemy; however, all the test sailors went crazy. But CIA men were made of sterner stuff and found it modern and convenient to "go zero" as they call it in a tight spot.

Porque no tiene	Because he doesn't have
Porque le falta	Because he lacks
Marijuana por fumar	Marijuana to smoke

On the wall were bullfight posters and *The Death of Manolete*. The poisonous colors made me think of arsenic green and the flaking green paint in the WC. It's a big picture and must be worth a lot of money, like a wooden Indian or *Custer's Last Stand*, which the Anheuser-Busch Company used to give out to their customers. I remember as an adolescent being excited by the green naked bodies sprawled about ass-up, getting scalped by the Indians, and especially a story about one man who played dead while he was being scalped and so escaped.

I drank the margaritas and ordered a combination plate and went to the green room. When I came back, "Thin Air" was gone. Kiki came and sat with me and had a Carta Blanca. I told him Jerry was dead.

	La cucaracha la cucaracha
"Cómo?"	"How?"
"Ahorcado."	"Hanged."
Ya no quiere caminar	Doesn't want to run round anymore
"Nudo?"	"Naked?"
"Si."	"Yes."

Kiki nodded philosophically and a face leered out, the face of a middle-aged man with a cast in the right eye. This must be Kiki's macambo magic master, I decided.

"It was his destiny," Kiki said. "Look at these." He spread some postcards circa 1913 out on the table. The photos showed soldiers hanged from trees and telephone poles with their pants down around their ankles. The pictures were taken from behind. "Pictures get him very hot. He want me pull scarf tight around his neck when he come." Kiki made a motion of pulling something around his neck.

"Jerry's spirit has got into my assistant. Only you can call him out."

"Why me?"

"Jerry's spirit has to obey you because you fuck him the best."

Kiki's eyes narrowed with calculation and he drummed on the table with his fingertips. I was thinking I could use an interpreter on this trip ... after all, expense account. My Spanish is half-assed and in any case he could find out more than two nosy *gringos*.

"Like to come along with us to Mexico and South America?"

I named a figure. He smiled and nodded. I wrote the address of my loft on a card and handed it to him. "Be there at eleven in the morning. We make magic."

When I got back to the loft Jim was there, and I explained that we were going to perform this ritual to get Jerry's spirit out.

He nodded. "Yeah, he's half in and half out and it hurts."

Next day Kiki showed up with a bundle of herbs and a head of

Elleggua in a hatbox. As he was setting up his altar, lighting candles and anointing the head, I explained that he would fuck Jim and evoke Jerry to bring Jerry all the way in—and then I had good strong magic to exorcise the spirit. Kiki watched with approval, one magic man to another, as I set up the altar for the noon ritual and lit the incense. It was ten minutes before noon.

"*Todos nudos ahora.*"

Kiki was wearing red shiny boxer shorts, and when he slipped them off he was half-hard. Jim was stiff and lubricating. I drew a circle around our bodies. We were facing south for the noon ritual and I had set up a red candle for fire, which was Jerry's element. The amulet was on the altar and there was a tube of KY by the unguent jar.

"When I say *ahora*, fuck him."

Kiki picked up the KY and moved behind Jim, who leaned forward over the altar, hands braced on knees. Kiki rubbed KY up Jim's ass and hitched his hands around Jim's hips, contracting his body as his cock slid in. Jim gasped and bared his teeth. His head and neck turned bright red and the cartilage behind his right ear swelled into a pulsing knot.

Holding the amulet, I took a position on the other side of the altar. Jerry's face was in front of me now, as the red color spread down Jim's chest and his nipples pulsed erect. His stomach, crotch and thighs were bright red now, and the rash spread down his calves to his toes and the fever smell reeked out of him. His head twisted to the right as I touched the amulet to the crown of his head, to the forehead between the eyes, and to the cartilage behind both ears.

"Back to earth. Back to air. Back to fire. Back to water."

For a split second Jerry's face hung there, eyes blazing green light. A reek of decay filled the room. Someone said "Shit" in a loud voice. We carried Jim to a couch. Kiki got a wet towel and rubbed his chest, face, and neck. He opened his eyes, sat up, and smiled. The decay smell was gone. So was the fever smell.

At two o'clock O'Brien called: "Well, I think we've found your head for you—or what's left of it. Can't be sure until we check the dental work...."

"Where did you find it?"

"At the airport. Crate labeled MACHINE PARTS sent by air freight and addressed to a broker in Lima, Peru, to be picked up by Juan Mateos. The crate was being loaded onto the plane when the workmen accidentally dropped it and it split open. It was airtight and strongly built . . . it just happened to fall right on a seam. They tell me the stink was enough to knock a man down. One of them puked all over the crate."

"When did this happen?"

"At noon. We sent along a duplicate crate and contacted the Lima police to tail anyone who calls for it."

"Was the crate lined with magnetized iron?"

"Yes. We duplicated that too. The Lima police have two men planted in the customs broker's to watch anyone who calls for other crates in case he tries to check out the head crate in any way. A compass would tell him it is magnetized. We've got a wax head inside, so even with X-ray equipment . . ."

"Very good. You seem to have thought of everything. But just one more point: an object like that gives out very strong psychic vibrations that a sensitive could pick up on. . . . You might tell them to watch especially for an adolescent who comes for another crate and touches or brushes up against the head crate."

"That's already been done. Captain Graywood told them to watch for an errand boy who might brush against the crate, especially with his ass or his crotch."

O'Brien said this in a matter-of-fact voice, as if it were routine procedure. Dimitri, Graywood, and now O'Brien. Who the hell were these so-called cops?

NECESITA AUTOMÓVIL

I hadn't been in Mexico City in fifteen years. Driving in from the airport I could hardly recognize the place. As Dimitri said, a selective pestilence may be the only solution. Otherwise, they will multiply their ass-holes into the polluted seas.

Kiki, Jim, and I checked into a small hotel off Insurgentes, which was a few blocks from John Everson's Mexico City address. Then we split up. Jim and Kiki went to John Everson's address to see what they could pick up from the landlady and the *vecinos*. I went to the American Embassy, found the Protection Department, and sent in my card. I saw the girl hand it to a man at a desk. He looked at the card and looked at me. Then he did something else. I waited twenty minutes.

"Mr Hill will see you now."

Mr Hill didn't get up or offer to shake hands. "Yes, Mr uh ..." He glanced down at the card. "... Snide. What can I do for you?"

There is a breed of State Department official who starts figuring out how he can get rid of you without doing whatever it is you want done as soon as you walk into his department. Clearly, Mr Hill belonged to this breed.

"It's about John Everson. He disappeared in Mexico City about two months ago. His father has retained me to locate him."

"Well, we are not a missing-person service. So far as we are concerned, the case is now with the Mexican authorities. I suggest you contact them. A colonel, uh ..."

"Colonel Figueres."

"Yes, that is the name, I believe."

"Did John Everson pick up his mail at the embassy?"

"I uh don't think ... in any case, we don't encourage ..."

"Yes, I know. You are also not a post office. Would you mind calling the mail desk and asking if there are any letters there addressed to John Everson?"

"Really, Mr Snide ..."

"Really, Mr Hill. I have been retained by an American citizen— rather well connected, I may add, working on a US government project—retained to find an American citizen who is missing in your district. So far, there is no evidence of foul play but it hasn't been ruled out."

He was also the type who backs down under pressure. He reached for the phone. "Could you tell me if there are any letters for John Everson at the desk.... One letter?"

I slid a power of attorney across the desk which authorized me among other things to pick up mail addressed to John Everson. He looked at it.

"A Mr uh Snide will pick up the letter. He has authorization." He hung up.

I stood up. "Thank you, Mr Hill." His nod was barely perceptible.

On the way out of the office I met that CIA punk from Athens. He pretended to be glad to see me, and shook hands and asked where I was staying. I told him at the Reforma. I could see he didn't believe me, which probably meant he knew where I was staying. I was beginning to get a bad feeling about the Everson case, like gathering vultures.

I waited almost an hour to see Colonel Figueres, but I knew he was really busy. He'd been a major when I last saw him. He hadn't changed much. A little heavier, but the same cold gray eyes and focused attention. When you see him he gives his whole concentration to you. He shook hands without smiling. I can't recall ever seeing him smile. He simply doesn't give himself occasion to do so. I told him I had come about the Everson boy's disappearance.

He nodded. "I thought you had, and I'm glad you are here. We haven't been able to give enough time to it."

"You think something may have happened to him?"

Figueres doesn't shrug. He doesn't gesticulate. He just sits there with his eyes focused on you and what is being discussed.

"I don't know. We have checked Progreso and all surrounding towns. We have checked airports and buses. If he had gone off on another dig, he would be that much easier to locate. A blond foreigner off the tourist routes is very conspicuous. We have also checked all the tourist places. Apparently he was a level-headed, serious young man ... no indications of drug use or excessive drinking. Is there any history of amnesia? Psychotic episodes?"

"None that I know of."

Dead end.

Back at the hotel, Jim and Kiki had turned up very little from questioning the landlady and the neighbors. The landlady described Everson as a serious polite young man ... *un caballero*. He entertained few visitors and these were also serious students. There had been no noise, no drinking, no girls.

I sat down and opened the letter. It was from his twin sister in Minneapolis. It read:

Querido Juanito,
   He has visited me again. He says that before you receive this letter He will have contacted you. He says you will then know what has to be done.

> Your Ever Loving Sister,
> Jane

At three o'clock, I called Inspector Graywood in New York. "Clem Snide here."

"Ah yes, Mr Snide, there have been some developments in Lima. A boy did come to call for another crate and was seen to brush against the duplicate head crate. He was followed to a bicycle rental and repair shop in the Mercado Mayorista. Police searched the shop and found false identity papers in the name of Juan Mateos. The proprietor has been arrested and charged with possession of forged papers and with conspiracy to conceal evidence of a murder. He is being detained in isolation. He claims he did not know what was in the crate. He had been offered a fairly large sum to pick up the crate after it had cleared customs. The crate was to have been brought to his shop. Someone would arrange to pick it up there, and he would be paid an additional and larger sum. The customs agent who passed the crate has also been arrested. He has confessed to accepting a bribe."

"What about the boy?"

"There was no reason to hold him in connection with this case. However, since he has a record for petty theft and a history of epilepsy, he has been placed in a rehabilitation center in Lima."

"I wish I could be on the scene."

"So do I. Otherwise, I doubt if any important arrests will be made. In a country like that, people of wealth are virtually untouchable. People like the Countess de Gulpa, for example...."

"So you know about her?"

"Of course. The description of the man who contacted the customs broker tallies rather closely with your Identikit picture of Marty Blum. I have sent a copy to the Lima police and informed them that he is also wanted in connection with a murder here. Benson, it seems, was a pusher, small-time ... a number of leads but no arrests as yet. Have you found the Everson boy?"

"Not yet and I don't like the looks of it."

"You think something has happened to him?"

"Perhaps."

"I believe you have a contact from Dimitri." I had said nothing about this contact when I told my story in O'Brien's office. "Perhaps it is time to use it."

"I will."

"Your presence in South America would be most valuable. It so happens that a client who wishes to remain anonymous is prepared to retain you in this connection. You will find thirty thousand dollars deposited to your bank account in Lima."

"Well, I haven't finished this case yet."

"Perhaps you can bring the Everson case to a speedy conclusion." He rang off.

It would seem that I had been called upon to act. I got out a map and couldn't find the Callejón de la Esperanza. There are small streets in Mexico City you won't find on a map. I had a general idea as to where it was and I wanted to walk around. I've cracked cases like this with nothing to go on, just by getting out and walking around at random. It works best in a strange town or in a town you haven't visited for some time.

We took a taxi to the Alameda, then started off in a northwesterly direction. Once we got off the main streets I saw that the place hadn't changed all that much: the same narrow unpaved streets and squares with booths selling tacos, fried grasshoppers, and peppermint candy covered with flies; the smell of pulque, urine, benzoin, chile, cooking oil, and sewage; and the faces—bestial, evil, beautiful.

A boy in white cotton shirt and pants, hair straight, skin smoky black, smelling faintly of vanilla and ozone. A boy with bright copper-red skin, innocent and beautiful as some exotic animal, leans against a wall eating an orange dusted with red pepper ... a *maricón* slithers by with long arms and buck teeth, eyes glistening ... man with a bestial Pan face reels out of a *pulquería* ... a hunchback dwarf shoots us a venomous glance.

I was letting my legs guide me. Calle de los Desamparados, Street of Displaced Persons ... a *farmacia* where an old junky was waiting for his Rx. I got a whiff of phantom opium. Postcards in a dusty shop window ... Pancho Villa posing with scowling men ... gun belts and rifles. Three youths hanging from a make-shift scaffold, two with their pants down to the ankles, the other naked. The picture had been taken from behind—soldiers standing in front of them watching and grinning. Photos taken about 1914. The naked boy looked American—you can tell a blond even in black and white.

My legs pulled me in, Jim and Kiki following behind me. When I opened the door a bell echoed through the shop. Inside, the shop was cool and dim with a smell of incense. A man came through a curtain and stood behind the counter. He was short and lightly built and absolutely bald, as if he had never had hair on his head; the skin a yellowish brown, smooth as terra-cotta, the lips rather full, eyes jet-black, forehead high and sloping back. There was a feeling of age about him, not that he looked old but as if he were a survivor of an ancient race—Oriental, Mayan, Negroid—all of these, but something else I had never seen in a human face. He was strangely familiar to me and then I remembered where I had seen that face before. It was in the Mayan collection of the British Museum, a terra-cotta head about three inches in height. His lips moved into a slow smile and he spoke in perfect English without accent or inflection, eerie and remote as if coming from a great distance.

"Good afternoon, gentlemen."

"Could I see that postcard in the window?"

"Certainly. That is what you have come for."

It occurred to me that this must be Dimitri's contact, but this was not the address he had given.

"The Callejón de la Esperanza? The Blind Alley of Hope was destroyed in the earthquake. It has not been rebuilt. This way, gentlemen."

He ushered us through a heavy door behind the curtain. When the door closed, it shut out all noise from the street. We were in a bare whitewashed room with heavy oak furniture lit by a barred window that opened onto a patio. He motioned us to chairs and got an envelope from a filing case and handed me a picture. It was an eight-by-ten replica of the postcard in the window. As I touched the picture, I got a whiff of the fever smell.

Three youths were hanging from a pole supported by tripods, arms strapped to their sides by leather belts. There were two overturned sawhorses and a plank on the ground below them. The blond boy was in the middle, two dark youths hanging on each side

337

of him. The other two had their pants down to their ankles. The blond boy was completely naked. Five soldiers stood in front of a barn looking up at the hanged men. One of the soldiers was very young, sixteen or seventeen, with down on his chin and upper lip. He was looking up with his mouth open, his pants sticking out at the fly.

The proprietor handed me a magnifying glass. The hanged boys quivered and writhed, necks straining against the ropes, buttocks contracting. Standing to one side, face in shadow, was the officer. I studied this figure through the glass. Something familiar ... Oh yes—the Dragon Lady from "Terry and the Pirates." It was a woman. And she bore a slight resemblance to young Everson.

I pointed to the blond boy. "Do you have a picture of his face?"

He laid a picture on the table. The picture showed the boy's face and torso, his arms strapped to his sides. He was looking at something in front of him with a slack look on his face, as if he had just received an overwhelming shock and understood it completely. It was John Everson, or a close enough resemblance to be his twin brother.

I showed him a snapshot of Everson I had in my pocket. He looked at it and nodded. "Yes it seems to be the same young man."

"Do you know who these people were?"

"Yes. The three boys were revolutionaries. The blond boy was the son of an American miner and a Spanish mother. His father returned to America shortly after his birth. He was born and raised in Durango and spoke no English. He was hanged on his twenty-third birthday: September 24, 1914. The woman officer was his half-sister, three years older. She was finally ambushed and killed by Pancho Villa's men. I can assure you that young Everson is alive and well. He has simply forgotten his American identity. His memory can be restored. Unlike Jerry Green, he fell into comparatively good hands. You will meet them tonight ... Lola La Chata is holding her annual party."

"Lola? Is she still operating?"

"She has her little time concession. You will be back in the days of Allende. The Iguana twins will be there. They will take you to Everson. And now ..." He showed us out the back way onto an unpaved street. "I think you will get a ride to Lola's."

Lola's was quite a walk from where we were, and it was not an area for taxis. Also I was a little confused as to directions. A Cadillac careened around the corner and screamed to a stop in a cloud of dust. A man in a glen plaid suit leaned out of the front seat.

"Going to the party? Get in, *cabrones*!"

We got into the back seat. There were two *machos* in the front seat and two on the jump seats. As we sped through the dirt streets they blasted at cats and chickens with their 45s, missing with every shot as the *vecinos* dove for cover.

POR CONVENCIÓN ZAPATA

The General's car stops in front of Lupita's place, which in a slum area of unpaved streets, looks like an abandoned warehouse. The door is opened by an old skull-faced *pistolero* with his black jacket open, a tip-up 44 Smith & Wesson strapped to his lean flank.

The *pistolero* steps aside and we walk into a vast room with a high-beamed ceiling. The furniture is heavy black oak and red brocade, suggesting a Mexican country estate. In the middle of the room is a table with platters of tamales and tacos, beans, rice, and guacamole, beer in tubs of ice, bottles of tequila, bowls of marijuana and cigarette papers. The party is just starting and a few guests stand by the table puffing marijuana and drinking beer. On a smaller table syringes are laid out with glasses of water and alcohol. Along one wall are curtained booths.

Lola La Chata sits in a massive oak chair facing the door, three hundred pounds cut from the mountain rock of Mexico, her graciousness underlining her power. She extends a massive arm: "Ah, Meester Snide ... El Puerco Particular ... the Private Pig ..." She shakes with laughter. "And your handsome young assistants ..." She shakes hands with Jim and Kiki. "You do well by yourself, Meester Snide."

"And you, Lola.... You are younger, if anything."

She waves a hand to the table. "Please serve yourselves.... I think an old friend of yours is already here."

I start towards the table and recognize Bernabé Abogado.

"Clem!"

"Bernabé!"

We go into an embrace and I can feel the pearl-handled 45 under his glen plaid jacket. He is drinking Old Parr scotch and there are four bottles on the table. He pours scotch into glasses as I introduce Jim and Kiki. "Practically everybody in Mexico drinks scotch." Then he laughs and pounds me on the back. Clem, meet the Iguanas ... this very good friend."

I shake hands with two of the most beautiful young people I have ever seen. They both have smooth greenish skin, black eyes, a reptilian grace. I can feel the strength in the boy's hand. They are incredibly poised and detached, their faces stamped with the same ancient lineage as the shop proprietor. They are the Iguana twins.

Junkies arrive and pay court to Lupita. She rewards them with papers of heroin fished from between her massive dugs. They are fixing at the table of syringes.

"Tonight everything is free," says the Iguana sister. *"Mañana es otra cosa."*

The room is rapidly filling with whores and thieves, pimps and hustlers. Uniformed cops get in line and Lupita rewards each of them with an envelope. Plainclothesmen come in and shove to the head of the line. Their envelopes are thicker.

Bernabé beckons to a young Indian policeman who has just received a thin envelope. The policeman approaches shyly. Bernabé pounds him on the back. "This *cabrón* get cockeyed *borracho* and kill two people. . . . I get him out of jail."

Other guests are arriving: the glamorous upper crust and jet set from costume parties. Some are in Mayan and Aztec dress. They bring various animals: monkeys, ocelots, iguanas, and a parrot who screams insults. The *machos* chase a terrified squealing peccary around the room.

A rustle of excitement sweeps through the guests:

"Here's Mr. Coca-Cola."

"He's the real thing."

Mr. Coca-Cola circulates among the guests selling packets of cocaine. As the cocaine takes effect the tempo of the party accelerates. The General turns to a spider monkey perched on top of his chair.

"Here, *cabrón*, have a sniff." He holds up a thumbnail with a pinch of cocaine. The monkey bites his hand, drawing blood. The cocaine spills down his coat. *"CHINGOA* YOU SON OF A WHORE!"* The General leaps up and jerks out his 45, blasting at the monkey from a distance of a few feet and missing with every shot as the guests hit the deck, dodge behind chairs, and roll under the table.

Lupita lifts a finger. Fifty feet away across the room, the old *pistolero* draws his long-barreled 44, aims and fires in one smooth movement, killing the monkey. This display of power intimidates even the *machos* and there is a moment of silence as a servant removes the dead monkey and wipes up the blood. A number of couples and some trios retire to the curtained booths.

Another contingent of guests has arrived among whom I recognize American narcotics agents. One of them is talking with a Mexican lawyer. "I feel so sorry for these American boys in jail here

341

for the *cocaína*," the lawyer says. "And for the girls, even sorrier. I do what I can to get them out but it is most difficult. Our laws are very strict. Much stricter than yours."

In a search booth, which is also one of the booths at Lupita's party, a naked American girl with two uniformed police. The General and the lawyer enter from a door at the rear of the booth. One of the cops points to a packet of cocaine on a shelf. "She have it in her pussee, *señores*." At a gesture from the General the cops exit, grinning like monkeys.

"We feel so sorry for your pussee—frozen in the snow," says the General taking off his pants. "I am the beeg thaw."

A giggling *macho* pulls aside the curtain in front of the booth. "Good pussee, *cabrones*?"

Two Chapultepec blondes nudge each other and chant in unison: "Isn't he *marvelous*? Never repeats himself."

The *macho* pulls aside the curtain of the next booth. "He fuck her in the dry hole."

"Never repeats himself."

In the end booth Ah Pook, the Mayan God of Death, is fucking the young Corn God. As the curtains are jerked aside they reach orgasm and the young Corn God is spattered with black spots of decay. A nitrous haze like vaporized flesh steams off their bodies. The *macho* gasps, coughs, and drops dead of a heart attack.

"Never repeats himself."

Lupita gestures. Indian servants load the body onto a stretcher and carry it out. The party resumes at an even more hectic pace. The gas released by the copulation of life and death acts on the younger guests like catnip. They strip off their clothes, rolling around on mattresses which are spread out on the floor by wooden-faced servants. They exchange masks and do stripteases with scarves while others roll on their backs, legs in the air, applauding with their feet.

The Iguana touched my arm. "Will you and your two helpers please come with me? We have matters to discuss in private."

She led us through a side door and down a long corridor to an elevator. The elevator opened onto a short hall at the end of which was another door. She motioned us into a large loft apartment furnished in Moroccan and Mexican style with rugs, low table, a few chairs, and couches. I declined a drink but accepted a joint.

"The postcard vendor tells me you can help us locate John Everson," I began.

She nodded. I remembered that I had not heard her brother say anything. He had nodded and smiled when we were introduced. He sat beside her now on a low couch looking serene rather than bored. Jim, Kiki, and I sat opposite in three cedar chairs from Santa Fe.

"We have many places here. . . ." A wave of her hand brought the benzoin smell of New Mexico into the room. "It *was* a lovely place but they had to spoil it with their idiotic bombs. Oh yes, John Everson . . . such a nice boy, modern and convenient. You found him so, of course?" She turned to her brother, who smiled and licked his lips. "Well, he is in Durango with relatives . . . in excellent condition, considering the transfer of identities. Such operations may leave the patient a hospital case for months. This generally means that the operation has not been skillfully performed, or that discordant entities have been lodged in the same body. . . .

"In John Everson's case, there have been no complications. We had to give the Mexican identity sufficient time for a transfer to take place. Now it only remains to blend the two and he will recover his own identity, with fluent Spanish and a knowledge of rural Mexico which will be useful in his profession.

"In this case, the two identities are so similar that there will be no disharmony. And the spirit of El Gringo now has a home. He could not enter the cycle of rebirth because his karma required a duplicate death. This was done by electric brain stimulation which seems completely real to the patient. As you know, a difficulty in organ transplants is that they are rejected as a foreign body. Drugs must be administered to suspend the rejection. In this case, the shared experience of being hanged will dissolve the rejection that would otherwise occur, giving rise to the phenomenon of multiple personalities, where only one personality can occupy the body at one time. The hanging experience acts as a solvent. The two personalities will blend into one. John Everson will contact his parents, and tell them that he suffered a lapse of memory owing to a light concussion but is now completely recovered."

I leaned back. "Well, that wraps that case up."

"You have been retained to act against the Countess . . . thirty thousand dollars. Does that seem enough to you?"

"Well, considering what we are expected to do—no."

"And considering that you are all inexperienced and susceptible, this is virtually a suicide mission. I am prepared to retain you at a fair price and provide contacts which will give you at least some chance of success."

She led the way into a bare room with chairs, a long table, and filing cabinets along one wall. I recognized the room as a replica of the room in back of the postcard vendor's shop. She went to the filing cabinet and handed me a short pamphlet bound in heavy parchment. On the cover in red letters:

CITIES OF THE RED NIGHT.

BOOK II

CITIES OF THE RED NIGHT

The Cities of the Red Night were six in number: Tamaghis, Ba'dan, Yass-Waddah, Waghdas, Naufana, and Ghadis. These cities were located in an area roughly corresponding to the Gobi Desert, a hundred thousand years ago. At that time the desert was dotted with large oases and traversed by a river which emptied into the Caspian Sea.

The largest of these oases contained a lake ten miles long and five miles across, on the shores of which the university town of Waghdas was founded. Pilgrims came from all over the inhabited world to study in the academies of Waghdas, where the arts and sciences reached peaks of attainment that have never been equaled. Much of this ancient knowledge is now lost.

The towns of Ba'dan and Yass-Waddah were opposite each other on the river. Tamaghis, located in a desolate area to the north on a small oasis, could properly be called a desert town. Naufana and Ghadis were situated in mountainous areas to the west and south beyond the perimeter of usual trade routes between the other cities.

In addition to the six cities, there were a number of villages and nomadic tribes. Food was plentiful and for a time the population was completely stable: no one was born unless someone died.

The inhabitants were divided into an elite minority known as the Transmigrants and a majority known as the Receptacles. Within these categories were a number of occupational and specialized strata and the two classes were not in practice separate: Transmigrants acted as Receptacles and Receptacles became Transmigrants.

To show the system in operation: Here is an old Transmigrant on his deathbed. He has selected his future Receptacle parents, who are summoned to the death chamber. The parents then copulate, achieving orgasm just as the old Transmigrant dies so that his spirit enters the womb to be reborn. Every Transmigrant carries with him at all times a list of alternative parents, and in case of accident, violence, or sudden illness, the nearest parents are rushed to the scene. However, there was at first little chance of random or unexpected deaths since the Council of Transmigrants in Waghdas had attained such skill in the art of prophecy that they were able to chart a life from birth to death and determine in most cases the exact time and manner of death.

Many Transmigrants perferred not to wait for the infirmities of age and the ravages of illness, lest their spirit be so weakened as to be overwhelmed and absorbed by the Receptacle child. These hardy Transmigrants, in the full vigor of maturity, after rigorous training in concentration and astral projection, would select two death guides to kill them in front of the copulating parents. The methods of death most commonly employed were hanging and strangulation, the Transmigrant dying in orgasm, which was considered the most reliable method of ensuring a successful transfer. Drugs were also developed, large doses of which occasioned death in erotic convulsions, smaller doses being used to enhance sexual pleasure. And these drugs were often used in conjunction with other forms of death.

In time, death by natural causes became a rare and rather discreditable occurrence as the age for transmigration dropped. The Eternal Youths, a Transmigrant sect, were hanged at the age of eighteen to spare themselves the coarsening experience of middle age and the deterioration of senescence, living their youth again and again.

Two factors undermined the stability of this system. The first was perfection of techniques for artificial insemination. Whereas the traditional practice called for one death and one rebirth, now hundreds of women could be impregnated from a single sperm collection, and territorially oriented Transmigrants could populate whole areas with their progeny. There were sullen mutters of revolt from the Receptacles, especially the women. At this point, another factor totally unforeseen was introduced.

In the thinly populated desert area north of Tamaghis a portentous event occurred. Some say it was a meteor that fell to earth leaving a crater twenty miles across. Others say that the crater was caused by what modern physicists call a black hole.

After this occurrence the whole northern sky lit up red at night, like the reflection from a vast furnace. Those in the immediate vicinity of the crater were the first to be affected and various mutations were observed, the commonest being altered hair and skin color. Red and yellow hair, and white, yellow, and red skin appeared for the first time. Slowly the whole area was similarly affected until the mutants outnumbered the original inhabitants, who were as all human beings were at the time: black.

The women, led by an albino mutant know as the White Tigress, seized Yass-Waddah, reducing the male inhabitants to slaves, consorts, and courtiers all under sentence of death that could be carried out at any time at the caprice of the White Tigress. The Council in Waghdas countered by developing a method of growing babies in excised wombs, the wombs being supplied by vagrant Womb Snatchers. This practice aggravated the differences between the male and female factions and war with Yass-Waddah seemed unavoidable.

In Naufana, a method was found to transfer the spirit directly into an adolescent Receptacle, thus averting the awkward and vulnerable period of infancy. This practice required a rigorous period of preparation and training to achieve a harmonious blending of the two spirits in one body. These Transmigrants, combining the freshness and vitality of youth with the wisdom of many lifetimes, were expected to form an army of liberation to free Yass-Waddah. And there were adepts who could die at will without any need of drugs or executioners and project their spirit into a chosen Receptacle.

I have mentioned hanging, strangulation, and orgasm drugs as the commonest means of effecting the transfer. However, many other forms of death were employed. The Fire Boys were burned to death in the presence of the Receptacles, only the genitals being insulated, so that the practitioner could achieve orgasm in the moment of death. There is an interesting account by a Fire Boy who recalled his experience after transmigrating in this manner:

"As the flames closed round my body, I inhaled deeply, drawing fire into my lungs, and screamed out flames as the most horrible pain turned to the most exquisite pleasure and I was ejaculating in an adolescent Receptacle who was being sodomized by another."

Others were stabbed, decapitated, disemboweled, shot with arrows, or killed by a blow on the head. Some threw themselves from cliffs, landing in front of the copulating Receptacles.

The scientists at Waghdas were developing a machine that could directly transfer the electromagnetic field of one body to another. In Ghadis there were adepts who were able to leave their bodies before death and occupy a series of hosts. How far this research may have gone will never be known. It was a time of great disorder and chaos.

The effects of the Red Night on Receptacles and Transmigrants proved to be incalculable and many strange mutants arose as a series of plagues devastated the cities. It is this period of war and pestilence that is covered by the books. The Council had set out to produce a race of supermen for the exploration of space. They produced instead races of ravening idiot vampires.

Finally, the cities were abandoned and the survivors fled in all directions, carrying the plagues with them. Some of these migrants crossed the Bering Strait into the New World, taking the books with them. They settled in the area later occupied by the Mayans and the books eventually fell into the hands of the Mayan priests.

The alert student of this noble experiment will perceive that death was regarded as equivalent not to birth but to conception and go on to infer that conception is the basic trauma. In the moment of death, the dying man's whole life may flash in front of his eyes back to conception. In the moment of conception, his future life flashes forward to his future death. *To reexperience conception is fatal.*

This was the basic error of the Transmigrants: you do not get beyond death and conception by reexperience any more than you get beyond heroin by ingesting larger and larger doses. The Transmigrants were quite literally addicted to death and they needed more and more death to kill the pain of conception. They were buying parasitic life with a promissory death note to be paid at a prearranged time. The Transmigrants then imposed these terms on the host child to ensure his future transmigration. There was a basic conflict of interest between host child and Transmigrant. So the Transmigrants reduced the Receptacle class to a condition of virtual idiocy. Otherwise they would have reneged on a bargain from which they stood to gain nothing but death. The books are flagrant falsifications. And some of these basic lies are still current.

"Nothing is true. Everything is permitted." The last words of Hassan i Sabbah, Old Man of the Mountain.

"Tamaghis ... Ba'dan ... Yass-Waddah ... Waghdas ... Naufana ... Ghadis."

It is said that an initiate who wishes to know the answer to any question need only repeat these words as he falls asleep and the answer will come in a dream.

Tamaghis: This is the open city of contending partisans where advantage shifts from moment to moment in a desperate biological war. Here everything is as true as you think it is and everything you can get away with is permitted.

Ba'dan: This city is given over to competitive games and commerce. Ba'dan closely resembles present-day America with a precarious moneyed elite, a large disaffected middle class and an equally large segment of criminals and outlaws. Unstable, explosive, and swept by whirlwind riots. Everything is true and everything is permitted.

Yass-Waddah: This city is the female stronghold where the Countess de Gulpa, the Countess de Vile, and the Council of the Selected plot a final subjugation of the other cities. Every shade of sexual transition is represented: boys with girls' heads, girls with boys' heads. Here everything is true and nothing is permitted except to the permitters.

Waghdas: This is the university city, the center of learning where all questions are answered in terms of what can be expressed and understood. Complete permission derives from complete understanding.

Naufana and Ghadis are the cities of illusion where nothing is true and *therefore* everything is permitted.

The traveler must start in Tamaghis and make his way through the other cities in the order named. This pilgrimage may take many lifetimes.

A COWBOY IN THE SEVEN-DAYS-A-WEEK FIGHT

Tamaghis is a walled city built of red adobe. The city stirs at sunset, for the days are unbearably hot at this season and the inhabitants nocturnal. As the sun sets the northern sky lights up with a baleful red glow, bathing the city in light that shades from seashell pink to deep-purple shadow pools.

It is a summer night and the air is warm and electric with a smell of incense, ozone, and the musky sweet rotten red smell of the fever. Jerry, Audrey, Dahlfar, Jon, Joe, and John Kelly are walking through a quarter of massage parlors, Turkish baths, sex rooms, hanging studios, cubicle restaurants, booths selling incense, aphrodisiacs and aromatic herbs. Music drifts from nightclubs, sometimes a whiff of opium smoke—the Painless Ones who run many of the concessions smoke it.

The boys pause at a booth and Audrey buys some Red Hots from a Painless One. This aphrodisiac causes an erogenous rash in the crotch, anus, and on the nipples. It acts within seconds, taken orally, or it can be injected—but this is dangerous since the pleasure is often so intense that it stops the heart. Adolescents of the city play red-hot dare games known as Hots and Pops.

The boys are dressed in red silk tunics open on their lean bodies, red silk pants, and magnetic sandals. At their belts they carry spark guns and long knives, sharp on both edges, that curl slightly at the end. Knife fights are frequent here since Red Hots can set off the raw red Killing Fever.

The virus is like a vast octopus through bodies of the city, mutating in protean forms: the Killing Fever, the Flying Fever, the Black Hate Fever. In all cases the total energies of the subject are focused on one activity or objective. There is a Gambling Fever and a Money Fever which sometimes infect the Painless Ones—eyes glittering, they draw in the money with a terrible eagerness, trembling like hungry shrews. There is also an Activity Fever: the victims rushing about in a frenzy organizing anything, acting as agents for anything or anybody, prowling the streets desperately looking for contacts.

Red Night in Tamaghis: Dog Catchers, Spermers, Sirens, and

the Special Police from the Council of the Selected who are infiltrating Tamaghis from Yass-Waddah. The Dog Catchers will seize any youths they encounter in the Fair Game areas and sell them off to hanging studios and sperm brokers. The Spermers are pirates operating from strongholds outside the city walls, attacking caravans and supply trains, tunneling under the walls to prowl in the rubbly outskirts of the city. They are outlaws who may be killed by any citizens, like cattle rustlers.

Two boys, faces blazing with alertness, slide from one red shadow pool to another. A patrol of Dog Catchers passes. The boys crouch in the darkness by a ruined wall, teeth bare, hands on their knives. The Dog Catchers are muscular youths with heavy thighs and the deep chests of runners. Naked to the waist, they carry a variety of nets and handcuffs around their shoulders, and bolos that can tangle legs at twenty yards. On leads are the hairless red sniff-hounds, quivering, whimpering, sniffing, trying to fuck the Dog Catchers' legs. Audrey's lips part in a slow smile. This is one of his infiltration tactics: the dogs are trained to wrap themselves around a Dog Catcher's legs and trip him up.

Audrey and Cupid Mount Etna are in a populous area with wide stone streets. A flower float of Sirens passes. In conch shells of roses they trill: "I'm going to *pop* you naked darling and *milk* you while you're being *hanged*. . . ."

Idiot males are rushing up, jumping on the hanging float to be hanged by the Sirens, many of whom are transvestites from Yass-Waddah. The floats wind on towards the Hanging Gardens where the golden youths gather with their Hanging Exempt badges. Like characters in a charade they pose and pirouette in the red glow that lights trees, pools, and diseased faces burning with the terrible lusts of the fever.

Audrey decides on a detour. Four Special Police from the Council of the Selected stand in their way. They are crew-cut men in blue suits, looking like religious FBI men with muscular Christian smiles.

"What can we do for you?"

"Drop dead." Audrey snaps. He draws his spark gun and gives them a full blast. They fall twitching and smoking. Officially the SPs have no standing in Tamaghis, but they are bribing the local police and kidnapping boys for the transplant operation rooms of Yass-Waddah.

The boys sprint around the bodies and turn into an alley, police whistles behind them. Possession of a spark gun is a capital offense. Dodging and twisting through a maze of narrow streets, tunnels, and gangways, they lose the patrol.

They are on the outskirts now, near the walls, walking down a steep stone road. There is a road above them and a steep grassy slope leading up to it. Suddenly, a World War I ambulance truck stops on the high road and six men jump out got up as pirates with beards and earrings. They rush down the slope, eyes flashing with greed.

"Spermers!"

Audrey drops on one knee, raking the slope with his spark gun. The Spermers scream, rolling down the slope, clothes burning, setting the grass on fire. The truck is burning. Audrey and Cupid sprint on as the gas tank explodes behind them.

SCREEN PLAY/PART ONE

It is on the second floor. A brass plaque: "Blum & Krup." A metal door. A bell. I ring. A cold-eyed young Jew opens the door a crack.

"Yes? You are client or salesman?"

"Neither." I hand him my card. He closes the door and goes away. He comes back.

"Mr Blum and Mr Krup will see you now."

He ushers me into an office decorated in the worst German taste with pictures of youths and maidens swimming with swans in northern lakes, the carpets up to my ankles. There, behind a huge desk, are Blum and Krup. A vaudeville team. Blum is Austrian and Jewish, Krup is Prussian and German.

Krup bows stiffly without getting up. "Krup von Nordenholz."

Blum bustles out from behind the desk. "Sit down, Mr Snide. I am the master here. Have a cigar."

"No thanks."

"Well, we will have some fun at least. We will have an orgy." He goes back to his chair on the other side of the desk and sits there watching me through cigar smoke.

"And why have you not come here sooner, Herr Snide?" asks Krup in a cold dry voice.

"Oh well, there's a lot of legwork in this business . . ." I say vaguely.

"*Ja und Assenwerke.*" (Yes and asswork.)

"We want that you stop with the monkey business and do some real business, Mr Snide."

"We are not a charitable institution."

"We do not finance ass fuckings."

"Now just a minute, Blum and Krup. I wasn't aware that you were my clients."

Krup emits a short cold bray of laughter.

Blum takes the cigar out of his mouth and points the butt across the table at my chest. "And who did you think was your million-dollar client?"

"A green bitch synthesized from cabbage?"

"Well, if you are my client, what am I expected to do exactly?"

Krup whinnies like a cynical horse.

"You are to recover certain rare books now in the possession of a certain Countess," Blum says.

"I am not even sure I would know these books if I saw them."

"You have seen samples."

"I am not sure the samples correspond in any way to the alleged books I am retained to recover."

"You think you have been deceived?"

"Not 'think.' *Know*."

The room is so quiet you can hear the long gray cone of Blum's cigar fall into an ashtray. Finally he speaks. "And suppose we could tell you exactly where the books are?"

"So they are in someone's private bank vault surrounded by guards and computerized alarm systems? I am supposed to sneak in there and carry out a carton of books slung over my shoulder in a rare tapestry, stamps and first editions in all my pockets, industrial diamonds up my ass in a finger stall, a sapphire big as a hen's egg in my mouth? Is that what I am expected to do?"

Blum laughs loud and long while Krup looks sourly at his nails. "No, Mr Snide. This is not what you are expected to do. There is a group of well-armed partisans operating in an adjacent area, who will occupy the Countess's stronghold. You will have only to go in after them and secure the books. There will be an outcry against the partisans who have so savagely butchered a rich foreign sow.... Then stories will filter out about the Countess and her laboratories, and there'll be something in it for everybody. The CIA, the partisans, the Russians, the Chinese ... we will have some fun at least. Might start a little Vietnam down here."

"Well," I say. "You have to take a broad general view of things."

"We prefer a very specific view, Mr Snide," says Krup looking at a heavy gold pocket watch. "Be here at this time Thursday and we will talk further. Meanwhile, I would strongly advise you to avoid other commitments."

"And bring your assistants and the books what you got," adds Blum.

When Jim and I go to see Blum and Krup on Thursday, we take along the books the Iguanas have given me. Krup looks the books over, snorting from time to time, and as he finishes leafing through each one, he slides it down the table to Blum.

"Mr Snide, where are the books you are now making?" asks Krup.

"Books? Me? I'm just a private eye, not a writer."

"You come to make with us the crookery," snaps Blum, "we break you in your neck. Hans! Willi! Rudi! Heinrich! *Herein!*"

Four characters come in with silencered P-38s, like in an old Gestapo movie.

"And now, your assistant will get the books while you and your *Lustknabe* remain here. Hans and Heinrich will go with him to make sure he does not so lose himself."

Hans and Heinrich step behind Jim. "Keep six feet in front of us at all times." They file out.

In half an hour Jim is back with the books. B & K spread them out on the table and both of them stand up and look at them like generals studying a battle plan.

Finally Krup nods. "*Ach ja.* With these I think it is enough."

Blum turns to me, almost jovial now, rubbing his hands. "Well, you and your assistant and the boy, you are ready to leave, *hein?*"

"Leave? Where to?"

"That you will see."

Hans, Rudi, Willi, and Heinrich march us up some stairs onto a roof and into a waiting helicopter. The pilot has a blank cold thuggish face and he is wearing a 45 in a shoulder holster. He looks American. The guards strap us into our seats and blindfold us and we take off. The flight lasts about an hour.

Then we are herded out and into another plane, a prop job. Dakota, probably. About three hours this time, and we set down on water. They take off our blindfolds and we now have a different pilot. He looks English and has a beard.

The pilot turns around and smiles. "Well, chaps, here we are."

They untie us and we get out on a jetty. It is on a small lake, just big enough to set the plane down. Around the lake I see Quonset huts and in an open space something that looks like an oil rig. A barbed-wire fence surrounds the area with gun towers. There are enough armed guards around for a small army.

In front of a Quonset hut several men are talking. One comes forward to greet us: it is that CIA punk Pierson.

"Well, Snide," he says. "Welcome aboard."

"Well, Pierson," I say. "If you can't lick them join them."

"That's right. How about some chow?"

"That would be just fine."

He leads the way into a Quonset that serves as a dining room. There are long tables and tin plates and a number of men eating. Some of them look like construction workers, others like technicians.

My attention is drawn to a table of about thirty youths. They are the best-looking boys I have ever seen at one time, and all of them are ideal specimens of white Anglo-Saxon youth.

"Our genetic pool," Pierson explains.

A fat mess sergeant slops some fish and rice and stewed apricots on our plates and fills tin cups with cold tea.

"Army-style here," says Pierson.

After we finish eating, he lights a cigarette and grins at me through the smoke.

"Well, I guess you are wondering what this is all about."

"Yeah."

"Come along to my digs and I'll explain. Some of it, at least."

I know quite a bit already. Much more than I want him to think I know. And I know that the less he tells me the better chance I have of getting out of here alive. I've already seen that the oil rig is a rocket-launching pad. Things are falling into place.

He leads the way to a small prefab. He turns to Jim and Kiki: "Why don't you two look around? Do some fishing. You can get tackle at the PX. The lake is stocked with largemouth bass . . . You'll do well here. . . ."

I nod to Jim and he walks away with Kiki. Pierson unlocks the door and we go in. A cot, a card table, some chairs, a few books. He motions me to a chair, sits down and looks at me. "You saw the launching pad?"

"Yes."

"And what do you think it will be used for?"

"To launch something, obviously."

"Obviously. A space capsule that will also be a communications satellite."

I am beginning to understand what they are planning to communicate.

"Now, just suppose an atom bomb should fall on New York City. Who would be blamed for that?"

"The Commies."

"Right. And suppose a mysterious plague broke out attacking the white race, while the yellow, black, and brown seemed to be mysteriously immune? Who would be blamed for that?"

"Yellow black brown. Yellow especially."

"Right. So we would then be justified in using any biologic and/or chemical weapons in retaliation, would we not?"

"You would do it justified or not. But the plague might well decimate the white race . . . destroy them as a genetic entity."

358

"We would have the fever sperm stocks. We could rebuild the white race to our specifications, after we ..."

The table of thirty boys flashed in front of my eyes. "Pretty neat. And you want me to write the scenario."

"That's it. You've written enough already to get the ball rolling."

"What about the Countess de Gulpa? How does she figure in this?"

"Ah, the Countess. She doesn't figure. She is not nearly as important as you may have thought. She would hardly go along with destroying the blacks and browns, because she makes her money out of them. She still thinks in terms of money."

"Her laboratories?"

"Not much we could use. Certain lines of specialized experimentation ... interesting, perhaps. She has, for example, succeeded in reanimating headless men. These she gives to her friends as love slaves. They are fed through the rectum. I don't see any practical applications. We had thought of using her in scandals to discredit the rank-and-file CIA ... but that won't be necessary now."

"I daresay you could wipe her out with rockets from here."

"Easily. Or we could use biologic weapons."

"The Black Fever?"

"Yes." He pointed to the radio. "In fact, I could give the order right now."

"So what do you want from me?"

"You will finish the scenario. Your assistant will do the illustrations."

"And then?"

"You have been promised a million dollars to find the books. You have found them. Of course, money will mean nothing once this thing breaks, but we will see to it that you live comfortably. After all, we have no motive to eliminate you ... we may need your services in the future. We're not bad guys really...."

How nice will these nice guys be once they get what they want from me? If I am allowed to live at all it will certainly be as a prisoner.

I am trying to stall Blum with a sick number called *Naked Newgate* about a handsome young highwayman and the sheriff's daughter. Blum isn't buying it.

"Any thousand-dollar-a-week Hollywood hack could write such a piece of shit."

Then Pierson asks me over for a drink and a "little chat." It sounds ominous.

"Oh uh by the way ... Blum isn't exactly happy about the screenplay."

"Nize baby, et up all the screenplay."

He looks at me sharply.

"What's that, Snide?"

"It's a joke. Fitzgerald in Hollywood."

"Oh," he says, a bit intimidated by the reference to Fitzgerald ... perhaps something he should know about ... He clears his throat.

"Blum says he wants something he calls *art*. He knows it when he sees it and he isn't seeing it now."

"What I like is *culture*! What I like is *art*!" I screech in the tones of a crazed Jewish matron.

He gives me a long blank sour look.

"More jokes, Snide?"

"I'll give him what he wants. I'm staging a little theater production tomorrow ... *very artistic*."

"This had better be good, Snide."

A slim blond youth in elegant nineteenth-century clothes stands on a scaffold. A black hood, laced with gold threads, is drawn over his head.

RUBBLE BLOOD PU
(END OF PART I)

Stuck in dead smallpox nights of the last century. This satined ass in yellow light.

(Yellow-flecked storm waves ... palm trees ... wide strip of sand ... a corduroy road ... I don't remember hitting ... I really don't think so ... the truck shadow ... trees tasting cement ... green dark water.)

"Good English soldier of fortune, sir. Work for you, yes no?"

Spelling years whisper the lake heavy red sweater, trash cans in yellow light. The sigh of a harmonica flags in the sad golden wash of the sunset singing fish luminous sky fresh smell of damp violets. Man smell of dirty clothes red faces breath thick on tarnished mirrors.

Sunset, train whistles. I am on the train with Waring. Red clay roads and flint chips glitter in the setting sun.

Pilots the plane across time into a waiting taxi, steep stone street, boy with erection yellow pimples turn-of-the-century lips parted ... red hair freckles a ladder.

A young face floats in front of his eyes. The lips, twisted in a smile of ambiguous sexual invitation, move in silent words that stir and ache in his throat with a taste of blood and metallic sweetness. He feels the dizzy death weakness breathing through his teeth, his breath ice cold.

The boy in front of him lights up inside, a blaze of light out at his eyes in a flash as Audrey feels the floor drop out from under him. He is falling, the face floating down with him, then a blinding flash blots out the room and the waiting faces.

ÉTRANGER QUI PASSAIT

Farnsworth, Ali, and Noah Blake are moving south across the Red Desert, a vast area of plateaus, canyons, and craters where sandstone mesas rise from the red sand. The temperature is moderate even at midday and they travel naked except for desert boots, packs, and belts with eighteen-inch Bowie knives and ten-shot revolvers chambered for a high-speed 22-caliber cartridge. They have automatic carbines of the same caliber in their packs, with thirty-shot clips. These weapons may be needed if a time warp dumps an old western posse in their laps.

The only provisions they carry are protein, minerals and vitamins in a dried powder concentrate. There are streams in the canyon bottoms where fish abound and fruit and nut trees grow in profusion.

They carry collapsible hang-gliders in their packs.

They have stopped at the top of a thousand-foot cliff over an area littered with red boulders. Here and there is a glint of water. The sandstone substrata form pools that hold water and even in otherwise arid patches there are usually fish and crustaceans in the pools.

The boys unpack and assemble the gliders. As always, they will take off one at a time so that the lead glider will indicate to the others the air currents, wind velocities, and updrafts to be expected.

They draw lots. Noah will go first. He stands on the edge of the cliff studying the terrain, the movements of dust clouds and tumbleweeds. He looks up at the clouds and the wheeling vultures. He runs towards the edge of the cliff and soars out over the desert. The glider is out of control for a few seconds in an updraft. He goes into a steep dive and pulls out, coming in smoothly now he lands by a pool. He waves and signals to the others; a tiny figure by a speck of water. They move a hundred feet down the cliff and take off.

By the pool they eat dried fruit washed down with water. Ali stands up and points.

"Look there."

The others can't see anything.

"There . . . right there. . . ."

They pick out a lizard about four feet high standing on two legs fifty feet away. The lizard is speckled with orange-red and yellow blotches, so perfectly camouflaged it is like picking a face out in a picture puzzle to see him. The lizard knows he has been seen and lets out a high-pitched whistle. He runs towards them on two legs with incredible speed, kicking up a trail of red dust. He stops in front of them, immobile as a stone, while the dust slowly settles behind him. Seen at close range he is clearly humanoid with a smooth yellow face and a wide red mouth, black eyes with red pupils, a patch of red pubic hair at the crotch. A dry spoor smell drifts from his body.

The lizard boy now leads the way setting the fastest pace the others can maintain. As he moves his body changes color to blend into the landscape. In the late afternoon they are making their way down a steep path into a canyon. Leaves spatter the lizard's body with green. They come to a wide valley and a river with deep pools. The boys take off their packs and swim in the cool water. The lizard dives down to the bottom and comes up with a fourteen-inch cutthroat trout in his jaws and flips it onto the grass by the pool. Ali and Farnsworth are picking strawberries.

Next day they set out to explore the canyon. The river winds between red cliffs. Here and there are cubicles cut in the rock by ancient cliff-dwellers.

We are heading for the river towns of the fruit-fish people. The staple of their diet is a fruit-eating fish which attains a weight of thirty pounds. To cultivate this fish they plant the riverbanks with a variety of fruit trees and vines so that the smell of fruit and fruit blossoms perfumes the air, which is a balmy eighty degrees.

Our boat rides high in the water on two pontoons of paper-thin dugout canoes sealed over to form a sort of sled on which we glide, propelled by a gentle current, past youths in the boughs of trees, masturbating and shaking the ripe fruit into the water with the spasms of their bodies as their sperm falls also to be devoured by the great green-blue fish. It is this diet of fruit and sperm which gives the fruit fish its incomparable flavor.

Little naked boys walk along the banks throwing fruit into the water and masturbating while they emit birdcalls and animal noises, giggling, singing, whining, and growling out spurts of sperm that glitter in the dappled sunlight. As we pass, the boys bend over, waving and grinning between their legs like sheaves of wheat parted by a gentle breeze that wafts us to the jetty.

Who are we? We are migrants who move from settlement to settlement in the vast area now held by the Articulated. These

363

voyages often last for years, and migrants may drop out along the way or adventurous settlers join the migrants. We carry with us seeds and plants, plans, books, pictures, and artifacts from the communes we have visited.

On the jetty we are welcomed by a tall statuesque youth with negroid features and kinky yellow hair. It is late afternoon and the boys are trooping back from the riverbanks and orchards and fish hatcheries. Many of them are completely naked. I am struck by the mixtures here displayed: Negro, Chinese, Portuguese, Irish Malay, Japanese, Nordic boys with kinky red and blond and auburn hair and jet-black eyes, blacks with straight hair, gray and blue and green eyes, Chinese with bright red hair and green eyes, mixtures of Chinese and Indian of a delicate pink color, Indians of a deep copper red with one blue eye and one brown eye, purple-black skin and red pubic hairs.

Arriving at the port city after a long uncomfortable train journey from the capital, Farnsworth checked into the Survival Hotel. The hotel was a ramshackle wooden building of four stories overlooking the bay, with wide balconies and porches overgrown with bougainvillea where the guests sat in high-back cane chairs sipping gin slings. A promontory of red and yellow sandstone a thousand feet high cut the town off from the sea, which entered by a narrow channel between the rock and the mainland. Looking down from the balcony of his room on the fourth floor, Farnsworth could see the beaches around the lagoon, where languid youths stretched naked in the sun. Fatigued from his journey, he decided to take a nap before dinner.

Someone touches his shoulder. Ali is looking into the dim light of early dawn.

"What is it?"

"Patrol, I think."

We are out of the reservation area and the penalty for being caught here without authorization is the white-hot jockstrap. We will not be taken alive. We have cyanide shoes, a cushion of compressed gas in a double sole under our feet. A certain sequence of toe movements and we settle down in a whoosh of cyanide as the Green Guards clutch their blue throats and we streak out of our bodies across the sky. We also have rocketfuel flamethrowers, very effective at close range.

This is not a patrol. It is a gang of naked boys covered with erogenous sores. As they walk they giggle and stroke and scratch each other. From time to time they fuck each other in Hula-Hoops to idiot mambo.

"Just leper kids," Ali grunts. "Let's make some java."

We drink it black in tin cups and wash down K rations.

WE ARE HERE BECAUSE OF YOU

Woke up in the silent wolf lope. There is the river. No sign of Yass-Waddah. I must be above or below it.

I reach the bank. Across the river I can see the rotting piers and sheds of East Ba'dan. To my right is what remains of a bridge, the upper structure rotted away, leaving only the piles protruding from green water.

I am standing where Yass-Waddah used to be. The water looks green and cold and dirty and curiously artificial, like a diorama in the Museum of Natural History.

A blond boy enters from my right where the bridge used to be, walking on the green-brown water. He moves with a stalking gait as if he were playing some part in a play, mimicking some actor with a touch of parody.

The boy is wearing a white T-shirt with a yellow calligram on the chest surrounded by a circle of yellow light, rainbow-colored at the edges. He is wearing white gym shorts and white tennis shoes.

A dark boy in identical white gym clothes is standing to my left on the bank at the top of a grassy hillock. He has planted a banner in the ground beside him and holds the shaft with one hand. The banner is the calligram in the rainbow circle stirring gently in a wind that ruffles his shorts around smooth white thighs.

The blond boy walks up from the water and stands in front of his dark twin. The dark boy begins to talk in soft flute calls, clean and sweet and joyful with a sound like laughter, wind in the trees, birds at dawn, trickling streams. The blond boy answers in the same language, sweetly inhuman voices from a distant star.

Now I recognize the dark boy as Dink Rivers, the boy from Middletown, and the other as myself. This is a high school play. We have just taken the west side of the river. This is the conquest of Yass-Waddah.

Good evening, our chap. A good crossing. Yass-Waddah disintegrated.

A slow insouciant shrug of rocks and stones and trees spreads a golf course along the river now several hundred yards away. Two caddies stand in a sand trap. One rubs his crotch and the other makes a jack-off gesture. Music from the country club on a gust of wind. Red brick buildings, cobblestone streets. It is getting darker. Dusty ticket booth.

A sign:

The Billy Celeste High School presents:
CITIES OF THE RED NIGHT

I lead the way through rooms stacked with furniture and paintings, passageways, partitions, stairways, booths, cubicles, elevators, ramps and ladders, trunks full of costumes and old weapons, bathtubs, toilets, steam rooms, and rooms open in front. . . .

A boy jacks off on a yellow toilet seat . . . catcalls and scattered applause.

We are in a cobblestone alley. I look at my companion. He is about eighteen. He has large brown eyes with amber pupils, set to the side of his face, and a long straight Mayan nose. He is dressed in blue-and-brown-striped pants and shirt.

I open a rusty padlock into my father's workshop. We strip and straddle a pirate chest, facing each other. His skin is a deep brownish-purple gray underneath. A sharp musty smell pulses from his erect phallus with its smooth purple head. His eyes converge on me like a lizard's.

"What scene do you want me to act in?"

"Death Baby fucks the Corn God."

We open the chest. He takes out a necklace of crystal skulls and puts it on. There is a reek of decay as he drapes me in the golden flesh of the young Corn God.

We are in a vast loft-attic-gymnasium-warehouse. There are chests and trunks, costumes, mirrors, and makeup. Boys are taking out costumes, trying them on, posing and giggling in front of mirrors, moving props and backdrops.

The warehouse seems endless. A maze of rooms and streets, cafés, courtyards and gardens. Farm rooms, with walnut bedsteads and hooked rugs, open onto a pond where boys fish naked on an improvised raft. A Moroccan patio is animated with sand foxes and a boy playing a flute . . . stars like wilted gardenias across the blue night sky.

A number of performances are going on at the same time, in many rooms, on many levels. The spectators circulate from one stage to another, putting on costumes and makeup to join a performance and the performers all move from one stage to another. There are moving stages and floats, platforms that descend from the ceiling on pulleys, doors that pop open, and partitions that slide back.

Audrey, naked except for a sailor hat, is tipped back balancing in a chair while he reads a comic book entitled: "Audrey and the Pirates."

Jerry comes in naked with an envelope sealed with red wax.

"Open it and read it to me."

"Oh sir, it's battle orders."

"Wheeeeeeeeeeee!" Audrey ejaculates.

On deck, naked tars throw their hats into the air jacking off and leaping on each other like randy dogs: "Wheeeeeeeeeeeeeee!" They scramble into uniforms as bugles call them to battle stations.

The Fever: A red silk curtain scented with rose oil, musk, sperm, rectal mucus, ozone and raw meat goes up on a hospital ward of boys covered with phosphorescent red blotches that glow and steam the fever smell off them, shuddering, squirming, shivering, eyes burning, legs up, teeth bare, whispering the ancient evil fever words.

Doctor Pierson covers his face with a handkerchief. *"Get it out of here!"*

Yen Lee looks at a painted village with his binoculars. Taped voice: "We see Tibet with the binoculars of the people."

In a stone hut, a naked boy lies on a filthy pallet. Bright red luminescent flesh-clusters glow in the dark room. He rubs the clusters with a slow idiot smile and ejaculates.

Yen Lee sags against a wall with a handkerchief in front of his face.

"It's the pickle factory."

"A health officer is on the way."

The Health Officer is on the nod on his porch over a sluggish river. The huge bloated corpse of a dead hippopotamus floats slowly by. The Health Officer is oblivious. Taped voice: "For he had a sustaining vice." On a riverbank with Ali standing over him, he looks with horror at his torn pocket and empty hand. Backdrop shifts to another bank. With the same expression, Farnsworth looks down at his naked body covered with red welts a dusky rose color on his reddish-brown skin.

Marine band plays "Semper Fi".

Picture of a privy on a door with a bronze eye under the sickle moon. Audrey, as Clem Snide the private eye, is sitting in a sunken room open at the top. The audience is looking down into the room so they can see what he is looking at: photos of Jerry—baby pictures

... age fourteen holding up a string of cutthroat trout ... naked with a hard-on ... Jerry live onstage, naked with his hands tied, face and body covered with red blotches, a baneful red glow behind him. He is looking at something in front of him as his penis stirs and stiffens. Scattered applause and *olés* from the audience.

Banner headlines in red letters: MYSTERY ILLNESS SPREADS.

On a hospital bed, Jerry spreads his legs with a slow wallowing movement, showing his bright red asshole glowing, pulsing, and crinkling like a randy mollusk. He twists his head to the right, eyes sputtering green flashes as he hangs.

A sepia cutback to the hospital bed. He ejaculates, kicking his legs in the air. Jimmy Lee, as a male nurse, catches his sperm in a jar.

Thunderous applause ... *"Olé! Olé! Olé!"*

The jar is passed to four Marine guards and rushed to a top-secret lab. A scientist looks through a microscope. He gives the OK sign.

Bouquets of roses rain on stage.

Red-letter headline: NATIONAL EMERGENCY DECLARED.

Stop lights. Quarantine posts.

Soldiers with their pants sticking out at the flies clutch their throats and fall.

Newscaster: "It is impossible to estimate the damage. Anything put out up to now is like drawing a figure out of the air."

A diseased face with a slow idiot smile is projected onto the newscaster's face from a magic lantern. ...

"The world's population is now approximately what it was three hundred years ago."

Boys on snowshoes reach the *haman*. Steam and naked bodies fade to a misty waterfront. Opium Jones is there with patches of frost on his face as the boys sign on in the ghostly cabin of *The Great White*.

Dinner at the Pembertons. Candlelight on faces that suggest madeup corpses. Only Noah, his boyish face flushed, looks alive. The conversation is enigmatic.

"Are they doing mummies to standard?"

"This is the aunt's language."

"We still don't have the nouns."

"You need black money."

"A master's certificate to be sure. ..."

"Suitable crops."

"Are you in salt?"

"Bring a halibut."

"Ah good the sea."

They all look at Noah, who blushes and looks down at his plate.

"Draw the spirits to the *plata*...."

"The family business ..."

"It probably belongs to the cucumbers."

"Cheers here are the nondead."

The boys are back on *The Great White*. A shout from the cabin boy brings them out on deck. Jerry, with a noose around his neck, grins a wolfish smile. Then he hangs, as the western sky lights up with the green flash.

Captured by Pirates: Boys swarm over the rail with knives in their teeth. One with an enormous black beard down to his waist swings his cutlass at imaginary opponents with animal snarls and grunts and grimaces until the crew of *The Great White* rolls on the decks, pissing in their pants with laughter.

"*Guarda costa ...*" the boys mutter.

One puts a patch over one eye and scans the coast with an enormous wooden telescope.

Kiki fucks Jerry, pulling a red cashmere scarf tight around his neck and grinning into his face. As Jerry ejaculates, blood gushes from his nose.

Slowly, a room in an English manor house lights up. A picture on the wall shows an old gentleman wrapped in red shawls and scarves propped up in bed, with laudanum, medicine glass, tea, scones, and books on the night table beside him. Taking to his bed for the winter....

A light shines on a huge four-poster bed. A man with a nightcap sits up suddenly. A naked radiant boy is standing at the foot of his bed. The man gasps, chokes, turns bright red and dies of apoplexy, blood gushing from his mouth and nose.

Cities of the Red Night: Spotlights bathe the papier-mâché walls in red light. The boys camp around putting on disease makeup. Juanito, the Master of Ceremonies, puts a red rubber flesh-cluster in his navel.

"My dear, you look like Venus de Milo with a clock in her stomach."

The boys pose with expressions of idiot lust. The spectators roll of the floor laughing. One turns blue in the face.

"*Cyanide reaction! Medics on the double!*"

Boys in white coats rush in and shoot him with a blackout dart.

Piper Boy with a bamboo flute in Lima ... blue sky, color of his eyes. Smell of the sea. Dink is fucking Noah who turns into Audrey and Billy.

"It's me! It's me! I've landed! Hi, Bill! It's two hundred years, Bill! I've landed!"

The pilgrimage may take many lifetimes. In many rooms, on many levels, the ancient whispering stage . . .

Moving age with his binoculars, Audrey lays back in a chair masturbating. Bright pirates. Jerry comes in red wax. We see Tibet for a few seconds, people. A sepia cutback to the hospital. Depraved smile, sperm in a beaker.

He plays "Semper Fi" to four Marine guards. Baby pictures declared in red letters of cutthroat trout. Red anticipation of fever drifts from the bed. See what he is looking at onstage.

National Emergency, age fifteen, holds up a string of stoplights. Jerry's radiant ghost may take many lifetimes. Jerry, the cabin boy, stands over the hills and far away.

"Lima, flash, it's me. The Piper Boy in Lima. Dink, I've landed. Long way to find you."

Noah is in the library studying diagrams of mortars and grenades. He is drawing a cannon. A Chinese child in the doorway throws a firecracker underneath his chair. As the firecracker explodes, the cannon barrel tilts up at an angle. A backdrop of burning galleons falls in front of him.

Audrey's boys are back on deck. Gas tank explodes in Tamaghis. Flintlock rifle on the library table. Hans and Noah take off their shorts.

"Wenn nicht von vorn denn von hintern herum." If not from the front then around by the back way.

As Noah bends over, the flintlock breaks at the breech. As Noah ejaculates, breech-loading rifles pour withering fire into a column of Spanish soldiers.

A float of a Spanish galleon moves slowly and ponderously across the gymnasium floor. On the deck, we see the Inquisition with stakes and garrotes, the Conquistadores, the patróns and governors, officers and bureaucrats and their modern equivalents, *machos* and *politicos* swilling Old Parr scotch and brandishing pearl-handled .45s.

Immigration police in dark glasses . . . *"Pasaporte . . . Documentos . . ."*

Kelley as Ah Pook, spattered with black spots of decay, is fucking the young Corn God in a pirate's chest overflowing with gold ducats and pieces of eight. As they come, a yellow haze like gaseous gold streams off them and wafts across the deck of the galleon. *Machos* clutch their throats, spit blood, and die.

Noah hangs ejaculating in the same yellow haze of magical intention. The curtain is drawn for a moment and guns are piled up in front of him—from his first cartridge rifle to M-16s and bazookas, rocket guns and field pieces.

He is lowered with a slow sinuous movement by the Juicy-Fruit Twins. The twins are naked except for their sailor hats and white sneakers.

Offstage, a voice bellows: *"All right, you jokers.*... Battle stations."

Noah and the twins are in the gun turret making calculations, taking the range....

"Yards: twenty-three thousand ... Elevation: point six ..."

The galleon is in the cross hairs of the sight. Jerry turns bright red as he presses the Fire button. The galleon blows up and sinks into a prop sea.

Panorama of Mexico, Central and South America ... music and singing ... naked Spanish soldiers washing in a courtyard, jetting the soap around like a soccer ball and tackling each other, washing each other's backs. In trees by a river boys with idiot expressions jack off, snapping and gurgling like fish as they shake fruit into the water.

Audrey is naked against a background of jungle and ruined pyramids. He gets a hard-on and levitates as it comes up. He lands from a hang-glider in a red desert.

Jerry, the cabin boy, meets him in a lizard suit that leaves his crotch and ass naked. "Me lizard boy ... very good for fuck." Rainbow colors play over his body.

Spanish galleon ... movement by the Juicy-Fruit Twins ... on the deck we see white sneakers ... bureaucrats calculating the range ... hand hair turns bright red on Fire button ... The Galleon *Pasaporte Documentos* is blown out of the water and so a vast territory as Ah Pook spatters the panorama with insurgents. All the boys in yellow haze of skintight magic transparent for a moment come to attention in a line from the first cartridge gun to M-16s ... naked haze like gold gas....

"TENSHUN!"

Audrey and Noah ejaculating angels in rainbow intention....

"AT EASE."

Naked soldiers sniff bazookas and field pieces....

Peace does not last forever....

Red Night in Tamaghis. The boys dance around a fire, throwing in screaming Sirens. The boys trill, wave nooses, and stick their tongues out.

This was but a prelude to the Ba'dan riots and the attack on Yass-Waddah. The boys change costumes, rushing from stage to stage.

The Iguana twins dance out of an Angkor Wat—Uxmal—Tenochtitlán set. The "female" twin peels off his cunt suit and they replicate a column of Viet Cong.

The Countess, with a luminous-dial alarm clock ticking in her stomach and crocodile mask, stalks Audrey with her courtiers and Green Guards. Police Boy shoots a Green Guard. Clinch Todd as Death with a scythe decapitates the Goddess Bast.

Jon Alistair Peterson, in a pink shirt with sleeve garters, stands on a platform draped with the Star-Spangled Banner and the Union Jack. Standing on the platform with him is Nimun in an ankle-length cloak made from the skin of electric eels.

The Board enters and takes their place in a section for parents and faculty.

Peterson speaks: "Ladies and gentlemen, this character is the only survivor of a very ancient race with very strange powers. Now some of you may be taken aback by this character. . . ."

Nimun drops off his robe and stands naked. An ammoniacal fishy odor reeks off his body—a smell of some artifact for a forgotten function or a function not yet possible. His body is a terra-cotta red color with black freckles like holes in the flesh.

"And I may tell you in strictest confidence that he and he alone is responsible for the Red Night. . . ."

Jon Peterson gets younger and turns into the Piper Boy. He draws a flute from a goatskin sheath at his belt and starts to play. Nimun does a shuffling sinuous dance singing in a harsh fish language that tears the throat like sandpaper.

With a cry that seems to implode into his lungs, he throws himself backward onto a hassock, legs in the air, seizing his ankles with both hands. His exposed rectum is jet-black surrounded by erectile red hairs. The hole begins to spin with a smell of ozone and hot iron. And his body is spinning like a top, faster and faster, floating in the air above the cushion, transparent and fading, as the red sky flares behind him.

, A courtier feels the perfume draining off him. . . .

"*Itza* . . ."

A Board member opens his mouth. . . . "*Itza* . . ." His false teeth fly out.

Wigs, clothes, chairs, props, are all draining into the spinning black disk.

"ITZA BLACK HOLE!!"

Naked bodies are sucked inexorably forward, writhing screaming like souls pulled into Hell. The lights go out and then the red sky. . . .

Lights come on to show the ruins of Ba'dan. Children play in the Casbah tunnels, posing for photos taken by German tourists with rucksacks. The old city is deserted.

A few miles upriver there is a small fishing and hunting village. Here, pilgrims can rest and outfit themselves for the journey that lies ahead.

But what of Yass-Waddah? Not a stone remains of the ancient citadel. The narrator shoves his mike at the natives who lounge in front of rundown sheds and fish from ruined piers. They shake their heads.

"Ask Old Man Brink. He'll know if anybody does."

Old Man Brink is mending a fish trap. Is it Waring or Noah Blake?

"Yass-Waddah?"

He says that many years ago, a god dreamed Yass-Waddah. The old man puts his palms together and rests his head on his hands, closing his eyes. He opens his eyes and turns his hands out. "But the dream did not please the god. So when he woke up—Yass-Waddah was gone."

A painting on screen. Sign pointing: WAGHDAS-NAUFANA-GHADIS. Road winding into the distance. Over the hills and far away. . . .

Audrey sits at a typewriter in his attic room, his back to the audience. In a bookcase to his left, we see *The Book of Knowledge*, *Coming of Age in Samoa*, *The Green Hat*, *The Plastic Age*, *All the Sad Young Men*, *Bar Twenty Days*, *Amazing Stories*, *Weird Tales*, *Adventure Stories* and a stack of *Little Blue Books*. In front of him is the etching depicting Captain Strobe on the gallows. Audrey glances up at the picture and types:

"The Rescue."

An explosion rumbles through the warehouse. Walls and roof shake and fall on Audrey and the audience. As the warehouse collapses, it turns to dust.

The entire cast is standing in a desert landscape looking at the sunset spread across the western sky like a vast painting: the red walls of Tamaghis, the Ba'dan riots, the smoldering ruins of Yass-

374

Waddah, and Manhattan, Waghdas glimmers in the distance.

The scenes shift and change: tropical seas and green islands, a burning galleon sinks into a gray-blue sea of clouds, rivers, jungles, villages, Greek temples and there are the white frame houses of Harbor Point above the blue lake.

Port Roger shaking in the wind, fireworks displays against a luminous green sky, expanses of snow, swamps, and deserts where vast red mesas tower into the sky, fragile aircraft over burning cities, flaming arrows, dimming to mauves and grays and finally—in a last burst of light—the enigmatic face of Waring as his eyes light up in a blue flash. He bows three times and disappears into the gathering dusk.

Selected Bibliography

By William Burroughs

(Published by John Calder except where otherwise indicated)

Junkie, 1953 (Penguin)
The Naked Lunch, 1959
The Soft Machine, 1961
The Ticket That Exploded, 1962
Dead Fingers Talk, 1963
Nova Express, 1965 (Cape; to be republished by Calder)

Minutes to Go, 1960 (with Sinclair Beiles, Gregory Corso and Brion Gysin; out of print) (Paris; partly in *The Third Mind*)
The Yage Letters, 1963 (with Allen Ginsberg; out of print)
The Job, 1970 (with Daniel Odier; temporarily out of print) (City Lights)

The Last Words of Dutch Schultz, 1970
The Wild Boys, 1972
Exterminator!, 1973
The Book of Breething (in one volume with *Ah Pook*), 1974 (with Bob Gale)

Port of Saints, 1976 (Paris; to be republished by Calder)
Electronic Revolution, 1971 (in one volume with *Ah Pook*)

The Unspeakable Mr Hart, 1970 (temporarily out of print)
The Third Mind, 1979
Ah Pook is Here, 1980
Cities of the Red Night, 1981

Not yet published
The Place of Dead Roads
Collected Essays

About William Burroughs

Interview with William Burroughs: Gregory Corso and Allen Ginsberg, *Journal for the Protection of All Beings*, edited Michael

McClure, Lawrence Ferlinghetti, David Meltzner, San Francisco 1961

Interview: *The Paris Review* No. 35 (with Conrad Knickerbocker), 1965; *Writers at Work*, edited George Plimpton, London 1968

William Burroughs Interview: Jeff Shero, *Rat: Subterranean News*, October 4–17, October 18–31, 1968

Interview with William Burroughs: Robert Palmer, *Rolling Stone* No. 108, May 11, 1972

'Look at Uncle Bill': An Interview with William Burroughs: Bill Butler, *Frendz* No. 31, July 14, 1972

William Burroughs: An Interview: Lawrence Collinson and Roger Baker, *Gay Sunshine* No. 21, San Francisco 1974

A Descriptive Catalogue of the William S. Burroughs Archive, compiled by Miles Associates for William Burroughs and Brion Gysin, London 1973

William Burroughs: The Algebra of Need: Eric Mottram, London 1977

With William Burroughs: Victor Bokriss, New York 1981

William Burroughs
Cities of the Red Night £2.50

His most important book since *The Naked Lunch*.

'An obsessive landscape which lingers in the mind as a fundamental statement about the possibilities of human life' PETER ACKROYD, SUNDAY TIMES

'Not only Burroughs' best work, but a logical and ripening extension of all Burroughs' great work' KEN KESEY

'Burroughs is an awe-inspiring poetic magician. I believe *Cities of the Red Night* is his masterpiece' CHRISTOPHER ISHERWOOD

'The outrageousness of *Cities of the Red Night* suggests it was written in collusion with Swift, Baudelaire, Schopenhauer, Orwell, Lenny Bruce, General Patton and John Calvin' SAN FRANCISCO CHRONICLE

Hugo Williams
No Particular Place To Go £1.95

Hugo Williams went looking for the America he'd been dreaming of most of his life – B-movie, back-lot, rock 'n' roll America. He found it in bars and Greyhound buses, clubs, beds, record stores and mean streets. With the excuse of a poetry-reading tour, he zigzagged across the country, missing nothing with his watchful poet's eye, and coming back with a freight of strange, hilarious, unforgettable impressions.

'Rich scraps of lunacy which seem to promise some imminent insight into the much plundered American psyche but, in the meantime, are simply very funny' TIME OUT

'Martian picture-postcards' THE TIMES LITERARY SUPPLEMENT

Italo Calvino
If on a Winter's Night a Traveller £2.50

A fiction about fictions, a novel about novels, a book about books. Its chief protagonists are its author and his reader. Its progress traces the reading of a novel and the consummation of a love affair. In its course a whole shelf of novels are begun and – for reasons at the time entirely reasonable – never finished. Its characters are the myriads of beings involved with the process of creation, construction and consumption of The Book.

'I can think of no finer writer to have beside me while Italy explodes, while Britain burns, while the world ends'
SALMAN RUSHDIE, LONDON REVIEW OF BOOKS

Richard Brautigan
The Tokyo–Montana Express £2.50

The 'I' in this book is the voice of the stations along the tracks of the Tokyo–Montana Express . . . Or, to put it another way, a sparkling series of short stories and sketches in the best Brautigan style: *My Fair Lady* in Japanese; the prisoners' menu on Death Row, San Quentin; the curious new light thrown on the Kennedy assassination by a lack of pancakes; the man in the undershirt on the railing of the Golden Gate Bridge . . .

'Style, fantasy, an imagination appropriating everything it encounters'
LONDON REVIEW OF BOOKS

'Set principally in Japan and America, two of the most crassly commercialized cultures on earth . . . [Brautigan] peers with wilful jokiness at the bottom left-hand corner' SUNDAY TIMES

Gabriel García Márquez .
In Evil Hour £2.50

The people of the nameless small town in the nameless South American republic face, as usual, a dripping, sweaty autumn. The rain falls in torrents, the mice are eating the church foundations, the people groan under a far-away dictatorship. Someone starts nailing lampoons to people's doorways at night. There is a shooting. The mayor (and chief of police) dawdles cynically into action, which can only mean more tragedy . . .

'Not just about one specific bad time but about all times when doubt, secrets, corruption, double-dealing and guilt come to a head . . . a masterly book' GUARDIAN

Samuel Beckett
Company £1.50

'Imagine yourself old and reviewing your life. You are at the mercy of your memory, which dins in your ear stories of those scenes that made your life what it was. And if in addition you perceive yourself remembering . . . then you have split yourself yet again: into the voice of memory, the unwilling rememberer, and the unhappy perceiver. Essentially this is what Beckett has done in *Company*' NEW YORK TIMES

'There is in it a vivacious sense of despair that tears at the nerve ends. But its real richness lies in its language. What a master Beckett is . . . the finest verbal artist of the twentieth century' PETER TINNISWOOD, THE TIMES

edited by Raymond van Over
Smearing the Ghost's Face with Ink £2.50
a Chinese anthology

Folktales, fables, stories of love and morality, of the fantastic and the supernatural, selected from the finest writers of the Chinese literary tradition stretching back 2,500 years. The reader is transported into a luminously vivid world where cruelty coexists with tenderness, freshness with sophistication, precise observation with extraordinary imaginative flights – an informative and entertaining insight into the richness of Chinese literature.

Fritz Zorn
Mars £1.95

The author of this devastating book died of cancer at the age of thirty-two. His answer to the terrible question 'Why me?' is simple and harrowing: 'My parents' neuroses were responsible for producing my neurosis; my neurosis was responsible for producing my lifelong despair; my despair is responsible for my being ill with cancer; and my cancer will be the cause of my death.' This insight came too late for Zorn, but his book remains. It is an uncomfortable experience, but an important and moving one in the bitter tradition of Sartre's *La Nausée* and Camus's *L'Étranger*.

'Fritz Zorn is a pseudonym, chosen spitefully and well. In German, Zorn means anger. This testament is the work of a sensitive mind slowly unhinged, a howl against the inhuman condition. It is a sound familiar to doctors. Occasionally, if the writer is skilled enough, laymen can hear it. In *Mars* even the whispers are deafening' TIME

Arthur Koestler
Bricks to Babel £3.95
selected writings with author's comments

'Carrying bricks to Babel is neither a duty, nor a privilege; it seems to be a necessity built into the chromosomes of our species' ARTHUR KOESTLER

'Koestler is perhaps the one remaining writer in English who deserves the French eighteenth-century term *philosophe* . . . Like the *philosophes* his books have been banned and burnt . . . everything he writes carries a fluttering banner of challenge, an appeal against culpable ignorance or insularity or complacency. He has assembled the present anthology from fifty years of controversial books, journalism, pamphlets and keynote addresses. It is a massive compendium, part intellectual autobiography and part bibliographic guide' THE TIMES

Picador

☐	The Beckett Trilogy	Samuel Beckett	£2.75p
☐	Making Love: The Picador Book of Erotic Verse	edited by Alan Bold	£1.50p
☐	Willard and His Bowling Trophies	Richard Brautigan	£1.25p
☐	Bury My Heart at Wounded Knee	Dee Brown	£3.75p
☐	The Price Was High, Vol. 1: The Last Uncollected Stories of F. Scott Fitzgerald	edited by Matthew Bruccoli	£2.95p
☐	The Road to Oxiana	Robert Byron	£2.50p
☐	Our Ancestors	Italo Calvino	£3.50p
☐	Auto Da Fé	Elias Canetti	£2.95p
☐	Exotic Pleasures	Peter Carey	£1.50p
☐	In Patagonia	Bruce Chatwin	£2.25p
☐	Sweet Freedom	Anna Coote and Beatrix Campbell	£1.95p
☐	Crown Jewel	Ralph de Boissiere	£2.75p
☐	One Hundred Years of Solitude	Gabriel Garcia Márquez	£2.75p
☐	Nothing, Doting, Blindness	Henry Green	£2.95p
☐	The Obstacle Race	Germaine Greer	£5.95p
☐	Household Tales	Brothers Grimm	£1.50p
☐	Meetings with Remarkable Men	Gurdjieff	£2.75p
☐	Roots	Alex Haley	£3.50p
☐	Growth of the Soil	Knut Hamsun	£2.95p
☐	When the Tree Sings	Stratis Haviaras	£1.95p
☐	Dispatches	Michael Herr	£1.95p
☐	Riddley Walker	Russell Hoban	£1.95p
☐	Stories	Desmond Hogan	£2.50p
☐	Three Trapped Tigers	G. Cabrera Infante	£2.95p
☐	Unreliable Memoirs	Clive James	£1.75p
☐	China Men	Maxine Hong Kingston	£1.50p
☐	The Ghost in the Machine	Arthur Koestler	£2.75p
☐	The Memoirs of a Survivor	Doris Lessing	£1.95p
☐	Albert Camus	Herbert Lottman	£3.95p
☐	The Road to Xanadu	John Livingston Lowes	£1.95p
☐	The Cement Garden	Ian McEwan	£1.50p
☐	The Serial	Cyra McFadden	£1.75p

☐	**McCarthy's List**	Mary Mackey	£1.95p
☐	**Short Lives**	Katinka Matson	£2.50p
☐	**The Snow Leopard**	Peter Matthiessen	£2.50p
☐	**A Short Walk in the Hindu Kush**	Eric Newby	£1.95p
☐	**Wagner Nights**	Ernest Newman	£2.50p
☐	**The Best of Myles**	Flann O'Brien	£2.75p
☐	**Autobiography**	John Cowper Powys	£3.50p
☐	**Hadrian the Seventh**	Fr. Rolfe (Baron Corvo)	£1.25p
☐	**On Broadway**	Damon Runyon	£1.95p
☐	**Midnight's Children**	Salaman Rushdie	£2.95p
☐	**Snowblind**	Robert Sabbag	£1.95p
☐	**The Best of Saki**	Saki	£1.75p
☐	**The Fate of the Earth**	Jonathan Schell	£1.95p
☐	**Sanatorium under the Sign of the Hourglass**	Bruno Schultz	£1.50p
☐	**Miss Silver's Past**	Josef Skvorecky	£2.50p
☐	**Visitants**	Randolph Stow	£2.50p
☐	**Alice Fell**	Emma Tennant	£1.95p
☐	**The Flute-Player**	D. M. Thomas	£2.25p
☐	**The Great Shark Hunt**	Hunter S. Thompson	£3.50p
☐	**The New Tolkien Companion**	J. E. A. Tyler	£2.95p
☐	**Female Friends**	Fay Weldon	£2.50p
☐	**The Outsider**	Colin Wilson	£2.50p
☐	**The Kandy-Kolored Tangerine-Flake Streamline Baby**	Tom Wolfe	£2.25p
☐	**Mars**	Fritz Zorn	£1.95p

All these books are available at your local bookshop or newsagent, or can be ordered direct from the publisher. Indicate the number of copies required and fill in the form below   6

....

Name_____
(Block letters please)

Address_____

_____

Send to Pan Books (CS Department), Cavaye Place, London SW10 9PG
Please enclose remittance to the value of the cover price plus:
35p for the first book plus 15p per copy for each additional book ordered
to a maximum charge of £1.25 to cover postage and packing
Applicable only in the UK

While every effort is made to keep prices low, it is sometimes
necessary to increase prices at short notice. Pan Books reserve
the right to show on covers and charge new retail prices which
may differ from those advertised in the text or elsewhere